WILD PEOPLE QUIET

TARA GEREAUX

PUBLISHED BY SCRIBNER CANADA

New York   Amsterdam/Antwerp   London
Toronto   Sydney/Melbourne   New Delhi

SCRIBNER
CANADA

An Imprint of Simon & Schuster, LLC
166 King Street East, Suite 300
Toronto, Ontario M5A 1J3

For more than 100 years, Simon & Schuster has championed authors and the stories they create. By respecting the copyright of an author's intellectual property, you enable Simon & Schuster and the author to continue publishing exceptional books for years to come. We thank you for supporting the author's copyright by purchasing an authorized edition of this book.

No amount of this book may be reproduced or stored in any format, nor may it be uploaded to any website, database, language-learning model, or other repository, retrieval, or artificial intelligence system without express permission. All rights reserved. Inquiries may be directed to Simon & Schuster, 1230 Avenue of the Americas, New York, NY 10020 or permissions@simonandschuster.com.

This book is a work of fiction. Any references to historical events, real people, or real places are used fictitiously. Other names, characters, places, and events are products of the author's imagination, and any resemblance to actual events or places or persons, living or dead, is entirely coincidental.

Copyright © 2026 by Tara Gereaux

All rights reserved, including the right to reproduce this book or portions thereof in any form whatsoever. For information address Simon & Schuster Canada Subsidiary Rights Department, 166 King Street East, Suite 300, Toronto, Ontario, M5A 1J3.

This Scribner Canada edition March 2026

SCRIBNER CANADA and colophon are trademarks of Simon & Schuster, LLC

Simon & Schuster strongly believes in freedom of expression and stands against censorship in all its forms. For more information, visit BooksBelong.com.

For information about special discounts for bulk purchases, please contact Simon & Schuster Special Sales at 1-800-268-3216 or CustomerService@simonandschuster.ca.

Interior design by Wendy Blum

Manufactured in the United States of America

10 9 8 7 6 5 4 3 2

Online Computer Library Center number: 1517556269

ISBN 978-1-6680-6056-8
ISBN 978-1-6680-6057-5 (ebook)

For Clarence

In 1869, Prime Minister John A. Macdonald sent the lieutenant governor of the North-West Territories to Rupert's Land to negotiate terms with Louis Riel and his Métis supporters for entry of the prairie territory into the confederation. Macdonald told a colleague: "I anticipate that [he] will have a good deal of trouble, and it will require considerable management to keep those wild people quiet."

I use beadwork to infer a sense of history and to celebrate beauty within our culture ... to make the statement that Métis culture is not fossilized, but alive. I use beadwork as a tribute to my ancestors, as a way of saying, "You don't have to worry, our struggle is not as dire. We have survived."

Christi Belcourt,
Métis in the Twenty-First Century Conference, 2003

PART ONE

FLOWERS

AUGUST 1946

Torduvalle, Saskatchewan

THE AIR SIZZLES in from the hopper window. The heat's been excruciating this past week. Florence nudges the bathroom door closed so the air doesn't warm the house and reaches for the peroxide under the bathroom counter. She pours some into the spray bottle and dilutes it with water from the tap, measuring by eye only. A faded towel wrapped around her shoulders, she works at her hair in sections, using a brush to guide the mixture as close to her scalp as possible, covering the brown roots that are just beginning to show. A Saturday-night ritual every other week for nearly thirty years.

No one has ever asked her about her hair. Most don't even know, though there have been a few women in town in recent years who've commented, either praising her particular shade or deriding her not quite out of earshot for trying to emulate those Hollywood starlets. She's flattered they would think that of her, that she would be the type of person to aspire to looking like a star.

Florence sits on the toilet lid and waits for the peroxide to tingle, never using a timer now, knowing by instinct the moment when the roots will be lightened to the perfect hue but before the skin on her scalp blisters. She plans her day tomorrow. Church at ten; return home to prepare the pork roast, gravy, and potatoes. She'll also make a pot of tomato and macaroni soup to eat with some cold roast pork buns for the workday evenings when she'd rather read or listen to the radio than prepare a meal.

A wave of heat rolls in and she looks up at the slit of sky. A branch from the Manitoba maple in her front yard stretches into view. It's not quite September but its leaves are already turning at the edges, bright and golden yellow. The colour is startling. Searing. She holds her breath.

Colours used to consume her. She spent so many of her waking hours, and sometimes her dreaming ones too, thinking about colours and how to work them into her floral designs. How to craft a story with her beadwork. She was careful when selecting a particular hue, deliberate in her choices, because colours held meaning and feeling. Meaning and feeling that was different for everyone. A shade could ignite joy in one person, pain or regret in another. Colours could spark memories, sometimes ones you'd tried to forget.

Florence pushes back her thoughts as she forces the window shut. It's all just history, all in the past now. She waves the towel shawl around herself to create a breeze. She is Florence Banks, a secretary at Pratt's Insurance and Real Estate in the town of Torduvalle and a respected member of the community for the past eleven years. She blends in with everyone else. The tingle on her head turns to a sting, almost a burn, while her dark hair fades to a perfect shade of blonde.

FLORENCE STEPS OUT OF the tub and pulls out the plug. The drain glugs and spurts, choking down the water. A cool bath before bed for a better sleep. She slips on her cotton nightdress and inspects her drying hair in the mirror. A soft sand or even hay colour. Not radiant or luminous, but she wouldn't want that anyway. She can hardly wait until it's all silvery grey and sparkly and she won't have to dye it anymore, but even at fifty-one she still has a ways to go. At least she has the curls that everyone wants, no curlers or bobby pins needed.

Down the hall to the kitchen she goes to fill the kettle, set it on the stove, and place a cup and saucer beside the canister of tea bags on the counter for the morning. The last thing she does every night before bed. As she lifts a cup and saucer from the cupboard, the doorbell rings, and Florence freezes, arms midair. It's well after nine at night. Who's at her door at this hour? Another peal of the bell, followed by a loud knock. Her legs fill with lead.

"Florence? Are you there?"

Jennie Broughton. Her neighbour. An emergency, maybe? The kids? But why come here, why not a house with more people, with a husband? Someone who could do something to help.

Florence forces herself to the door.

"Oh, goodness, I startled you," Jennie says, "I'm sorry." She stands there, cool in her culottes and summer blouse, nothing awry about her or her disposition. No emergency, then.

Florence is suddenly aware of her bare feet, sweaty soles on the linoleum. Nails unpainted. Her thin summer nightdress fluttering loosely in the night breeze, and no brassiere. She might as well be naked.

"I . . . was in the bath." Florence stumbles over her words.

"Are you okay?"

She left out the bottle of peroxide. Left it on the edge of the sink in the bathroom, on display. Fumes perhaps still in the air. But it's a common household cleaner. That's all. Still.

"I'll be right back," Florence says and heads to the bathroom. Tucks the peroxide bottle under the sink, finger-combs her hair, and grabs the housecoat hooked on the back of the door. It's far too warm for it but she puts it on and ties it around her waist anyway.

"I saw the lights were on!" Jennie shouts from the door.

"Is everything all right?" Florence asks, heading back.

"Yes, I didn't mean to give you a scare." Jennie shifts on her feet in the doorway. "It's just . . ." She pauses, waves to her own house next to Florence's and to the empty driveway. "Garth and the kids are away and the house is so quiet tonight." She shifts again.

"I'm sorry, come in," Florence says, compelled to find her manners and stepping back to make room for her.

Jennie glances around the living room as she crosses the threshold. She's never come over like this before. Unannounced, uninvited. Florence doesn't invite guests over. *Private*, everyone calls her. Keeps to herself. Is respected for it.

"This is the first time I've been inside your house. Isn't that crazy, after all these years?" She wanders through the living room as if through a gallery or museum.

"Nonsense." Florence feigns shock.

"It's true. I've popped my head in once or twice before but I don't remember you having so many lovely things."

Florence feels a small ripple of pleasure. Grandmother wall clock, walnut, with a Westminster chime. Delft-blue vase on the antique French side table. Two painted atmospheric seascapes from another country, framed in gold. The Cogswell, reupholstered with soft green velvet, hand-embroidered doilies resting on its arms.

Jennie scans the room, seeming to appreciate what she sees.

"I purchase them as I find them," Florence says. But she doesn't just find them; she hunts for them. Tracks them down. Pores over catalogues, mines the papers for news of estate sales, garage sales, and yard sales. Never knowing what she's looking for but always finding something she desires, each item calling to her as if it will safeguard her or offer her some kind of protection. Her precious purchases are insulation against the poverty she never wants to know again.

"That's beautiful," Jennie says, looking at the candy dish in the china cabinet.

Milk glass with diamonds cut in relief and a finial lid. Funny that Jennie notices that piece. Florence bought that dish specifically for the Chicken Bones candy that Jennie gave her as a housewarming gift when she first moved in. Florence starts to tell her this but stops herself, worried it would make her sound strange.

"It's one of my favourites," Florence says instead.

"I can see why," Jennie says, eyeing it a moment longer before stepping away from the cabinet. "Were you just about to make tea?" Jennie says when she passes by the doorway to the kitchen and sees the teakettle on the stove.

"I was getting it ready for breakfast . . . but I—"

"I suppose it is too late for tea. Perhaps a nightcap, though?" Jennie looks away, embarrassed by her own brazenness.

Florence has noticed in recent weeks that Jennie awkwardly prolongs conversations between them in the driveway and finds excuses to be outside in the yard at the same time as Florence. There's a neediness in her of late. Florence feels her own twinge beneath her ribs. "Of course, please sit. I'm going to change first."

"There's no need, Florence. We're friends and we'll both be off to bed soon. Please."

But Florence throws her a smile and goes to the bedroom anyway, shuts the door behind her. A loose gingham skirt and a short-sleeved button-up blouse. Open-toed slippers to cover her feet. *Friends.* They are, aren't they? Neighbours for over six years and always pleasant. Chatted across their lawns. Helped each other carry groceries, push the mower, shovel walkways. They've even walked to church together a few times and sat at the same table during fundraising teas. But they've never visited each other. It's never been just the two of them.

Florence heads to the kitchen for the Harveys Bristol Cream. Maybe it's silly to be so distressed about a guest. Six years in this house, eleven total in town. It's fine. No reason to feel like her skin has come right off just because her neighbour wants company and a drink. Deep breath. She finds the bottle in the fridge and closes the door. Carries it back to the living room.

"I can't have nice things at my house with those two little terrors. It's always a mess and I can never keep up," Jennie says, taking a seat on the settee when Florence returns.

"You said everyone's away?"

"Yes, the kids are with Garth's parents at the farm this weekend," she says. "They've been missing their grandparents." A wistful afterthought.

Florence grabs two ruby red sherry funnels from the china cabinet. "It's only natural." When Garth went overseas and Jennie took a job at the post office, Garth's parents stepped in to help. The kids even lived at the farm for a while.

"I suppose," Jennie says, watching Florence pour the sherry.

"Is Garth at the farm too, then?" Strange Jennie wouldn't also be there, but she won't ask that. Garth—Mr. Broughton when they're at the office—works at Pratt's Insurance and Real Estate too but she hardly knows him. He was hired as a junior agent just before the war and was there only a few weeks before he signed up and left. When Garth returned, Pratt's was in the midst of its ever-growing expansion and immediately promoted him to a senior agent. Moved him upstairs to his own private office where Florence goes only to pick up and drop off paperwork. The Second-Floors keep to themselves.

"He's in the city for the night."

"Senior management had meetings there yesterday, didn't they?" Florence hands Jennie a glass.

"They did."

The Second-Floors have been commuting somewhat regularly to the city, but no one tells the Bottom-Floors what it's all about, and Florence doesn't poke her nose in. It's not her job. That's one reason why she's so respected at her workplace—her discretion.

"Apparently, the meetings went very well, so they stayed to celebrate." Jennie stops, then smiles as if deciding whether to share. "He said they met Tommy Douglas." She sips her drink.

"He met the premier?"

Jennie lowers her voice and says, "He was at one of the meetings," then adds quickly, "But Garth's a man of few details and even fewer when you ask."

Hard to imagine why Pratt's would meet with the premier of the province, especially when so many of the Second-Floors thought his socialist government was as bad as Hitler's National Socialists. Such silly nonsense, but again, it's none of her business. She sips her own drink. "Are you no longer working at the post office?"

"Mr. Klein is back full-time so I'm superfluous." She shrugs it off playfully, but it's clear it bothers her. "He caught some shrapnel in his left leg and has a limp now, but he says he's ready to return. It's quite a physical job, though. You wouldn't think sorting mail would be, but it is. I was so exhausted at the end of the day." She smiles, proud.

"Will you look for other employment, then?"

"No." Jennie takes a large sip, mood changing. "Garth thinks things have been too topsy-turvy for the kids and we should get back to normal." A tautness surfaces.

Florence understands the need to work. Her own job at the insurance office sustains her, and not just in the monetary way. Yes, she can buy her precious things, but the work itself keeps her going. She can't imagine her life without it. She'd never be in Jennie's position, though. She'd never want anyone who told her what she could and couldn't do. She's lucky in that way, not to have anyone to constrain her—no husband, no children; no one, period. Her whole life has been about getting to this point. This town, with this house and her job—a life without constraints. She's worked hard for it.

"Hmm," Jennie says, something coming to her as she swallows, "did you hear about the Sanderson twins?"

"Graham and Isla's boys down the street?" Seventeen but already like grown men, their frames topping six feet and their faces with perpetual five-o'clock shadows.

Jennie nods. "They got into a bit of trouble," she says, a mischievous lilt in her voice.

"What kind of trouble?"

"I can't believe it, really." She shakes her head, then leans forward to divulge. "Bootlegging. Illegal home brew."

"Those boys?" Florence says. They've always been so helpful, offering to shovel her sidewalk or rake her leaves. You never know the other sides to people. She sips, and the raisin-y metallic syrup slides down her throat.

"They purchased it—didn't make it," Jennie clarifies. "But still. They bought it in town, apparently."

"From whom?"

"That's what I'd like to know, but they haven't said." She downs the rest of her glass with one swallow. "But . . . *bootlegging*. In our town."

It is shocking. "How's their mother taking it?"

"I haven't spoken with her." Jennie looks away. "I only heard her telling Mrs. Larsen when I tried calling Garth's parents yesterday," she says.

Hazards of the party line—you never know who's listening in. Florence tightens her grip on her glass. "The twins are all right, though?"

"Yes. They were stopped just after their purchase, so they hadn't gotten into any of it. Thankfully. You never know what's in moonshine, if it's safe or not. Remember when all alcohol was illegal? There were all kinds of stories about people making their own and then falling seriously ill. Dying, even. I can't believe people are still doing it when you can just buy it off the shelf now." Jennie shakes her head.

Florence nods in agreement. Prohibition doesn't seem that long ago, but when she thinks about it, the Sanderson boys wouldn't have even been born then.

"This town," Jennie says, "it's changing." She worries the empty funnel in her hands.

Florence tops up her glass.

"Don't you feel that, Florence? That this town is changing? And fast?"

"I do." The town has grown busier since the men returned from the war. It's busier than before the war, and she liked it when it was quieter. It's why she came here.

"Hard to believe those boys would get up to something like that. Just goes to show you that people are always full of surprises."

They are, indeed. Florence downs her glass, then reaches for the Eaton's catalogue she received a few weeks ago. Best to get back to safer ground. "Have you seen the latest issue?"

Jennie peruses it, commenting on the latest styles and fashions. They make fun of the hats that are too ostentatious, the undergarments that are too impractical.

Jennie stops at a dog-eared page. "You're buying a new skirt?"

"Bought. It came in the mail yesterday but needs alterations."

"Which one? No, no, let me guess." There are four on the page. Four slim, blonde models wearing four different skirts. "The tattersall wool."

"How'd you know?" It's the most expensive. Not by much, but still. She should save more, though. She's been saying that for years.

"It's elegant but understated. It's you." Jennie continues browsing. "Have you ever thought of something like this?" She points to a dress, a gold silk gown with off-the-shoulder sleeves.

"Where would I wear that?"

"A dinner party."

"I don't go to dinner parties."

"Why not? You'd turn heads in something like this."

"Those days are done for me." She never turned heads when she was younger—or maybe not never, but never the heads she wanted to turn.

"Your dinner-party days don't need to be done, Florence. Any man would be lucky to win you."

"There was only one for me." Florence looks at the fourteen-karat yellow-gold band on her finger. Bought at a Goodwill in the city just before moving to Torduvalle.

"Gerald. Was that his name?" Jennie's voice is gentle.

Florence nods. Sips.

"How long were you married?"

"Almost twenty years." Florence smiles as if remembering happy memories. She tells everyone that she was married when she lived in Regina, and when her husband passed, that's when she decided to move to a small town. For a quieter life. It's easier—widows draw less suspicion from people than women who have never married.

"I wish I'd met him."

A small silence in the room.

"You are lucky, though. You can just order a skirt when you want. You can have all this nice furniture and not have it ruined. No husband, no kids to look after—" Jennie stops herself. "Oh, I'm sorry. That was inconsiderate. I didn't mean it to be."

"It wasn't, and I'm fine." Florence had tried for children. Tried and tried, and it just never happened. At least, that's what she tells people when they ask. In a way it's true. "I'm very happy with the life I had then and with my life now." Most of that is true as well.

"I often think about where I want to be in the future," Jennie says, then pauses. "And when I do, I sometimes think of you." Jennie's crossed leg gives a little bouncy kick.

For the first time, Florence realizes she's almost old enough to be Jennie's mother. The thought is shocking but funny too. It makes her want to giggle. Or maybe it's the sherry.

Florence pours them both some more. Her whole body tingles; she's enjoying the surprising turn of the evening. She's sitting in her living room with her neighbour on a Saturday night. She's sitting in her living room with her friend on a Saturday night.

∞

THE PHONE RINGS AS Florence pulls the pan from the oven to check on the pork loin. It'll be Mrs. Clarkson's mother again—she always calls the Clarksons on Sunday around this time and she always dials the wrong number. The Clarksons live across town but their number is only one digit away from Florence's and the elderly woman seldom gets it right. Florence takes her time, poking and basting the roast, before she answers on the seventh ring.

"Florence," Jennie says on the other end, surprised. "I was just about to hang up. If you're busy I can call later."

"No, it's fine," Florence says, any annoyance she felt immediately dispelled. "I was just busy at the stove. Is everything all right?" Jennie wasn't at church this morning.

"Everything's fine. Lovely, actually." Then Jennie's voice drops as if she's confessing: "I'm still in my pyjamas."

"It's the middle of the afternoon," Florence blurts out before she can stop herself.

"I know! I'm having a wonderfully lazy day," she says, and Florence can practically hear her smiling through the line. "Though I should get dressed soon because Garth said he'd be home with the kids before supper. But,"

Jennie continues, "I was calling because . . ." She trails off. "Well, last night was such fun—it's rare I get to spend time with adults." A breezy laugh. "And I was wondering if you'd like to come to the city with me next Saturday. With school just around the corner, I need to go to the department store for new clothes and supplies, and I thought you and I could do a little shopping together."

"A trip . . . to the city," Florence stammers as she processes this.

"Only if you want," Jennie says. "I just thought we could both do with a girls' day out, and there's a new restaurant on Scarth Street Garth's been raving about that I thought we could check out." Jennie pauses. "But please don't feel obligated to say yes."

"I'd love to," Florence says, hoping she doesn't sound too eager. She hasn't been back to Regina since she moved to town, and in all those years it's surely changed as much as she has. It'd be nice to see it again. And with company too.

"Perfect. Let's chat later this week," Jennie says.

When Florence hangs up, she heads to the closet in her bedroom to plan her outfits for the week, with special focus on Saturday's attire.

UP AT SIX. TEA and toast with butter and marmalade. Cooler this time of day already, so it's her blue brushed-wool cardigan, which will be far too hot by the afternoon but that's just how it is. Headscarf knotted snugly under her chin. Purse and package under her arm and she's out the door. When the weather's poor, she drives, but she prefers the *clip-clip* of her shoes on the way to work when everyone else is just getting dressed or still lounging in bed. *Clip-clip-clip*, like the chirp of a bird.

Torduvalle. A small, square town with rows of straight, square streets. A game board with houses and cars for pieces and easy-to-understand rules. She'd taken the bus from the city for an interview with Mr. Hicks for the secretarial position at Pratt's eleven years ago. Caught the earliest one so she could walk around the town first and see what it had to offer. Within an hour she had covered all the streets that bordered Pratt's and still had three more to go until her interview, so she crisscrossed the remaining residential streets, then looped back to Main for a late lunch. She knew before her cream of mushroom soup arrived she wanted the job. More than that—she wanted to live here forever. It wasn't the smallness of the town that attracted her—she'd interviewed for jobs in tinier places—it was something else. There were no statues of its first residents, no historical buildings with plaques to describe their past importance. It was a town with no history. It was perfect.

She breezed through the interview and demonstrated her skills: seventy-five words per minute with one hundred percent accuracy. At forty years old, she was middle-aged, but her life was really just beginning.

Key in the lock, *ka-thunk* of the bolt, *flick* of the lights. Always the first one to arrive. It's a nine-to-five job and she's been told she doesn't need to come in before nine, but the time between seven thirty and nine—between her arrival and everyone else's—is her favourite part of the day. She gets so much accomplished when no one else is around. Today, there's dictation for the Schneider file to type, two correspondence letters to draft for review and type once approved, the accounts receivables and payables for the previous business day, and the contracts to prepare for the new clients' signatures. And all the other daily tasks and emergent jobs.

Some might say it's easy work—it's just pressing keys, moving paper—but she doesn't see it that way. It takes concentration, real concerted effort, because you can't make mistakes. The stakes are too high. A decimal point in the wrong spot or an extra *l* in *MacDougal* means documents do not get filed by the deadline, which means dates get pushed back, which means lives are thrown into turmoil. Not everyone can be so precise. It's why she has the reputation she does in town. Other employers have tried to lure her away from Pratt's, and honestly, she considered a couple of those offers, but when it came down to it, why rock the boat? She's perfectly happy where she is. She's a small cog in a giant wheel, a cog that's easily overlooked, and she likes it that way. Invisibility doesn't diminish her importance.

She slides a fresh sheet of paper in her typewriter and the carriage catches it, curls it around the roller. Her Remington Rand. The clack of its hammers is musical. Reminds her of that one time she saw the Regina Symphony Orchestra at Darke Hall. When she reaches peak speed, when her fingers have found their rhythm, her chest even lifts. No, this work is not easy but when it's done right, there's something about it that makes life easier. Manageable. She knows what is expected of her and she meets those expectations. Plus, she's always at her best when her hands are busy. It's when her mind finally calms, unwinds itself. She discovered this as a child with thread and a needle. Those small beads in every colour. Typing has replaced beading. Florence hits the carriage return and pushes the thought away.

Refocuses.

At twelve minutes after nine, Florence has finished the dictation, processed the receivables from Friday's clients, and prepared the cheques for the Second-Floors' signatures for the bills that are due. And at twelve minutes after nine, Shirley arrives for the day. Shirley seems to subtract two minutes from her start time every year she's there. But Florence doesn't mind. It makes her own performance stand out.

"Good morning," Shirley singsongs, removing her homburg-style hat. Always the latest fashion for Shirley—blazing and bright, like her personality. Her bubbly presence fills up a room, and that's why Mr. Hicks hired her six years ago. They needed someone to welcome clients to the office. Greet them, serve them, converse with them to make them feel comfortable and at ease. Florence needed to focus on the actual work required and not the pleasantries. Chin-wagging only increases her stress levels. It's upsetting to listen to someone go on about how their Scottie dog chased a coyote from their yard when a claim has to be filed that very day. She was relieved when the Second-Floors suggested another hire. It eliminated a significant amount of pressure for her.

"How was your weekend?" Shirley asks.

"Jennie Broughton came over for a visit on Saturday night," she says, pleased that she actually has something to share.

"Really? No theatre program on the radio?" Shirley's shocked.

"We even had a little sherry." Silly to disclose such a detail.

"Look at you, Flossie, I always knew you had a wild streak," she teases.

"It was just a visit," Florence says, waving it off as if it were nothing. But she had such a pleasant time. And plans for a trip to the city for some shopping on Saturday to top it off. But Florence doesn't tell Shirley this, afraid that saying it out loud might jinx it somehow.

"How was yours?" Florence asks instead.

"We've switched places, it seems," Shirley says. "It was my turn to stay in and read a book all weekend."

Florence nods, recognizing a lie when she hears one. They're harmless, though. Little white lies just so that no one feels uncomfortable. It was clear to Florence that when Shirley was hired, she was having an affair with Mr. Hicks, the longest-serving Second-Floor at Pratt's and now the president. Mr. Hicks had hired Florence all those years ago when he was just a senior underwriter, but the way he's always treated her compared to how he treats Shirley is quite different. He's been fatherly with Florence since day one, but with Shirley, who's nearly a decade younger than Florence, Mr. Hicks is stricter, more critical. Perhaps to make up for their dynamic when not at work. But it's none of Florence's business and she respects people who keep things to themselves.

"By the way," Florence says when Shirley returns from spending an inordinate amount of time tidying the kitchenette and putting the kettle on, "there's nothing in the calendar for this morning—no meetings or appointments—and no one's called in to say they're running late, but none of the Second-Floors are here yet." She scans the entries in the days ahead to see if there are any mistakes. The Second-Floors generally start arriving at nine thirty and most are through the door before ten, but it's nearly ten o'clock now, and aside from the new juniors, no one's here.

"A meeting for this morning was scheduled at the end of the day last Friday. They're all over in Forsyth and should be back after lunch."

"All of them?"

Florence is always the one to lock up, the last out the door, so the meeting must have been scheduled after hours. Florence doesn't ask any more questions—she and Shirley have built their trust up through discretion. She picks up her favourite fountain pen and updates the calendar, her cursive as neat and proficient as typeface, while Shirley ambles around the office, watering and dusting the plants. Her bum is never in her seat until after ten.

By quarter after ten, her break time, Florence has drafted the two letters by hand for the Second-Floors' review. She places them in the review file, carries the file upstairs, and leaves it on the inbox tray in the hallway. Then, purse and package under her arm, she heads out for her break. The day has warmed and it's already too hot for her sweater, but she keeps it on because the wind has picked up as well, blowing dust and dirt every which way. Once she rounds the hardware store onto Main, the buildings block most of the current, and the air comes at her in short clips instead. She straightens, lifts her head to the day.

Up the street and near the Wells Brothers Grocery, three Native men are gathered on the sidewalk chatting, one holding his hat to his head so it doesn't blow away. Florence avoids them and jaywalks to the other side, passing by Mr. Schmidt and Mr. Ivanenko, who both tip their hats to her.

"Been more of them in town lately," one man says to the other.

Florence catches this comment on the wind. She picks up her pace, eyes on the pavement all the way to Third Avenue, where she turns. The wind, now at her back, pushes her towards Nelson's Tailoring and catches the door as she pulls on the handle. The door flies from her grasp and strains against the hinge. She steps inside and tugs it closed with both hands.

"That wind is vicious today," Hilde Nelson says, rising from her sewing cabinet in the corner. A white pillowcase with delicately embroidered edges is caught in the Singer's tooth. Hilde's husband, Clifford Nelson, opened the shop long before Florence moved to town, but he returned from war with battle fatigue and it's only Hilde who runs the place now.

Florence unties the knot beneath her chin, slides her scarf off. "Almost blew me away."

"What do you have there?" Hilde asks, reaching for Florence's package. She unwraps the tattersall wool skirt that came in the mail last week. "I was eyeing this one myself in the catalogue."

"It could be yours if it can't be let out."

"Too small?"

"About an inch. Too many baked goods lately."

"Quality items such as these always have some extra fabric to work with. If not, I'm sure I can match this fabric very closely," she says, looking through her bookings, "but I do have a bit of a backlog." She reaches for her ticket pad.

"I'm in no rush."

"It's actually an easy job if you have a needle and thread at home."

"Oh, goodness, n-no," Florence sputters. "I can't be trusted. Whenever you get to it is fine."

"You couldn't do it even with a little instruction?"

"I'm sure I'd muck it up. It's best left to the professionals."

"I can try to squeeze this in sometime late next week." She hands Florence a ticket.

Voices on the street outside break through the wind.

"Of course. Best of luck with the backlog." Florence tucks the ticket into her purse and steps to the door, but movement outside the window stops her. The three Native men she saw near the grocery store are now walking up Third towards the shop. She turns back around to face Hilde. "Actually, what day next week do you think you might be free to tackle my skirt?"

"Oh," Hilde says, and looks through her calendar. "Is Thursday fine? I might get it done earlier, and I can call you if I do."

"Thursday's great." Florence turns back to the window and sees the three men are just walking by. She will wait until they've passed before reaching for the door handle.

"Are you all right?" Hilde asks as Florence lingers by the door.

"Yes, thank you. Just bracing myself for the weather." Florence pulls open the door and steps out into the wild wind.

CUTLERY PINGS IN THE grease-filled air. Friday. End-of-the-week lunch at Nick's, a tradition for as long as Florence has worked at Pratt's. The days flew by this week, but they always do when it's busy. Florence wrapped up the paperwork on four claims and archived all the files from the 1940–41 and 1941–42 fiscal years that her and Shirley hadn't been able to get around to. Took them all down to the basement filing cabinets on her own. It feels good to have that sorted, especially before the long weekend and the start of another month. So good, she might even order dessert today.

When she first started working for Pratt's, it was only her, Mr. Hicks, and Mr. Pratt, who founded the business and is now retired, and they all fit into a single booth. Even when Mr. Henry was hired on as junior underwriter in 1938, and then Shirley in 1940, they continued to squish into one booth despite the lack of elbow room. But now, with Mr. Broughton—Jennie's husband—and the two junior agents, Peter and Jeremy, who share the first floor with Florence and Shirley, they're spread over two booths. Florence and Shirley often sit with the junior agents, but today they're in the booth with the Second-Floors, which happens when the Second-Floors don't want to be bothered by clients who are also dining at Nick's—clients feel less inclined to approach and talk business when the secretaries are present.

When the waitress brings their orders to the table, the bell on the restaurant door jangles. All their heads turn towards the sound. As they take in the arrivals—the three Native men Florence saw earlier in the week—a quiet settles in the room. Conversations don't stop, but tones change. The men amble to a booth by the front window. The Formica tabletop glows red from the sun streaming through the painted sign on the glass, *Nick's Diner* in sloppy script. Patrons exchange furtive glances while food is lifted to mouths. Some shift in their chairs so sidelong looks are less noticeable.

"Obviously not from around here," Mr. Broughton says to Mr. Hicks and Mr. Henry, who both shrug as if it's none of their business. Shirley continues to gawk, watching to see how things will unfold.

The three Native men flip the coffee cups in front of them so they're right-side up in their saucers. As the waitress approaches their booth, one of them leans back in his seat to give her room to pour, but she walks right past them, the full coffeepot in her hand.

Florence looks away. She stirs her beef barley soup and stares at the club sandwich she hasn't yet touched.

"Eat up, Florence," Mr. Hicks says to her. "Don't want your food to get cold."

She picks up one triangle of her sandwich and takes a small bite, tries to put the men at the other table out of her mind, but seconds later the cook comes out from the kitchen and approaches the men's booth.

Florence pretends to eat, pretends she isn't watching the table by the window, but she is. And so is everyone else.

There are never any outright rules banning them from the place, only endless excuses.

"That table is reserved," the cook says to one of the men, the one with the blue plaid work shirt.

The man scans the room, trying to make eye contact with every single person in the place, even Florence. She's the only one who meets his gaze. It's brief, and she immediately turns back to her soup, eyes cast down. On the other side of the booth, Shirley bumps the underside of the table as she uncrosses and crosses her legs.

"If you want to order food to go, or sit outside, we can do that and bring the food out to you," the cook says to the men.

The men sit there awkwardly for a moment, then place their orders, stand, and walk to the front door. They leave the diner and head to a picnic table on the scrappy patch of lawn in the empty lot beside the building. There's no umbrella or overhang to protect them from the blistering summer sun.

Mr. Hicks salts his fried ham steak and eggs, then taps his lips together, a sign that he's thinking but prefers to keep his thoughts to himself.

"Shame," Shirley says under her breath.

Florence isn't sure what she means. Is it a shame the men weren't served inside or a shame they wanted to be? Florence forces herself to eat even though her stomach protests.

Mr. Broughton attempts to change the topic entirely and asks Florence if she's looking forward to her trip to the city with Jennie tomorrow. She politely answers, then someone else mentions the new Gregory Peck Western playing in the theatre there. And somehow that spins into a discussion about the almanac's precipitation forecast for the coming winter. While the others converse, Florence occasionally steals glances out the window at the three men. Clearly manual labourers, likely hired on at a farm nearby from the looks of them. Steel-toed boots, jeans, and work shirts from Simpson's. Dusty, sweat-stained collars like all the other farmers from town. The only differences are the shades of their skin, ranging from a dried foxtail to the deep brown of an old penny.

When the waitress clears their plates, it's already a few minutes to one, but the Second-Floors order dessert, another round of coffees. It's usual for them to take a lazy approach to Friday afternoon; some even nip out the door before five, but Florence often stays late. And though she'd thought she might partake in dessert today, she no longer wants to and would rather get back to the office. They tease her about this, her inability to relax, call her a robot that's always wound up. But she prefers to work than loll about.

Florence reaches into her handbag for her coin purse.

"Put that away, Florence," Mr. Hicks says.

They always pay the bill, but she never likes to assume.

"I'll be right there." Shirley sips her Coke through a straw.

"Take your time," Florence says. They both know Shirley will return when the last of the Second-Floors struggle in.

The bells on the door chime as Florence exits the diner and steps out into the heat of the day. As she turns up the sidewalk, she bumps into one of the men from the picnic table, the one she made eye contact with. He's carrying the greasy newspapers that held their burgers and fries.

"Excuse me," he says, stepping to the side and dumping garbage into the bin near the door. Florence smiles politely and continues along the sidewalk, heading towards Bay Avenue where the trees, nearly touching at the top, will provide some welcoming shade.

"Florence!"

She's almost at the corner when she hears her name.

"Florence!" the man calls again when she doesn't respond.

She turns. The man from the picnic table jogs towards her, skin shiny with sweat and wrinkled at the tops of his cheeks from the smile stretching across his face. A hot breeze blows over her, so damp and heavy it's hard to breathe.

"Florence, it's me," he says with that accent, that mix of French and Cree in a staccato cadence she remembers so well.

"I . . . I'm . . ." Florence stammers, sweat forming on her brow.

"Clancy," he says, hands spread wide and eyes full of happiness.

"I'm sorry," she says. "You must be confusing me with someone else." A cold washes through her despite the heat.

He lets his hands drop and watches her a moment. "I know my own sister when I see her. It's been—what? Over thirty years?" He waits for a reaction.

Florence looks away and tucks her purse tight under her arm.

"The hair is different, for sure, and you're all done up in fancy clothes." He smiles.

"I don't know what you're talking about," she says, her voice clipped and measured.

She glances back at Nick's. Sees heads turning to look through the window at the hubbub down the street. They're watching every move, seeing what's going on here on the sidewalk between her and . . . this man. Even Shirley, who's seated near the aisle, is leaning far over to look out the window, her curious face peering through the glass.

"Florence?" Clancy asks, his tone changing. "No one knew what happened to you."

"I'm not Florence." It comes out harsh. "I mean . . . I'm Florence—Florence Banks. My last name is Banks." She folds a stray lock behind her ear.

"Did you marry?" he asks, noticing the ring on her finger.

She tucks her hand out of view, then hears the diner door open. Mr. Hicks exits with Mr. Broughton hovering behind him.

"Florence, everything all right?" Mr. Hicks calls out.

"Yes, it's fine. I'm fine," Florence replies. She turns to Clancy. "I'm not who you think I am."

Clancy watches her a moment, confused anger on his face, then he takes a step back from her, pulls a kerchief from the pocket of his jeans, wipes his brow. When he's done, the anger is gone and his face is blank. "I understand.

Sorry to have bothered you." He turns his back on her and walks to the picnic table where his friends are waiting for him. After a minute, Mr. Hicks and Mr. Broughton go back inside Nick's.

Florence's body won't move; she's stuck there on the street. Should she go back to the diner, explain she was mistaken for someone else? Or maybe that would bring more attention? She wills her feet to move, one foot in front of the other, back towards the office. Type the covering letters for the information packages requested. Log this week's expenditures. File all the papers on Mr. Hicks's desk that he never puts away himself. Everything will be tidied before the end of the day.

Florence's heels *clip-clip* on the sidewalk as she heads back to Pratt's. Her blouse is wet under her arms, the band of her bra damp and constricting.

SPRING 1908

The Nest, Saskatchewan

FLORENCE SCANS THE road, looking for him. From the top of the hill, she can see quite far. It's still white with snow, but it's soft enough now in the warmer weather to crumble under the weight of horses' hooves and the wheels of the wagons. Others have already travelled it now that the worst of the winter is over, which is how she knows Paapaa will be coming home soon.

For five days in a row Florence has climbed this hill between her chores to watch and wait, wanting to be the first to see him, but three days ago Clancy discovered what she was up to and now he's always here too. Sitting next to her, glued to her side and always talking and fidgeting. Now he's going on and on about the size of the rabbit he found in a trap this morning.

"If you gather enough round stones, we could play marbles," she says, interrupting him.

"Really?" He hops to his feet.

"They have to be *round*-round, though."

He's already kicking snow aside and bending down to search.

He's exhausting. More so this winter because it was their first without Paapaa, and Florence had to mind him more than usual, which was unfair because she's only four years older than him and when she was seven—nearly eight—she never needed anyone to mind her. But she and Clancy are different—he's loud and reckless and wants everyone's attention, and she just wants to be left alone.

"There's still too much snow." He pouts.

"I saw some patches of ground peeking through back there when I came up that way yesterday." She points behind her and he descends the far side of the hill and disappears.

She turns back to the road. Still empty. Movement directly below catches her eye but it's just smoke rising from the Boyers' shack. She counts how many of the others have fires burning. Four of the seven homes have billowing grey clouds that idly rise up, disappear into the sky. The Nest. There's no sign to say that's the name of the place but that's what it's called. She asked her mother if the Nest was a village or a hamlet; she knows it's too small to be a town. But Maamaa said it was neither of those things, said it was land the government claimed it owned. But the government also owns towns and villages. Maamaa wouldn't say any more. There are some things she never wants to talk about. Whatever the Nest is, it feels exactly like what it's called—though their houses are built in a straight, narrow line and not a round circle, it's just as snug, their houses the eggs cupped inside.

Behind her and down the hill, Clancy shouts but she can't make out the words and doesn't want to either. She closes her eyes and shuts everything out for a while, until Clancy returns, carrying his woolen cap in his arms like a kitten.

"That enough?" Clancy asks, a cheeky grin on his face as he holds it out. The cap is filled with stones, more than they could possibly need.

"We need more," she says, wanting to be alone for longer.

"You're lying!"

But Florence ignores him and shoots to her feet. There's movement on the road. A horse and wagon. Clancy follows her line of sight and they both stand still, breath held tight in their chests. Florence looks for the shapes of two men because Paapaa went south with Napoleon Morin and both should be returning.

"That's just old Joe Boyer and Remy coming back from Quincy Lake," Clancy says.

"That's not his horse," Florence says. And Uncle Joe didn't take any of his sons with him when he left this morning. Florence starts down the hill. It could just be visitors passing through on their way north. She picks up the pace anyway.

"Florence, wait for me!"

But she bends her knees and angles her body so she can move faster.

Clancy yells again and there's anger in his voice this time. He drops to his bottom and starts sliding down the hill, but there are too many lumps of sagebrush and sedge grass for a clear route and she reaches the road before he's even halfway down. The snow on the road is stickier and tries to swallow her boots, hand-me-downs from the Boyer boys last year and still too big and floppy. She slows but is easily going to beat Clancy to the wagon that's arriving and whoever is driving it.

It's hard to keep it in focus as she runs over uneven ground. Then one of the men stands and she pushes harder. "Paapaa!" Florence can't hear Clancy behind her anymore, can't hear anything but her own breath whooshing in and out of her. By the time she rounds the slight curve, Paapaa's already out of the wagon and is kneeling on the ground, arms open. Her legs are wobbly as she nears him but she makes it all the way before losing her balance and he scoops her up.

"You've grown so big, my girl," he says, holding her tight.

His hair is longer and whiter than when he left in the fall but it smells the same, earthy and piney from his pipe. She closes her eyes and inhales it.

"There he is!" Paapaa lets out a whoop of laughter. "Honeybee!" he calls out. The nickname he gave Clancy because of his sweet tooth. But he's also chubby like a bee too—round face, round belly. And busy like one, always wants to be everywhere all the time. *Buzz-buzz.*

"Kaa kaashkihtaan!" Paapaa shouts as Clancy struggles in the snow. Paapaa shifts Florence in his arms and walks forward, hauls Clancy up when they finally meet. He carries them both back to the wagon, doesn't even stumble once, and Uncle Nap slides over on the bench seat to make room for them all.

"Is Maamaa at the Duncans'?" Paapaa asks. Florence's mother works part-time at the Duncans' farm a mile north of the Nest, helping Mrs. Duncan with housekeeping and other chores. Her father and others from the Nest work there too in the warmer months.

"She's home," Florence says. Darning clothes for Mrs. Duncan and other neighbouring farm women in exchange for canned goods, clothing, or other items the women no longer want.

"Let's go surprise her." He smiles and winks at her.

Uncle Nap clicks his tongue to get the horse to start moving.

"Ni miyeuytayn," Paapaa says, one arm around Clancy, the other around Florence. "Ni miyeuytayn."

Florence is happy too. Paapaa, Napoleon, and Albert LaRose left the Nest together last fall after harvest season at the Duncans'. They went south to work for another farmer who was hiring half-breeds to clear trees and rocks from newly purchased land. They worked there until winter set in, and on their way back, they heard the coal mine in Estevan was desperate for workers and so made their way there. But Albert said the mine told them "half-breeds get half the rate," so he came back home. Paapaa and Nap stayed on, though, figuring they could still save some money. But the longer Paapaa was away, the shorter Maamaa's temper grew. It's a relief to have him home.

She fights the urge to ask him when they'll go to Quincy Lake. He promised her a trip before he left and it's all she thought about while he was away. But she's more mature now and can see he's tired. Worn down, even. She'll wait until he's had some rest.

Maamaa's sitting at the kitchen table sewing with Aunt Lillian, who's nibbling on the end of her ever-present and unlit pipe, when they enter. Maamaa stops mid-stitch and stares at them, all three squished together in the doorway. Her mouth twitches until she's smiling, something she did very little of all winter. "Well, come inside, don't let the cold air in." She sets her sewing aside. "I'll start some tea." She stands and reaches for the ladle in the pot of water on the stove.

But Paapaa strides towards her and grabs her by the waist. "Not without a kiss first."

"Irwin," Maamaa scolds him, but she's also pleased.

"Ugh." Clancy jumps on the bed and covers his face in the pillows, hiding from the sight of the kiss.

Auntie begins to pack up her sewing things. Florence steps closer to look at her work, but it's just sewing stuff, not her beadwork. As if reading Florence's disappointment, Aunt Lillian removes the pipe from her mouth and leans over to speak in her ear. "I started a new pair of gauntlets, I'll show you later," she says, voice low, because even though Maamaa loves beadwork, she doesn't want Florence to learn it. Says only half-breeds bead, and Florence only needs to know how to sew.

"Can we all sleep in the bed tonight?" Clancy asks on the verge of another pout.

While Paapaa was gone, Maamaa let them sleep in the bed with her instead of piling clothes and blankets on the floor every night and putting them away in the morning. Florence dreams of them being able to add on a second room like the Boyers did last summer.

"Not tonight. Tonight, you'll be sleeping at Auntie's," Paapaa says. Then he looks to Aunt Lillian to see if it's all right.

"Wii," Auntie says, both grinning and shaking her head.

"Aw," Clancy whines in protest.

But Florence doesn't mind because now she can see the gauntlets.

"If you complain, you won't get your presents," Paapaa says, teasing.

For a moment, there's just the crackle of the fire as Clancy immediately falls silent.

"Aashtum oota," Paapaa says, and Clancy races to him.

"English." Maamaa pokes Paapaa in the ribs. She never wants Florence and Clancy to speak Michif. She says they'll get along better in the world if they don't sound like half-breeds, that others will treat them better if they don't. But Paapaa always has to be reminded.

"You too," he says to Florence, and she steps forward.

Paapaa holds out two whole rolls of Necco Wafers.

"That's too much," Maamaa says.

But Paapaa ignores her. "You have to promise me two things," he says as he hands them over. "That you'll share with Auntie and that you won't come home tomorrow until the sun is up."

Clancy nods right away and tears his open, but Florence tucks hers into her pocket. She'll wait until Clancy is asleep tonight and then eat them one at a time, savouring each one slowly to keep herself awake. Because no one knows that Florence has learned a lot about beading already, that Auntie has been secretly teaching her.

AUGUST 1946
Torduvalle, Saskatchewan

WHEN SHIRLEY RETURNS to the office after lunch, she quietly approaches Florence at her desk. Glances around before speaking. "Was everything okay at Nick's... with that man?" she asks in a whisper.

"Oh, yes. He just mistook me for someone else, then asked for directions. No bother." Florence twists a letter out of the typewriter and examines it before placing it in the file for signatures.

Shirley stands there a moment as if about to say something else, then turns away. "I'm glad it was nothing," she says, returning to her desk.

No one else says anything to her about it. Not even Mr. Hicks. It was just a little blip. Everyone's too busy with their own work, their own lives. Florence can pretend it never happened. She winds a fresh piece of letterhead into her Remington, starts another letter, and buries herself in productivity until four thirty rolls around and the juniors rise to leave, a little early—but it is, after all, the Friday before a long weekend.

"Good night, ladies," Jeremy says as he and Peter head to the door.

"Have a wonderful weekend." Florence nods goodbye.

"Don't get into too much trouble, boys," Shirley teases. When the door closes, she glances dolefully at the clock. "All the Second-Floors have gone too." A not-so-subtle hint.

Florence hands her the mail she completed that's ready to be posted.

"There's no need to come back to the office afterwards—you can get an early start on your weekend too."

Never one to pass up an opportunity to leave early, Shirley does a little shoulder dance as she gathers her things. But she stops when she looks at the addresses on the envelopes.

"I think there's a mistake," she says, and carries the envelopes back to Florence. "The Kleins live in town, don't they? And the Hubers on a farm?"

"Goodness, that's right . . . I—I'm sorry." The words splutter out as Florence sees she's incorrectly labelled them.

"Do you want me to correct them?"

"No, no, off you go. I'll fix this and go to the post office myself."

"Are you sure, Flossie?"

Florence nods.

Shirley starts to go but stops. "Are you all right?"

"It's all this hot weather, I'm sure."

"It's enough to throw anyone off. Have a good night."

After Shirley leaves, Florence tries to shrug it off, but it rankles, her mistake. She never makes careless errors like this. She decides to look over the other tasks she completed to make sure they are correct. She stays so late, she almost doesn't get to the post office before it closes. The day has been an unsettling one and she can't wait for the end of it.

She hopes a slow, relaxing walk home will settle things, but it doesn't. In fact, she feels worse. And when suppertime arrives, she has no appetite, her stomach thick with nausea. Thinking about the trip to the city with Jennie tomorrow exacerbates it even further. What if she runs into someone else she knows there? The chances are slim, but just the thought is another layer of distress she can hardly bear. Right before eight, she calls Jennie.

"I'm so sorry," she tells her, "I'm not well and won't be able to come with you to the city tomorrow."

"Oh, no, that's awful. Can I bring you anything?"

"Don't trouble yourself. A good, long sleep is what I need."

When Sunday arrives, she uses the feigned illness as an excuse to stay home from church, glad to miss it for a week. But in the afternoon, she finds herself restless, wishing it weren't a long weekend and she could return to work tomorrow. She cleans the house from top to bottom, and on Monday she tackles the yard.

She gathers up the few leaves that have prematurely turned and fallen, then uses the push mower to trim the lawn to a short, even length, diagonal lines crisp and clean. The flower beds are next. Her knees rest on one of the railway ties that frame her largest hexagon-shaped bed. Inside the border, three circles of flowers, and each one a different variety, shape, and shade. Marigolds, pansies, violas. And in the centre, a forsythia bush. Its spiky, sun-coloured fronds stick out like a threatened porcupine's quills.

Florence knew a yard would be a lot of work. Her family had kept a vegetable garden when she was growing up, and it was endless labour—she'd spent hours tending potatoes, squash, carrots, beans. They grew most of what they ate and canned what they could for winter. The garden was for sustenance; it was a necessity. But this garden, her yard now, is different. It's designed to harmonise with the other yards on the block, to impress and awe. Designed for a different kind of need.

Florence digs deep into the dirt, her muscles burning, but the soil is cool on her fingers. The smell of it grainy. Musty. So rich she tastes it in the back of her throat. She could hollow out a burrow and crawl into it like a womb. She pulls up a root and brings herself back into the moment and to the task at hand.

Hours pass and she's spent, exhausted. There are still the beds that line the front of her house, but she can't do any more. She stands, takes in her property, letting the sight fill her. The best garden on the block. She never tires of hearing others talk about how beautiful it is.

On the way inside, she spots a dandelion nub, its stem so short that its yellow head is almost flat against the lawn, hiding. Dandelions were abundant in the fields around her childhood home, and they were always a surprise. Bright and shocking among the dry, dull grasses or rising from ground that was too sandy for almost anything else. But there they were, defiant and resilient. They called them wildflowers then, and she would pick handfuls for her mother, who would make tea with them but always save a couple and set them in a jam jar filled with water. Centre them on the kitchen table. Circles of yellow shining in the room.

Something inside Florence's chest clenches. She bends, digs deep into the earth with a flathead screwdriver, a trick she learned to get right down to the root where it begins, and pulls it up. Holds it a moment, its gilded petals almost glowing in the sunlight. She adds the dandelion to the pile of weeds she's collected and discards it on the gravel driveway in the back to dry and wither.

SPRING 1908
Quincy Lake, Saskatchewan

"**D**ON'T GO WHERE you're not wanted," Maamaa says as she unpacks the wagon at the campsite.

"I know," Florence says, annoyed but trying to hide it. Florence knows how to keep out of the way, how to move about without drawing attention. Maamaa doesn't need to ruin it with all her warnings.

"And mind Honeybee," Maamaa says, reaching in the wagon for a stack of wool blankets to carry to the tent.

"What?" Florence bursts out, and looks at her brother, who's on all fours wrestling with the Boyers' dog, who followed their caravan all the way from their home at the Nest. All she wants is some time away from him.

"Did you hear me?" Maamaa asks. Maamaa didn't even want to come to town after Paapaa organized the trip with Uncle Nap and the Boyers and relented only when Florence said she'd get the groceries so Maamaa could stay at the camp. Clancy wasn't part of the arrangement.

"Yes, I heard you!" It comes out sharply.

But Maamaa whirls around to her, a look of silent steel on her face, and Florence changes her tone.

"I'll watch him," Florence says, compliant. Clancy ruins everything.

Paapaa, who's helping the Boyers set up their tent, catches the interaction and walks over. "Kwaayesh natoohta kii maamaa," he says, but his voice is calm and even; he always settles things before they boil over.

"I *am* listening," Florence says to him. "I'll watch him, I promise." She'd rather go with Clancy than not at all.

"Si kwaarek," Paapaa says, and turns to face Maamaa. "Si boon. Kaaya ooshaam naakatwayhta," he says and kisses her forehead.

Maamaa softens, then starts off to their own tent, blankets piled in her arms. "Speak English," she says to him on the way.

"Can we go now?" Florence asks, voice as light as possible.

"Just wait," Paapaa says. He reaches into his pocket, pulls out two silver coins, and hands one to her and one to Clancy.

"Five cents?" Clancy jumps up, ecstatic.

Florence can hardly believe it and stares at the coin in her palm, glossy and glinting in the sunlight. It's money he made at the mine, but Florence doesn't care and is glad to spend it now.

"Now, go on, then," he says, pointing with his lips towards town.

"Let's go!" Clancy takes off running.

"Be back for supper," Paapaa shouts after him.

Florence follows Clancy through the field, coin clutched in her fist. When they reach the grid road and the first houses on the edge of town, they're both winded, throats on fire, and slow to catch their breath.

"Hold on," Florence says and stops. She pulls her drawstring pouch from her pocket. The moosehide is a rich brown and soft; the darkness of it contrasts with the bright rose beaded on its front. Florence picked the three shades of pink herself: blush, salmon, and a shade so deep it's almost cherry.

"Does Maamaa know you have that?" Clancy asks.

"Auntie helped me make it," Florence says, both answering and not answering his question. Florence needed help with the intricate petals—they fold over and in on themselves and hide an infinity symbol in the rose's centre. She made it especially for this trip. Florence drops the nickel inside and it clanks against the other coins—the two pennies she earned from helping Auntie with her beadwork and the change Maamaa had given her to buy the groceries she requested.

Stepping onto the first residential street, they both fall quiet. The houses are bigger than she remembered, and the newer ones even larger. Rooms are stacked on top of rooms, and there are windows on every side—there'll always be a corner flooded with light. Some houses are ringed with colourful bushes, others with rows of obedient flowers. The air even smells different in town, but she can't describe how.

They hear Main Street before they reach it, and Florence picks up the pace, pulled by the rush of it. By its energy. Voices call out; so many horses are clip-clopping, and in the midst of it all, the deep rumble of car engines, so low and loud, it makes her heart shake. She stops when she gets there just to take it in.

"Where's McCloud's?" Clancy asks, looking up and down the street for the one store they know they can enter. Everyone from the Nest shops there. Rumour has it the mother of the man who owns it was Michif, but no one's confirmed. You can't ask someone a question like that.

"It's over there." She points to the store with the red awning. "But let's look around first," she says, watching a woman with a hat as wide as a parasol swoosh by, skirt rippling behind her.

"Let's go!" he says, jogging on the spot, eager to head straight there. Florence grabs his shoulder to calm him. This is exactly why she didn't want to bring him. All he cares about is sweets, but she wants to experience the town itself, to see it and feel it. To be swallowed up by it.

"Come on." Clancy draws the words out, impatient.

"No, I have to get oats and flour and sugar for Maamaa and also tea for Auntie. I don't want to lug all that through town. We'll look around first, then go to McCloud's."

Clancy whines, but she starts walking and he relents. She heads in the opposite direction of McCloud's. She'll walk down one side first, then up the other so she doesn't miss anything. Clancy follows behind initially, but then he races ahead to examine a car, laughing at its headlights.

"They look like bug eyes!" he says, then races farther up to look at something else, dodging people and the goods they carry. He catches scornful looks, which is bad enough, but worse, he doesn't even know he does. He's still such a child—she can't look in even one window because she has to keep an eye on him.

"Listen," she says, rushing to catch up to him, "why don't you go straight to McCloud's and wait for me there."

"Yes!" He hops up and down. "I'm going to get toffees and peppermints—"

"Wait for me there!" she repeats, but he's already dashing back up the street to the red awning. Florence waits until she sees him enter.

On her own, Florence walks slowly, mindful to keep out of everyone's way while still able to glance through the windows as she goes. There's a furniture store with rocking chairs and stained-glass lamps. A grocery store with a row of angled crates outside it, all of them stuffed with apples. So many apples that if you didn't pick them out carefully, they'd topple down onto the street. Another store with windows lined with various bottles and vials filled with what must be tinctures and medicines. Every need and want met in one single place. You'd never have to go anywhere else.

At the end of Main, a small clutch of people are gathered around the last store on the block. She slows as she approaches, keeps her distance. The store has two great glass windows, one on either side of the door, and hanging across the top of them are paper chains, the links alternating in red and white. Below the decorations are bright signs in various colours and types of lettering. Once a few people have moved inside and it's less congested, Florence steps forward. In the corner of one window, a porcelain tea set is on display, gold-rimmed and painted a pale blue with flowers the colour of a sunset. Stacked behind the cups and saucers are tins and tins of different kinds of tea. She didn't know there were so many kinds. She starts to head to the other window.

"Don't be shy," a man in the doorway says to her. "We've got the best deals in town and products you can't find anywhere else."

Florence freezes. He's talking to her.

"Hollinger's Groceries and Provisions. Just opened this week, come in and look around."

"I . . ." she starts but is unable to voice any of the words stumbling around in her head. He's actually inviting her in.

"Thank you," she says, and steps back, imagining the scolding she'll get from Maamaa. But she bumps into a couple who are being solicited by the same man who just spoke to her. "I'm sorry," she says, but they stare at her, waiting for her to enter. Her stomach burns, and the burn spreads.

"Are you going in?" one of them asks.

But wouldn't Maamaa and the others be pleased to know there's another store they can shop at? Perhaps a new store would entice Maamaa to come into town herself. Florence steps up and enters.

Inside and along either side of the walls are two long glass cases that stretch the length of the store and, behind those, shelves that reach the ceiling, stacked with jars and tins and bottles. Florence has to keep sidestepping other shoppers because the place is so full.

"Can I help you, young lady?" a woman behind one of the glass counters asks Florence. She's wide with a wide smile to match.

"Yes, please." Her voice comes out quiet, but the woman still hears her.

Florence lists all the items Maamaa instructed her to get, plus the tea for Auntie.

"Are you doing the shopping all on your own today?" the woman asks, impressed.

Florence nods.

"Good for you," she says and pokes the man who's standing beside her. The man, whose moustache hangs over his lip like a comb, gives Florence an approving smile, and she blushes because others now look at her too. "Our children weren't as helpful when they were your age," the woman says, nodding to the young man at the doorway, the one who welcomed Florence in. She rings up the items on the till. "I can pack these up," she says, and reaches for the folded cloth bag Florence pulls from her skirt pocket.

Florence takes out her drawstring pouch from her other pocket, places it on the counter, and loosens the leather strings. She pours the coins onto the glass display case.

"Look at that," the woman says. She stops packing the items and stares at Florence's pouch. "Is that yours?"

Florence nods, proud of her work, but senses a shift in the woman's demeanour.

Her husband—the man with the moustache—looks over the woman's shoulder at the pouch, then eyes Florence. "One of them half-breeds down the way," he says to his wife in a tone that's no longer approving.

The others who stopped to watch Florence begin turning away.

"Crawled out from the rats' nest," one of them says.

"Saw a few of them setting up on the edges of town on my way in," another adds.

"How many?"

Florence counts out the coins, her hands trembling, pretending not to hear.

"Three or four families."

"Someone better inform the cops."

"I'm sorry," the woman says to Florence, "we don't serve your kind here. Did you not see the sign?"

Florence saw the signs in the window but she has no way of knowing what they mean. Besides, the woman's son invited her in. But she can't say either of these things and only shakes her head.

"McCloud's is at the other end. They'll take your lot." The woman removes the items from the cloth bag, and Florence scrambles to pick up her coins from the glass counter. But the more she rushes, the more they slide from her grip. She finally drags them to the counter's edge and pushes them into her pouch. As soon as she's done, the woman's wiping down the glass Florence touched with a rag. Florence snatches the empty cloth grocery bag and hurries out the door. Runs around the corner to a side street and stops when she's put enough distance between herself and Hollinger's.

Maamaa would be furious. Florence will get a tanning for sure if she finds out. But it wasn't her fault. It was the shopkeeper's son's fault—he made the mistake, not her. Still, Maamaa wouldn't see it that way. Florence can't tell anyone.

She makes her way back to McCloud's through the residential streets, not wanting to risk any more trouble.

Clancy's leaning against the side of McCloud's when she finds him, chewing his candy like a cow, absent-minded and uninterested in anything but the contents of the paper funnel in his hands. Honeybee. She refuses to call him that. Maybe it's because Paapaa hasn't given her a nickname.

"You have to buy some of these," he says, pointing into his funnel at some kind of toffee.

"I'll just be a few minutes," she tells him and heads inside. It's a different place entirely from the stores at the other end of Main. It's dusty and dank, with far fewer things on the shelves, some of which are completely empty. It feels uncared for, and suddenly Florence doesn't want any candy. Doesn't want to buy anything from here. She wanders the aisles to get the things she couldn't at Hollinger's, and at the till, she decides she better buy something for herself; if she doesn't, it'll raise suspicion. She picks a single Hershey bar.

Outside, Clancy teases her for spending an entire nickel on one item, but she doesn't argue or justify her purchase. Doesn't even open it, just slides it into the bag with the other items for later. Her mind's too preoccupied, turning over every moment of what happened earlier and how each event unfolded. She reaches into her pocket to feel the moosehide pouch. They walk back to camp, both of them slow and sluggish, but for different reasons.

When Clancy complains of a stomachache and has to take a break, she guides him to some shade under a spindly tree, and he sits down, puts his hands over his cramping belly. It's then, while watching him, his eyes closed and unaware he's being watched, Florence sees herself in a new way. When the two of them are together, you see the similarities—same mouth shape, same eyes. But when they're apart, you see the differences: Clancy has Maamaa's soil-black hair and Paapaa's dark skin, but she has Paapaa's brown hair, and skin like Maamaa's, as light as dried prairie grass in the fall. Her own stomach tingles.

SEPTEMBER 1946

Torduvalle, Saskatchewan

TEA AND TWO small buttermilk pancakes and syrup for breakfast, an apple packed for her midmorning snack. Tuesday. The start of a new workweek. The previous one—and all its disruption—is long gone. It's over and behind her. At six thirty, she locks her front door and heads down her walkway, the stars twinkly in the expansive sky above. *Clip-clip* on the way to the office. *Ka-thunk* and *flick* when she arrives.

She unties her headscarf and slides off her coat. There are items already in her inbox. Mr. Hicks often works on the weekends. Florence once tried to come in on a Saturday herself, but Mr. Hicks said she already did too much and it would weigh on his conscience if she worked the weekends too. He forbade it. He laughed and said he would fire her and bring in someone less competent to teach her a lesson. It was only a joke. Still, she's never come in on the weekends since.

Florence sorts through the tasks: A letter to type to their client Mr. Oborowsky detailing the results of his property assessment for his claim, more meetings with prospective clients to add to the Second-Floors' calendars, a list of requested supplies to order from their vendor. A little shiver of relief runs through her. Shirley says she sometimes feels like a hamster in a wheel at Pratt's, running around and around and not getting anywhere. But Florence likes the image of herself as a hardworking hamster. She'd rather be moving and breathless, exhausted with effort, than be sitting in a corner of a cage stagnating with nothing but her own thoughts to occupy her. Besides, the point of their job is to keep things running; their hamster wheel actually fuels the office, it's the beating heart keeping it alive. And hearts are hidden under muscle and bone and flesh. They aren't meant to be seen.

"Morning, Florence," Mr. Hicks says. He's the next to arrive, as always.

"Morning, Mr. Hicks. How was your weekend?"

"Good. Mrs. Hicks was visiting her family in the city, so I was able to focus on work."

"So I see." Florence holds up the letter she's completed.

"Thank you," he says, taking the paperwork and heading up to the second floor.

With Mrs. Hicks away, Shirley likely had things to focus on as well. But again, not her business.

Minutes later, the other junior and senior agents trickle in: Peter and Jeremy first, then Mr. Henry, followed by Mr. Broughton.

"You're feeling better today, Florence?" Mr. Broughton asks as he passes her desk.

"Right as rain," Florence says.

"Wonderful. Jennie asked me to check in with you."

"That's kind of her. I'll ring her this evening."

"She'd like that," Mr. Broughton says as he tromps up the stairs.

It's almost a quarter after nine when Shirley finally arrives. She breezes in with a smile on her face.

"I had just the best weekend, Flossie," she says.

"I'm glad to hear it." It's clear that Shirley would love to tell her more, but Florence won't ask questions. Boundaries must be kept.

When it's time for Florence's break, the office is full and humming steadily. She slices and eats her apple in the kitchenette, then heads out for her walk, a brisk four-block loop to get her heart pumping. When she returns, the mood in the office has changed. Mr. Henry and Mr. Broughton are on the main level, milling about oddly, and Peter and Jeremy stand near their desks, made awkward and nervous by the presence of their superiors. Florence looks to Shirley for clues, but she only shrugs, just as befuddled.

"Gentlemen, is there something I can help you with?" Florence says, heading to her desk.

"We're just waiting," Mr. Broughton says.

"Actually," says Mr. Hicks, who's descending the stairs, "would you mind locking the door and flipping the sign for a minute, Florence?"

"Certainly." But a small knot ties itself in her stomach. When she returns, Mr. Hicks is perched on a low filing cabinet against the back wall, unusually casual for him.

"I have some good news," he says, removing his glasses and tucking them into his breast pocket. "Thanks to the hard work of everyone on this team, the high standards we set, and the excellent service we provide our clients, we are continuing our expansion." He pauses. "Mr. Broughton, you were the real push behind this next step. Why don't you make this announcement?"

Mr. Broughton smiles bashfully, but then strides to the back wall and takes the stage. "After some careful planning and research, and a lot of negotiations—"

"He means wining and dining," Mr. Hicks puts in.

"That too." Mr. Broughton laughs. "We have acquired Lewis and Wright Insurance in the town of Forsyth."

"Huzzah!" Peter says, and claps along with Jeremy.

"That's incredible," Shirley says. "Isn't it, Flossie?"

"It is, it's wonderful news." Florence turns to Mr. Hicks. "Congratulations." Then to the other Second-Floors: "Congratulations to you as well."

"Congratulations to us all," says Mr. Hicks. "You included, Florence. You ladies keep us running a tight, efficient ship, which has contributed to our company's success."

Florence beams. She is a part of it, isn't she? Pratt's has certainly grown in the years Florence has been there, but purchasing another business is a whole new level.

"But rather than run two offices in two separate locations, we will be merging Lewis and Wright Insurance into our location here. Our client base will increase by twenty-five percent, and we will be gaining another senior agent, a junior agent, and a junior adjuster, which I'm sure makes Mr. Henry happy, since he's been the sole adjuster here."

Mr. Henry nods and smiles to himself. Pleased as punch to finally have his own underling, no doubt.

"Aren't there five staff members at Forsyth?" Peter asks.

"That's correct, but their president is retiring, and their secretary has found other employment in Forsyth."

Florence calculates in her head the additional filing cabinets they'll need for all the incoming clients, wonders where the new employees will sit. If they bring in two more desks for the new juniors, her desk and Shirley's will need to be moved forward, and they'll be practically sitting in the foyer. On the one hand, it means more work, and her teachers at the Queen City School for Secretarial Training always told her that the reward for good work was more work. But on the other hand, Florence doesn't want to have so much on her plate that she can't keep on top of it. That's not a reputation she wants, not the person she wants to become.

"This merger will require some logistical adjustments in the office," Mr. Hicks says. "We'll be clearing out the storage room upstairs to accommodate two of the incoming staff."

Storage room? Hardly. It has two filing cabinets and one bookshelf, but it also has three armchairs, each with its own side table, and one large trolley cart stacked with glasses and bottles with varying levels of alcohol.

"And now is as good a time as any to share with you all that in light of this new growth, which was largely initiated by Mr. Broughton's keen research and innovative approach, he will become Pratt's new—and first—account manager."

More applause and congratulations. Mr. Hicks pulls Jeremy aside and asks him to run upstairs, and when he returns, he's carrying a bottle of champagne.

"Please pour some for everyone," Mr. Hicks instructs him, and Jeremy tours the room to distribute the champagne in mugs, glasses, whatever's handy. Shirley laughs as he pours some into her teacup.

"We will, of course, have a much larger celebration to welcome our new members, some of whom plan to relocate here to Torduvalle with their families. We plan to host a banquet at the end of the month so all our families can get to know one another."

"How wonderful," Shirley says, sipping from her cup.

Florence has already started drafting a letter to the incoming clients in her head, a welcome letter to express how delighted Pratt's is to work with them. It's the kind of thoughtful service Pratt's is known for, that she's helped to create. But now there's also a banquet to plan. A venue to book, caterers. All these new clients and new staff, and still, there's just her and Shirley to handle all the secretarial work.

Across the room, Mr. Broughton's glass is filled a second time. Success comes easily to some. She handled some of his files when he was away in Europe; she stepped up and worked directly with his clients herself when the company needed it. But that's just how the world is. Some people are born into certain places, certain positions, and there's nothing anyone can do about it. There might be some businesses in larger cities that allow women in higher positions, but this is Torduvalle. She's happy with what she's achieved, even if she knows she could do more.

"We'll need to get a list of the clients from Forsyth as soon as possible," Florence says to Shirley, and heads back to her desk to update her list of tasks with all the new work that's required for the merger while the others continue to celebrate.

Later, when the champagne bottle is empty and people are trickling back to their desks, Mr. Hicks approaches Florence and asks to see her upstairs. She brings her updated task list, which has grown exponentially, and the draft content for the welcome letter that she scribbled in her notepad for his review.

"Close the door and have a seat," he says when they enter his office. The smell of cigarette smoke permeates everything: the wallpaper, the leather chair, the leather-bound books on his shelves.

Florence begins going over her list with Mr. Hicks and creates a timeline in her head as she does. She'll organize it all again later. "And I've started to draft a letter to our new clients." She reads out loud what she's written so far.

"That's fine, that's fine," Mr. Hicks says, "I'm sure whatever you have will be perfect. It always is."

"I wouldn't want to type it up without your review first," Florence says, tearing the draft from her pad and placing it on his desk.

"Of course. I'll read it later," he says, smiling. "This isn't why I asked you up here, Mrs. Banks." He pauses. "In all the years you've been here, you've done exemplary work. You're dedicated, thorough, assiduous. And on top of it all, you understand that this business is sometimes sensitive and requires confidentiality."

"Absolutely." They handle clients' private information all the time—Florence knows much more about some people in town than they're likely comfortable with.

"Quite simply, you're trustworthy."

Florence looks down at the notebook on her lap. It's silly to feel flattered for just doing her job. Her cheeks warm.

"You're the most trustworthy person I've ever worked with." He meets her eye.

He is referring to her trustworthiness in the office, of course, but he also might be obliquely referencing his ongoing relationship with Shirley. Florence nods.

"And there are more exciting events on the horizon—things too premature to disclose yet, but it means that senior management will no longer have time to do some of the things we've done in the past." He pauses. "We've decided, Mrs. Banks, to promote you to senior secretary."

"Goodness." The word escapes her mouth, airy and breathless.

"Given that all other areas of our company are growing, we'll need to grow our secretarial pool, naturally. This is one of the areas we'd like you to manage."

"Me?"

He nods. "The senior secretary will be responsible for hiring and training all the new girls. You will take a load off our plates, Florence. For now, we'll start with two new hires."

She writes *Two* in her notepad to keep focused, but her palms are sweaty. She never would have guessed this was a possibility.

"Are you up to the task?" He winks. "Of course you are. You're a model employee, Mrs. Banks, one of the hardest workers I've ever known. We lucked out when you moved here, and now with the town and other businesses growing, we know we need to challenge you to keep you."

This is another reason why she never wanted to leave Pratt's—Mr. Hicks has always appreciated her. Always understood her in ways that others didn't.

He lights a cigarette. "This promotion also means you will move up to the second floor and directly assist those of us here with the more sensitive files."

"Of course," she says, adjusting in her seat to hide the trembling in her knees.

They begin to discuss the logistics of her promotion—the timing of her move and the installation of a phone, as she'll triage the calls that get routed upstairs—but most of what they exchange is a blur. Florence is so stunned by this turn of events that she's having trouble comprehending it all. She's getting a promotion. She's being entrusted with sensitive files.

"I didn't want to make this announcement publicly downstairs," he says when they've finished discussing logistics, "because I know you don't like the attention."

"I appreciate that, Mr. Hicks." It would have been awkward, too much fuss. She will celebrate at home in private. Maybe she'll call Jennie tonight and tell her.

"We can discuss more of the particulars in the coming days," he says, looking at his watch.

Florence rises, understanding that he has other business to get to. "Of course. Thank you for this opportunity, Mr. Hicks." She could gush profusely like others might, but it's best to remain professional.

She leaves his office, closes the door behind her, and stands there a moment on the landing, taking in the space where her new station will be. It's small, cramped even, so she'll have to downsize to a smaller desk, but it'll be fine. Her own little warren. She's always believed that you succeed by keeping quiet and working hard. She believed it and it must be true because here she is. On the second floor. Not truly a Second-Floor, but she will work there amongst them nonetheless. She balances on the top step, hovering while she hears the sounds from the main floor rise up. She feels the weight of all that she's accomplished gather, a flutter in her chest.

WALKING HOME AT THE end of the day, Florence takes a different route. She retraces the path she took the day of her interview. The town's grown a bit since then; there are a few more blocks with new houses and another new street under construction. But she follows the same streets as before and ponders all that she's achieved in her life. She wouldn't have gotten to this point if she'd remained Florence Campeau. It wouldn't have been possible. The decisions she made were the right ones. There was no other way.

It's almost six thirty when Florence turns up her street. Before she's at the door, Jennie's rushing towards her across her lawn.

"Congratulations!" She waves a bottle in her hands. "Garth spilled the beans over the weekend," she says, following Florence into the house, "and I had to keep my mouth shut until now."

Jennie says she'll stay for one glass only and then let Florence get on with her evening, but Florence is pleased to talk about some of her plans for the new secretarial pool. Even just calling it a pool is pleasing. They top their drinks up and Florence forgets all about the trout and green beans she had planned for her supper.

"Who do you think you'll hire?" Jennie asks, expression open, expectant.

"Are you interested?"

"Oh, heavens, no. Garth would have a fit." A pensive look flashes across her face. She brushes the thought away. "Did he tell you about the banquet?"

"Yes, he did—it's thoughtful."

"Isn't it? It's a lovely way to welcome the new staff and their families to Torduvalle."

"It will also be a lot of work," Florence says.

"Yes, but don't worry—I'll be helping you organize it!" Jennie says, bouncing in her seat.

"You?"

"Yes! I suppose Garth's throwing me a bone so I'll stop thinking about having a real job, but I'll take what I can get. So don't worry about having too much to do, Florence—I'm ready to jump right in."

"That's wonderful. We should begin with writing up a list—"

"But not tonight, Florence," Jennie says. "Tonight, you relax and bask. Bask!" She throws her arms wide, exaggerating.

Florence laughs.

"What's funny about that? You should reward yourself—buy something special, take a trip. Somewhere grand and flashy."

"I don't know about that."

"We went on vacation twice after we got married—before the kids. Seems a lifetime ago. When was your last vacation?"

"Vacation? I've never had one," Florence says as if it's just dawning on her.

Jennie gasps. "No."

"It's true."

"Then you must. If anyone deserves a vacation, it's you."

Florence shakes her head at the idea, but then she smiles.

"If you could go to one place in the world, anywhere at all, where would it be?"

"Venice." A twinge in her gut. She wants to reach out and grab the word, stuff it back in her throat.

"Why Venice?"

"It was a place my husband always dreamed of going." She swallows, but her mouth is dry. "I don't know why, but I still think of going. Even without him."

Jennie smiles sympathetically. "It might be different now, though. All those places in Europe. So changed . . ." Jennie wrinkles her brow. "I'd like to go to Las Vegas or Miami. Maybe Hawaii."

Florence relaxes. She didn't give anything away after all. Jennie isn't interested in Venice, doesn't press. She doesn't know about Venetian beads, doesn't know what it's like to hold those round specks of glass in her palms and wonder where and how they were made. But this is exactly what happens when you let people get too close. You grow too comfortable and forget where the lines and the lies are. She has to be more careful.

SPRING 1908
Quincy Lake, Saskatchewan

"**D**ID YOU HAVE any trouble in town?" Maamaa asks when she and Clancy return to camp.

Florence shakes her head. "But Clancy's sick," she says to direct the attention elsewhere.

"What's wrong?" Maamaa asks as Clancy walks up to her for comfort, hunched and clutching his stomach.

"Too much candy," Florence says.

Maamaa uses the end of her skirt to wipe the candy evidence from the corners of his mouth. "Go lie down until supper," she says to him.

For the rest of the afternoon, while the women drink tea around the fire and gossip, and the men are drinking at the one pub in town that will serve them, Florence sits off by herself thinking about what happened at Hollinger's. In the evening when Maamaa asks her to help prepare supper, she chops potatoes and onions silently, still consumed with the day's events. She doesn't notice when the women start to get angry because the men haven't returned yet and the rubaboo has long been boiling on the flames.

"Go easy on 'em," Uncle Joe says. He had declined to join the men, saying he was far too old. "It was a rough winter for them." He's referring to the mine, which none of the men will talk about.

Maamaa doesn't like to talk about the past and about being Métis, and

Paapaa doesn't like to talk about the mine. And now Florence has something she doesn't want to talk about too.

Maamaa and the other women eventually decide to eat without the men, and Florence dishes up the food. Clancy declines a bowl, but Maamaa forces it on him, saying he needs real food after all the sweets. After supper, Uncle Joe takes out his fiddle and plays a tune to distract everyone, and it works. With more than just candy in his belly, Clancy finds new energy and begs Joe for a faster tune so he can jig and show off. He even gets Maamaa up on her feet to do the chi galop and she discards her shawl to keep up.

Uncle Joe is between tunes when the sound of horses approaching breaks through the black night. Their own horses are secured behind their tents, so the air over the camp grows taut. Florence catches Maamaa and Genevieve Boyer exchange glances across the fire. The Boyers' dog growls and gives a warning bark, then hushes when Aunt Genevieve snaps her fingers.

"Go to your sister," Maamaa says to Clancy and nudges him towards Florence, who's farthest from whoever's arriving.

"Is it Paapaa?" he asks.

Florence shrugs. The shadows resolve into two men walking slowly and weaving slightly. Behind them are two horses, each with a rider. Florence puts her arm around Clancy.

Joe rises and both he and Genevieve move to Maamaa's side. "Evening," Uncle Joe calls out.

"I believe these belong to you," a man answers. The light from the fire finally reaches them, illuminating two officers on the horses shepherding Paapaa and Nap like cattle back from town. Judging by the men's loose, clumsy gait, the assistance may be necessary. "They overstayed their welcome," the same man says, climbing down off his horse.

The other uniformed man, whose hair seems too long for an officer's, also dismounts and walks towards the fire.

"No one likes a half-breed, even a happy one," Paapaa says, smiling, and then he shrugs, feigning shock.

"Watch it," the officer behind him warns.

"Kiiyaamaya," Maamaa says to Paapaa, her anger apparent.

Nap laughs at Paapaa's joke and loses his balance, collapsing on the ground. That sets Paapaa off laughing. Paapaa's had spirits before—he often does on special occasions, like the others do—but this feels different because when his eyes catch the firelight, they're glassy and wet, like they belong to someone else.

"I feel sick," Clancy whispers.

"It's okay," Florence says but doesn't believe it herself.

The shaggy-haired officer has moved around the fire and is now in the shadows by their tents, inspecting their belongings, looking through crates, and even opening their tent flaps. But he doesn't barge in or rummage through their things roughly like others have. He moves slowly and carefully.

"You fellows sleep it off tonight and I suggest you head back first thing," the officer behind Paapaa says, but he's looking at Joe, who's stepping towards Nap to collect him. "We'll circle back here in the morning."

"Is that a suggestion," Paapaa says without turning around to face the officer, "or an order?" His tone has changed, the playfulness now gone.

No sound but the crackling of the fire. Florence tenses with each pop.

"Irwin, stop," Maamaa hisses at him.

"Excuse me?" the officer behind Paapaa steps forward, bearing down on him.

The shaggy-haired officer stops searching and heads back to the fire. His movements are still slow, almost gentle, but Florence sees his hand move to his holster.

"I'm just curious because we planned to stay until Sunday," Paapaa says, but he says it to Maamaa and not the officer. "That's what we decided."

The officer leans over Paapaa, his chest against Paapaa's back. "It's an order," he says right into his ear.

"I don't feel well," Clancy whispers to Florence, which catches the shaggy-haired officer's attention.

Florence doesn't dare say anything; she only pulls Clancy tighter.

"Is there going to be a problem?" the officer asks Paapaa.

A long silence.

"No, sir," Joe says. "We'll be out when the sun's up."

"I'm not convinced until I hear it from this one." The officer waits for

Paapaa's response. "What do you say?" He shoves Paapaa's shoulder and someone gasps.

Paapaa closes his eyes and drops his head, hunching over, as if he's about to topple like Nap. But he doesn't. "Yes," he finally says. "We'll be out."

The officer nods and then steps back from Paapaa. Florence slowly lets out the air she was holding trapped inside.

"Florence..." Clancy says and pulls away from her. "I'm—" He stops because a thick mess of rubaboo and half-digested candy snakes out of his mouth.

Everyone turns to look.

"Is Clancy okay?" Paapaa squints over the fire towards them.

Florence pats Clancy's back as he leans over. "Yes," she says, her voice unsteady.

"Let's go," the officer behind Paapaa calls to the other and turns to walk away.

Maamaa speaks to Paapaa in Michif, giving him hell, and Clancy moans again.

"Wait," Paapaa calls out to the officer returning to his horse. "My wallet!"

Clancy vomits a second time, and the shaggy-haired officer steps towards them. "Is the little guy all right?" he asks Florence and bends down to look at Clancy.

As he does, Paapaa turns to follow the officer receding into the shadows, but he trips over a branch and stumbles forward. He picks up his pace to keep from falling, arms reaching out. But when the shaggy-haired officer turns to look up, all he sees is Paapaa rushing towards his partner as if about to tackle him.

The officer nearing his horse hears Paapaa rush up behind him and turns. He raises his hands to prepare for the impact. "Hey, hey, hey, wait!"

It all happens so fast, Florence doesn't have time to tell the shaggy-haired officer that he's got it wrong, that he's making a mistake, when he reaches for his revolver.

When the crack rings out, something inside Florence shifts. She doesn't look ahead, doesn't dare take her eyes off the shaggy-haired officer. The only thought in her head is a question: She wonders whether the shaggy-haired officer thinks she looks like a half-breed too.

SEPTEMBER 1946

Torduvalle, Saskatchewan

THURSDAY MORNING. FLORENCE slings the messenger bag used for office errands over her shoulder and decides to take a longer break. *Clip-clip* down the street and then up Third Avenue. Her own errands first. At Nelson's, she finds Hilde bent over the sewing machine, so focused on the length of cloth moving through the machine's teeth that she doesn't hear the chime of the door when Florence enters. Satin, cobalt blue. Shiny, and so long its folds pour down the side of the sewing desk almost to the floor. Florence studies her a moment. The arc of her back. The way her neck, head, and shoulder all curve forward over her work, almost encircling it, protecting. Her posture is familiar to Florence, and her own body twinges as if yearning. "Morning," Florence says to break the moment. She sets the messenger bag on the counter and digs out the ticket from her purse.

"Oh, morning," Hilde says, then rises to collect the tattersall skirt. She places it in a paper bag.

"Looks beautiful." Florence motions to the blue dress.

"It will be the death of me—I'm working from pictures only and creating a pattern as I go." Hilde hands her a magazine photo of a willowy blonde-haired woman wearing an elegant flowy gown. The model is turned away from the camera but looks back towards it coyly, a large diamond-encrusted orb on her earlobe.

"That's magical."

"And it's magical thinking that makes Mrs. Hendrickson think she's going to look the same in such a slim-fitting cut." They laugh, and Florence pays, then tucks the skirt under her arm and pushes out the door to finish the rest of her errands for work. Near Main Street, the smell of gas hits her as she passes the station on the corner at Third. Perry, the attendant, crouches over two jerry cans as he fills them; he dribbles some gas on the ground as he pulls the pump out and places the nozzle back in its hook. Kid's always been sloppy. Florence waves and he nods back.

Behind him, a few feet away, is Frank Huber's half-ton with Frank himself behind the wheel. Florence would have waved at him but he's looking away. Perry twists the tops back on the cans, and a man rises from the bed of Frank's truck and reaches down to hoist the cans up. Florence's stomach wavers. The man from Nick's Diner—Clancy. He looks up, sees her watching. And nods. Florence snaps her head forward and marches to the bank, jaw clenched so tight her teeth ache.

There's a line at the bank and she tucks in at the end. She can see the gas station through the door when someone else enters. He's still here. And obviously hired on with Mr. Huber. She keeps glancing back at the station whenever the doors open for other customers.

"Good morning, Florence," Lyle Lesley says when she reaches the teller window, his pencil-thin black moustache so shiny under the lights, it almost glows. Mr. Lesley's the friendliest and most charismatic person in town—she always thought if anyone in Torduvalle could be a Hollywood star, it would be him—but not even he can put her at ease right now.

Florence pulls the office's ledger from the messenger bag but her body clenches, every muscle rigid and stiff. She wrestles with the bag to release the book, and both her purse and the bagged skirt slip from her other arm, fall to the floor. Everything tumbling down.

"You all right?"

"All thumbs today." She forces out a laugh, but her hands shake as she collects her things.

"You look wan, dear," he says as she rises. There's genuine concern on his face, and she's hit with a different kind of pang. The people in Torduvalle have always been so kind to her, right from day one. Silly to be so rattled, so out of control.

"I'm fine, thank you."

"What can I do for you today?"

"Deposits," she says, handing the book to him along with an envelope of cheques. He sorts through them, date-stamping, signing, logging his own records. Florence turns her head back to the doors but they're closed, and the bank's slim, rectangular windows that line Main Street are too high up to see the gas station.

"How are things at Pratt's?" Mr. Lesley asks, bringing her attention back to him.

"Pardon me?"

"Pratt's—we've heard about the merger."

"Yes, yes. Lots to do, very busy."

"Must be exciting?"

"Yes," Florence says, still flustered, not able to engage on the topic, all thoughts colliding in her head. "Listen," she says, her voice a bit quieter, "do you happen to know who Mr. Huber—Frank—has working for him?"

Mr. Lesley looks at her as if he's waiting for her to say more, but she doesn't. "Do you mean the Indian?"

"I just saw Mr. Huber outside with some new help, but he didn't look like someone from town."

"Strange that he's hiring outsiders, isn't it?" he says. "There are still good local men looking for work." He points to the teller next to him. "Bernice's son, for one."

"I'm sure he'd work a lot harder too," Florence says, and the back of her throat tightens.

Mr. Lesley smiles awkwardly and then nods. "He might be going to the city," he says, closing the ledger and handing it back to Florence.

"Mr. Huber's helper?"

"Bernice's son. To find work. A shame, don't you think?"

"Yes. A shame, isn't it?" Florence learned long ago that this is what you're supposed to say when someone has to leave Torduvalle.

"Can you imagine? Going off overseas, doing your part, and then coming home to no work? Bernice is so worried."

"It's just awful." Florence slips the ledger back into her bag. Two more weeks, maybe. Three, maximum. After that, the harvest would be over and Huber's helpers would move on.

"By the way, we're starting to collect funds for the Christmas pageant. It's early, I know, but we want to purchase entirely new costumes this year. Would you be interested in donating?"

"Of course." She slides two fives from her wallet. Too much. That amount would cover groceries and sundries for the rest of the month, but she's not a penny-pincher, not anymore. She hands them to Mr. Lesley. It's funny, the impulses that never seem to leave her, even after all this time.

"Wonderful," Mr. Lesley says. "It's nice to know our community can always count on you, Mrs. Banks. The reverend will be pleased."

Another impulse surfaces. "Listen, while I'm here, I'd like to make a withdrawal from my personal account."

"Certainly. How much would you like?"

She considers her needs for the month, the raise she'll receive in next week's paycheque, and the generous Christmas bonus that Pratt's always provides its staff just before the holiday. "This may sound strange, but I would like to take out what's remaining."

"Everything?" Mr. Lesley asks.

"Yes." No sense in doing things by half measures, not at this point.

Mr. Lesley hesitates. "Are you sure?"

Florence nods.

"Are you going to another estate sale?" he says as he starts to process her request.

"I've actually been thinking about a new car." She looks back at the doors again. "With the promotion, I thought I'd get something more reliable."

"I heard about your new role. Congratulations," Mr. Lesley says. "A new car sounds like just the thing to purchase."

Florence compels herself to smile.

When she pushes through the doors, she's grateful to see the gas station lot empty aside from Perry, who's washing down the pavement with a hose, soaking his own trousers in the process. But even if Clancy is just here for harvest season, it won't do. She could run into him anywhere.

Back at the office, she busies herself with sorting through client files, boxing up older ones for archiving in the basement, watching the hours and minutes pass on the clock. When the workday is over, she waits until everyone has left and locks the door behind them. Then she picks up the phone and calls the Huber residence.

Mrs. Huber answers. The two women hardly know each other, since Mrs. Huber rarely comes to town. Florence doesn't tell her who's calling; she simply says, "Tell Clancy his sister phoned." It's the first time she's said his name out loud in decades. It feels strange on her tongue.

"What is the number where he can reach you?"

Florence gives her the office number, which is risky, but it's safer than her party line at home.

In less than thirty minutes, Clancy calls back.

"I need to speak with you," she says and doesn't give him time to reply. "Can you come to my house at eleven tonight?"

"That's late," he says.

The neighbourhood would be in bed by then. "It's urgent."

"I suppose I can."

She gives him her address, tells him to park one street over and come through the alley to her back door. She will leave the back porch light off and her curtains drawn.

SPRING 1908
The Nest, Saskatchewan

MAAMAA STILL HASN'T said anything. Not a single word. Florence can't read anything on her face either, it's blank, but her hands clench the reins as she steers the wagon back home in the dark, the moon mostly hidden behind a veil of clouds. The others are behind, trying to keep up. None of them dare to call out and caution Maamaa to slow down.

Maamaa might have said something after the shot rang out, after she rushed to Paapaa's side, but if so, Florence didn't hear; she was held in place by Clancy and her own fear. She didn't dare step forward. Florence has only flashes of what happened next. Aunt Genevieve whisking her and Clancy into the Boyers' tent. The officers' voices, tense and shouty, filtering through the darkness and the canvas walls. Florence's chest tightening as if gripped in a claw. Clancy's wet face on her neck. The dog's teeth chattering as it hid behind the trunk in the corner.

Time passed and disappeared at once. Then things were being packed up around them, haphazard and messy. In the rush, a few items were left behind when they pulled away in the dark: a bowl near the fire, a strewn blanket near the trees, their own tent, one side drooping because someone had started to take it down but never finished.

Florence holds on to the wooden bench for balance as they plow through the night, her hands stiff in the cold air. Her body aches with every lump and bump on the road. But she won't reach for a blanket in the wagon bed, won't ask Maamaa to slow, preferring to focus on this pain rather than the one that's quietly searing in her chest.

When they turn off the main road and onto the path that leads to the Nest, the dog leaps out of the Boyers' wagon at the rear and races up ahead, barking to announce their arrival home. As the dog passes Florence and Maamaa at the front, its tail is wagging as if it's forgotten the terror it felt earlier, as if the home they're returning to is the same one they left.

The dog and the sounds of the wagons returning in the middle of the night wake the others who didn't join the trip to town. Albert and Elsie LaRose step outside their shack and onto the path, blankets over their shoulders. Nap's wife, Suzette Morin, stands in the entry of her home, door only partially opened, no doubt with her children crowded behind her, hovering to find out who's arriving so late and why.

"Marie?" Albert calls out as Maamaa halts the wagon. But Maamaa just climbs out and strides up the path, leaving Florence to scramble out on her own.

"What's going on?" Elsie asks as Maamaa moves past them towards their own home, the fourth house in the line of seven. Elsie steps forward to help Florence. "Where's Clancy? And Irwin?" A look of concern on her face.

Florence opens her mouth to speak but her throat seizes up, and she suddenly can't get any air in.

"Slowly," Aunt Elsie says, rubbing her back. "Slowly now," she repeats as Florence tries to suck breath back into her body.

The other wagons start pulling in behind them.

"I'll go and see," Albert says and heads off, first handing his blanket to Elsie to wrap around Florence.

The others can tell them what happened. Florence doesn't know how. Paapaa was there, he was standing there, and then he wasn't. Let the others explain, because Florence can't. She pulls the blanket around herself but still can't get warm.

"Taanishi ishpayihk?" Aunt Lillian says as she approaches from the darkness, also awake from the commotion, despite her house being the last in the line at the far northern end and almost hidden behind bushes and trees.

Florence races to her, almost knocks her over when she runs into her arms.

"Taanishi maaka, ma fii?" Auntie asks.

"Paapaa . . ." Florence is finally able to get one word out, but that's all, because the other words are drowned out by her crying.

Aunt Lillian holds her until Joe approaches, carrying Clancy, who's fallen into a deep sleep. Joe tells Lillian to take them back to her home and places Clancy in her arms. Auntie nods without questioning and turns around. As they pass Florence's home, Maamaa is exiting with a basket of laundry, one of the four she brought home from the Duncans' farm on Friday to wash when they returned from Quincy Lake. She sets it down by their firepit and starts to make a fire, though it's far into the night, and morning is still a long way off. But everything else about the day has been strange too.

Lillian's home is Florence's favourite, even more than her own, partly because of its smell. There are always flowers drying—sunflowers, prairie lilies, violets, and Auntie's favourite, asters. Tied in batches with twine and hanging from nails on the walls. Even when the flowers are dried, their scent fills the air. Florence also loves it because of the colours. On her bed, Aunt Lillian has the thickest quilt Florence has ever seen, made with scraps of patterned material in bright pinks and greens and yellows. Material that was gifted to her in exchange for the most colourful thing of all at Auntie's: her beadwork.

People from all over ask Aunt Lillian to bead them things and she always has various projects going at once. Tonight, there's a man's jacket hanging on a kitchen chair, a pattern drawn on its yoke with the paste Auntie makes with flour and water, now dried and ready for beads. There's a pair of moccasin vamps on the table along with a fire bag almost complete. And among the items are bottles and tins and envelopes of beads in every shade and colour possible.

Lillian places Clancy in her bed, putting him close to the wall so there's plenty of room for Florence to climb in, but Florence isn't tired.

"I want to bead," she says to Auntie and gathers her own beadwork from a tea tin she keeps under Auntie's bed.

Auntie watches her a moment, considering. "Kiiyaam, ma fii," she finally says, and lights some candles for Florence at the kitchen table. Then she pulls on the man's wool cardigan she always wears and goes to the door. "Payho oota," she says before heading back outside.

But Florence only wants to stay here anyway, only wants to get lost in the rhythm of beading.

Florence, seated across from the window, sees the moon emerge from behind a cloud as she spreads the containers of beads out before her. She doesn't know what to bead but senses something coming to her. She threads a needle and, guided by instinct, scoops up some yellow beads with its point. She's never beaded freehand before but follows her gut, exhaling as the thread whooshes through the hide, inhaling as she pulls the thread back up. The familiar motion calms her.

When the moon has moved across the window and disappeared from view, Auntie returns and examines her work.

"Zhalii," she says, impressed. "You are better than I was at your age, maybe even better than me now."

The beads are smooth on the hide, all snugged up against each other with no extra spaces, and there's no puckering in the hide. As she examines the flower and the dark leaves surrounding it, she finally understands what she's beading and who she's beading it for. She'll need to make a second flower that's exactly the same and starts to work on that one. Auntie tries to stay up with her and bead too but manages only a few mouse tracks on the fire bag before she crawls into bed with Clancy.

The sun is starting to rise when Florence finally finishes the other flower, but instead of going to sleep, she searches through Auntie's things for something to draw on. She finds a few sheets of old newsprint in the bottom of a crate. She takes one and goes outside and down the path to her home. She expects to find Maamaa in bed sleeping, like everyone else, but she's still outside, sitting by the firepit, hunched over and spent. The loads of laundry she's washed and wrung out now hang on the lines around her, almost glowing in the dawn.

"Maamaa," Florence says, approaching her. "Maamaa?" she says again when there's no response.

But Maamaa doesn't look up, continuing instead to stare at the ashes and burnt logs in the pit that have long since grown cold. Her lips look nearly as pale as the ash.

"We should go inside now," Florence says and tugs her arm, but Maamaa doesn't budge. Florence goes in the house alone, finds her mother's woolen shawl, brings it outside, drapes it around her shoulders.

"I made something for you, Maamaa," Florence says as she bends down and removes her mother's boots. "But I need to measure before I can finish."

Florence reaches into the pit, picks up a piece of charcoal, and begins to trace her mother's foot onto the newsprint, slowly and carefully to ensure a perfect fit. Maamaa doesn't twitch once. When Florence is done, she tries to coax her inside again, but there's still no response and her eyes are empty. Her mother is broken.

Florence should be too because she has felt the same thing trying to take hold of her all night, trying to crush and shatter her. Flatten her into nothingness. But instead of breaking, Florence decides to split, like a thread frayed in two, and part of her will have no memory of this night.

SEPTEMBER 1946
Torduvalle, Saskatchewan

AT EIGHT MINUTES after eleven, there's a light tap on the door. Florence answers it right away and he's barely inside before she's closing it swiftly. Her arm brushes up against his and knocks loose a small package tucked under his arm. He catches it before it falls, and a waft of tobacco puffs out from his clothes into the small entryway.

"Boon swayr," Clancy says, removing his hat, the tracks of a comb's teeth still evident in his hair.

"Come in," Florence says, pointing to the living room.

Clancy plants himself in the Cogswell, filling it with the full size of him. He's bigger than her now. Taller, wider. Like a cottonwood. And there's something else about him that stops her a moment. It's not his bulk or how his skin's grown thick and coarse in age. It's not even that tinge of sadness that's hovered around him since they were young. He has a depth that wasn't there before, a heaviness that she feels seeping into her from across the room.

"Tea?" she asks.

"Please."

Heading to the kitchen, she realizes he's the first male guest she's had in the house. Other men have been inside—Mrs. Sanderson's husband to look at her hot-water tank and then the pipes under the kitchen sink. Repairmen. But none have sat down to visit. She returns with a tray holding cups and saucers and a teapot. She places the tray on the coffee table, then hands him a cup and saucer and pours him tea before stepping around the coffee table to the settee. The springs squeak with her weight as she sits, a small screech in the silence.

"Miiyooshin aen waapamitaan miina," he says.

She hasn't spoken Michif since she left the Nest thirty-five years ago. Once she reached Regina, she never spoke the language out loud again, using only English. Sometimes, especially when she was flustered or if she made a mistake at work, a Michif word would pop up in her head instinctively. Aykooshi. Gishiwaashin. But over time, and with effort, she forced them out.

"You've forgotten?" he asks, seeing she doesn't understand.

"It's been too long." Strange to phrase it like that, like it was accidental.

"Is your husband home?"

"He passed."

"I'm sorry," Clancy says, leaning forward to set his tea down.

"It was years ago now, before I came here," she says, "but I'd prefer not to talk about it." Hinting at tragedy always prevents further discussion on the matter.

Clancy nods and looks away for a moment. "How are you . . . now?" he asks.

"Quite fine, thank you." She pours her own tea and stares at the cup in her hands. "And you?"

"You can sum up more than three decades just like that?" He laughs.

She smiles and shrugs.

"You've done well for yourself. This is a beautiful house. You own or rent?"

"Own. It's small but suits me just fine."

"Built with care. You can tell by the details. The Victorian mouldings." He nods up at the ceiling and points with his lips.

The gesture makes her stomach buzz. She's buried so much of her past that she couldn't pull it forth even if she wanted to, like she was no one before Torduvalle, like she didn't even exist. But here is proof, sitting across from her. It's unnerving and reassuring at once.

"You know about houses?" she asks, though she hadn't been planning to engage in conversation.

"Some. Did some carpentry work for a few years before the war. Loved it." He slides a pipe from his chest pocket. "Do you mind?"

Florence shakes her head.

He stuffs the pipe with tobacco. Funny to see him with one—he hated the smell of it when he was young. He shakes the fire off his match and sets it in the saucer. The tobacco smells piney, like he's brought the forest with him.

"We built houses and shops in and around Quincy Lake before I signed up, but when I got back, most of the people I'd worked for had moved on."

"You signed up . . . for the war?" Florence can hardly imagine him in a uniform.

Clancy nods, leaning back in the chair.

"You went overseas?"

"Twice." He puffs. "In '42 and again in '44. First France, then Belgium."

"I had no idea . . ." She trails off.

"No idea about what? That half-breeds fought in the war? Or that someone who couldn't shoot a slingshot for shit when he was a kid was actually a decent soldier?"

He was a horrible shot. She was okay, but Auntie was the best. She once knocked a mug of moonshine out of Uncle Joe's hands from yards away when he'd had too much and was telling fibs. She looks up and Clancy's watching her smile.

His voice drops a notch: "I thought a lot about the Nest when I was over there." He holds her gaze. There's a softness in his eyes but it's too much for her.

"What brought you to Torduvalle?" She looks back to her tea.

"Same thing that led me to Europe and that leads me anywhere—a job, some money."

"How long has Mr. Huber hired you on for?"

"Nothing's set in stone but at least another month. After that, we'll see."

Before she can ask any more questions, he leans over and picks up the package he brought with him.

"You didn't need to bring anything."

But he holds it out to her until she takes it.

She places it on the empty cushion next to her. "Where do you plan to go once your work with Mr. Huber is over?"

"Won't you open it?"

"Now?"

"Please."

The newsprint it's wrapped in is wrinkled and faded, the ink smeared with fingerprints. The bundle is lighter than it looks. She pulls on the fraying string holding the paper together, and underneath is a shortbread tin, blue and black with silver letters. Inside that, more paper, crinkled into haphazard balls. She pulls out the wads of paper as if plucking bloody bandages from a wound and reveals a pair of moccasins. Her heart crumples.

The five-petalled flower, identical on each vamp. The first design she was taught. The petals a rich lemon and the round centres another yellow but just a hue darker. She wasn't confident in choosing colours so similar, but she'd followed her gut and was glad she did. She wanted the five-petalled flowers to catch the eye, and they do; even after all these years they're pleasing. She chose a deep green for the leaves and stems, and the contrast makes the flowers explode off the hide. They're big and bright like suns. Dandelions.

The first pair of vamps she'd beaded all on her own.

Silence stuffs itself into the room as Florence runs her fingers over the beads. They're smooth, almost silky. The points of the leaves gave her the most trouble and she restitched them over and over until they were sharp. She wanted them to be perfect.

"Try them on," Clancy says. "They may fit you."

"They won't."

"How do you know if you don't try?" He leans forward, and the lines on his face are deep, the creases filled with shadow.

"I can tell just by looking at them." Florence sets them back in the tin and buries them under the scrunched-up newspaper.

"Do you still bead?"

She shakes her head.

"That's a shame." There's a hint of something in his voice, dismay or disappointment.

A twinge of anger rises in her. Can't he see that someone like her wouldn't bead? "Life here keeps me very busy," she says instead. "I've been here eleven years now—"

"How long did you stay in Regina after . . . you left?" he asks, both cautious and prodding.

"Over twenty years," she says. "It took me that long to get on my own two feet and put myself through school in order to move here for the job I wanted . . . which is why I asked you here tonight."

"Yes. Why did you ask me here?"

"My life here is good. Better than it's ever been." She catches him wince in her periphery. "I wouldn't want to change it." The words are clipped and not coming out right. "Do you understand?"

He nods, then leans back and rests both arms on the sides of the Cogswell. "You should have at least come back for Maamaa's funeral."

The muscles in Florence's arms twitch. She'd been living in Regina for over a year when she got word. She wasn't surprised—her mother had left the world long before she actually died.

"We buried her beside Paapaa."

Electricity jolts through her body—it's all too much. Too much at once. She stands, steps to the window, and pulls back the curtain to look out at the night, but the idea of prying eyes makes her drop it.

"I didn't mean to upset you."

She stays standing at the window, facing the closed curtain, and puts her hand on the sill to steady herself.

She turns and sees Clancy step towards her, but she skirts around him and stops at the credenza. She takes a moment to settle herself, then pulls out the envelope from her purse and returns to the settee.

"Eleven years is a long time," she says, gripping the envelope in both hands, smoothing it with her thumbs. She keeps her head down but glances up at him. He's listening, his face unreadable as he sits back down. "I want to continue living here. As I have been. Do you understand?"

He sighs heavily, and the mood changes in the room.

"I called you here tonight because I'd like you to consider moving on from this town sooner. I know the going rate for farmhands in this area, and in here," Florence says, setting the envelope on the coffee table, "is the equivalent of almost eight weeks' pay."

Clancy just eyes her, not saying a word.

"Please." She pushes the envelope closer to him.

A moment passes, then he picks it up and looks inside.

"It's rather a good deal, especially if you find something quickly," she says. She drinks down all the tea in her cup, pours herself some more, and holds the pot out to Clancy.

He shakes his head. He still hasn't said anything.

"If farm work or any other work is hard to come by and you still haven't found anything by Christmas, you can write me. I'll send more money if need be."

More silence. He picks up his pipe and puffs on it.

"Is it not enough?" she asks. "Is there a problem?"

"I get it," he says, chewing on the lip of the pipe. "I understand wanting to live this way." He motions around her living room.

For some reason, the gesture brings heat to her cheeks.

"Others have made the same decision you have, but"—he pauses and taps the bowl of his pipe with his free hand—"when I knew you before . . . I don't know, maybe I shouldn't be surprised, but I am."

"You're not the only one surprised," she says.

He snaps his head up, a look of confusion in his eyes.

"You just told me you joined the army," she says. "When I knew you before, I never would have expected that." The words come out fast and sharp.

"How is that the same as you? As this?"

It bursts out of her: "Fighting someone else's battles—that's what you would have called it back then. Fighting alongside the same army, the same government that hanged Riel." Florence stops herself there, swallows her anger. "So who's the one who's changed?"

Clancy blows the smoke out of his nose like there's a fire inside him. "Right," he says.

"So you'll take the money, then?" Florence's voice is quiet but firm.

"I want you to come with me somewhere first."

"What?"

"On Sunday. And it's not anywhere here in town," he adds.

"Where?"

"The place I'm staying."

"The Huber farm?"

"No."

"Don't they give you room and board?"

"They do. Sort of. I stay there only when I have to. I have my own place near the town of Forsyth—you know it?"

"Yes. It's the next town over."

"You don't have to worry about seeing anyone you know."

"I'm not sure, Clancy."

"We'll meet at the edge of Torduvalle. There's a row of houses just being built," he says, pointing east.

"Colburne Street."

"That's right. I'll wait for you there."

"I don't think it's a good idea."

"Seems a shame that the last time we see each other, we spend it arguing."

A laugh swells in her throat and spills out of her, a silly, embarrassing laugh that hangs in the air between them.

"After you come visit me, I'll take the money and leave Torduvalle for good." He taps the ashes from the bowl of his pipe into the saucer.

"You will?"

"Yes. We'll meet at three on Sunday."

"Can we go in the evening?"

"Under cover of night?"

Florence doesn't respond.

"Can't. I have to be back at the Hubers' in the evening."

It's one short visit, then it's all done.

"It's a deal, then," he says, rising before Florence can say anything more.

After he leaves, Florence notices the envelope is still on the coffee table, all the money left inside. She folds it and places it back in her purse, then picks up the tin he gave her and carries it to the bedroom. She sets it on the bed and pulls out the moccasins, slides a foot into one, then the other.

Takes a few steps in them, turns around. They're snug but not too tight. Her mind flashes to the night she made them and she returns to the bed, kicks them off.

Florence packs them away in the tin and places the tin on the highest shelf in her wardrobe. She flicks off the light and moves through the shadows to the bed. The smell of pine from down the hall floats into the room and keeps her awake all night.

PART TWO

LEAVES

SEPTEMBER 1946
Torduvalle, Saskatchewan

HER LaSALLE SPUTTERS through town towards the new development. She's been sputtering all morning too. Tripped over her words at church a few times, she was so nervous. No one at church seemed to notice her state, but she regrets agreeing to Clancy's terms. The springs in the seat bite her bottom and she shifts a little to the left, away from a particularly pointy spring digging in. Doesn't want a hole in her Kerrybrooke houndstooth slacks. Her favourite for the office and chosen for today because they pair nicely with her poppy-red blouse. *Spiffy and smart,* Shirley said of the outfit when she first wore it to work. An outfit to impress. Others at church had admired it too. Silly to want to wear it today.

Florence rounds the end of Saunders Street onto Colburne, which is still just a dirt road. Mounds of upturned earth and stacks of lumber here and there. Skeletons of houses on what will be a new block in town. A crescent, actually. The first for Torduvalle. The plan is for other, larger crescents to be built behind this one as the town grows, one street hugging the other. There was some talk about whether the streets should be kept in straight lines—there are no rivers or lakes that require a curved road—but ultimately the town council approved the crescent on the theory that it would add value to the town. Improve its character. Florence thought it was all silly, but driving along the curving street, imagining the finished homes, green lawns, and some trees, she thinks it will be pretty. There's even a circular boulevard in the centre where a flower garden or a bunch of lilac or azalea bushes could be planted and make the block burst with colour and scent. She could put her own little house up for sale, maybe, and move into something more modern, easier to maintain.

Florence inches along the dirt road. No sign of Clancy. The clouds are a thick wool blanket in the sky and dark at the edges, like the weather could turn. She drives the entire length of the crescent and still no sign of him. She could head home, pull on her flannel housecoat, and spend the rest of the day reading. But the envelope is still in her purse. She starts another loop, feeling a fool.

When she's partway around, a croaky horn honks, and Florence brakes. Mr. Huber's truck is parked behind a partially built two-storey, the truck's back end hidden by the house skeleton. The horn croaks again. Florence climbs out of her own car, pulls her coat collar up against the cool air, and glances around, but the rest of the street is empty. She totters through piles of gravel and dirt, past stacks of plywood and two-by-fours.

Clancy rolls down the window. "Climb in," he says, and motions for her to walk to the passenger side.

As she nears, her foot lands in a pocket of mud and a glob sticks to her loafers—inappropriate for such an excursion, but they completed her outfit. "I'd rather follow you in my own vehicle."

"I'm that ugly?" He chuckles, though there's friction there too.

"I'd prefer it that way." She scrapes the mud off her shoe on a nearby rock, scratching the leather in the process.

"Fine. Get on the highway and head east. I'll wait for you to catch up." He rolls up the window and reverses at the same time.

She trudges back to her car, stones and pebbles now sticking to the mud on her shoes.

On her final tour of the crescent, she sees Clancy in her rear-view driving straight through the empty field behind the bare-bones houses, the truck bobbing over the broken ground, cutting its own course, then partially disappearing into the overgrown prairie grass.

Florence turns onto the highway just as rain begins to fall. The car makes a racket as it gains speed, protesting. About a mile ahead, Clancy is parked on the side of the road, waiting for her, and he pulls out in front when she nears.

The raindrops soon grow fat and fall hard. Sound like hail on the roof, and the wipers have a hard time keeping up. The weather is turning too soon. The changing of seasons can be seamless or vicious and you never know which it will be.

It's not long before the truck begins to slow but there's nothing but empty fields on either side of them. He's not signalling either. He goes slower and slower. Florence is almost up to his bumper when the barricade comes into view—police cars bisecting the highway. Officers wave Clancy to the side, where he stops. They speak with him a moment through the car window, then he gets out as three officers begin examining the truck.

The cops wave Florence forward to the barricade.

She rolls down her window for the officer approaching. "Good afternoon," she says.

"Afternoon." He bends to her window.

"Officer Purleigh?" She pulls her headscarf back. Alec Purleigh. Assigned to Torduvalle two years ago, moved from Alberta with his wife and two young children, though he's just a kid himself. Barely thirty, if that. Shortly after his arrival, he set up his property and personal automobile insurance through Pratt's.

"Mrs. Banks," he says, smiling. "I didn't recognize you at first, I'm sorry."

"Everything all right?" she asks.

"Yes, just routine inspections."

"Should I get out?"

"Oh, no, you're fine, Mrs. Banks." He motions to the other men. "You can continue through," he tells her.

"Thank you. Stay warm out here, this weather's awful," she says.

"It is, so you drive safe, now." He knocks on the roof of her car.

She presses the gas and passes Clancy, who's hunched over in the cold rain, still waiting for the cops to finish searching his truck. He wipes the soggy curls from his brow but doesn't acknowledge her as she drives by. It's not until she passes him and he's in her rear-view, his back to the uniformed men, that he waves to her, letting her know he's fine.

Routine inspections. Only for some.

Florence putters on below the speed limit, and in ten minutes, Clancy catches up and passes her in the oncoming lane. As he goes by, she glimpses his profile—the boy she knew back then is clear and obvious. That high forehead and slight curve of his nose. The edges of his lips, the bottom one much fuller than the top. Florence flicks on the radio, and Gene Autry's voice fills the car. A new song, one she hasn't heard yet but she half sings, half hums along with it anyway, drowning out her thoughts.

Another long stretch of time before Clancy's signal lights flash, followed by his brake lights, though they're still ten miles from Forsyth. She slows the LaSalle to follow his turn and her breath slows too, the air leaving her chest in one long stream. They're off the highway and on a trail heading north, a rutted dirt path with bushes and fields on either side. A spasm in her chest. The Nest was like this too, off in the corner where others didn't look. Crown-owned land, set aside for roads. Sixty-six feet wide. Long, narrow strips where people built homes. *Set-aside people on set-aside lands.* Clancy had laughed when they'd heard someone say that and said they'd been booted aside, not set.

Soon, the outlines of homes in the distance, the size of ice shacks on a frozen lake. Her whole body stiffens. She parks behind Clancy, who's out of the truck and pulling out his pipe. The rain's now subsided into a drizzle, and his match ignites on first strike.

"Know where we are?" he asks, the smoke puffing out of him like a cotton balloon.

"Yes and no," she says matter-of-factly. "It's a road allowance."

"Seedy Creek. You heard of it?"

"I haven't."

"Maybe a little too far from Torduvalle. Forsyth's just that way," he says, pointing east. "That's what they called this place—Seedy." He chuckles, then strides off, leading the way.

The shacks stretch on in a straight row into the distance. She counts two, then three, then five, and a couple more beyond. No signs, no streetlights, no power lines. Just rough paths between the shacks. Clancy got off the road allowances; he even went overseas and saw places she never will; it doesn't make sense that he's come back. And why bring her here? It only validates the decisions she's made.

She steps around the muddy puddles that have collected on the path. Alongside the shack on the end closest to them is a lopsided wagon, one wheel off and lying in the grass, its broken spokes waiting to be mended.

There's movement to her left in the bushes—two children darting through the thicket—then squeals of laughter.

"Why are you staying here if you have a room at the Hubers'?" There is no judgement in her voice, she makes sure of that, but he continues on as if he doesn't hear her.

A man stands in the doorway of another shack, leaning against the frame, a lit cigarette dangling from his lips and one fraying suspender holding up his pants. He exchanges greetings with Clancy, nods at Florence, and watches her pass.

Clancy turns onto a narrow footworn path and heads towards the shack it leads to. There's a slim window beside the door and through it, a thin green medicine bottle perched on the sill, sprouting dried flowers. Asters. A shiver runs up Florence's spine. In a few short hours, she'll be home. She just has to get through whatever this is.

Clancy pushes open the door.

She sucks in a final lungful of outside air, bracing herself, then steps into the shack.

The room is warm, hot, even, and the smell of the fire hits her nose first. In the corner, a stove burns off the damp chill from outside. Its flames are big and bright and tended to. But the two chairs at the table are empty. Florence turns to the asters in the window. It's not possible. It can't be. But there, on the bed in the other corner, a woolen blanket over her legs and another around her shoulders—a lump rises at the back of Florence's throat, and she stops breathing.

She's changed so much. Her mop of dark, curly hair now white, her curved back even more hunched, and her features more lined and pronounced with age. She's propped up against pillows, but her head lists to the side in her sleep.

"Auntie?" Florence whispers, her breath finally releasing.

Clancy turns from warming his hands by the fire, his face lit up by the orange flames. "She can't hear you unless you're up real close." He slides his jacket off and hangs it on a nail on the wall. "Her eyesight is failing too."

"I didn't know she . . ."

"Was still alive?" Clancy says, finishing her thought for her.

"She must be in her eighties now."

"About that." He sets a pot of water on the stove, then takes Florence's jacket and purse, hangs them on the back of a chair at the kitchen table—the only furniture in the house aside from the bed in the corner, which is just a mattress balanced on wooden crates. Then he steps to Lillian and crouches over her gently, his mouth almost touching her ear.

"Auntie," he whispers, then says it again more loudly.

Lillian stirs, lifts her head to him and pats his arm. Says something that Florence can't hear. Lillian shifts, about to get up, but then stops, turns her head to Florence, who still hasn't moved from the door.

"Taanday ma yayns?" Lillian says to Clancy.

The sounds of the words are familiar but their meaning is now foreign to Florence.

"You'll have to speak English, Auntie—it's been too long." Clancy motions to Florence to join them, but she's rooted to the floor. Clancy and Lillian exchange more words in Michif. Lillian takes her pipe from an overturned milk crate beside the bed, places it in the corner of her mouth as she always did, and pats the bed beside her. Florence finally steps forward.

"She's old but she won't bite," Clancy says loudly. Lillian swats him. "Or maybe she will." He laughs and sits on a chair at the table a few feet away.

Florence approaches the edge of the mattress, sits. The light catches Lillian's eyes. Once midnight black, they're now tinged with white. Lillian's fingers travel down Florence's arm until they find her hand. She clasps it tight.

"Ma fii. Taanishi kiiya?"

"English," Clancy reminds her.

Lillian ignores him. "Aashtum, aashtum." She pulls Florence closer until her leg is up against Lillian's folded knees.

"Lii sooyii moo," Lillian says. "Ootihtikoon?"

"As you can see, she's still as stubborn as always." Clancy shakes his head.

"I'm sorry, what's she asking?" Florence says.

Clancy rises and takes the pot of water off the stove, pours the steaming water into three tin mugs. "Wants to know if you got the moccasins." He drops a single tea bag into the first and second cup and two bags into the third.

"I did," Florence says to Lillian.

Lillian taps Florence's hand, nods. She says something else in Michif.

Clancy carries over the tea and hands the mug with two bags to Lillian, who frees Florence's hand.

Lillian waits for Florence to respond.

"I'm sorry," Florence says, and shrugs. "I don't understand."

Clancy grins at her, clearly enjoying her discomfort, then returns to his seat at the table. "She said she kept them for you after Maamaa passed," he says.

Lillian nods and puts her pipe back on the milk crate to drink her tea.

A couple of sparks fly out from the stove, land on the floor, and send up a short burst of smoke before going out.

Lillian continues talking in Michif. Florence catches a familiar name here and there and realizes Lillian's filling her in. Telling her what's happened in the past thirty years to all the people Florence had known when she was still a Campeau.

When Florence made the decision to leave her former life behind and live as a different person, she imagined that if she ever returned—ever returned to her family—she'd be met with anger. She imagined shouting, loud and fierce. She hadn't imagined this, Lillian simply catching Florence up as if she has been on a long vacation, as if she didn't turn her back on them at all. It'd be easier if there were anger.

Lillian finishes and asks a question. Clancy translates. "She wants to know about you," he says, his voice turning soft. "I already told her you're a widow and . . ." He looks away. "She was sad to hear about that."

Now it's Florence's turn to look away as something snags inside.

"But she wants to know everything," Clancy continues, "everything that's happened in your life since she last saw you. What you've been doing, where you've been."

"I'm the senior secretary at an insurance company now, Auntie," Florence says. "I manage all the administrative functions for the office."

Lillian listens and nods, then prods her for more, even though to Florence, that's her biggest piece of news.

"There's not really much else to tell," she says. "After I got to Regina, I worked at a hotel. Doing laundry and cleaning rooms and saving as much money as I could." She looks down, not wanting to remember those years. Just like she did with her life at the Nest, she's stored it all away, and it's easier to leave it there, packed up neat where it won't bother anyone. "Eventually, I used my money to put myself through secretarial school. Studied at night and worked all day. It was a lot but I managed it." It's boastful, she hears that in her voice, but it's true too.

Lillian asks something else and Clancy answers for Florence. He turns to her. "I told her you're not beading anymore."

Lillian says something, then shakes her head.

"She says it's a shame," Clancy translates. "You were the best she ever knew." He taps his mug on the tabletop as if distracted. "But I guess some things are easy to just put aside."

Florence stares at the tea bag in her mug, bobbing in the still steaming liquid.

Lillian pulls the tea bags out of her mug with her fingers, squeezes the water out of them, and discards them in an empty tuna tin on the small table beside her. "Clancy. Aen biskwii."

"Auntie . . ." he says, dragging the word out.

"Aen biskwii!"

Clancy apparently caves and he grabs a tin from the far end of the table. He holds it out for Lillian. Rounds of bannock, still greasy on the surface.

"Noo, noo." Lillian pushes both the bannock and Clancy away from her. "Si koom enn rosh."

"She doesn't like my bannock. Says it's too hard for her teeth, but that's just an excuse."

"An excuse for what?" Florence shakes her head when Clancy offers her a piece. He takes two for himself.

"An excuse for her to eat these." He reaches for another box. This one is full of assorted store-bought cookies.

Lillian puts a hand inside and digs around, feeling one and then another, until she finds one with nuts.

"Still has a bloody sweet tooth."

"Kiiyaamaya," Lillian says, dunking the cookie into her tea.

"You can dunk your bannock in the tea too," he says.

Lillian shakes her head. Florence fights a smile, but Clancy catches it. He finds another cookie with nuts and sets it on the side table for Lillian.

"Which kind would you like?" he asks Florence, holding out the box.

"I'm fine, thank you."

"That's not a flavour we have." He continues to hold out the box.

Florence takes a gingersnap.

When Lillian finishes her cookies, she pulls a brown paper grocery bag from under the bed and pours out long strips of rags. She selects three strips and nudges Florence's arm.

"Kaa wiichihinn chiin?" Lillian asks.

"I don't understand—" But before she finishes, Lillian grabs the tea from her hands and sets it on the side table. She takes both of Florence's hands and places the ends of three strips of rags in them.

"Michimina shiishtamoohk." Lillian begins to braid the strips.

"She doesn't bead or sew anymore but she still makes these for others to sew together." He shows Florence a bag of already completed braids for rugs.

"Clancy, how long has she . . . why . . ." Florence stops, trying to slow the thoughts in her head. "I'm confused. Why are you and Lillian *here*? I thought you said you've been travelling around for work since you got back from the war?" Florence asks.

"I was. I went back to Quincy Lake first thing, but when I couldn't find any work, I set off. Was thinking of maybe making my way to Winnipeg—some soldiers I was with said there was work there."

"So how did you—and she—end up here?" she repeats.

"Ask her."

"Auntie," Florence says and pauses after the word, wondering where to begin, "when did you leave the Nest?"

"Quincy Lake gii itoohtaan—" Lillian says.

"English, Auntie!" Clancy says. "So stubborn." But he's smiling and Lillian continues in Michif. Clancy translates when she's done. "She moved to Quincy Lake just after I joined up," Clancy says. "The McKays took her in when they moved there. You remember them?"

Florence shakes her head.

"They lived at a settlement on the other side of Quincy Lake but moved to town when more farmers set up around there—a few Michif families did. She was still there with the McKays when I got back. They were treating her real well, taking good care of her. But after I left, the town council raised property taxes. Needed money for infrastructure," he says, a note of sarcasm in his voice, "and, lo and behold, the poor Michif families could no longer afford their homes." He pops an entire cookie in his mouth as if to stop himself from saying more.

"I'm sorry, Auntie," Florence says.

"The McKays have cousins here," Clancy says. "I got word through the moccasin telegraph that they brought her here. And now she's grown lazy," he says, sliding a log in the fire. "Wants other people to look after her."

Lillian mutters something at him.

"But there's work in Winnipeg, you said?" Florence asks.

"It's what I'm told."

"Are you still planning to head out that way when you leave here?"

"Taanday itoohtayyenn?" Lillian asks.

"It's nothing, Auntie."

"You haven't talked to her about it," Florence says, more a statement than a question.

"Taanishi ishpayihk?" Lillian asks.

Clancy picks up the bag of braided rugs. "I have to deliver these," he says, ignoring them both.

"How long will you be? It's getting cold, and with that rain—"

But he's out the door. A blast of cool air rushes in and the flames flutter before settling again. Lillian asks her something in Michif.

"Auntie," Florence says, "I haven't spoken Michif since I left."

"That's okay, ma fii," Lillian says, then begins to sing. "'Alouette, gentille alouette.'" She nods at Florence, inviting her to join in.

"It's been too long, Auntie, I—"

"'Alouette, je te plumerai,'" Lillian continues.

"I don't remember the words—"

"'Je te plumerai la tête.'" She stops singing, waiting for Florence to join in.

"The last time I sang—" But Florence stops herself and gives in. "'Je te plumerai' . . .'"

"'La tête.'" Lillian helps her with the words.

"'Et la tête,'" Florence sings, tentative.

"'Alouette, a-a-a-ah.'" Lillian joins in with her. As she comes to the end of the strips, Lillian adds more scraps to the braid. Never the same length—additions are added at irregular intervals, and the braiding continues. One length over the other. Lillian's hands are like knotted tree branches, bulbous knuckles, fingers slanted in odd angles. Her skin's even the shade of bark. Still singing, Florence rises and stokes the fire, stirring up some warmth, and when she returns to the bed, she studies Lillian's face. The length of her nose, the hook of her jaw, the long grey hairs in her eyebrows.

Lillian stops singing. Florence does too. After setting the braid aside, Lillian pulls Florence to her, her blanketed arms like wings enveloping her, their heads touching. The smell of Lillian's hair hits Florence's nose: bear grease. That pungent fatty oil she squirmed away from whenever her own mother tried to rub it into her hair to soften and tame it. The scent travels to the back of Florence's throat, slides down, and lodges somewhere beneath her ribs.

Florence pulls away and grabs a strip of fabric that must have come from suit pants, and this time Florence adds to the shortest length of braid and continues plaiting while Lillian holds the end. When Florence is ready to add another strip, Lillian feels her handiwork with her fingers and laughs. Undoes everything Florence braided. "Too loose," she says, and starts from the beginning.

A laugh shoots up Florence's belly but she catches it in her throat.

"Kaykwy, ma fii?"

"Nothing."

Lillian side-eyes her and waits.

"Remember when my beadwork was too tight?"

Now Lillian laughs. "You were so mad at me," she says in English, though Michif inflections are still thick in her words.

"I had worked so hard. For *hours*." The yokes on a man's jacket. Lillian had discussed the design with him and they'd settled on pink roses, daisies, and Saskatoon berries, each element meaning something special to him. Lillian sketched it all out on paper, then basted it onto the jacket.

"But you were angry when you did it, so it had to be undone."

It was true. She'd fought with Clancy that morning and went to Lillian's to avoid him, but Lillian had gone to visit a cousin that day, so Florence started beading on her own, anger pulsing through her as she stabbed the beads onto her needle, yanked the thread through the leather. She didn't even go home for supper because she didn't want to face Clancy or her mother.

Lillian secures a slack knot at the end of the braid so she can continue later. Points to the box of cookies on the table and nudges Florence to get them. Florence does and they each take another. They dunk and chew.

"It looked fine," Florence says.

"It didn't! Those beads were so tight, they couldn't breathe—you strangled them with the thread." Another laugh. "Even the leather was choking."

It was after supper before Lillian returned that day. She'd taken the jacket from Florence's hands to inspect it and reached for the embroidery scissors.

"What are you doing?" Florence was stunned. "You can't!" But in went the sharp end of a blade and *snip*. "Auntie!" *Snip-snip-snip*. Lillian held the jacket so the beads collected into a little pile on a tea towel as they came loose from the thread. *Snip-snip.* "No!" Florence rushed forward to stop her, reaching for the scissors, but she leapt too hard and too fast, and she knocked the table off-balance. The beads spilled to the floor. Lillian continued snipping, more determined now and not bothering to catch them. Letting them all fall to the floor.

"How would he have felt wearing all that anger on his body?" Lillian says now.

"I never did it again, though," Florence says. She had stormed out and vowed never to come back, but of course she had. Three days later. And the beads were still scattered on the floor, waiting for her to pick them up. After she collected them, she washed them gently in a bucket of water. Started all over again.

"You never did tell me what you were so angry about that day."

"It seems silly now," she says, shrugging it off. Clancy had eaten the Hershey bar she'd hidden in her apple box. She couldn't believe he'd snuck into her personal things and stolen it. Not only that, but he'd put the empty wrapper right back where he'd found it when he was done. Rubbed it in.

"That boy had a naughty streak," Lillian said. "You took good care of him, though, ma fii."

But she hadn't, had she? She hated the responsibility. It would burn up inside her and she'd become cruel to him sometimes. Florence pushes that memory away and presses her hands against herself, tries to keep it all tamped down inside.

"Ma fii?" Lillian asks.

That term of endearment makes it worse and Florence stands. Tries pacing in the tiny room, a sauna now, with the fire going so strong. She steps to the door and opens it; the blast of bitter air is shocking. "It's cooling and I'm worried about the roads. I should go."

Lillian nods and rises herself.

"Do you know where Clancy went?"

Lillian answers in Michif and points north.

"I'll go find him," Florence says.

"Payhtaa," Lillian says, then bends and pulls some items out from under the bed. Two suitcases and a small wooden chest. Inside the chest, a cloth bag. "Aashtum." Lillian pours the contents onto the bed. An envelope of needles, spools of thread, pieces of hide and stroud and calico. Two pairs of embroidery scissors. And small medicine bottles filled with beads. Florence sits and picks one up, and the beads tink in the glass container, cool in her hand. She picks up another bottle, then another, something stirring inside. Amber, vermillion, cotton-candy pink, jade. Seed beads. Each one a small, round world on its own. The mint-coloured beads are charlotte-cut and their flat sides catch the flickering firelight, sparkle in their clear casing.

"When you get home, bead for me," Lillian says, not asking.

"I can't, Auntie," she says, rising. "I really should go." She collects her things from the chair. "Before the roads get icy."

"Enn fleur." Lillian gathers the materials back into the bag.

"I don't remember—"

"Payek." She holds up a single finger, then hands the bag to Florence. "Pchi," she says, motioning with her fingers: *small*.

Florence gives in and takes the bag, eager to exit, but turns when Lillian speaks again.

"Koochiihk, ma fii," Lillian says. "Koochiihk."

The word enters Florence's brain; its meaning circles, then lands. *Try.*

"Okay, Auntie," Florence says, "I will." And immediately regrets it because either way, whatever she does, she'll just disappoint. It's how she moves through life. It's only when she's pretending to be someone else that she excels.

She pulls Lillian into a perfunctory embrace. "It was so good to see you, Auntie." Because what else is there to say? She's just been cracked open, snapped in half.

She steps outside. A cold wind has moved in, whipping and whirling, and it's cleared away the rain clouds. There are only a few trails of grey left, streaking across a blueberry sky. There are three other homes in the row and the first is dark, but loud voices and laughter emanate from the second. Florence knocks on that door. A man answers, and Florence recognizes him. He was with Clancy that day back in August when they were asked to leave Nick's Diner.

"Florence!" Clancy shouts from inside the shack, where he and a few other men are gathered, sitting on stools or crates or on the floor. One man has turned a crate into a makeshift table, and a notebook and papers are spread on top of it.

"Name's Delbert," says the man who opened the door.

Florence nods brusquely and steps inside. As she does, the man with the papers folds them as if hiding them from Florence—as if she would care. He watches her suspiciously as she passes him. Clancy's sitting in the far corner holding a cup, a large glass jug half full of clear liquid near him. There's a pungent, yeasty smell in the room. A hint of turpentine or gas.

"I'm going now," she says.

"You're done already?"

"The sun's gone down."

"Quick glass first?" he asks, holding up his tin cup.

"No, thank you." It comes out sharper than she wanted.

The others exchange words in Michif. Chuckle. But she doesn't have time for this nonsense.

"Can I see you outside?" she says to Clancy.

"Hold on, I'm coming with you." He downs what's in his cup. "Have to head back to the Hubers' tonight." He says his goodbyes to the others, then follows her out and back down the path.

"Do you think that was wise?" she asks.

"Visiting friends?"

"Drinking before driving on the highway—especially in inclement weather."

"It's not as bad now," he says, looking up at the sky, "and it was just one drink."

"A strong one, by the smell of it." She takes quick, sharp strides down the path. "And it looked like more than just visiting," she says, reproving.

But Clancy doesn't respond.

"Does she stay by herself when you're not here?" she asks as they pass Lillian's.

"She knows her way around a fire, even with her eyesight fading. And the

McKays are just a couple doors down." He quickens his pace to walk beside her. "Was it a good visit?"

"It was." He must feel smug now, like he's pulled one over on her. "It was a nice visit and I'm ready to go home."

"That's all you have to say?"

"I hope you'll take her with you when you go."

"To Winnipeg?"

"It'd be better for her than staying here, wouldn't it?"

"It'll be up to her, but she has people here."

"But no running water, no electricity. And still outhouses, I assume?"

"Not everyone can afford the luxuries you have—"

"Running water is hardly a luxury nowadays."

"Only for some." It bites.

They reach the vehicles and Florence stops to face him. "Winnipeg will be good for her. Much better than this place." She pulls the envelope of cash from her purse. "It'll be more expensive to take her, but like I said, I can send more if you let me know where to mail it."

But he doesn't reach for the envelope.

"I've done what you asked me to do." She holds it out. "What did you think would happen when I came out here? That I'd want to move back?"

"No," he says, wooden. "You're too ashamed for that."

"I'm not ashamed."

"Then why do you look the way you do?" He reaches up to the curls sneaking out from her headscarf, caught in the breeze. He twists one in his fingers, and she grips the handle of the cloth bag, a current of anger rippling through her.

She steps back. "Then why did you want to bring me here?"

"It's not about what I want," Clancy says, voice growing soft. "She's old, Florence, and I know she wanted to see you."

Florence looks away and out into the dark fields in the distance, waiting for a wave of emotion to pass before speaking. "It was nice to see her," she admits. "But I don't think she should stay here. When do you think you'll leave?" She holds the envelope out again.

"I need to talk with her first—"

"You know she'll go with you if you ask."

"I also just can't up and leave Mr. Huber—it's a busy time, and his reference will be helpful."

"A couple of weeks?"

He scoffs.

"Well, how long, then?"

"Gimme a month," he says, resentful, and snatches the envelope from her.

"That's a long time—"

"You don't get a say." Clancy turns and heads to his truck. Gets in, snaps the door closed behind him.

There's no more rain but it turns pitch-black on the way home, and Florence leaves the radio off to avoid any distractions. The evening has left her wobbly enough. The tires whoosh along the highway and spit stones against the undercarriage, every ping and pop like gunshot. Her life, under fire.

She expects to lose Clancy's headlights behind her when she turns off into town, expects him to continue down the highway towards the Huber farm. But he turns too. Follows her all the way to her street, stops at the corner. His headlights are still there when she enters the house and closes the door behind her.

SUMMER 1909

Quincy Lake, Saskatchewan

UNCLE JOE'S WAGON approaches town, and they come close to last year's campsite and the site of Paapaa's last moments. As they pass, Joe doesn't say anything; he doesn't even turn his head to look. Florence doesn't either because that's how they live their lives—if they don't acknowledge it, it's like it never happened. Michif lives are all about silence, about keeping things bottled up: feelings, history, anger. Everything. But she also knows that doing so will eat you up from the inside, which is what's happening to Maamaa. And it'll happen to her too if she fails today. Her heart jolts against her ribs.

"Here's fine," Florence says after they pass the site.

"I can take you all the way," Uncle Joe offers.

But she tells him she wants to walk the last bit and stretch her legs, because if he takes her all the way into town, he'd give her away in an instant. The way he looks and sounds. She can't risk it. What she tells him is not really a lie because a walk will get out the cramps from the wagon and let her get her bearings.

She ambles slowly down the road until the wagon is out of sight, then she slips into the overgrowth off to the side. Hidden in the bush and trees, Florence takes off her stained gingham dress that she's nearly outgrown and opens one of the cloth bags she brought to carry the groceries. Inside is a cotton cream dress covered in brown paisley with a pleated ruffled yoke around the neck. It's nothing showy or loud; its prettiness is subdued and perfect for her needs. Florence knew she wanted to wear it for this trip months ago, when she first saw it among the clothes Mrs. Duncan had sent to be laundered. It belongs to Mrs. Duncan's oldest daughter, and the next time Florence received it for a washing, she arranged a ride with Uncle Joe, who had deliveries this way. She'll return it next week with the rest of the items Mrs. Duncan sent her.

Florence stuffs her own dress into the bag, then unbraids her hair and twists it up into a bun high on the back of her head. She practiced at home using her reflection in the window, astounded that it made her look so different, more mature. Each time she rehearsed, her excitement grew, but so did her fear. She's been waiting over a year for this. Florence heads back to the road that leads to town. Puts one foot in front of the other.

Afraid she'll lose the nerve if she thinks too much about it, Florence takes the quickest route through the residential streets to Main, doesn't bother pining over the houses. She stops right before stepping into the fray. A few deep breaths to slow the rattle in her chest, then out she goes onto the sidewalk and into the flurry and charge of rushing bodies. Head up this time and looking at every face she passes, testing, daring. Nothing half-hearted because she has to know if she can avoid her mother's fate. Maamaa has become a shell of herself since Paapaa died.

After they buried Paapaa last year—travelling all the way to Colchester because none of the nearby churches would allow Paapaa in their cemeteries—Maamaa fell ill with pneumonia. She was sick all summer, pale and sweating in bed, her lungs so clogged, they prevented her from speaking. When fall came around, her body started to recover, but the rest of her didn't. She still spends her days in bed, barely eating and talking even less. The sickness left her body, but the anger remained. That's what her illness is. A festering rage from having to live life on the edges and in the shadows. Florence knows that's what it is because she feels it under Maamaa's skin when she washes her, brushes her hair, changes her clothes. It's the same rage trying to take hold of Florence herself.

No one seems to notice Florence at first; they whizz past on their own missions. A woman in a blue bell-shaped skirt and a lace blouse meets her eye, then smiles a greeting. A man in a straw boater hat moves to the side to let her pass, tipping his hat as she does. A laugh wants to rise from her belly but she holds it in—it's too premature. A simple glance is not enough. She won't know for sure until she interacts with them, which is why she heads straight to the place that barred her before.

Clancy's reaction to Paapaa's death was the opposite of Maamaa's. He suddenly started helping with chores, doing them without complaint and without anyone prompting or nagging. He asked Nap and Joe to teach him how to clean and gut fish, how to set his own snares. Though he's barely grown in size in the past year, he's grown in age and maturity, filling every moment of the day with being useful. A few months ago he even asked the Duncans if they had odd jobs for him. He'd feed their chickens, brush down their horses, haul pails of water from their well. Now he's there nearly every day and he's helping the other men with their work. His response to Paapaa being gone from their lives was to take his place.

Florence's days are just as busy as Clancy's. She makes the meals, cleans Maamaa's bedpan. She still helps Auntie with her beading when she's asked to, but she no longer beads herself; it doesn't mean the same thing anymore. She's even taken on some of Maamaa's laundry work for Mrs. Duncan and handles any repairs and alterations she requests. But Florence doesn't enjoy her work like Clancy does his. He's driven to it, fulfilled by it; Florence does it only out of necessity. She doesn't complain, though, because what it has allowed her is time. Time to think and imagine. To plan.

Florence arrives at Hollinger's and doesn't stop to peruse the window displays or wait for someone to invite her in. She pulls open the door herself and enters. There are not as many people as there were last year, but there is a small queue of people at one of the two glass counters waiting for service, and a couple of customers are selecting nuts and other goods from the barrels and baskets arranged in the centre of the single aisle.

"I can help the next person over here," the man says from behind the counter on the opposite side of the store. Still with the same moustache. A patron at the front of the line steps out of the queue and over to the man, and Florence joins the back of the line. There's no need to be nervous. If they catch her, she walks out. Then she knows and can stop wondering, obsessing. Either way, there'll be some relief.

She glances around the store. It's just the couple running the shop today; there's no sign of their son. A little disappointment takes hold of Florence, and the reaction surprises her. As she waits her turn, she looks at the items in the aisle, at the stacked cans of goods with pictures of peas, corn, or tomatoes on the front. She touches as many as possible just because she can, as if claiming them.

"What can I do for you, miss?" the woman says to Florence when it's her turn.

Heat rises to her face, but Florence ignores it and steps forward. She looks right into the woman's eyes; they're a strange golden colour, warm and sharp at once. Florence opens her mouth but the words catch in her throat as the woman focuses on her.

The shopkeeper waits. Her head tilts, and her brow slightly furrows. Florence fights the impulse to flee. To race out and give up. Instead, she steps even closer, so close the edge of the glass case cuts into her stomach. She wants the woman to see everything. Florence has to know.

"Miss," the woman says, "are you all right?"

Florence exhales the breath she was holding. "Oats and flour, please. Five pounds of each."

The woman gathers the items from the shelves behind her. "Twenty-five cents."

Florence pulls the change straight from her pocket this time, counts it out in her palm, and puts the money on the display case.

"Thank you," the woman says. "Have a nice day. Next, please."

Florence gathers her purchases and keeps looking at the woman, who doesn't pay her any mind now that she's assisting someone else. Outside, Florence tucks herself close to a display window, away from foot traffic, and absorbs what's happened. There was no skepticism or suspicion. No one had even a mild inkling that Florence didn't belong. After all those months of anticipation, she finds the whole thing anticlimactic. It can't be this easy.

She enters another store and buys sugar. Then a third for lard. And another, where she splurges on a jar of honey that she'll wrap up for Clancy's birthday next month and let him have all to himself. And in each store, no one questions her; not a single person looks doubtful. It's more than relief, what she feels. With her bags stuffed and arms full, Florence takes a moment to step out onto the street when there's a gap in traffic, just far enough out that she can see it from end to end. She's invisible in an entirely new way. Now she laughs.

She crosses to the other side and goes into another store for Auntie's tea and the biscuits she requested. She's about to pay the shopkeeper when she notices, in the display case just to the side of the register, arranged on a length of red velvet, six coin purses. One in particular catches her eye. It's round and silver and finely etched with delicate flowers. Inlaid in its centre is an oval of mother-of-pearl, iridescent and shiny.

"It's hand-engraved," the shopkeeper says. "And comes with a chain that attaches to your wrist." He pulls it out of the case and places it in Florence's hands.

There's no way she can afford it. As if sensing her thoughts, he offers to give her a deal, but if she buys it, she won't have enough for the tea and biscuits. She holds the purse and realizes she has to have it. She needs it more than Auntie needs tea. She needs something to remind her that another life is possible. Auntie won't believe Florence if she says she couldn't find tea, but she will believe her if she simply says she forgot. It will be Florence's first outright lie with no hint of truth. But she doesn't care—it hurts no one.

Florence wears the coin purse when she leaves the store, feels the chain on her wrist, the weight of it dangling as she heads back through town to the edge to wait for Uncle Joe. After changing into her own clothes, she leaves the purse on her wrist and tucks it into the sleeve of her dress, enjoying the cool metal against her skin. There are two separate parts to her now, two different ways to be in the world, but she feels whole, more complete, like she never has before.

SEPTEMBER 1946

Torduvalle, Saskatchewan

A REAL ROLE MODEL. That's what Mary Beth Watkins called her. The young woman came into the office last Monday morning, right after the job advertisement appeared in the weekly paper, wearing a smart two-piece slacks suit and coral lipstick and projecting a ton of confidence. Not in an off-putting way either. She'd graduated high school last year and had brought in her final marks to show that she excelled in typing. She also brought a letter of recommendation from her teacher. Miss Watkins had been contemplating going to the city to study at the same secretarial school Florence had but didn't want to leave Torduvalle. Saw her procrastination as a sign when she heard Pratt's was hiring.

"Why learn in school when I can learn on the job with the best?" she said.

Girls these days have a conviction, a self-assurance, that wasn't available to Florence when she was younger. It's refreshing. Uplifting. Florence wanted to hire her on the spot but scheduled her for an interview and a typing test anyway. And she's glad she did because there have been four more inquiries since then, and all their interviews and typing tests are scheduled for next week. Strange to think that so many young women in town are clamouring to train with her. *Clamouring.* That's too strong a word. Still.

Her new desk arrived this week, and a phone. Main calls will still go through downstairs, and only those for the Second-Floors will be routed through Florence. The phone is mostly for her own business needs. She's not upstairs full-time just yet, but she moves between the floors more and more often. It's a different world on the upper floor. Quieter. The Second-Floors are frequently out at meetings, and when they are in the building, they mostly keep their doors closed. A lot of the time, it's just her.

And now at the end of the week, Florence is filled to the teeth with happiness. The feeling is still with her when she arrives home, and it's this feeling that prompts her to dig out the bag of materials Lillian gave her. Just to see if she still has the knack. No harm in that.

There is still a bit of time before Clancy and Lillian depart for Winnipeg, and the least she can do is follow through on Lillian's request. Even if her beadwork is sloppy and messy, even if she warps the material because she no longer knows how to keep the thread properly taut, it won't matter. The fear of making something that isn't perfect is not as strong as her desire to please Lillian. To give her a final gift. She never said goodbye the first time.

Florence lays the glass bottles and tins on the settee beside her. Places her hands over them as if they emanate heat. Then she sorts through the fabric and hide and selects a large piece of dark stroud cloth, large enough for two panels. Opens a tin of pineapple-coloured beads and pours some into a saucer, the sound like trickling water. The cotton thread unwinds easily from the spool, memories unwinding with it.

She slides a yellow bead onto the needle and sews it onto the cloth. A single bead for the very centre of the flower. She slips seven more yellow beads onto the needle to encircle the centre, the movements familiar, her muscles remembering. Even her bones. She should have sketched the design on the cloth first—too much time has passed to begin with freehand—but she follows the feeling that's guiding her.

Without even thinking, Florence threads a second needle. She always used to bead with two, one for the beads and one with just thread to tack the beads down. Lillian never used two because her threads would tangle together, but she told Florence about the method, and Florence figured it out on her own. The technique allowed Florence to work faster, to get out all the ideas and feelings she had bursting inside her.

She can't work fast now, but the impulse is still there.

When the centre is complete, Florence starts on the petals, using a light mauve, the shade of asters. Always Lillian's favourite. The first line goes smoothly, as she uses her thumb to guide the beads into a clean curve, but the next wobbles in places and she cuts it out. Starts again. When the five petals are complete, she does two more flowers, slightly smaller, one on either side of the larger one. *It must be balanced.* Lillian's voice in her ears. Balanced, in harmony. *Just like life.* Body, mind, spirit, emotions. Even if it's an asymmetrical design, there should be balance in the final composition.

She pushes the needle down, pulls the needle up. Her hands in rhythm with her breath. Her life hasn't really been balanced. More split. Separated. But it had to be that way. Has to be that way. It's too hard to be two people at the same time. Too risky, and there's no point in trying.

Around the mauve, she beads some dark-coloured buds for contrast. When she's done with this piece, she'll bead the same design on the second panel, then sew the panels together and line them with scraps of that old sheet she saved to be cut up for rags. The corners of it are still in good shape, still thick and not pilled. A cozy to keep Lillian's tea warm.

The evening passes quickly and Florence stays up late. Doesn't even feel tired when it's her bedtime, but when the clock chimes eleven, she forces herself to bed. Lies there, thinking. Her whole life, she's focused on being a single person. First one, then the other. But since that Sunday at Seedy Creek, she's thought about Clancy and Lillian several times, and she can't deny that a part of her was happy to see them again. If they ignore each other in Torduvalle, not let on they know one another—and if she is careful—why can't she keep visiting them? Live as two people. Others do the same. But her thoughts fade as sleep pulls her under.

In the morning, before she has her tea and toast, she finishes the leaves on the first panel. The leaves that feed the flowers, make them grow. And she spends the rest of the morning and afternoon on the stems. The stems that support it all, that whirl and curl and join everything together. *Everything is connected, ma fii.* Before suppertime arrives and before she finishes the last stem on the first side, Florence slips one bronze bead onto her needle in the midst of the double-curvilinear vines. A little spot of orange in the green flow of the stems. A spirit bead. *To humble yourself, because no one is perfect.* Lillian's lessons returning, welling up from below. Her spirit bead is bronze, for the fire she's feeling inside.

ON WEDNESDAY, WHEN ALL the Second-Floors are either out of the office with clients or locked away in the boardroom having private meetings and discussions, Florence uses the newly installed phone at her desk to call Clancy at the Hubers'. Once again, she doesn't give Mrs. Huber her name, just tells her that she's Clancy sister.

"One moment," Mrs. Huber says, "I'll catch him before he heads back to the barn." She doesn't seem surprised or concerned that Clancy is getting a phone call, and she's not known as a gossip, so no need to worry.

When Clancy gets on the line, Florence asks him when would be a good time to visit Lillian. He laughs at the question.

"If you want to know when we're leaving, just come out and ask," he says.

She hates that he sees right through her. "I was wondering because I have a gift for her and wanted to know if there was a better time than others."

"She's not some city socialite."

"I was just trying—"

"Doesn't have a calendar that needs booking."

"To be considerate," she finishes.

There's a pause, and Florence feels his annoyance through the line.

"Next Wednesday," he finally says.

"A week from now? That's when I should visit?"

"That's when we're leaving."

"Oh." Seven days left. Florence twists the phone cord in her fingers. "You've talked to her, then?"

"Yep."

"Did you find a place?"

"With a buddy of mine and his wife."

"Right in the city?"

"With a shitter that flushes and everything."

"It will be good for her." She ignores his sarcasm. "Maybe I'll visit her tomorrow after work."

"I'll be there Saturday," he offers.

"Ah." Silence. "Might be best to go during the day," Florence says, contemplating. "The highways at night . . ."

"And you're a nervous Nellie behind the wheel," Clancy adds.

She smiles and it's as if he hears it because he says, "I'll see you there, then," and hangs up.

Saturday is good. That will give her time to bead mouse tracks along the borders of both panels before sewing them together and adding the lining.

So focused on Clancy and Lillian's departure, Florence nearly forgets about the banquet-planning meeting that afternoon and is reminded only when Shirley calls up to tell her that Jennie's arrived. Florence rushes downstairs to greet her and quickly makes a pot of tea before bringing her upstairs, along with Shirley, who doesn't want to be left out of anything and nearly begs to help.

Florence booked the boardroom for them earlier that week when Jennie suggested a meeting so they could work undisturbed. Florence knocks on the boardroom door at three, but Mr. Hicks and Mr. Broughton are still in there, even though their meeting with some government officials from the city ended at two and the officials have long since left.

"I'm so sorry," Florence says to Mr. Hicks, "I thought you were finished."

"That's fine, Florence, we've overstayed and will vacate," Mr. Hicks says. "You have important company business as well." He thanks the three of them for their work with organizing the banquet and exits the room.

Mr. Broughton, however, is obviously annoyed at the interruption. He gathers his things, and when Jennie teases him about leaving the room so the women can get down to real business, he grows even more irritated, mutters something in her ear when he passes. Jennie just rolls her eyes, smiling, and closes the door behind him.

"Is he always so sour at work?" she asks Florence.

He's never been cheery but it wouldn't be polite to say so. "It's been very busy lately, and some of the men have been putting in longer hours than normal."

"Something's definitely in the works," Shirley says—as if it's anything they should be discussing. "Do you think Pratt's is buying up another shop?"

That wouldn't explain the meetings with government officials and the increased trips to the city, but all Florence says is, "I've not been made privy. I trust we'll learn things as we need." Her tone is a little more chastening than she intends, but neither of the women seem to notice.

Shirley pours everyone a cup of tea while Jennie begins the meeting by talking about themes and colour options for the banquet. Florence takes a seat at the far end of the table, and something on the chair beside her catches her eye. A folder, strangely without a label. Florence picks it up—she'll ensure it's returned to the proper person. Inside, there are a couple of letters, both of which are addressed to Mayor Williams and carry the subject line *Community Pasture Program*. They're both red-stamped *Confidential* at the top, but Florence didn't stamp them. She's never seen the letters before. She closes the file immediately and slides it under her own notebook and papers to deal with later.

"Florence," Shirley says, "what do you think?"

"I'm sorry, I was momentarily distracted."

"For the centrepieces. Jennie's designed two options," she says, pointing to the drawings that Jennie's placed in the middle of the table.

Centrepieces, for heaven's sake, as if the companies are marrying. "I like the smaller one—it's simple but stylish, and tables always get so cluttered with dishes and whatnot."

"The smaller ones will take me less time too," Jennie says, making a note on the selected design and moving on to talk about balloons and streamers for the room.

Florence looks back down at the file under her notepad. Pratt's does a lot of work for the mayor and the town council, and much of it's confidential, but there's been nothing new recently. At least, nothing that she's been brought into yet. She forces herself to concentrate on the task at hand, though she's glad Shirley wriggled her way into the project because Shirley's far more invested and interested in it than she is.

As soon as the meeting's over and Florence has seen Jennie out, she carries the file directly to Mr. Hicks's office and discreetly presents it to him in case he was the one who left it behind. But he tells her it's not his, that it belongs to Mr. Broughton. Mr. Broughton isn't in his office, and because it's marked confidential, she doesn't want to leave it on his desk without his knowing it's there, so she carries it back to her own desk. While waiting for him to return, she opens it again. She shouldn't—and she normally wouldn't—but they moved her up here precisely because they know they can trust her with all the company's matters. She scans the contents of the letters. They're from the provincial government to the mayor and indicate that, under the federal Prairie Farm Rehabilitation Act, they are establishing a community pasture in the area. There's a map attached to one of the letters. She only glances at it at first, but something niggles, and she looks at it again, and she's glad she does. The proposed community pasture encompasses all the land between Torduvalle and Forsyth, including the road allowance.

When Mr. Broughton finally returns, it's the end of the day and he's come back only to collect some paperwork to take home with him. As he's packing up his briefcase, Florence walks to his office and stands in his doorway, her coat and gloves already on.

"I think this belongs to you," she says, holding out the file.

Mr. Broughton looks bewildered as he stares at the file in her hands.

"I found it in the boardroom this afternoon just after you left," she says to explain.

He strides to her and takes it from her hands without saying a word.

"If you'd like, I can make you a label for the file—" she starts.

"That won't be necessary," he says, sliding it into his briefcase. "This file will be handled strictly—and only—by myself."

"Certainly," Florence says, and considers the matter resolved. But as she exits the building, her thoughts linger on the image of the map.

FLORENCE PULLS ON HER tattersall wool skirt and her cashmere cardigan, her one and only. Reddish rust like a fox's fur. It always catches compliments.

In the living room, she opens a drawer of her credenza and pulls out the tea cozy, heavy with all the beads. It's a gift and should be wrapped. She heads back to the bedroom to see if there's something in her wardrobe closet she can use. But on the bed, the box that holds her cashmere cardigan is open, waiting for the sweater's return at the end of the day. She still stores the cardigan in the box it came in because it's the most expensive piece of clothing she's ever purchased. She bought it brand-new. Other items might have cost more originally—her winter coat with the fur-trimmed collar—but she got them secondhand. The box is just the right size for the cozy. She places it inside, and the box's walls perfectly frame it.

It's already after one. Out the door she goes, *clip-clip* to the car. The sun is bright, the sky clear. It's a good day for a drive. The Broughtons' house is quiet. Kids are at the farm again, Garth is who knows where, and Jennie's gone to the city in her Studebaker, running errands for the banquet, with Shirley in tow. They're supposed to be buying decorations—balloons and streamers and materials for the centrepieces. Jennie's designing the invitations and making them herself with a special calligraphy pen and thick paper. It's all a bit much. But Jennie's loving every second of it. Even if there's a hint of desperation underneath it all, as if she's trying to prove something to herself or, more likely, her husband. Florence hasn't really had to do much of anything except act as a sounding board and approve certain things. With Jennie so busy with the planning, she hasn't popped over unannounced for a tipple in the evening recently, and Florence was able to finish the cozy for Lillian.

The sweater box is wedged beside her, tight and protected against her thigh, preventing it from falling off the seat as she gets onto the highway heading towards the town of Forsyth. She tries to recall the turnoff for Seedy

Creek. It was almost hidden by a thatch of tall spindly birches, but the trees will look different now with their leaves mostly fallen. Though there was one tree with a crooked branch, likely purposely broken, the way Paapaa and others used to do to point to a hunting ground or trapping area. Or a settlement. A hitch inside her as she thinks about the file she found at the office and what it means for Seedy Creek. There will be implications, she knows. But it shouldn't bother her because Clancy and Lillian are leaving in four days. They won't be affected by whatever's being planned.

Smoke curls up from the stacks at Seedy Creek and climbs towards the clouds. Near the end of the line of shacks, a couple of vehicles are parked—a Tin Lizzie like hers and Mr. Huber's truck, which means Clancy is already here. In the field behind the homes, a group of kids have built up a mound of fallen leaves and take turns jumping into it. As Florence walks up the path to Lillian's, a neighbour steps out of his front door and calls to her. A man in a green newsboy cap. He shouts again from his doorway but the words are indecipherable.

"Morning," she says, heading over to him.

He says something in Michif, one side of his cheek bulging from a wad of chewing tobacco. He spits a ball of black juice into an empty can in his hand.

"I'm sorry," Florence says, watching her footing on the rough and rocky footpath that leads to his place. "I don't speak Michif. Is Lillian not home?"

"There," he says, pointing farther down the line of shacks. "At the McKays'."

Florence glances back at Lillian's. "Maybe I should just wait for her."

"I'll take you there," he says, setting the can down just inside his shack and closing the door. He walks towards her, hobbling on one leg and pitched forward, as if tumbling downhill.

Florence transfers her box to one hand and holds out the other to assist him, but she moves too quickly and loses her grip on her package. It topples to the ground; its lid pops open when it lands, ejecting the cozy. The man gasps, reaches down, and grabs it immediately. He doesn't give it back, though. He examines it, holding it close to his face and looking at every inch of it. He emits a low, quiet moan from deep in his chest. "You do this?"

She nods.

"Ni maamaa used to do the same. Katawashishiw." He turns it over to look at the other side. Even though it's identical, he takes the same amount of time with it. "Katawashishiw," he says again. "Could you make one for me?"

"I only made this as a gift."

"Mine would be a gift too. For my sister."

"I wish I could—"

"I don't have much to trade—I'm heading to Prince George soon, so I've been keeping light—but I have a little money saved and my sister would love one. Would take the sting out of me arriving on her doorstep with my bags." He laughs a hoarse laugh, places the cozy back in the box when Florence picks it up.

"This was just a one-time thing, for Lillian. My aunt."

"I know. Lillian and I are cousins. So we're related too somehow. Third cousins six times removed?" He winks at her, then latches his hand onto her arm. "Shipwayhtaytaak." He leads the way, slowly with his limp. "Name's Hank."

"Florence."

"Know that too. Met you when you were just little. Barely walking."

"Really?"

He nods. "It's been a long time since I saw your mother, but looking at you brings her right back."

This jolts Florence, sends a shock through her limbs. In all the years that have passed since she last saw her mother, Florence has never been able to bring her image, full and complete, to mind, only flashes. A glimpse of her cheekbone in profile. The corner of her mouth in a smile, a couple of teeth exposed. She can't see her whole face at once. It's never occurred to her to look for her mother in a mirror. Hank pats her arm with his free hand as if sensing her thoughts.

They shuffle farther down the path to another shack in the row that a young couple are heading towards from the opposite direction. When they arrive, the front door is open and a clutch of people hover in the doorway because there are already too many inside. Hank simply totters up and inside, winds his way through the crowd as people part for him. He tugs on Florence's sleeve and pulls her in with him.

The heat hits her like a punch. The air is thick and steamy and filled with pipe smoke. Underneath it all, a whiff of something savoury.

"Taanishi, taanishi," Hank says to everyone gathered in the room, moving smoothly despite his leg.

"Excuse me," Florence says, trying to follow and not bump anyone too roughly.

They pass the stove, where a giant pot takes up the entire surface. A woman drops in some diced potatoes as a man uses a ladle to fish out a round meatball. Boulette soup. But the woman swats him away before he can get the morsel into his mouth.

"I'm sorry," Florence says after stepping on a foot. But the owner of the foot just nods and smiles, trying his best to make way for her. Then, in a rush of motion, Hank pulls her forward in front of himself and towards Lillian, who's on a stool and leaning against the wall. Florence bends to her ear and announces herself, and Lillian belts out a laugh, claps her hands, then pulls Florence to her side so she's nudged up beside her aunt.

She puts the box down by her feet. "How are you, Auntie?"

"Ji bayn," she says. "I'm fine, ma fii." She leans into Florence and wraps an arm around her waist.

"What's this about?" Florence asks. The energy in the room makes her skin rise with gooseflesh.

"Laniversayr," she says, pointing to the woman making the soup and the man beside her. "Marguerite and Norris McKay. Traant."

Anniversary. Thirty years. Florence is surprised she remembers the Michif words, but then another thought takes hold. She has spent a similar amount of time living as another person. In a way, she's as old as the couple celebrating now. A part of her is. She pushes the thought away. "Where's Clancy?" she asks. "I saw the Huber truck here."

"Clancy, atooshkew."

"Auntie . . ."

"Atooshkew." She says it slowly, enunciating. "Working."

"Doing what?"

But Lillian is pulled into a conversation with her neighbour.

People mingle and move about, and Lillian introduces Florence as they pass by. They stop to converse. Some, like Hank, met her when she was young, but Florence has no memory of them. Florence mostly nods and smiles, lets Lillian do the talking. A plate of cookies is passed around from one direction, then a plate of crackers from the other. Florence sends them along without taking anything.

"These go quick," says Hank, who's managed to tour the room and visit and is now on the other side of her, holding another plate of cookies. "Won't be coming around again, so best grab one now." He lifts the plate towards her. Florence gives in and takes a cookie. It's smooth and buttery and falls apart in her mouth. When he sees that she enjoys it, he takes a second off the plate and hands it to her. The soup is ladled into mugs, and a young woman carefully carries four of them like a barmaid and gives them to the older ones. Hank and Lillian each get one.

Across the room, Clancy and his friend Delbert enter, and though the shack is full, people squeeze even closer together and make room. Clancy looks for Lillian immediately, spots Florence beside her, grins. Mischievous look in his eye that gives it all away. He knew there was a party. Knew there was a party today and didn't tell her because he also knew she wouldn't come if he did. She doesn't want to grin back but it happens involuntarily. She shakes her head at him and turns to Lillian.

"Auntie, I know you and Clancy are leaving here soon, so I came to give you something," Florence says.

But Lillian reaches out for a mug of soup that's being passed through the room and hands it to Florence. "Miitsho. Eat, ma fii."

It's like she's eight again and all her years of careful independence have been erased. Florence obeys, takes the cup in her hands. There's no spoon, so she blows on its surface, then opens her mouth wide to drink in the pieces of potato and even wider for the single boulette at the bottom that clunks into her mouth. It's so big it's hard to chew, but the meat is savoury and juicy and worth the awkwardness.

Florence tries a few times to take her leave, but with each attempt, Lillian hands her something else to eat or calls someone else over to introduce her to. But finally, when enough food has been shared and stomachs are full, conversation dies down, and Florence picks up the box that was tucked behind her legs against the wall. "Auntie, I really do have to go, but I brought you this. To take with you to Winnipeg." She places the box in Lillian's lap. Her aunt opens it and feels the gift first, running her hands over the beadwork. Then she pulls it up close to her face, so close she can take in only one section at a time.

The room grows oddly quiet and Florence looks up. A few are watching Lillian as she studies the cozy, but most are watching Florence, looks of awe on their faces. Florence tenses and tries to step back but bumps into the wall.

"Wii, wii," Lillian says, nodding. She starts to say something else but pauses, too overcome, and embraces Florence instead. "Kiiya kishkishi." She passes the cozy around the room, and others admire it, compliment it.

The woman who made the soup shouts from the corner, "Could you make me one too?"

"Me first, though," Hank says, and winks at her.

Florence fumbles for words. "I wish I could," she finally says, "but I don't have any more materials. And this was just . . . something for Lillian."

"I love it, ma fii." The cozy makes its way back to Lillian, and when she boxes it up, conversation begins again, at a quieter pitch than before. Then a younger man near the opposite wall begins to tune a fiddle. The mood in the room changes. She should go now. Push off from the wall and wind her way back out. But the man begins to play. The tune comes to her almost immediately: "Peekaboo Waltz." The room is crowded, but it doesn't stop people from shuffling their feet. Even Hank, who's perched on a stool, kicks his feet in time to the music. Lillian claps her hands on her legs.

The shack grows even hotter and fills with the sour smell of sweat as people move with the music. Bodies so close they're always touching, always connected. Some have gathered outside the door and they're moving too. The man with the fiddle starts in on another tune, a faster one, and Florence watches the others' feet. Step one, two, three, kick. She imitates in tiny movements, but Lillian catches her and encourages her, giving instructions. Delbert, moving by, overhears and stops, reaches out his hand to Florence, inviting.

"No, no, I can't—"

But he's already leading her through the room, around the others and out the door. The cold air snaps cool on her skin, her scalp.

"Careful, she jigs like a horse with shoes that don't fit," Clancy says as Delbert whirls her into the group of other jigging couples.

"I'll take my chances." Delbert lifts her hand and twirls her around, his other hand firm on her back, guiding. Before the tune comes to an end, the next starts up, "Whiskey Before Breakfast," then a third. The tunes bleed into one another as if they're one long piece of music. Florence loses her breath; she's drenched in sweat, and the muscles in her legs burn. Still, she dances two more before finally pulling away. She sits on a log near the house, and Clancy comes over to join her.

"Not bad," he says. "Only stepped on the poor guy five or six times." He pulls a flask from his pocket and takes a swig. Offers her some.

"This the same stuff from the other time?"

He nods. She takes it anyway. It burns going down but in a way that wakes everything up inside.

"That was a nice thing you did for her," he says, watching those still jigging. "The beading."

She doesn't tell him how much she enjoyed it. How much it occupied her thoughts when she was at work, walking through town, running her errands. How much doing it again made her feel whole in a way she'd forgotten. Instead, they talk about other things. His time in the war, what living in the capital city was like for her, movies they'd seen in the theatres. They sit and talk until the sun has lowered in the sky. When it's almost dark, Lillian steps out of the doorway.

"You're done visiting, Auntie?" Clancy asks.

"Ni noohtayshin."

"I should go too," Florence says, rising from the log. "I'll walk you home."

"Clancy, aashtum," Lillian says.

The three of them head down the path, music fading behind them as they go. A teenage girl races towards them, lit by the sliver of moon. She stops in front of them. "I did it, Auntie," she says, proud. "I did what you asked and there's a lot there," she says.

"Bonn ouvraazh, ma fii." Lillian pats the girl's head, praising her, and the girl runs back to the gathering.

"What are you up to, Auntie?" Clancy asks, but she only smiles in response.

When they enter Lillian's shack, she sets about making tea, readying her cozy for its first use.

"I can't stay," Florence says. "I've been gone too long already."

"Okay," Lillian says, "but take that with you." She points to an old battered toolbox on the floor at the foot of the bed.

"What is it?"

But Lillian only motions for her to open it. Hinges squeak as Florence lifts the lid. It's filled with tins and little glass medicine bottles. And each of the tins and bottles are filled with beads. Underneath the top drawer are more pieces of hide and cloth. Velveteen, stroud, and something thick and satiny.

"Where did this come from?" Florence asks, overwhelmed.

Lillian responds in Michif. Florence doesn't catch any of the words.

"Colleen went hunting for her," Clancy says. "The girl we just saw, the McKays' youngest. She collected from here and there."

"This is too much," Florence says, taking it all in.

"Now," Lillian says in English, "you can bead more."

"That was just for you," Florence says, but she doesn't turn away from the toolbox.

Lillian pours hot water into the pot and puts the cozy over it. "The others should have their beadwork too," Lillian says. "Makes them proud."

Florence closes the lid and picks the toolbox up; it's heavier than she expected. Lillian pushes Clancy forward to take it for her. "Thank you, Auntie," Florence says, embracing her.

"Maarsii," Lillian corrects her.

"Maarsii." Florence holds on to Lillian for a long time.

"You visit, ma fii. Come to Winnipeg and visit."

"I will." Florence finally lets go and Clancy follows her out, the toolbox clanging against his leg.

"Is it always that easy for you?" Clancy asks when they're back on the path to her car, the sounds of the party at the other end of Seedy Creek carrying on the night air.

"What?"

"Lying. You're not going to visit her."

That easiness that was there between them earlier instantly dissipates. Florence does up the top button of her coat, trudges on. But maybe she could visit. Winnipeg is a huge city; there'd be little risk. She could take a week off work in the spring or summer. Stay in a hotel. But there's no point in bringing it up. "Did your friend find you any leads on work?"

"You don't need to pretend you're interested." That gruff shell of his is back.

There's no reason for him to be difficult now—he's agreed to go. They reach the car, and Florence opens the trunk so Clancy can place the toolbox inside.

"It's actually a good time for you to go." She wasn't going to say anything about the file, but if that map was correct, they would have to leave anyway. He should know.

"What do you mean?" he asks, suspicious.

"After I called you earlier this week, I found something at work. Documents. It seems the government has plans for this land. Something about a community pasture."

"Right. I bet they also said something about the Prairie Farm Rehabilitation Act?" he says, disdain obvious in his voice.

"They did," Florence says, surprised. "You've heard about it?" If Clancy already knows, she hasn't divulged anything she shouldn't.

He drags in a deep breath, then leans against the car. "What else did those papers say?"

"There were two letters and a map. The map was of this corner of the province and it showed an entire section blocked off," she says, then pauses.

"And that section was the area between Torduvalle and Forsyth, including this land here."

"Explains why others have seen some suits out this way," says Clancy. He falls silent, distracted by his own thoughts.

"Do you know what it all means?" Florence asks, hesitant.

But he's still thinking.

"Has Mr. Huber told you something?"

He shakes his head. "We heard about it from a couple of the locals near the Manitoba border."

His words confuse her. *We?* And what does he mean by *locals*? He's a hired hand on a farm, and there are no unions for hired hands. "Is this something to do with the army?"

He turns to her, an incredulous look on his face. "Hardly," he says.

"Well, I don't know what you're saying," she says, stung.

"The Saskatchewan Métis Society. You've heard of it, right?" he asks, but it's more of a statement.

"I haven't," she says, lifting her head to look right at him. She won't be shamed for not knowing things she doesn't want to know.

"Well, you should. It's an organization that's doing important things," he says. "Its membership numbers are growing fast and there are locals all over the province now."

Florence regrets bringing up the documents. She should have just kept her mouth shut. "Well, whatever's happening here, you and Lillian will be safe in Winnipeg."

"And what about everyone else?" he asks, frustration creeping into his voice.

"I don't know," Florence says, throwing her arms up. This is hardly her fault.

"Bloody bastards! Keep everything secret and don't tell us a thing. Why don't they just come and talk to us? We're human beings. If they came and just talked things over with us . . . instead, they plan in secret, then tell us what to do."

"You told me you wanted to go to Winnipeg, that you were working your way there," she says to remind him he doesn't need to be so upset by this.

"That's not the point. I'm sick of it. Sometimes I just want to"—he pushes himself off the car, turns away to kick at some rocks—"tell them no. Tell them they can't do that to us anymore."

His anger hangs off him like a coat, and the moonlight catches on his hunched shoulders. When he finally turns to her, there's an expectant look on his face. He wants her to say something, agree with him, maybe, but there's no point in that. No point in whining and wishing for things to be different. That never helps anything.

Another moment passes, then Clancy nods, as if unsurprised she'd have nothing to say. "Goodbye, Nimish." He turns and heads back to the others.

She watches him disappear into the darkness, his shoulders slumped forward. His life has been full of disappearances. Their father's death was one kind of disappearance. Their mother disappeared inside herself. And Florence up and gone away from him too. A pang in her chest. The toll that must have taken.

SUMMER 1910
Quincy Lake, Saskatchewan

"**Where would you** like to go today?" the man asks, pointing to each dessert on display under the glass. "To the Scottish Highlands with a slice of Dundee cake or the streets of Paris with a madeleine?" He puts on an accent for each location. "And this here, this apple strudel, will take you all the way to the mountains of Austria."

Florence laughs. Clancy would think all of this is stupid, but she doesn't care. She wants to taste every single one, travel the world with her taste buds. Her eyes land on a strange long cylinder that looks like a giant candy.

"That? That's a Swiss roll and it will take you to a quaint village in Switzerland," he says. Then he leans across the counter and whispers, "It's not really Swiss, but don't tell anyone." He puts his finger to his lips, a secret between the two of them.

The café is on the main floor of the new hotel that just opened, the Aylesbury. Three storeys high and the biggest building in town, constructed over the past year at the same time as the station house and freight shed were expanded to accommodate a new north–south railway line. With that has come an explosion of people, nearly a thousand in Quincy Lake now; there's even talk of it becoming a city. The new developments have also brought many more visitors through town, and the influx means Florence floats in and out without anyone remembering her. This is already her fourth visit since the spring thaw.

Clancy made her angry last night when he said she comes to town so often only because she wants to get out of her duties, but all she does is work from morning to night. Sometimes even in the night when Maamaa can't hold it. Clancy goes out fishing with Nap and his boys and goes to the farm nearly every day. The Duncans even took him all the way to Weyburn when they went to pick up a new piece of farm equipment. He's always out and about, but she's stuck, every day the same as the last. Florence was so angry she wanted to spit on his food.

Aunt Lillian doesn't understand either. She's happy with things as they are, letting each day roll over her as if there is nothing more to life. It's what she chooses, and that's the difference. What choices did Florence make? None. And, more important, what choices can she make to change things? None. A life without choices is a stagnant one, a lonely one. But none of those things bind her when she's here in town—every time she comes, she has a million choices. She can decide where she's from, who her family is, who she is, where she wants to go, and what to buy. It's never lonely.

Florence pays for her order, counting out the change from the coin purse on her wrist.

"Will you be sitting inside or outside today?" the man asks.

"Outside."

"I'll bring it out to you momentarily," he says, when another couple steps up to the display case.

The best part about the new hotel's café is that it has a veranda that sits above Main Street where patrons can watch people and cars pass by a few feet below. Despite all the dust and dirt kicked up from the roads, you still feel above it all, like it doesn't reach you. The day is cool and overcast, but there's a large awning that will protect her if the sky lets loose some rain. Florence pushes out the doors and selects the table at the far end, where the veranda runs along the side street. If she swivels, she can see the train station in the distance.

Before she's even settled, the man from inside approaches. "Bon voyage," he says, placing her tea and the dessert on her table, and winks before returning inside.

The Swiss roll is on a mint-green plate with French-pearl edges, the soft green highlighting the rich yellow of the sponge and the thin red line of jam. The white dusting of sugar on top like snow. Florence stares at it for a moment, her mouth watering, before picking up the fork.

It tastes like a cloud. Fluffy, airy, sweet. Her first instinct is to eat it quickly, but she wants the moment to last. She doesn't know when she'll be back—her trips always depend on her work and Uncle Joe's delivery schedule. She sets the fork down, forcing herself to take a break between bites. She sips her tea. Within seconds, she picks the fork back up but holds the cake in her mouth, letting it dissolve slowly. She closes her eyes as she does, imagining what a Swiss village would look like. When she swallows, she hears someone call her name. It's a common name and there are so many people around, but it rings out again, and this time she recognizes the voice. She freezes. The whole world freezes.

Florence puts her fork down, her appetite gone.

Clancy walks up to the edge of the veranda, happy to find her. "Michael Duncan came into town with a load and asked me to help," he says, proud of himself. "I didn't think I'd see you, though."

Florence doesn't answer. Doesn't move.

A moment passes as he registers the surroundings.

"What are you doing up there?" he says, his voice pinched. He wraps his hands around the balusters of the railing, pokes his head through to look at the place, unaware how inappropriate it is, how wrong.

Others at the tables start to take notice. Florence still doesn't look at him but he's large in her periphery.

"How'd you get in there?" he asks, confused but a hint of irritation taking hold. "What are you wearing?"

Florence feels the other patrons on the veranda watching. She folds her hands in her lap and stares down at the planks at her feet, studying the cracks in the wood, the places where it splinters. She shakes her head imperceptibly, either to warn Clancy away or perhaps to convince herself it isn't happening. She isn't sure which.

"Why are you ignoring me?" His voice is louder. "Say something."

Florence remains a statue. Solid stone.

"I'm coming up." Clancy starts to walk around to the front of the café.

One of the men from the tables folds his newspaper and gets up from his seat. He stands at the top of the stairs, blocking the entrance, but he faces Florence. "Young lady, are you being disturbed?" He's in a three-piece camel-coloured suit, the jacket off and draped over his chair. A gold chain curves like a rib bone from a button to his vest pocket.

Florence opens her mouth but nothing comes out, a heat in her body rising to the surface of her skin.

Clancy ascends the stairs until the man stops him.

"Please, boy, leave the young lady alone and move along," the man says, extending a single hand to block the way.

"Lady?" Clancy laughs. There's no spite in it; he genuinely finds it funny.

"That's enough, now, go on." The man waves his paper at Clancy like he's an errant cat.

"Florence, tell him—"

But then the man backhands Clancy on the arm with the paper. It isn't hard, but it thwacks loudly, startling all who witness it. Florence jolts in her seat. A silence falls and the man prepares to do it again, holding the paper high in the air.

"She's my sister," Clancy says in his defence, barely audible.

The man turns to Florence again, grinning as if he can't believe the gall of the boy. "Is that true?" he asks, the smile starting to fade, as if he can read Florence's thoughts on her face.

Florence looks at her brother, who is now leaning against the railing to see around the man, waiting for her to respond. Clancy. Chubby cheeks like a baby's despite his nearly twelve years. Rust-coloured skin and curly, mussed hair that's damp-soil dark. His black eyes normally shine like glass beads, but in that moment the light is gone, replaced with something else. Florence sees the bits of dried grass in his hair, the fraying threads on his collar. The repairs and patches on his clothes where the fabric split and was sewn back together, a constellation of thin scars and round scabs. With the man in his suit standing beside Clancy, she sees what the man does. She sees everything her brother will never be, will never be allowed to become. He's unkempt, dirty. Wild. Something to be swatted away.

Florence turns back to the man, who's waiting for her to answer. "He's not my brother," she says, shaking her head.

Thwack.

Florence sees shock flash in Clancy's eyes, and she scrunches her own shut. She hears Clancy's footsteps race down the stairs, then pound in the dirt as he heads back up the road. And she hears chair legs scrape the veranda as the man resettles himself, then the rustling of the paper as he unfolds it.

Florence keeps her eyes closed a long time. So long that when she finally opens them, the afternoon is almost over. It's still overcast, but the clouds have thinned, and the possibility of rain is gone. The crowds on Main Street have thinned too. Most people have gone home to prepare meals, start fires; the other tables on the veranda are nearly empty. The last few morsels of the Swiss roll lie on the plate, now dry. She gathers the bags of groceries and other items she purchased for home. As she rises from the table, a fly settles on the roll. It skitters over it from edge to edge as if measuring the size of its treasure. Florence turns and descends the stairs, leaving the fly to its feast.

SEPTEMBER 1946

Torduvalle, Saskatchewan

IT WAS A harmless mistake. She caught it before anyone else did so there was nothing to be upset about.

Florence pulls on her alpaca coat in front of the mirror and selects her brown headscarf with polka dots.

She almost sent copies of Mr. Colthart's new insurance papers to Mr. Brubaker, a prospective client. She somehow scooped them up when putting together a package of general information for Mr. Brubaker. It was days ago now, but it still bothers her. The papers included life and property insurance and documents with personal and private information—details on his medical and physical health, particulars on his income and other assets. That's not the kind of thing that anyone wants in the wrong hands. She can't imagine Mr. Brubaker would have done anything with the papers except return them directly to the office. But it still would have been a mark on Pratt's solid reputation. A mark made by her.

She steps out her door and locks it behind her.

Thank goodness she caught the error. The day was harried enough as it was. Two of the new staff from Forsyth had come in to get acquainted and learn the ropes, and both the new secretaries—Mary Beth Watkins and Emma Richardson—had started that Monday, and there was so much more instruction involved than Florence had anticipated.

Also, it was Wednesday.

That whole day she kept wondering if Clancy and Lillian had made an early start or if they were spending the morning loading things up and saying their goodbyes. She wondered if they were taking a train or if they had found a ride with someone. She wondered what time they would arrive in Winnipeg. Would the sun still be up or just going down and at their backs, setting the cityscape alight as they arrived? Would they feel as excited as she had when she first arrived in Torduvalle?

The thoughts kept intruding all day, kept her on edge. It was why she'd made the mistake. But in the evening, long after supper, when she knew the day was also over in Winnipeg, something settled. It was done. Back to her life as it was. There was a relief, but also a small hole of sadness inside her. It was this sadness that made her finally open the toolbox that night.

She strides to her car, the crisp fall air stinging her cheeks.

She chose bright shades of blue and yellow for Hank's cozy, colours like his laughter. And Saskatoon berries in a rich purple for balance and because she saw how much Saskatoon berry jam he'd spooned onto his bannock at the anniversary party. For Marguerite, she chose shades in more muted tones—clover, chestnut, navy. The colours corresponding to a feeling Florence sensed when speaking with her. A gravity, a kind of introspection. If Marguerite were a season, she would be winter. But Florence also selected pearl and spring-green beads to use as accents. To make the darker shades stand out and highlight whatever was running deeper within her.

But that was Wednesday. This is Saturday, and there's much that needs to be done before the banquet this evening, so she needs to focus.

She climbs into the LaSalle and checks her wristwatch. It's ten to nine and Jennie's Studebaker is not in her driveway. They agreed to meet at the town hall at nine to decorate, but she must have left early. It really is too much work and a lot of hullabaloo for a welcome supper. But the event keeps snowballing. Even the mayor and town council have been invited, branding Pratt's success as the town's success, and now it's a big event.

But with so many people coming, Jennie had worked herself into a tizzy on Thursday night, panicking about the seating plans. Came over unannounced and Florence had to scramble to put away all her beading materials before opening the door. She stuffed them into drawers of the credenza, but beads can always get away from you. Sure enough, as Jennie was taking her seat on the settee, she spotted a bead in one of the cushion's button tufts. She pinched it in her fingers to examine it.

"What's this from?" she asked, dropping it in Florence's hand.

"Maybe my white cardigan with the pearls and beads on the cuffs? Or my beaded clutch?" Florence said, her voice trembling. She owned neither of those things, but she had to say something. She hoped it sounded believable. But what surprised Florence the most in that moment, the moment when Jennie dropped that single bead into her palm, was that the lie she'd formed in her head was not about keeping something from someone; it was about keeping something to herself. There was a difference. A difference that she couldn't explain but only feel.

In the end, she didn't have to lie any further because Jennie didn't wait for an explanation. She was too concerned about past squabbles and rows between townsfolk and how those disagreements affected the seating arrangements. The two of them worked for hours that evening, pencilling in names and erasing them until they were satisfied. It had to get done that night because Jennie and Shirley were heading to the city the following morning to get more decorations and then stopping in Hoagland, a town halfway between Regina and Torduvalle, to meet with the Ukrainian caterers. Even though Florence knew the two women would be shopping for more than just banquet items, she'd approved the day as a work trip for Shirley.

Now Florence starts her car and puts it into drive, but just as she's about to signal, someone shouts her name. It's Jennie, rushing down her walkway towards the LaSalle.

"Jennie?" Florence rolls down her window.

"Could I get a ride? I meant to call last night but the evening flew by and when I remembered, it was far too late."

"Of course." Florence waits for her to climb in. "Where's your car?"

"Shirley and I got a flat yesterday on the way back from Hoagland—"

"Oh, goodness."

"It was fine. Didn't have to wait too long for help. When I got back, though, Garth took the car to the shop just to make sure everything was shipshape, but they're short-staffed at the moment. Lucky if I get the car by Monday." Jennie rolls her eyes. "Serves me right for telling him."

"I'm sure he just wants it to be safe."

"He didn't care at all that we were stranded on the highway—thought it was amusing to think of me, run ragged these past couple of weeks and then stuck there, unable to do anything at all. A 'stop and smell the roses' lesson, he said. He got his feathers ruffled only when I told him it was one of those Natives who was kind enough to stop for us. Changed the tire lickety-split. Friendly too. But you know Garth, doesn't trust anyone he doesn't know. So into the shop it went, and now I'm on foot."

"It's always best to get things double-checked," Florence says to cover the cringe she can't control.

Shirley's car is parked outside the town hall. They go through the front doors and see a glittery welcome sign in the foyer, and in the hall, glittery streamers are wrapped around the pillars. Shirley's wrestling with the folded tables leaning against the wall.

"Impressive, Shirley," Jennie says as they head over to help.

"Thought I'd get an early start. There's so much to do and only a few hours before the caterers get here."

Jennie helps her half carry, half drag a table to the front of the room while Florence pulls chairs from the stack next to the tables and follows them.

"And I finally remembered how I knew that man," Shirley says to Jennie, then turns to Florence. "Did she tell you about our adventure yesterday?"

"The flat? Yes."

"The man who helped us was the same man who stopped you outside Nick's a few weeks back. I knew I'd seen him somewhere before and it came to me right before bed. Finally. It's how it always is."

"I don't remember," Florence says, snapping the legs of the table into position so they can flip it while her stomach twists. It was so long ago—why does Shirley remember? And—more important—Shirley and Jennie went shopping on Friday morning, and Clancy had told her he and Lillian were leaving on Wednesday.

"Don't you? He thought he knew you from somewhere."

"That man who changed our tire?" Jennie asks.

"I vaguely recall." Florence wipes invisible debris from the tabletop. Why won't Shirley let it go? "We should wipe all these down."

"We have tablecloths." Shirley points to some boxes along the wall.

"Still, they should be cleaned first. I'll get a rag." Florence escapes through the swinging doors to the kitchen, knees weak. Did Clancy postpone their departure? Did Mr. Huber offer him a raise to keep him on? Did he and Lillian change their minds? It could be a million things. She glances out the pass-through window and watches them heave another table across the room. She slips to the back of the kitchen, where there's a small desk with a phone. Picks up the receiver. "R-R-five-one-four, please." The number now fixed in her mind. Mrs. Huber answers.

"I'm sorry to bother you again, but is Clancy there?"

"He's out in the barn right now."

"Is there any chance you can call him in?"

A silence as Mrs. Huber contemplates this.

"It really is important. Is there any way I can speak with him?"

An annoyed sigh on the line. "His sister, right?"

"Yes. Again, I'm sorry for the trouble."

"What's your number?"

"I can wait on the line," Florence says.

"It may be a while."

"I'll wait," Florence says, then she pulls the phone from her ear to listen for the others. She sets the receiver down, grabs a rag from under the sink, and wets it. Rushes back to the doors. "This kitchen is a real mess. I don't know who used it last," she says.

"Was it the Shriners?" Jennie asks.

"Maybe, but I'd hate for the caterers to arrive and have to deal with this.

Are you okay out here while I clean up in there?" Florence tosses the damp rag to Jennie.

"Of course."

Florence races back to the phone, keeping her eye on the swinging doors.

"I know why you're calling," Clancy says when he gets on the line.

"We have to talk."

"I know."

"But not on the phone."

"Fine." A quiet huff. "I can come by again tonight—"

"No. I'll come to you."

"Okay—"

"Today. This afternoon."

"I can't. I'm leaving shortly."

"Can you wait half an hour?"

"I don't know . . ." he says, deliberating.

"Florence?" Jennie's voice from the pass-through.

"Please, just half an hour," Florence whispers in a panic, then hangs up. She races back to the sink and blasts the hot water when the doors swing open.

"I thought I heard voices," Jennie says.

"Just me. Talking to myself."

"You okay?" Jennie asks.

"Another heachache seems to be taking hold."

"Oh, goodness, I hope you're not coming down with something."

"Me too."

"It is that time of year, though—flus and colds."

Florence nods. "I really don't want to miss tonight. Do you think you and Shirley would be able to handle setting everything up? I'm feeling rather awful."

"Of course, and Shirley can drive me home. You go and get yourself to bed."

Florence walks back to her car, legs shaky, brow sweaty, like she really is coming down with something. She heads for the highway, turns left, then accelerates. Drives so fast down the road, the world's a blur around her, smeared and harsh. One dull colour bleeding into the next. Her car bucks and rattles in protest all the way to the Huber farm.

A long, narrow lane leads off the grid road to their two-storey A-frame. Robin's-egg blue with white trim and a deck that wraps around two sides of the house. But Florence drives past the house to the next lane, the one that leads to the barn and where Frank's truck is parked. She parks her own vehicle on the side of the barn where her car can't be seen from the highway and strides to the open barn doors, where Clancy's loading milk cans into the truck.

"I have a delivery to make right now," he says, moving back inside the barn.

Florence paces, her shoes crunching on the gravel with each pounding footstep. "You can't spare a few minutes?" she asks when he returns with another load, anger obvious in her voice.

"I'm free tonight."

"I'm not."

He doesn't respond.

"How long will you be?" she says as he places the crate in the truck.

"All day. I have one trip this morning, another this afternoon." He tightens a lid on a can. "You can come with me."

"On your delivery?" she says, scoffing.

"First one's not far."

"Unbelievable." She wants to smack him, hit him with everything she's got.

"It's just a few miles west." He nods in that direction, pointing with his lips. "We're not going into town."

"Whose farm is it?"

Clancy wipes his brow. "Remus."

"Never heard of him."

"Maybe I got the name wrong but I've been there before."

She pauses. "How long exactly?"

"That depends," he says. "How fast do you drive?"

"What do you mean?"

"We can take your car."

"Are you playing games with me?"

"This truck has broken down on me on both of my last trips," he says. "It keeps overheating. It'd be better to take yours."

"My trunk won't hold all that." She points to the milk cans.

"Most of those are for the second trip. It's just one crate for the first trip. It'll fit."

"This is ridiculous, Clancy. Just tell me now why you haven't left. Actually, no—just tell me when you'll be leaving."

"I will. I do owe you an explanation, but I also really need to make this delivery on time. Can we please take your vehicle?"

He's being sincere, and some of her anger dissipates. "Just on the highway?"

"Yes. I'll sit in the back. If anyone asks, you can say my truck broke down and you picked me up."

Florence looks back to the highway in the distance. Shirley and Jennie will be at the town hall all day. "Fine." She walks to her car and opens the trunk. "Won't those leak?"

"Lids are tight and I'll tuck a blanket over the top for good measure."

Florence waits in the car for him, engine on for the heat. The car rocks when he loads in the crate and again when he climbs into the back seat. As she heads down the uneven road to the highway, she regrets her decision. It's too loud for a normal conversation, and with him in the back, it's even more awkward. Minutes pass and he remains quiet, doesn't offer anything. A seed of anger starts to take hold again.

She shifts in her seat to glance at him in the rear-view. "So?" she asks, but he doesn't hear her over the thrum of the car. He's looking out the window, off somewhere else, his face softer and eyes relaxed. Her ribs pinch. She raises her voice: "You're still here."

He turns and meets her eye in the mirror. "I planned to go. I made all the arrangements."

She waits. "And?"

A long pause. "Auntie." He looks back at the sprawling fields.

"Is she all right?"

"I think so." He says something else but at a volume too quiet for her to hear.

"I'm sorry?"

Clancy shifts in his seat, leans forward. "I called the guy I know in Winnipeg and arranged to pay Eldon, a friend of Delbert's, to drive us there. We were going to leave Wednesday night as soon as Eldon was done with his shift at the poultry plant. I spoke with Mr. Huber, and that was hard because he's been good to me. He's a real good boss. But he understood. I spent as much time as I could at the farm to help him out beforehand." He stops, shakes his head as if in regret. "I left Auntie on Sunday and she just had a cough. Thought it was a cold. But when I hitched back to Seedy Creek on Wednesday, she was coughing and hacking so much, she could barely breathe. The McKays had wanted to take her to a doctor in Radford earlier in the week, but you know her . . . come Wednesday night, Eldon drove us to Regina, to the hospital, instead."

"And?" Florence looks over her shoulder quickly, then turns back to the road.

"Bronchitis and pneumonia." He taps his fist against the back of the seat in front of him. "They kept her for two days and wanted to keep her longer, but she didn't want to stay. And hospital bills are not cheap." *Tap, tap.* "Plus, her medication costs money, and they want her to see another doctor to follow up." *Tap, tap, tap.*

The rapping pulses through the seat, persistent against her spine.

"So, yes, I took your money and I had every intention of going. But I spent it—I had to. I will pay you back, though. Mr. Huber hadn't hired anyone else yet—he actually wasn't planning to, since it's the end of the season, but he's a kind man and is finding jobs for me to do—"

"You're staying?" She straightens to see him in the mirror and her foot hits the gas harder as she does, jerking the car forward. He stops tapping.

"I won't stir things up for you, Florence. I'll do my job at the farm, head to Seedy Creek when I can, and avoid Torduvalle. If I have to go to town for Frank, I'll pretend we're strangers."

Florence's hands tighten on the wheel, the skin on her knuckles thin and taut. "How long?"

"Will I stay?" He shrugs. "Until she's fit to travel. A few weeks, maybe, and then we'll see if the weather allows, but . . ." He meets her eye in the rearview. "I will pay you back. I've got a few irons in the fire, so I'll pay you back and I'll save for the move."

The drone of the car turns to white noise in Florence's ears. A few weeks is a long time. Her anger subsides but is replaced with fear. So much can happen in just a few weeks. Her vision tunnels to a single point on the horizon.

"Did you hear me?" Clancy asks, voice loud.

"Sorry." Florence nods and wills herself to calm down. He's promised to ignore her—it will be fine. Nothing is going to change. She focuses on the road, on the things under her control in this moment.

"I thought hospital stays were supposed to be free now," Clancy says after a while. "Isn't that what Tommy Douglas promised?"

"In the new year. Beginning in January," Florence responds, still in a haze but relieved to be talking about something else. "They're also working on a bill that will make all health services free."

"So maybe we shouldn't move to Winnipeg, then?" A sardonic laugh.

"Why is that funny?"

"It's not. It sounds great." But there's still a mocking tone. "Are you just as enamoured with ol' Tommy as everyone else?" He's smiling in the mirror.

"He's doing good things."

"Sure, yeah. But only for certain people—only for those who can already afford it. Right?"

She doesn't answer.

"Isn't that right? It'll be free for those who pay taxes?"

"I'm not sure," she lies.

"Not for us squatters," he says, emphasizing the last word. "What kind of health policy is that? Same as their education policy—as all their policies."

"That's not true. Education has changed now—all kids can go to school no matter where they live, no matter if their families pay taxes or not."

"Good ol' Tommy." He slaps his knee. "Sounds good, doesn't it?"

She remains silent, not wanting to go down this road with him.

"They sound like kind, caring people," he says, continuing on anyway. "Free education, even for those poor people who don't pay taxes. Sure." He huffs out a breath. "But what about their Prairie Farm Rehabilitation Act?"

Florence can't help but look at him in mirror because she doesn't see the connection.

"Do you know what they're doing under the guise of that act? The act they say is to help improve land quality? They're using that piece of legislation to forcibly remove the people from that land."

Forcibly. The word sticks in Florence's head, rolls around. Clancy's always so dramatic.

"So what non-tax-paying people are they talking about? They're making sure there are none." He pauses. "Are they really so kind and caring?" He stops again. "And who are those people they're forcibly removing?" He glares at her in the mirror. "Our people, Florence. Our own people from our own lands."

Now Florence huffs.

"Do you not believe me?"

"Living on a road allowance is never permanent. Everyone knows there will come a day when you'll have to move." It's hardly so harsh as he makes it sound.

"This isn't just packing up and moving, Florence. We just heard from another Métis local farther west that over the past couple years, the government has gone into three different Métis communities and took people— *took* people—right from their homes. Gave them very little warning to pack up anything and just drove them miles and miles away."

There's a hint of fear in his voice that gives Florence pause.

"Delbert's aunt and uncle were two of those people," he says, his tone a few degrees lower.

"You believe they're going to do that here?" she asks, thinking of Lillian.

"They might," he says, but then, as if sensing her concerns, he continues. "That local out west said they do it only in the spring and summer. They move them to farming colonies they've set up elsewhere. For rehabilitation."

"Lillian will be better before then," she says, but it's also a question.

"It's just . . ." he says, frustration ramping up. "How do they get away with it? Over and over again. These are our lands. We are from this land, Florence. *Born* of it. So, tell me, how is it possible that our people, who were created here on this land, do not have any land ourselves?"

"How much farther?" she asks, deflecting, but he doesn't take the bait.

"It's because everything governments do—federal, provincial, municipal—every policy or law they put into place is designed to keep us from our own land. They took it, and the greedy bastards won't give it up. Not even a single piece. They just keep pushing us here and there. They'd be happy to push us right off the ends of the earth."

"Are we close?" she asks. *Stolen land. Broken promises.* The same refrain since childhood.

Clancy reads her thoughts. "You know our history, sis."

"Yes, I know our history. And you know what else I know? What you're ranting about now is what Napoleon Morin and the Boyers ranted about all those years ago. Even Paapaa did when the mood struck, and I'm guessing you've now taken up the mantle." She glares at him in the mirror. "And I'm also guessing it's what you and Delbert and the others in your local and the Métis Society or whatever rant about, don't you?"

"Yes, because we're still angry!" he says. "And I don't understand how you're not. How you're not fucking seething."

"Because it happened. It's done."

"It's just all in the past to you?"

"What do you want me to say? Do you want me to be mad for the rest of my life? Rail and yell and kick my feet?" She shakes her head. She's done with all that.

"But that's exactly what they want. They want us to roll over and forget. But it's not the past. We're still here," he says, leaning forward, "we're still here. This is still our land, our home. We're still owed."

His breath is on her neck, warm and cool at the same time. "I don't want to live like that." She shifts away.

"Like what?" There's an edge in his voice.

"My hand always out. Always asking and waiting."

"You think my hand is out?" His anger is obvious now. "You think people who want what's been promised—what's rightly owed—are *begging*?"

"I just—I don't . . . I don't want to fight anymore. Can't you see it's easier if you just—"

"Just what? Be like you and ignore it all?"

She starts to answer, then stops, focuses on the road ahead instead.

"I can't do that," he says. He falls back against his seat. "Justice isn't begging. If that's what you think then they've succeeded."

Neither one speaks. The car clatters along the highway, Florence's insides along with it.

"You should have told me how far it is. I barely had half a tank when I left."

He leans over the seat and looks at the gauge. "You'll be fine. Turn's coming up," he says, and sinks back again, still annoyed.

Florence watches him in the mirror. He pouts just like he did when she or Maamaa scolded him, and she softens. Funny the things that change and those that don't.

"What's that?" He's pointing at a group of cars up ahead.

Florence squints. "An accident?" Silence as they drive. Four cars come into view, blocking the road. Patrol cars, and officers milling about. They wave down a car approaching from the other direction.

"Those buggers are relentless."

Florence slows. "Another search?"

"Do you know these guys?"

Florence scans the officers. "Don't think so."

"Tell them like we said—my truck broke down and you're giving me a ride to the nearest farm."

"The Remus farm?"

"No," he says harshly, "just say the nearest farm."

"Why?" She glances in the mirror at Clancy, but he has leaned far back in his seat, his body twisted to face the passenger-side window. "Clancy?" A ripple of fear rises in her.

"Stay calm, it's fine."

But it's clearly not. She nears the officers and loosens her grip on the wheel. She comes to a stop and waits. Across the lane, two officers are inspecting the other vehicle. "I think that's Alec Purleigh."

"Honk at him."

"I can't do that—"

"Get his attention." Clancy whispers urgently.

But another officer is approaching. Florence rolls down her window and pulls back her headscarf, letting her blonde curls spring free.

"Good morning, ma'am."

"Morning." She smiles. "How are you?" Her throat is tight and she has to force the words out.

"Where are you headed today, ma'am?"

"Is that Officer Purleigh?" She hopes he doesn't notice the strain in her voice. The officer doesn't respond as he scans the inside of the car and sees Clancy. "I've done some work for him at Pratt's in Torduvalle."

"Who's your passenger?" he asks.

"A farmhand—his truck broke down . . ." Her voice wavers, making her more insecure. "Officer Purleigh," she calls out to mask her panic. He doesn't hear.

"Ma'am—"

She presses the horn and Officer Purleigh looks over. She waves, a little too enthusiastically. He smiles and motions to the other officer, who lets her through.

"Thank you," she says to him and moves off as another car comes up behind her. As she passes Alec Purleigh, she waves again and sees him notice the passenger in her back seat. An odd look crosses his face. She waits to speak until they're some distance away. "Clancy, what was that about?"

"Same as before, I assume."

"I meant you. Why were you so nervous?"

"Wouldn't you be if you looked like me?" There's a bite in his tone.

She could argue with him. Remind him that after the police searched him when they were headed to Seedy Creek, they let him go. But there's no point. She turns on the radio so they don't have to talk anymore. A few ads, then a Dale Evans song.

"You want to take the next left, about a mile up," he says.

She turns, and the LaSalle labours over a rough gravel road. Patches of trees and bush on either side. No sign of a house or barn.

"How far is it?"

"There's a dip up ahead—"

"I see it."

"When you get to the other side, at the top of the hill, just pull to the side of the road."

"By the trees? Is there a house there?"

"He'll be there."

"Remus?"

A throaty chuckle from Clancy. "Yes, Remus," he says.

The descent is steep and sharp but short. At its base is a slough on one side, thin and redolent. The car fights to climb up the other side.

"Right here," Clancy says.

"There's nothing here—" she starts, but then, off behind the clutch of trees, she sees a truck. And a man leaning against it, smoking.

"Is that him?"

"Yeah."

She heads towards him but the ground is too uneven and she parks just off the road. Clancy hops out and opens the trunk. Her gut grumbles. It's Delbert. In an empty field. Clancy wasn't delivering to a farm.

He lugs the crate to the other vehicle. She pushes her door open and steps out of the car.

"Clancy!" Florence calls, louder than she needs to. Her feet tromp through patches of grass.

"Wait in the car," he shouts over his shoulder.

"What's going on here?" She trips on a rock and loses her balance, stumbles. Rage bubbles up. "Stop!" She manages to stay upright.

Clancy sets the crate down and moves to help her.

"I'm fine," she says, continuing forward to the crate. She pulls back the blanket. Not the milk cans she saw him moving in the barn but bottles of clear liquid.

"How dare you!" she says, out of breath with anger. He just risked her entire life like it was nothing. "We could have been caught! What if they'd searched us?"

Delbert walks forward but Clancy puts up his hand and stops him. "They didn't."

"They could have," she says. She puts her hands to her temples. She can't even imagine.

"Not with you in the car—"

"You don't know that," Florence says. "If they did, we'd both have been arrested!" She would've had to leave Torduvalle. Leave everything behind. That is, if she didn't go to jail. She steps away from him to grasp all this.

Clancy uses the moment to pick the crate back up and give it to Delbert.

"Everything all right?" Delbert asks as he takes the crate.

Clancy nods, waving it off, and Delbert heads back to his truck, eager to avoid the altercation.

"Listen," Clancy says to Florence, "I would have told them what I said before—my truck broke down and you picked me up on the side of the road and you didn't know anything about it."

"Jesus Christ, Clancy." She draws in a long lungful of air to slow her hammering heart, and then it hits her. "Remus," she says, putting it together and turning around to face him. "George Remus."

He chuckles, and it riles her up again.

"We're not kids anymore. This is not a game—my life is not a game."

"No," he says, serious now. "Me having to bootleg to make ends meet is not a game."

"You used me."

"Doesn't feel good, does it?" He stares at her, challenging.

"I never used you."

"You tried to pay me off—"

"That's not the same."

"No?"

"It's certainly not illegal." The words like weapons out of her mouth.

"It's easy for you, isn't it? To be so high and mighty now that you—" He stops, strikes a patch of dried grass with his boot.

"Now that I what?"

"Now that you're living like them. You've forgotten everything about where you came from." He pauses, then grows oddly calm. "Maamaa and Paapaa would be ashamed of you."

A thread inside Florence's chest breaks, its ends fraying as she slowly turns and walks back to the car.

Clancy follows her, taking long strides to catch up. "And the only reason why Lillian isn't ashamed is that she doesn't know the truth. She doesn't know the real reason you dye your hair, doesn't know you're pretending to be someone else—that you've been lying your whole life! I've kept it all from her to spare her the shame too."

"I didn't ask you to."

"I didn't do it for you," he says. "You were always so selfish."

But Florence is empty now and doesn't respond.

"You know, you might not understand this, given your life now, but some of us have to do things we don't want to just to get by."

Florence gets to the car, pulls on the door, then turns to face him. "You have a job, Clancy. A paying job—why would you bootleg?" she says.

"You think a job that's paid mostly in room and board will cover the costs of medication and the doctor's appointments she needs? Never mind paying you back." He's livid now. "And you and I both know the money you gave me wasn't to help me and Auntie. It was to help yourself," he says, voice full of venom as he points an accusing finger at her.

A cold anger swells up inside her, but she climbs into the car.

"How am I supposed to get back?" he demands.

"Hitch," she says, and closes the door. She drives faster than she should back to the highway. The car slides on the gravel, the back end not following the front, kicking up and scattering stones behind. Her thoughts are scattered too. He's not leaving. At least not until Lillian's better. Auntie must've been worried. Scared. But she has medication now, and others to look after her at the road allowance. There's nothing Florence can do. It's not cowardly; it's practical.

She arrives back at the blockade in no time at all and pulls in behind another car. Officer Purleigh speaks with the driver. As that car pulls away, Officer Purleigh waves her forward, not making eye contact.

"Hello again," she says to him.

"Mrs. Banks—"

"Florence, please."

He nods and finally meets her eye but he's noticeably uncomfortable. "Where were you off to today?"

"I was just driving someone to the nearest farm to use a phone."

"The man you had with you before?"

"He's Frank Huber's farmhand, I believe."

"You know this man?"

"No. His truck had broken down on the highway."

"Nice of you to stop for a stranger."

"Well, I recognized him from town—saw him with Mr. Huber a couple times."

"Where did you take him?"

"To the nearest farm."

"Which one?"

"I honestly don't know." Florence pulls her headscarf back up, feeling the need for the protection. "I let him off at a side road. He said he'd walk to the house from there. The Willochs are along this stretch, aren't they? And the Arnolds." She tightens the knot under her chin. "Is something the matter?"

Alec Purleigh shifts on his feet. "I apologize, Mrs. Banks, but I'm going to have to look in your trunk."

"My trunk?"

"Yes."

"Of course. What for?"

"It's a routine inspection."

He walks to the back of her car. Her throat swells and it's hard to swallow. Clancy took the crate. Took it all. Didn't he? But she never checked. He closed the trunk and she never checked, just took off, didn't examine it herself. But she could say what Clancy said—that she didn't know. And she didn't. Clancy said he wouldn't implicate her. Would he still keep her out of it after all that they said back there? Or she could come clean right now. But then she hears the trunk slam shut.

"Thank you, Mrs. Banks," Officer Purleigh says as he walks towards her. "I'm sorry for the inconvenience."

"It's no trouble at all."

"Mrs. Banks," he says, stepping to the window, "in the future, you should be careful about who you pick up."

"Have I done something wrong?"

"Not at all." He pauses as if thinking about what to say. "There's been some unsavoury activity lately and you just never know."

"Oh, dear. I'm terribly sorry."

"That's all right. Just next time, be more careful."

As she pulls away, her fingers ache on the wheel. She loosens them, breathes. A throb at her left temple. A small tapping. And by the time she's back in town, it's her whole head. A hammer, *pound-pound-pound*ing. As if it's trying to crack her head open and let something out. When Florence finally gets home, she realizes she really is sick. Illness, self-fulfilled. It will be bed for her until the evening.

SUMMER 1910

The Nest, Saskatchewan

CLANCY WON'T EVEN look at her when she walks up the path to their home. He's stacking wood into a pile near the firepit, his face hardened with fury. But if she had confessed at the Aylesbury, if she'd come clean and told the man she was his sister, she would've gotten into much worse trouble than he had. He must know that. Besides, it was just a cuff, and they've both had much worse from Maamaa when they were younger. There's no reason for him to be so sour.

Behind him and on the other side of the woodpile, Aunt Lillian hacks at a downed tree with an axe. Maamaa is also outside, sitting in a chair by the open front door and staring into nothing. Auntie always brings her outside, saying the fresh air helps, but Florence never sees an improvement. Inside or outside, Maamaa doesn't seem to care where she is.

"I got everything everyone wanted," Florence says, holding up the bags in her arms.

"Si boon," Auntie says and puts down the axe.

"I'll put our things away, then deliver everyone else's," Florence says, and starts towards the house.

"Kaaya akooshiishi toota," Auntie says, and before Florence can ask why she shouldn't deliver them, Auntie tells Clancy to do it. He drops the log in his hands and walks to Florence, still avoiding eye contact. He yanks the bags from her arms and storms off down the path. Such a child still.

"Aashtum," Auntie says to her and walks towards the shack, takes a seat on a stump near Maamaa.

Florence senses Auntie's mood change as she goes to her. Clancy's told her, obviously, still taking any opportunity to get her in trouble.

"Api," Auntie tells her, pointing to an empty chair near Maamaa. She pulls her pipe from her pocket but doesn't light it, just chews on the end of it, her jaw muscles clenching.

Florence sits where she's told. Long moments pass.

"Joe won't be taking you to town anymore," Auntie finally says.

"What?" It bursts out of her, angry and panicked.

Maamaa flinches and Auntie reaches out to pat her knee.

"Someone else will go if things are needed."

Florence notices Auntie's switched to English now that they're near Maamaa, still respecting her wishes even if Maamaa wouldn't correct her anymore. It annoys Florence further, how Maamaa controls so much of everyone else's lives even when she's not living her own.

"It's too dangerous—" Auntie says.

"If I knew Clancy was also going," Florence says, cutting her off, "I wouldn't have gone today. I would've waited until the next time."

"This has nothing to do with Clancy."

"Of course it does—"

But Auntie puts up her hand, silencing her. "It's about everyone else," she says. "You remember what happens when just one bead is crooked?"

But Florence doesn't want Auntie's beading teachings right now. "Auntie, I know what I'm doing." If anything, today proved it—the people at the shop had believed her over Clancy. But she won't say that out loud.

"What if the Duncans spot you? See you wearing their clothes?"

"I won't wear them anymore, then, I'll wear my own—"

"Enough," Auntie says. "It has to stop, ma fii. We don't need any more reasons to bring the cops around here. You of all people know what can happen."

Maamaa rises from her seat and heads inside. Closes the door behind her.

Florence watches her go. Maamaa is still in so much pain from losing Paapaa. So is Florence, but it angers her that Maamaa can't see beyond her own pain to notice that it's also destroying Florence's whole life. A rage takes hold but Florence pushes it away, because even if Maamaa were well, would Florence's life be any different? A half-breed stuck on a road allowance. "It's all I have, Auntie," Florence says, choking it out.

"That's not true," Auntie says softly, pulling her into an embrace.

Florence lets Auntie hold her even though it's not comforting. She doesn't want to cry because there's no point in it, no point in feeling anything anymore. She wipes her face and heads inside to start supper. Douses out all the emotions inside of her.

Clancy doesn't speak to her that evening, or the next day, or the day after that. Over the following weeks, and as the weather turns cooler, a distance grows between them. He spends more time at the Duncans', sometimes staying overnight in the bunkhouse he helped build, or with the Morins and Boyers, talking about the past. About Riel and Dumont and Grant. Like it's his mission to learn about the history they weren't allowed to before. He rambles on to Auntie about his discoveries, about scrip and stolen land and other injustices. But Florence doesn't listen. Learning about the past doesn't change the present.

Florence sleepwalks through the days, goes through the motions, doing what's required of her. And in the middle of winter, she's convinced herself that she's succeeded, that she's surrendered to the life expected of her. Then, just before the weather warms again, Auntie comes to her after a trip to the farm and says she has good news.

"Lii Duncans . . . miiyowatishiw," Auntie says and unpacks another care package they sent. Eggs, biscuits, a jar of jam.

"They have been very kind to us," Florence says as she finishes mending a tear in Mr. Duncan's pants. "To Clancy, especially." And she means it, her resentment put away with everything else.

"And now you," Lillian says, smiling.

Florence snips the thread and looks at her, confused.

"They would like to offer you a position as a nanny."

"Nanny?" Florence says. Their youngest is older than Clancy. "Is Mrs. Duncan expecting?"

Lillian shakes her head. "Mr. Duncan's pchit seur. She's coming from Ontario in the summer. Her and her husband and their four children. Soon a fifth." Lillian pats her own belly. "They want you to live with them."

"Live there . . ." Florence says, setting the shears down and examining her stitches, pretending to hide her shock. "Is there enough room at the farm?"

"Not the farm." Lillian shakes her head. "In town." She grins at Florence. "I know that's where you want to be."

"Quincy Lake?" Florence says, hesitant.

Auntie nods. "Mrs. Duncan says they're buying a big house and there will be a room for you," she says, her eyes bright. "Pi," she continues. "Mr. Duncan's pchit seur . . ." She stops to think. "Elinor Ogilvie. She will teach you to read."

Florence stays silent.

"Miiyaashin, ma fii. It's good."

Florence forces a smile. "What about Maamaa?"

Auntie reaches into her pocket for her tobacco and pinches some into her pipe. "She will be fine."

"She can't do anything by herself anymore," Florence says.

"I will take care of my sister," Lillian says, lighting her pipe and heaving in a deep puff.

It's been settled; there's no point in arguing. "In the spring?" Florence asks, feigning interest.

"Wii." Auntie exhales a long length of smoke.

Living in a house. Her own room. Stable employment. Florence lists all the things she's ever wanted that will now be hers. Tries to tamp down the panic that's building. She'll learn to read. Books, newspapers, magazines.

Store signs.

Which means most of the town will now be off-limits to her. More than anything, Florence wants to pick up the scissors and slice the pants and all the other clothes she's darned into tiny pieces.

SEPTEMBER 1946

Torduvalle, Saskatchewan

WHEN SHE WAKES, it's already turning dark outside. She wants nothing more than to roll over and go back to sleep. Sleep for days, for weeks. For the rest of her life. When she chose to be Florence Banks, to slip out of her old life and become someone else, it was a choice she made to be free. To escape the burdens of being born a half-breed. But these past few weeks, and today especially, have felt like another kind of burden. She forces herself to get out of bed. Reaches for the fancy dress that she'd had cleaned for the occasion—canton crepe silk with long sleeves, a boat neck, and a black velvet belt—and puts it on. Applies her makeup. Watching herself in the mirror, she wills herself to find that sense of freedom again.

When she arrives at the town hall, cars are already parked along the street, guests in their fancy clothes already arriving. She pulls open the doors and enters.

Guests mill about, introducing themselves to one another. "Wow," Florence says, taking in Shirley, who's putting final touches on a centrepiece at a table. "You look lovely." Shirley's in a long, flared skirt, purple like a pansy and shimmering.

"Bought this a while ago but haven't had a chance to wear it. It's too fancy for tonight, but you only live once."

Florence catches her glancing to the other side of the room where Mr. Hicks is speaking with the Treadaways, Mrs. Hicks beside him, her arm hooked through his. So many others with their own burdens.

"Can I help you with anything?" Florence asks and puts a hand on Shirley's shoulder.

"I'll be fine," Shirley says. "Maybe I'll see if there's anything I can do in the kitchen."

The room fills quickly; everyone seems to arrive at once. Florence attempts to ease some of the congestion in the room by showing people to their assigned tables. She has just finished seating the Virks when Jennie spots her from the entrance and heads towards her, Garth in tow. Jennie weaves her way through the guests.

"How's the head?" she asks.

"Much better—thank you for taking care of all of this."

"It was nice to be out of the house, and the kids enjoyed time with their dad. Not sure it was mutual," she jokes and looks back to Garth, but he's already moved off to speak with the mayor. "Of course," Jennie says flatly. "Never not working. But I'm not thinking anymore about this event—it's out of my hands now. I'm just going to enjoy it."

"As you should," Florence says.

"Come, sit with me for a bit while my husband is occupied." Jennie tugs Florence to her table where they sit and ogle everyone's attire. Whisper about whose dress is a size or two too small. Whose suit has never seen an iron's soleplate. It's childish and wicked of them but so much fun. When Garth arrives they bite their tongues and sit up straight but then he immediately becomes engrossed in conversation with the person sitting on his other side, Ian Murray, one of the town councillors. Jennie rolls her eyes at Florence. "It never stops." She pours Florence a glass of wine. "This is how I get through it." Raising her glass, she says, "Here's to a well-planned event."

"Cheers," Florence says and takes a giant swallow.

"I think these might be our seats," says a man behind her.

Florence turns. Officer Purleigh and his wife. "Oh, goodness," she says, caught off guard. "I didn't know you—"

"The sergeant and his wife couldn't make it tonight," he explains, "and he sends his regrets, but my wife and I were honoured to take his place." He makes awkward eye contact with Florence.

"Of course." Florence rises to give up her seat. "I should go—"

"Lovely you could make it," Jennie says to Alec Purleigh. "I hope everything's all right with the sergeant."

"It is. It's work that's keeping him at the detachment."

"He could have brought it here." Jennie nods in Garth's direction. "Right, love?"

"What's that, dear?"

"We have more tablemates."

"Wonderful," he says, moving to pour them some wine. "Looks like we're short a glass, darling."

"Looks like we are." Jennie doesn't fall for the bait and looks back at Florence with a naughty smile.

"I'll fetch one," Florence says and moves off despite Jennie's protesting. When she returns, the caterers bring out bowls of soup, and people begin shuffling to their tables.

"Well, look at that," Jennie says, "like pigs to a trough."

"I should get to my table," Florence says.

"By the way, Mrs. Banks," Officer Purleigh says, pulling out a chair for his wife, "I do apologize for earlier today."

"There's no need. Really."

"Today?" Jennie asks.

"Yes, I was a bit rude with Mrs. Banks when I saw her on the highway."

"The highway?" Jennie snaps her head towards Florence.

"Honestly, it's fine," Florence says to Officer Purleigh. She turns to Jennie, whose eyes are locked on her. "I can explain," she says under her breath, "but not here."

The mood at the table shifts as the others sense the tension.

"But I should take my seat now if I want to be served." Florence plasters on a smile. "I hope you all enjoy your evening."

"Yes, you as well," Officer Purleigh says, taking his seat beside his wife.

When Jennie doesn't respond, Florence heads off, frantically thinking of what to tell her later. A private errand for Mr. Hicks or his wife—something Garth wouldn't know about or dare ask. Or a prescription that wasn't available in the town pharmacy. She finishes what's in her glass at the table and starts to pour another before she sits.

"Me too, please," Shirley says, turning her head from Mr. Hicks and his wife at a nearby table and holding out her empty glass. Despite her smiling face, there's a strain in her eyes. What would it be like if Florence and Shirley could talk openly? Florence fills both their glasses to the rim.

As people start on the first course, Mr. Hicks rises and taps a knife on his glass to get everyone's attention. The room hushes. "I'll keep this short, but I just want to thank everyone for coming tonight. This evening is about celebrating our expansion and welcoming our new employees to the Pratt's family. It's an exciting time for us, and, as they say," he says, raising his glass, "the future is bright."

Florence follows Mr. Hicks's gaze to a table at the back of the room where no one she recognizes is seated. Three men and their wives, all in sharp, expensive clothes. Must be from the city, judging from the looks of them.

"Who are they?" Florence asks Shirley.

"No idea," she says. "They were last-minute additions Mr. Broughton made just this afternoon." Shirley shrugs and they turn back around.

Throughout the meal, Florence and Shirley make small talk with the others at their table. Florence steals glances at Jennie's table, sees her engaged in conversation with Officer Purleigh. Only once does she catch Jennie's eye. Jennie turns away quickly, but it was there: a mixture of hurt and confusion. And now what? She looks at Shirley, who's laughing with the woman seated next to her. She has her own secrets, just like Florence, and yet if both their secrets came out, Florence doubts they would be treated the same. Some indiscretions are worse than others.

"Are you all right?" Shirley says, seeing Florence lost in her thoughts.

"Still a little fatigued, I suppose."

After the plates of carrot cake and lemon meringue slices are served, people rise from their seats and socialize. The din grows louder. Florence watches Jennie follow Garth to the table in the back, watches him introduce her to those people she doesn't recognize. Mr. Hicks and his wife head the same way, but Florence's tablemates stop them as they pass, and all of them are forced to chat. Shirley grows stiff beside her, unable to make eye contact with Mr. Hicks or his wife.

"Excuse us, we have to check on something in the kitchen," Florence says, putting her hand on Shirley's shoulder. She leads her across the room and through the swinging doors. In the kitchen, they go to the desk at the back, out of the way of the caterers.

"What was it you needed?" Shirley asks.

"A break from all that. Thought you might too."

"I did. Thank you." Shirley meets her eye and there's a sadness there. "I might just nip out early. Feeling fatigued myself."

"Of course."

"We have the morning to clean up."

"We do. Do you want me to get your things so you can leave out the back?"

Shirley nods. Once Florence has collected her coat and purse and Shirley has left, Florence steps back into the hall, where the crowd is already thinning. The Broughtons have moved to the other side of the room and stand with a small group of people.

Florence heads straight for Jennie. "Can I borrow you for a minute?"

"Can it wait?" Jennie asks, tension in her voice.

"It'll just take a moment."

Jennie turns to her husband. "Do you mind?"

"Don't be long."

"We're just about to head home," Jennie says to Florence, following her to an empty table. "The councilman and his wife are coming over for nightcaps."

"I just wanted to say . . ." But she doesn't know what to say. "You might be a little confused by what Officer Purleigh said earlier."

"A little," Jennie says, acerbic.

"I can explain."

"You can explain being on the highway when you were supposed to be home resting?"

Florence hangs her head. "Yes, I know that seems odd, but sometimes a long drive is relaxing—"

"And you can explain why you picked up that man you said you didn't know?"

Florence looks up, panic thrumming through her.

"Alec said he was a farmhand, an Indian. I assume it was the same one who helped me and Shirley. The same one who approached you at Nick's and you said didn't know." A moment as this lands.

"I don't know him, Jennie—or I do, but—"

"So you lied about that too?"

"Sort of, but not exactly." She's nauseated trying to figure out what to say.

Jennie looks back towards her husband. "Garth's waving at me."

"Can we talk later? After your nightcaps."

"It'll be late."

"Please, I would like to explain. Properly. I can come by when your guests leave."

Jennie watches her a moment as if she's considering it. But she doesn't answer, just strides away.

It's in the caterers' contract to clean and put away the dishes, but Florence stays. Washes, wipes, sweeps, dries. Even folds up the tables and stacks the chairs, fueled by an uneasy energy.

IT'S LONG AFTER MIDNIGHT when Florence finally sees Councilman Murray and his wife exit the Broughtons' and head to their car parked on the street. Jennie and Garth trail behind them down their walkway, seeing them off, laughing and tipsy, shouting pleasant farewells far too loudly for the hour.

As the Murrays' car moves off, Florence opens her door, steps out, and cuts across her lawn. "Jennie," she says. Her voice is quiet but they both hear her and turn around, surprised to see her. "Could I have a word now?"

"It's hardly the time," Garth says, suddenly sounding sober.

"I'll be quick," Florence responds but she's looking at Jennie.

Garth ignores her, goes to the front door, and turns around to wait for Jennie, who hasn't followed. "Jennie, come on," he says, as if calling a child or a pet.

Jennie bristles almost imperceptibly, but Florence catches it.

"A minute or two, that's all," Florence says. "Please."

"Jennie," Garth says again, and this time there's a warning tone.

"I'll be right back," Jennie says over her shoulder and steps forward. Garth shuts the door loudly behind them as they walk to Florence's house.

"Can I fix you anything?" Florence asks, holding the door open for her. Silly thing for her to offer so late at night but she's disconcerted.

"I'm still quite full from supper," Jennie says without looking at her. Her shoulders are tight as she steps inside.

Florence motions to the seating area where she's already set out the sherry on a tray. Florence pours one glass and starts to pour a second.

"None for me. I've had enough for the night."

Florence nods and takes two sips from her glass. "So," she says.

"So," Jennie says, offering nothing back.

"I'm sorry I haven't been entirely honest with you."

Jennie remains quiet, waiting for more.

"I do know that man." Florence pauses. "Or, rather, my husband did."

"Gerald?" Jennie asks.

"Yes. They worked together at the Regina plant—the automotive factory," she explains. Jennie watches her, her look unreadable. "It was only brief, though," Florence continues. "That man—Clancy—he wasn't there long so I'm surprised he even recognized me. I'd met him only once or twice, when I took Gerald his lunch he'd forgotten." It's too much. Too many details.

"Florence . . ." Jennie says, reproachful.

"What?" The question stretches out of her mouth as if time is slowing down.

"That's not true, is it?" Jennie asks. A glower on her face.

Lies are like beads—there can be hundreds or thousands in a single piece, but all it takes is one to come loose, just one, and the whole structure is weakened.

"Why didn't you tell that to Garth and the others at the office when you ran into him at Nick's?"

The word echoes in Florence's head: *Why?* But no answers, no explanations or rationales, come forward.

"And why not tell Alec Purleigh that earlier today? Why lie?" There's anger there now. "It doesn't make any sense to me."

It wouldn't, no. Florence nods in agreement, even though everything's unspooling. Her head hurts, and so does her chest, but underneath it all, she's surprised that she wants Jennie to understand. Her neighbour, her friend. "Jennie," she says.

"What?"

"Clancy's . . . he's my brother."

Jennie leans back as if she's been pushed. "Your brother?" She stares at Florence as if examining her for the first time.

"My name's really Florence Campeau."

"So you're . . . a . . ." A look of confusion on her face.

"Half-breed?" Florence says, then looks down.

Jennie falls quiet and Florence can't discern what she's thinking. The grandmother clock ticks across the room.

"I grew up on a road allowance near Quincy Lake," Florence says to break the silence. "In the southern corner of the province, not on a farm."

"A road what?"

"Allowance. Land set aside by the government to build future roads."

Jennie still doesn't understand.

"It's where many Métis live when they can't live—or aren't welcome to live—anywhere else."

Jennie absorbs this. "But I don't understand. Was your husband also . . ."

"No, Gerald Banks was not Métis." Florence hesitates, not sure how to continue.

"Did he know or did you lie to him too?" As Jennie looks at Florence, her face is hard, but Florence can tell her anger is tempered by her need for answers.

So many of her lies have been lies of omission, which always felt less damaging. Or at least, she convinced herself they were. She could do the same here. Let some lies remain to spare everyone more hurt. Or maybe just to spare herself more hurt. "He didn't know, but I didn't lie to him either." Florence pauses. "Gerald Banks was just someone who was kind to me once—"

"You were never married?" Jennie's voice is loud, incredulous.

Florence shakes her head.

"I can't believe this, Florence." She's shocked, and there's a hint of anger there too.

"I know, I—"

"So you never tried to have children, and your husband didn't die of cancer, and you're a . . . Native or a half-breed or whatever, and it's all been a bunch of lies."

Florence's teeth chatter as if she's cold. "I'm so sorry, Jennie."

"This whole time . . ." Jennie says, then rises and paces. "Everything you've said to me has been a lie." It's not a question.

"Not everything—"

"What is true, then?"

"I did go to secretarial school in the city."

Jennie laughs, but derisively. "Is that it?"

"No, but the things that matter—that really matter—are true."

"What does that mean?"

"Us. Our friendship—that's true," Florence says.

But Jennie walks to the door. "It's late. I have to go."

"Can we talk in the morning?" Florence asks, following her.

"I don't think so."

"But I haven't explained why—"

Jennie opens the door and the cold air floods into the room, shocking them both.

"I need some time," Jennie says, stepping outside and going down the front stairs.

"Will you come by again when you're ready?" Florence calls after her.

Jennie stops on the walkway and turns. "I'm not sure I ever will be."

"What do you mean?"

"I don't know who you are, Florence. If that's even your name."

"It is," Florence says, but Jennie's already walking back to her house.

Florence stands in the doorway watching her, the night air now so cold it bites her skin.

PART THREE

BUDS

SEPTEMBER 1946

Torduvalle, Saskatchewan

SUNDAY IS BRIGHT and clear. An early overnight frost makes the streets look lit up and sparkly. Florence debates whether to attend church. Word will have spread, of course. Jennie told Garth, no doubt, and from there, who knows. But Florence can't blame her—it's how things work here. On the one hand, avoiding church today will give everyone, especially Jennie, time and space to digest everything. But on the other, she'll have to face the whispers and the looks on Monday anyway, so why not get it over with? Besides, if she hides, it's like admitting she did something wrong. Others in town must understand why she did what she did, and surely that counts for something. Jennie will eventually understand too. Won't she? Won't they all? She's been a resident of this town for eleven years and they've got to know by now that she's one of them.

So she puts on her Sunday best and pulls on her coat and church gloves and waits by her door for the bells to ring. She'll be late on purpose, slip into a pew at the rear, and leave just before service ends. But when she opens the door and waits for her eyes to adjust to the gleam of the day, the Broughtons are up the street a ways, late as well. Jennie's in the lead, holding their son's hand, Garth a few steps behind them, then their daughter, skipping at a swift pace so her ponytail pops up and down. The four of them in the dazzling day. Stem, leaf, bud, and flower. Something falters inside Florence and instead of stepping out and closing the door behind her, she retreats inside, removes her gloves.

She pulls out the beading materials instead, the cozies for Marguerite and Hank. She slides several beads onto the needle and slips it through the black stroud. Each time she beads, her body loosens more as it remembers the familiar movements. Her arms were first, then her shoulders. Now the wide, shallow muscles that spread down her back relax into the rhythm. Her fingertips have started to harden too, callused from pushing the needle through the thick material.

She scoops more beads up and adds them to a curling white vine, using her second needle to tack every second or third bead down. Each bead connected to all the others by the thread running through their centres. The beads of the Saskatoon berry connect to the tip of the leaf surrounding the five-petalled turquoise flower in the other corner. The needle has been threaded many times and will be many more times to come, but it's still a continuous flow. Surprisingly, for certain moments throughout the day, she loses herself in the beading and forgets about the previous day. It's after five when she realizes she hasn't eaten since breakfast. She prepares a small meal, then puts away the cozies and materials, but she continues to think about the designs and the colours when she crawls into bed early, then falls asleep quickly.

FLORENCE ARRIVES AT THE office at her usual early hour on Monday and heads straight up the stairs to her desk to check her inbox. Mr. Hicks has left her a note regarding his off-site schedule for the morning, as well as instructions for a letter to draft to a client summarizing the policy changes the client requested. Business as usual in some regards. At nine, Peter and Jeremy arrive in tandem, quickly followed by Parker—the new junior agent—Emma, and Mary Beth. Their voices float up the stairs as they chitchat but Florence can't make out what they're saying. She has work to do anyway. Before she can complete the letter Mr. Hicks requested, she needs to get some information from the client's file, so she heads for the stairs.

When she descends, a quiet falls over the main floor. It unnerves her for a moment.

"Good morning," Florence says, voice as pleasant as usual as she approaches the filing cabinets.

"Morning," Peter says, but he doesn't meet her eye.

Word has gotten around, but she knew it would, so there's no need to be startled. "Did you all enjoy the banquet?" What else can she say?

"It was very nice, yes," Peter says, then coughs uncomfortably.

Jeremy throws her a look of misgiving before awkwardly stepping out of her way, spilling his coffee as he does.

"Did you two?" She turns to the new secretaries.

"Yes, Mrs. B-Banks," Mary Beth says, tripping on Florence's name as it leaves her mouth. Emma only nods.

"And how are things coming with your orientation?" Florence asks them as she finds the file she needs. She pulls it from the drawer. "Do either of you have any questions?"

"No, ma'am," Mary Beth says, and Emma stays silent again, only shakes her head.

"No questions?" They've been here only a couple weeks. They barely understand how the office functions.

"I can wait for Shirley," Mary Beth says, and looks down guiltily.

"Of course," Florence says. "I'm just upstairs if you or anyone else needs anything."

"Yes, ma'am."

They're quiet as mice as she returns to the second floor.

It's quarter past nine when Florence hears Shirley arrive, trilling her greetings exuberantly. Florence really must address the increasing tardiness, especially now that Shirley's a role model for the new secretaries. But best to wait a bit. Until things die down.

Almost half an hour later Shirley comes up the stairs carrying the day's mail for the Second-Floors.

"Good morning," she says, eyes down and a hint of awkwardness in her voice.

"Morning," Florence says. "Thank you." She takes the mail and starts to sort it right away, signalling she'd prefer not to talk.

But Shirley stands there, hovering by her desk.

If anyone is going to be professional and ignore things, it'll be Shirley, won't it? She has to grant Florence the same courtesy that Florence granted her regarding Mr. Hicks. She must. Their situations are not the same, but they are alike in a way.

Florence carries Mr. Hicks's mail to his office, hoping Shirley will take the hint and go, but she doesn't and is still at Florence's desk when she returns. An uneasiness settles over Florence as Shirley looks at her in a way she never has before, as if she's appraising her. Shirley's eyes land on Florence's wedding ring.

"I knew . . . you had secrets," she says, her voice a loud whisper. "But I never would have thought"—she pauses, searching for the words—"that you were . . . I mean, you don't look like one of them."

It's meant as a compliment and Florence forces an appreciative smile. "I'm sorry, but Mr. Hicks left me quite a bit of work to complete before he comes in," Florence says.

"I'll let you get to it, then," Shirley says but continues to stare at her as if trying to find the crack or flaw. Then she shrugs and heads back down the stairs.

Florence grabs her tea and drinks it all down to hold back the sob that wants to come out.

She's collected herself by the time Mr. Broughton arrives, just after ten. His demeanour is the same as the others—he keeps his head down, eyes fixed on the floor in front of him as he rounds her desk. He says a perfunctory good morning but quickly disappears into his office and closes the door. Throughout the rest of the morning, he comes out three times and walks by her desk each time without acknowledging her, as if she's a ghost. All three times he goes to Mr. Hicks's office, only to find it empty.

"He'll be in this afternoon," Florence says after his third emergence. "A personal appointment in the city." His wife's doctor's appointment, a regular checkup, and since she doesn't drive, Mr. Hicks takes time off, but it's up to Mr. Hicks to share that information if he wants.

"I see," Mr. Broughton says, standing in Mr. Hicks's doorway as if willing him to appear.

"He's expected in after lunch. Would you like me to schedule you in his calendar or notify you when he gets here?"

"No need." Mr. Broughton shuts himself back in his office. As soon as Mr. Hicks arrives, Mr. Broughton scurries right into his office and closes the door.

It's clear the discussion is about her, and, yes, she supposes Mr. Hicks should be informed, but the revelation doesn't change her work habits or the professionalism she's exhibited all her years at Pratt's. It's just a small detail of her past that will hopefully be forgotten soon. But after about fifteen minutes, Mr. Broughton returns to his own office, and Mr. Hicks calls her into his. He too has trouble meeting her eye.

"What can I do for you?" Florence pretends as if nothing is out of the ordinary, as if it's any other Monday.

"Have a seat." He motions to her, then swivels his chair away to face the window beside him. He stares out of it, seeming both contemplative and confused. "There have been a lot of changes of late." He pauses. "A lot." The words are heavy, laden.

"There have been. But we're all managing it fine, aren't we?" She swallows. "The new secretaries are quick learners—they've made a few mistakes, but we all do when we're just starting out. And one of my teachers always said that mistakes are important because once we make them, we learn and never make them again." Her palms grow sweaty.

"That may be true, but change can be difficult for some. We've grown quite fast in a short amount of time, and that can feel . . . topsy-turvy."

"I see that, but we are managing. We haven't missed a deadline, and the bills are paid and the invoices sent as they always have been. It may be unsettling for some, but things are running—and will continue to run—as normal as ever." She speaks too quickly, almost desperately.

Mr. Hicks continues to stare out the window, thinking. Then he twists back to face her. "That's good to hear."

"I really don't think anyone at Pratt's has anything to worry about."

Mr. Hicks nods. "Sometimes a little reassurance is all that's needed." He taps his desk for emphasis. "We're growing and changing in some ways, but we're still the same."

"We are."

"Good, that's that, then. I'll let the others know." He sits up in his chair as if to get back to business. "Now, next Wednesday night, the town council meeting."

"Yes."

"You'll be there as usual," he says, more statement than question.

"It's in my calendar."

"Mr. Broughton and I will also be in attendance, as we've been asked to provide some updates on our growth—it's of interest to council members as the town itself grows and looks to attract other businesses and investments. We're a success story that they'd like to highlight. Could you ensure—"

"That it's on the agenda?" Florence says, finishing for him. "Yes, I'll call Mrs. Rondelet to remind her."

"Thank you, Florence."

"Of course, Mr. Hicks." She rises but Mr. Hicks looks up at her and meets her eye. Holds it as if he's about to say something else. Florence is already unnerved and her legs grow weak. A moment passes before he nods at her and turns to the work in front of him. She's wobbly on her way back to her desk and plunks heavily down into her chair. Mr. Hicks has always been a level-headed man, one who knows that certain things are more important than others. That discipline and commitment to work are paramount in business. Florence draws in a long, deep breath, releases it gradually, and feels herself centering again as she looks up the number for the town council's office.

Mr. Broughton's door is still closed, but he'll have to come around now. And that means that Jennie will too. All her worst fears about the truth being revealed haven't really come to pass. Yes, there was a terrible fright after the banquet with Jennie on Saturday night, and surely there'll be some troublesome encounters to come, but in the grand scheme of things, it is as she hoped it would be—the people in Torduvalle who know her, who are closest to her, understand who she truly is. They know that she is a hardworking, loyal member of this community no matter her last name. No matter where she comes from.

SPRING 1911

Quincy Lake, Saskatchewan

FLORENCE STARES AT the Ogilvies' yellow brick house on the corner, wide as can be and three storeys high. She wonders which window at the top is the room meant for her.

"There's nothing to be nervous about," Uncle Joe says as if sensing her apprehension. He slows the wagon.

Florence clutches the bag in her hands, all the things she packed from home inside. Two dresses, her stockings, the kerchiefs Auntie gifted to her yesterday, all her undergarments, and, stuffed into the toe of one of the stockings, her metal coin purse. Inside it, the money she stole.

"You'll be fine," Uncle Joe says. "I'm sure they'll let you come home to visit whenever you need."

Florence climbs out of the wagon and holds on to the side for a moment to get her balance; her legs are shaky from more than just the ride. She took all the money from the tin that she and Clancy had saved that year. She was surprised when she counted it last night to find there was nearly six dollars. Two dollars and eighty cents was her contribution from her sewing and beading jobs; the rest from Clancy's wages at the Duncans'. But she needs it more than he does, so it's not really stealing. And she'll pay it back as soon as she can.

"You'll be fine," he repeats, and nods at Florence, encouraging her.

She stares at the ground beneath her feet and the weeds that are starting to break through the dirt. As if summoning their strength, she finally starts to walk towards the house. Behind her, Uncle Joe clicks his tongue to rouse his horse and turns the wagon around, heading off to continue his deliveries.

Florence moves slowly, nearer and nearer to the gate of the Ogilvies' property. Mrs. Duncan sent a message from the Ogilvies through Clancy last week telling her that if the family wasn't home when she arrived, she could wait for them in the house. Florence reaches for the latch, then looks back at Uncle Joe, who's disappearing down the street, and as soon as he's out of sight, she lets the handle go. She continues down the street, rounds the corner, and walks all the way to the train station.

The station house is long with three different doors, but it's the middle door that people are entering and exiting through, and Florence follows suit. Inside, as she stands in line at the ticket booth, she reaches into her bag, carefully unravels the stocking, and collects her coin purse. The task gives her something to focus on and it calms her.

"One ticket to Regina, please," she says when she reaches the window, pretending that she's done this before.

When she has her slip of paper, Florence goes to the far corner of the station instead of heading to the platform to wait. It's hot and sticky inside with no fans or open windows to circulate the air, but there's less risk of anyone she knows spotting her. She sinks onto a hard wooden bench as the magnitude of what she's doing begins to hit her. Is it even possible? Can she find a job and a place to live? And can she do it quickly enough? The city is expensive and five dollars and change won't last very long. Her stomach churns.

A small waft of air hits Florence when the door opens, both cooling and calming her. She has to break it down into smaller, manageable pieces. Bead by bead. Just focus on getting on the train. That's it. That's her only task right now. Once she gets to the city, she can focus on the next task.

By the time the train's whistle blows announcing its arrival, Florence is breathing normally again. She stands and puts one foot in front of the other all the way to the door and outside to the platform, then up, up the stairs and onto the train. She chooses a seat beside a window, across from a white-haired couple who have their noses in books and don't bother looking up. When the train picks up momentum, Florence's heart does too; her whole body vibrates with it when it reaches top speed, as if it's shaking things out, letting things go.

Out the window, she sees the land and the fields and the trees streak by fast. So fast it's like she's travelling through time, and her past, her old life, is already receding. Travelling so fast and so far makes everything—the world, her future—feel more possible and wieldy. Like nothing is as difficult as she thought.

When the train arrives in the city, Florence debarks onto the platform less nervous than before. She weaves her way through the crowd of bodies and approaches a man selling newspapers at a kiosk.

"Excuse me, I'm looking for accommodations in the city. Are there any you recommend?" she asks. Next step.

"There are some hotels downtown, just a few blocks south," he says and points in that direction.

A hotel would eat up her money quickly. "I'm looking for something more long-term. Are there any boarding houses you could vouch for?" she asks.

He writes an address on a piece of paper. "My wife's brother stayed there in the fall. Said it was clean and decent." He holds it out to her.

Florence takes the paper and stares at it. Stares at the pencil markings as if finding meaning in its lines and squiggles. She expects the self-doubt and fear to rise up again, but for some reason, she remains calm. "Is that . . ." she says, pretending to read the address.

"McIntyre Street," he says. "Just south of the downtown centre and Victoria Park. If you hit the lake, you've gone too far."

"Thank you," Florence says. She goes down the platform stairs, along the sidewalk, and across the street to the city centre.

She thought Regina would be like Quincy Lake, just bigger, but it's nothing like Quincy Lake at all. There are cars everywhere and hardly any horses and wagons. The buildings have more floors and rise so high, she feels dizzy when she looks up. Most of all, the smells are different, and they come at her in layers. Underneath, there's the familiar smell of dirt and gravel, blown through the streets by the wind. On top of that there's gasoline and musty exhaust from all the vehicles, harsh in her throat. Then there's the occasional perfume scents that waft off people as they pass by or spill out from a store's open door. But above all that, there's a smell she doesn't recognize; it's less noticeable than the rest but it's there, and she almost has to close her eyes to catch it. It's clear and clean somehow and she has no idea where it comes from. It must be the city itself, and she inhales it deeply.

She takes her time walking through the streets, allowing herself to adjust to the city's speed and temperament. To its energy. When the lake finally appears in the distance, she asks a passerby where McIntyre Street is, then makes her way there. She tries to match the numbers on the house to the lines on her paper, but it doesn't work. Up the street, there's a woman outside a house. She's minding a young child, who's stacking stones on the ground.

"Excuse me," Florence says, approaching her.

The woman looks up, but the child ignores her, too focused on his stones.

"I was told there was a boarding house on this street but I've forgotten the address already." Florence shakes her head as if annoyed by her own forgetfulness.

"The Vinduskas'," the woman says. "They're right there." She points across the street. "The one with the door propped open."

Florence thanks her and turns to the three-storey brick house with a slanted top floor the shape of a triangle. She climbs the front stairs and knocks on the open door, then goes in when no one answers. It's quiet in the entryway but clanging sounds from a room down the hall indicate someone's here. She follows the noise and finds a woman, older with long, greying hair pulled into a severe bun at the back of her head. She's setting several tables with cutlery that she carries in a bucket.

"Excuse me," Florence says, and the woman looks up but doesn't stop her task. "Hello, this is a boarding house, correct?" The woman nods and moves to the next table.

"It was recommended to me and I was wondering if there was a room available?" The woman is so unwelcoming, Florence wants to turn around and walk out.

"Are you alone?" she asks with an accent that Florence has never heard before. Then she leans over to look behind Florence and down the hall as if someone might be there.

"I am."

"Then, no, there's no room."

"Pardon me?" Florence hears the quiver in her own voice.

"My husband and I do not rent to single young women. We don't want trouble." She waves her hand as if to shoo her away.

"Trouble? I won't be any trouble. I just need a place to stay while I look for work." Her breath is shallow, faint.

"You don't have a job?"

"Not yet. It's why I came to the city. Just now . . . I took the train . . ." Her thoughts splinter and she can't form coherent sentences.

"And what kind of work do you do?" There's a tone in the woman's voice that's both critical and careful.

"Th-that," Florence stammers in a panic and points to the cutlery on the table. "I clean, cook . . . I have nanny experience," she lies. Minding Clancy doesn't count but this woman doesn't need to know he's her brother. "I can wash laundry, clean bedpans . . . anything and everything. In fact, if you need help here, I'd be happy to work for you."

The woman watches her, assessing. Then she smiles, and Florence starts to smile too, relaxing.

"I like that you're a hard worker." She nods her approval. "But no."

"I don't understand."

"We only have men here. Carpenters, bricklayers, factory workers—they work hard from dawn to dusk and abide by our curfew and rules when they return. They don't need a distraction, and Mr. Vinduska and I don't need trouble."

"I won't be a distraction, I promise. I just want to work too."

Mrs. Vinduska considers for a moment. "No," she says, but there's a softer tone. Then she leaves the room through another door on the far side.

Florence weighs her options. She could go back downtown to a hotel or ask someone else for a recommendation. It's nearly suppertime now, though. She follows Mrs. Vinduska through the door and into the kitchen, surprising her. "I'm sorry, I don't know if I should be back here, but I really need a place to stay and this place was recommended and you seem nice and . . ." The words stumble out because Florence has no idea what she's doing. "You said there's a curfew?"

"Yes, at nine p.m."

"What if I agree to an earlier one? What if I have a curfew at seven p.m. or whenever supper is over. I'll go straight to my room right after and stay there. Or even eat in my room if that makes things easier."

Mrs. Vinduska watches her with an expression Florence can't decipher.

"We could try it for a week and if you and Mr. Vinduska aren't happy, I will find another place."

Mrs. Vinduska opens the oven door and checks on whatever's inside it, poking it with a fork, unhurried. She finally turns around. "Okay, we'll try it for one week," she says, "but you eat down here. There's no food allowed in the rooms. Dishes get broken, mice come out—no."

"Understood," Florence says, "and I promise I won't cause you any trouble."

Mrs. Vinduska leads Florence up to a room on the third floor. The room is so tiny and the roof so slanted that Florence has to bend when she moves around. But she doesn't care. It's her own little space and it has a small window. She steps to it and looks out at the city. Its wide streets and buildings expand in front of her, like there's no end in sight. Her own lungs expand in response. Everything is before her, and she can't wait to see who she will become.

OCTOBER 1946

Torduvalle, Saskatchewan

THE TREES HAVE already shaken off their leaves but despite the chill, snow hasn't yet arrived. The streets feel naked and exposed as Florence walks to the town hall, wishing she'd worn something warmer than her alpaca coat.

When she rounds the final corner, she finds several vehicles parked down the block, almost as many as the night of the banquet. A momentary panic flares, but there's no reason for it. Over a week has passed since that night. There was the exchange with Mr. Hicks, but it ended fine. Everyone else at the office has been so busy getting up to speed on things with the new workload, they haven't had time for gossip. Sure, there have been looks on the street, murmurs as she walked by, but it's only to be expected. It will pass, as all things do.

Inside, things are arranged much differently than they were on banquet night: Chairs in neat rows like at a student concert, and only one table, a long one at the front for the elected officials and guests, including Mr. Hicks and Mr. Broughton. Florence heads up a side aisle and takes a seat at the end of the front row where she can hear everything but is out of the way. On the seat of each chair is an agenda for the meeting. She scans it for the Pratt's presentation. Item number five, and, amazingly, Mrs. Rondelet has spelled everything correctly.

She stops when she sees the next item: *Community Pasture Program.* Below it, a single bullet point for a description: *Federal request to purchase town land.* Clancy's voice is immediately in her head, sounding off about unfair policies and amoral governments. It bothers her that he can get under her skin even when he's not around. She pulls out her notepad and pen to focus her thoughts. She looks up when she sees Pratt's client Mr. Oborowsky and his wife approaching, eyeing some empty seats next to her.

"Good evening," Florence says.

"Good evening," Mrs. Oborowsky replies, but falters when she sees it's Florence and looks to her husband as if for direction.

A hitch in Florence's gut. "Hello," she says to Mr. Oborowsky. "I haven't seen you in the office in a while, but I trust all is well with your account."

"Mrs. Banks . . ." He grimaces. "Yes . . . it is." Then he lifts his head and scans the room. He waves at someone near the back. "Excuse us, I see Doug over there and we have matters to discuss."

"Of course," she says, forcing a smile as they retreat down the row to the middle aisle. She watches them walk to the back of the room and notices several heads turned her way. Another jolt of adrenaline as her worries resurface. Even Mrs. Rondelet, the secretary for the town office, is looking at her in a way that seems stern. Florence waves, but Mrs. Rondelet shifts in her seat, pretends she doesn't see. Florence snaps her face forward.

It's early days still. She just has to wait for the next spell of gossip to take hold, for someone else to be the centre of attention. She's lived here long enough to know that it takes more than a couple of weeks. She'll have to bide her time and prove herself again, just like she did when she arrived in Torduvalle. Keep quiet, lie low, focus on work. Florence starts writing again with her gold-capped fountain pen, glad to have something to keep her busy.

They start with the roll call, then approval of the agenda, which needs amendments because Mrs. Rondelet managed to get other names and dates incorrect. Then last month's meeting minutes need to be approved, and approvals are requested for the month's financial statement, and each item and cost is read out loud—phone bill, electric bill, postage, town permits, janitor's wages . . . and on and on. But Florence jots it all down; the notes Mrs. Rondelet takes are never detailed enough. As she does, she slowly relaxes because the room is now attuned to the business at hand and not her.

Nearly half an hour passes before Mr. Hicks and Mr. Broughton are invited to provide their update on Pratt's. They stand beside the long table, angled so they are addressing both the councilmen and the residents. Mr. Hicks is slightly behind Mr. Broughton, who looks tense. But as soon as Mr. Broughton launches into his presentation, all his nerves seem to disappear. Though every word has been practiced and rehearsed—Florence heard him behind his office door these past few days—he delivers it naturally, as if talking casually with friends. As Mr. Hicks mentioned to Florence before, Mr. Broughton references future expansions on the horizon but says that's all he can share at this time. It goes smoothly and there are no questions at the end, just praise and congratulations from some council members.

Florence glances up to see the reactions around the room but is careful not to make eye contact with anyone.

"The next item is another piece of good news," Mayor Williams begins. "Council was recently approached by the provincial government to sell the quarter sections of land the town owns just to the east. The government intends to establish a community pasture between here and Forsyth with the Crown land they already own and have requested to buy our land as well."

Florence's thoughts turn to Seedy Creek and Lillian and Clancy. And the last words she and Clancy spoke to each other. A current of regret runs through her.

The mayor looks at Ian Murray to his left, who nods his head. "I'll turn it over to Councilman Murray," the mayor says, "our town planning and development lead."

"Thank you," Councilman Murray says, leaning forward in his seat. Through his thinning hair, his shiny scalp catches the light. "I think most of you are aware of the program, as a number of community pastures have already been established in the province—by both provincial and federal governments—to great success. The program is designed to improve the quality of our land and prevent the kind of degradation and soil erosion that led to the difficulties we experienced in the thirties," he says, and pauses for effect, "which many of us well remember."

Solemn nods around the room.

"So it's an important program, and while land improvements will take time, there are immediate benefits as well."

Immediate repercussions too. The thought intrudes in Florence's mind but she pushes it away, willing herself to focus on her notes.

"This program will provide the farmers in our community with cattle-grazing and cattle-breeding opportunities, which I know for some of you is of particular interest. Especially those who are looking to expand their operations." He looks over to Mr. Hicks and Mr. Broughton. "Expansion seems to be the theme of the night."

"The little town that could," Mayor Williams says, and there's a ripple of laughter.

Florence smiles, too, to mimic the others.

"Since the request, I and my fellow councilmen have solicited thoughts and opinions from various community members and have heard resounding support. Given this, the council has decided that it's in the town's best interests—both long- and short-term—to sell the land, and we will enter into negotiations with the government. We will provide the community with updates on the timelines and progress for the program's implementation."

A smattering of applause.

"Thank you, Councilman Murray," the mayor says. "With that, we can turn to the next item, which is . . ." He reads the agenda. "Soliciting bids for a new garbage collector, now that Mr. Rymer is retiring."

"Excuse me." A voice from the back of the room.

Mayor Williams and the other councilmen look up. There's a visible shift in their demeanour.

Florence twists in her chair. A cold ripple through her body. It's Clancy. Seated beside him are Delbert and another man she saw at Seedy Creek.

Clancy falters and looks at Delbert briefly before turning to face the town council. "My name is Clancy Campeau and I'm here tonight on behalf of many people," he begins.

"Mr. Campeau, you said?" Mayor Williams asks, and motions to Mrs. Rondelet to ensure she gets the name down.

Florence turns forward and focuses on her notepad and on taking the notes that she's required to. She grips her pen and writes, her cursive script turning choppy and tight.

"That's correct. I'm here because we've heard about the plans for a community pasture—"

"Excuse me," the mayor says, "are you a community member?"

"Of Torduvalle?" Clancy asks.

"Yes."

"I work in the community—"

"You're Mr. Huber's farmhand, isn't that right?" Councilman Murray taps his pen on the paper before him.

"That's right."

"Is he here as well?" Councilman Murray looks around the room.

"No, but this has nothing to do with my employment." Clancy's voice is calm, measured, but an uneasiness grows in the room.

Councilman Murray waits a moment, registering the unease. Then he nods at Clancy to continue.

"I work for Mr. Huber and do stay at his farm occasionally, but I mostly reside on a stretch of land where this pasture is supposed to be going."

Florence writes everything out in full instead of shorthand—it takes longer, but she doesn't have to lift her head.

"That stretch of land is the one closer to Forsyth, is it not?" Councilman Murray asks.

"Yes, but I've already tried to speak with the elected leaders there," Clancy says, clearly sensing where Councilman Murray is going with the question. "Unfortunately, they were not helpful."

"Well, I'm afraid the same may be the case here, because that land is not ours," Mayor Williams says. "That land you are . . . occupying"—he drags the words out—"is Crown land."

"I'm aware—"

"So have you not thought, then, to approach the provincial government for answers to your questions?"

"Yes, I have thought to, and I have tried to approach them. I've called several times and have spoken with several different people, and all of them either pass me on to someone else who also passes me on to someone else or they take a message but no one ever calls back." He's trying to keep his voice level, but it's clear he's struggling.

Florence wills him to stop talking. To just let it go and walk out the door.

"Have you written them? Put your request in writing?" Councilman Murray asks. "A formal request might be best for a matter such as this. Though . . ." He stops, suddenly uncertain. "You wouldn't be able to receive a response at your location, would you?" The question is more of a statement.

"I have written them," Clancy says, ignoring his question, "but there's been no answer yet, and it's been my experience that the government may take weeks to respond." His comment elicits snickers from around the room.

"I'm sorry, Mr. Campeau, but this is a matter for the provincial government and one with which we are unable to help." Councilman Murray picks up the papers in front of him and taps them, signalling the discussion should end.

"Please," Clancy says, a desperate note in his voice. "There are about thirty of us living there, including children and old ones. And some of our old ones are ill."

Florence's pen falters. She prints Lillian's name in the margin. Scribbles it out.

"All we want to do is to speak with those who are in charge of the program. These are our homes, our families. We'd like to be kept informed of plans and how they will affect us. What are their plans for us?"

Glances flit among the councilmen at the table.

So senseless of Clancy—to come where he's clearly not wanted and where he should have known answers would not be provided. Florence's shoulders stiffen.

"We have a right to know," Clancy says.

Councilman Murray inhales sharply and starts to speak, but the mayor leans forward in his chair and waves to Councilman Murray, signalling he will take it from here.

"Mr. Campeau, I am sorry that you have not had the response from the government that you desire," he says, "but our only role in this matter is to negotiate the details for the sale of our land. We are not involved in the establishment or the operations of the program and therefore do not have any information that we can share with you."

"You can't even share with me the name and phone number for the government official you are dealing with?" Clancy asks. There's a tightness in his voice, a tightness that makes the room fall quiet.

The mayor attempts to smile but it's clear he's riled. "I can inform our provincial counterpart—"

"Inform? Why inform? Why not just give me a name and number?"

"I'm sorry, Mr. Campeau." Mayor Williams stands up and so do the other councilmen. "Your tone is out of order and I'm going to have to ask you to leave."

Delbert and the other man with Clancy now also stand.

"Leave?" Clancy asks. "This is a public meeting."

"Yes, for the lawful, taxpaying public of Torduvalle," the mayor says.

"Right," Clancy says.

There's a long silence in the room. Florence doesn't dare look up, doesn't dare shift an inch. Then she hears three sets of footsteps go down the aisle, all the way to the foyer, and out the door.

Murmurs among people until Mayor Williams suggests they move on to the remaining business on the agenda. People slowly settle in their seats and when the focus eventually returns to discussing garbage-collector bids, Florence finally lifts her head. Mr. Broughton is staring right at her, his face dark and intense.

Clancy had already heard of the program, so she really hadn't disclosed any of Pratt's confidential information. But she knows that telling Mr. Broughton that would only make things worse.

∞

THURSDAY. THE MORNING IS dark but sparkly from the stars. *Clip-clip* the five blocks to the office, but no key in the lock because she can see the dead bolt is retracted; the door has already been opened. The light near the stairwell to the second floor is lit. She heads around the side of the building to the lot in the back off the alley. Two cars already there. Mr. Hicks's and Mr. Broughton's. The last time anyone was here before she arrived was four years ago when they were being sued by Mr. Puglisi for violating the terms of his hail-insurance policy. It caused quite a stir and there were several meetings with lawyers to resolve it and lots of overtime. Turned out, Pratt's did make a mistake, but it was unintentional, and when they returned funds owed to Mr. Puglisi with a small added bonus, the case was settled and never went to court.

Florence hangs her coat and scarf on the rack and walks gently up the stairs but not so gently that they won't hear her—she doesn't want to catch them off guard or appear as if she's trying to be stealthy. But at the top, the door to the small meeting room is closed and there are voices behind it. She flicks on the lights, sets to work.

By nine, others have trickled in downstairs. Tea and coffee get made. Then the phone starts to ring. The door remains closed. When the two new Second-Floors arrive, Mr. Broughton pokes his head out and calls them in.

"Can I fetch anyone anything?" Florence asks when the door's ajar.

"We're fine." The door closes again but not for long. In less than ten minutes, Mr. Broughton and the two new staffers scuttle out and head straight to their respective offices like mice running back into their holes.

Mr. Hicks emerges last, slowly and as if weighted down. "Could I see you in my office, Florence?"

"Of course." She reaches for her pen and pad and follows him in. Finds him standing at the window, back to the room, shoulders hunched. She sits across the desk and waits. After a few moments, he straightens up and clears his throat, takes his seat opposite her.

"Is there an emergent issue?" she asks.

"I'm not sure I would phrase it that way." He rolls a pen between his fingers, studies it.

"But there is an issue?"

"Of sorts." He doesn't look up from his hands.

Florence writes the day's date in her notepad, ignoring the strangeness developing in the room, developing between them. "What do you need me to do?" she asks. It's a phrase she's learned by working at Pratt's—being useful dramatically reduces the stress on her superiors. It signifies she'll take on some of the load, that they don't have to bear it all.

"That's the thing, Florence," he says, "this is very difficult for me and I'm not sure how to begin."

Florence pastes on a smile, steeling herself. "I'll help in any way I can."

He emits a small, helpless chuckle. "As you know, we've just experienced some rapid growth, which led to your advancement in the company."

"Yes, we have."

"And as you also know, given this growth, I no longer make the sole decisions regarding the company's direction—others now have a say too."

Florence nods, feels the strain in her facial muscles.

"We may have grown a bit too quickly, is what this comes down to." Then he adds, as an afterthought, "I think." He bobs a leg up and down under his desk, the leather on his shoes squeaking. "We've been too rash, I'm afraid, and we need to restructure so that we can be in the best position for the next stage in our growth." He meets her eyes briefly, and it looks as if they're pleading, like he wants something from her.

"I see."

"Yes. This is quite difficult, but the company has decided we moved too soon on a senior-secretary role and that the creation of the position was premature."

"That's not such a huge problem," she says.

"No?"

"I can rescind the offers I made to the new junior secretaries—explain that our needs have changed—and I'm happy to return to my previous position. I'll even move back downstairs if that's more suitable." Florence notices he's flicking the end of his pen with his thumbnail, and small bubbles of worry blossom in her belly.

"Unfortunately, as I mentioned, others are also involved in the decision-making regarding the running of this office and it's been determined that the three ladies in the secretarial pool on the first floor will remain."

"Oh." It slips out. "Of course."

"It's not how I wanted this to occur at all. I really didn't think Pratt's would need to make this decision." He speaks quickly now, the words pouring out of him. "I was confident that it wouldn't come to this, but we exhausted all possibilities and there are concerns about potential impacts on the company's future."

Florence closes her notebook, and the gesture feels like a finale. An end come too soon.

"We will provide you with the requisite two weeks' pay in lieu of notice. And I will supply you with a reference letter that will surely assist you in your search for new employment."

"Thank you."

"Of course."

Florence rises, though her legs are numb.

"If you would like to stay until the lunch hour and leave while the others are on break, that's certainly acceptable. The keys, of course, can be left on the desk. We will not advise the other staff until after . . ." But he stops there.

"Thank you." Florence returns to her desk. In the time she has left, she types up two letters, prepares the cheques for all the accounts payables for the rest of the month, then writes up a numbered, step-by-step procedure list for all the tasks that she manages. She leaves it in a folder marked with Shirley's name.

SPRING 1911

Regina, Saskatchewan

FLORENCE PROMISED MRS. VINDUSKA that she wouldn't cause any trouble, and she didn't want any herself, but the problem was, trouble was all she felt.

It wasn't just how some of the men at the boarding house leered at her as they ate their meals, or whispered things to her as she passed—things she chose not to hear. She felt it almost everywhere she went. When she inquired about work at a grocery store, a man followed her out and said he would gladly hire her if she went with him into the alley. She soon learned there were areas of the city and certain streets she needed to avoid and understood the Vinduska's hesitancy to rent her a room. But it wasn't just that kind of trouble. It was also the trouble of her past.

Being someone else for a few hours every couple of months was completely different than living as someone else all the time. She felt like her past was always waiting for her. In every room she stepped into, on every new street she walked, and hovering on the edges of every conversation she had with every new person she met. It was always there, waiting to rear up and catch her out. It was the fear of being caught that made her flee at every potential threat.

A month into her first job as a maid at Regina College's residence for female students, she learned a second-year student there was from a town near Quincy Lake, so she abruptly quit. When she'd been nearly two months at the Vinduskas', Mr. Vinduska joked with a fellow lodger one evening during supper that the only good half-breed was a dead one. Florence couldn't sleep the whole night and checked out the next morning. At her second job, as a domestic servant for a politician and his family, she learned the head of the household was working on a project with the Indian Department, so she told the housekeeper that a family emergency required her to return home immediately. Being constantly on the move and telling spur-of-the-moment lies was exhausting. But mostly, it was risky.

It's while sitting in the room of her fourth boarding house on the night before she's about to search for her fifth job that Florence decides she has to make a change. If she wants to truly live as someone else, she can't carry her old life around with her anymore. Her old thoughts and memories. Old experiences. In order to live confidently in her new life, she needs to excise the old one. She begins with her hair.

Florence slips out to the pharmacy on Rose Street to buy a bottle of hydrogen peroxide, a staple in the laundry room at the college and in the politician's house. Half a cup in the washing tub made the sheets and shirts white-white-white. And it's rumoured to be used in the salons in France, according to the politician's head housekeeper. She locks herself in the shared bathroom on the second floor and starts with a tablespoon in a cup of water, dunking in just an inch of her hair that she can easily cut off if it doesn't work. But it does work. Too orange at first, and unnatural, but she adds another tablespoon of peroxide and dunks another inch, experimenting until every strand is a golden apricot.

When she enters the dining room the next morning, many of the boarders are already there eating breakfast, and as usual, they don't take notice of her, too busy shoveling hot sausages and eggs in before the workday begins. But as Florence pours herself some tea and carries it to an empty table, the owner, Mrs. Peckham, and her hired help watch Florence from the corner, disapproving looks on their faces. And just before Florence finishes her own toast and eggs, Mrs. Peckham's underling approaches her table.

"Mrs. Peckham would like to see you in the front room when you're done," she says.

"Is there a problem?" Florence asks, but she already knows there is because, before the young woman responds, she takes a long moment to stare at Florence's hair. Runs her eyes over it with a curl in her lip.

"You'll have to speak with her," she says and stalks off.

"I think you're in for it," a man at the next table says over his shoulder.

Florence glances at him, and he turns to her, a smile on his face.

"I think you're right," she says, and smiles back.

Sure enough, when Florence meets Mrs. Peckham in the front room, she tells Florence she'll have to leave at the end of the week. Once again, Florence is told they don't want any trouble, and Florence doesn't argue because, from their perspective, it would seem suspicious. But she can't explain to them that her change in hair colour is not to hide something; it's to allow something new to come forth. Florence doesn't stay until the end of the week. When she heads out the front doors and down the stairs with her packed bags, the man who spoke to her in the dining room is there smoking a cigarette. He sees her, her bags in hand.

"I'm sorry," he says to her. "They didn't need to do that."

"It's okay," Florence says, and oddly, it is. For the first time since she arrived, she's not leaving a place out of fear or panic; she's leaving because she's moving on. "I'll find somewhere else."

"I hope this doesn't make you late for work."

"It won't," she says and pauses. "Because I'm also out of a job." Florence laughs. She shouldn't—she came here for a better life, but after months she's still scraping by.

"King's Hotel on Scarth. Tell them Gerald sent you. Gerald Banks."

"Is that where you work?"

"Used to. Finished up the expansion there, but we're heading to Saskatoon on Friday for a job."

"Thank you," Florence says, and turns to head down the street.

"Hey!" Gerald calls after her. "If it's any consolation, it looks pretty on you." He tugs at a lock of his own hair and Florence blushes as she rounds the corner.

She finds a room at another boarding house east of Broad Street and close to the hospital, but it's worse than the others she's stayed in. The stairs are broken in places, and the front door doesn't lock, but at least the door on her room locks and she can slide the dresser in front of it for extra security if she needs to. The room is stale and damp, and there's a large dark stain on the hardwood floor. The window over the bed is cracked and so splintered in places, she pulls the bed away in case it decides to give way and shatter. She sinks onto the mattress, worried she's only traded one kind of poverty for another.

But the King's Hotel hires her on the spot to work as a chambermaid, and in many ways, it's perfect for her. Five floors of rooms on top of a busy restaurant and a café on the main floor means there is more staff than they can keep track of. She disappears into her work, and the supervisors barely remember her, recognizing her only by the signature black dress and white pinafore. She spends her days flinging bright bleached sheets onto the beds and dusting the tables and dressers, removing the evidence and history of others' lives from each room. While doing so, she feels her own history dissolving.

OCTOBER 1946
Torduvalle, Saskatchewan

"SIX-FOUR, PLEASE, OPERATOR," Florence says, her voice as warm and courteous as ever despite the lack of sleep. She looked a mess in the mirror this morning, eyelids swollen like worms fattened by rain and nose blotched and sore from the stiff, scratchy tissue.

"One moment."

"Good morning, Mr. Whitby, barrister and solicitor, how may I help you?" Miss Bosch answers. Like Florence, she's known for her committed work ethic but minus Florence's pleasant demeanour. As sour as vinegar, and that's on her best days. Some say it's why she's never married, despite being in her mid-thirties. It's also why Mr. Whitby had approached Florence discreetly over a year ago to see if he could entice her over to his office. There had been a few complaints, he said. Florence was flattered but explained to him that she was unable to leave Pratt's. He admired her loyalty, said that made her an even more interesting candidate, and offered to pay her more than her current wages. Still, she had to decline.

"Miss Bosch, it's Florence Banks."

An odd sound on the line, like something's caught in Miss Bosch's throat.

The news of her termination has spread. Florence wanted to wait longer before cold-calling. If she could, she'd wait an entire season, but two weeks' pay won't even cover all her expenses for next month. There's no time to wait.

"Flor . . . Mrs. Banks, yes, what can I do for you?"

"Is Mr. Whitby in the office?"

"He is," she says slowly, drawing it out.

"May I speak with him?"

"What's it in regard to?"

"A personal matter. I'm sure you understand."

"Of course," she says, but the judgement is obvious. "One moment." Florence waits on the line a lengthy amount of time. A length that Pratt's would consider inappropriate. "I'm sorry, Mrs. Banks, but Mr. Whitby is indisposed at the moment," Miss Bosch says, as if pleased to deliver the news. "May I take a message?"

"When would be a good time to call back?"

"His calendar is quite busy."

"It won't take a moment."

"Hold on."

Miss Bosch is clearly not used to persistence. After several minutes, during which Florence thinks Miss Bosch is expecting her to hang up in frustration, Mr. Whitby finally comes on the line.

"Good morning, Mr. Whitby, I hope you are doing well. I'm calling because you had mentioned there might be an opportunity for a secretary at your office."

"That was a while ago now," he says, voice crisp.

"It was, but the situation at your office has not changed and . . . as I'm sure you're aware . . . I am now available."

A pause. "I've heard, yes."

"Mr. Hicks has provided a recommendation letter, and you could certainly reach out to him directly."

"Unfortunately, Mrs. Banks, although the office is in the same situation, it is . . . not a good fit at this time." He ends there.

"I understand. Thank you." Florence hangs up. Calls the operator again. "R-R-two-nine, please."

"One moment."

"Good morning, Stegmeier and Associates." It's a voice that Florence doesn't recognize, but the secretary stops there. No other pleasantries, no offers to assist. It makes sense for the office, though—Mr. Stegmeier's accountant and auditing business has grown over the years but not as fast as Pratt's and not as smoothly. There's always been high turnover rates. He's a stereotypical accountant who's better with numbers than people, and those hired might be capable and congenial when they start, but it's not long before their shine comes off. But high turnover means frequent openings.

"Good morning, Mr. Stegmeier, please."

"Who's calling?" It's a demand more than a question.

"Florence Banks."

"Will he know what this is about?"

"He may. I'd like to discuss—"

"Just wait."

She expects another long wait but the second hand on her clock barely completes a full rotation before Mr. Stegmeier comes on the line. "Yes?" he barks. "Who's this?"

"Mr. Stegmeier, good morning, this is Florence Banks."

A moment as this registers. "You need my services?" It's said more in disbelief.

"I'm actually calling to inquire about possible employment opportunities at your office."

"I heard you were no longer at Pratt's."

"That's correct. I was wondering if you have any current needs for a secretary."

"No."

"Do you anticipate there will be any openings in the future?"

"No. Not for secretaries." She hears him take a drag on his cigarette. "I hired several months back. Another clerk—Michael Thornhill—to handle some of the office duties. Comes from good stock and can handle the pressure. Been less hassle with him on board. I've no intention to hire another secretary."

"Okay, thank you. I'm sorry to disturb—"

The line goes dead, abrupt and startling.

She can't handle another rejection today and takes out the beading materials from the credenza, but it's not the cozies she wants to work on. Instead, she opens an Old Gold tobacco container, the one that holds the bright yellow seed beads. *Honeybee.* The word's a little explosion in her head. Without thinking, Florence pours the beads into her palm, then into a tea saucer. She threads a needle, following her gut, and picks a piece of fawn-coloured hide.

She beads a short row, a slight curve to it. Then another alongside it. Then two black rows next to the yellow rows, hugging them; she adjusts the number of beads for each row so they taper and create an oval shape. Alternating yellow and black, yellow and black. It's not a flower or a petal. It's not a traditional design at all. It's something she's never beaded before. She beads anyway.

When she finishes the striped oval body with its round black head, she moves on to its wings. Then she beads a second bee near the first, then a third and a fourth. Each one from a slightly different angle. But they're not different bees, they're the same one. One bee flitting in the air. Around it, she stitches curlicues with light grey beads, similar to stems but coiled like corkscrews: Wind, trailing from the bee's wings as it lifts in the air and twirls back down to rise again. A single bee in motion, energetic and alive.

A drop falls to the hide. Florence doesn't wipe it away, lets the salty tear stain as she adds another whorl of wind. *Buzz-buzz,* under her own skin.

WINTER 1913

Regina, Saskatchewan

"You don't mind sharing a room with Nicole, do you?" Miss Boxall asks one evening in mid-January when Florence returns from a shift at the King's Hotel and finds another bed has been placed in her room. There's barely any space left to move about.

An unease takes hold of Florence, but Miss Boxall is standing in the doorway, waiting for a response. "Of course not," she says, because the decision has already been made and she would look ungrateful and unfriendly otherwise.

"The radiator in Nicole's room cracked this afternoon," Miss Boxall explains, waving Nicole in from the hallway, "and was leaking water everywhere. Her room will be closed off until it's repaired."

"I won't bother you a bit," Nicole says, carrying a hatbox, some dresses, and an armload of books as she enters, "I'm only in my room to sleep."

Florence moved from the dodgy rooming house near the hospital to the Boxall sisters' red-brick Georgian Revival in the Cathedral neighbourhood last fall after hearing about it from another maid. It's the private home of the sisters, two older women who never married and see it as their mission to help other single women. The sisters have created a home-like atmosphere at the house, which worried Florence at first; she thought there'd be nosy residents who'd poke and pry into her life. But it's been quite the opposite.

Most of the other residents are students at the college who are engrossed in their studies to become nurses or teachers, or women, like Florence, who have jobs that keep them running all day and who are too bone-tired in the evenings to socialize. Then there are a few women who come to the city only to be swallowed up by it and return home straightaway. Florence feels sorry for them, to come all that way and have their dreams crushed, but the city can be unforgiving. The rush and flurry of it is what makes it exciting, but it can also roll right over you, flatten you out.

Then there are some women who come to the city under the guise of attending school or finding employment but who are really only looking for men to marry. Florence spots them right away because there's an air of desperation about them, a kind of energy that Florence can't be around. The thing of it, though, is that these women are always successful, some within a few short weeks. It annoys Florence. But then, whenever she walks past a new building being constructed or an old one being renovated, she always slows her pace and scans the site, looking to see if Gerald Banks might be there. He could be hauling lumber or laying brick, having followed the work and made his way back to Regina. He never is, but she looks all the same.

Whatever the situations are for the other residents, Florence has never exchanged more than a few words with any of them. It's easy to keep her distance from them when they're just as preoccupied as her. And as Nicole said, she's hardly ever around, too focused on studying for her teaching degree. She's at the college campus nearly every day of the week, preferring to study there than at the Boxalls'. In fact, she's at the Boxalls' only because the women's residence on campus was full. In the mornings, Florence is up and out the door for her shift before Nicole rises, and she's in bed before Nicole returns. They hardly cross paths.

One Tuesday evening Florence returns to her room after supper and finds Nicole, fresh from a bath down the hall, rushing about pinning up her hair. Florence stands just inside the door, not wanting to get in the way.

"I'm late for my study group," she says, dropping a pin, "and we have a test tomorrow." There's panic in her voice. She scans the floor for the pin, gives up, and grabs her schoolbag. "Can you pass me my history textbook?" She points to the pile of books that are always scattered on her bed, sometimes even when she's sleeping in it.

Florence hesitates, but then steps into the room. She stares at the books on the rumpled blankets. Beside her, Nicole is gathering other items—pencils, a notebook, a handkerchief—and stuffing them in the bag.

"It's right there," Nicole says and points. "*The History and Geography of Canada*."

Florence looks in the direction she's pointing in, but there are three piled together, nearly on top of another. Florence panics and picks up all three and holds the stack out to Nicole without looking her in the eye.

There's a long moment before Nicole reaches out and pulls the middle book from the stack. "Thank you," she says, gingerly. Then she slides it into her bag and heads out of the room.

Later that night, when Nicole finally returns, Florence pretends she's sleeping as normal, and Nicole changes into her nightgown and crawls into bed as normal too. She turns off her lamp and the room is silent for a moment, but it's broken when Nicole whispers across the room in the dark, "Florence, how come you can't read?"

Florence swallows, though her mouth is dry. "I had to work. My family... we didn't have a lot of money."

"I didn't know," Nicole says. "I'm sorry about before."

The apology is unexpected, and touching. So touching, Florence wants to thank her, but instead she asks, "It's what you'll be doing, right? Teaching kids how to read?"

"Yes, and many other subjects too."

"Is it hard? To learn to read, I mean."

"Depends on the student, really. But I wouldn't imagine it would be hard for someone like you. The first thing the sisters told me about you is that you're hardworking and dedicated."

Florence feels her neck warm with the compliment. "Would you teach me?"

"Really?" There's a bright tone in her voice, and Florence hears her roll over in bed and face Florence's side of the room.

"I'd like to learn," Florence says.

"Then I'd love to teach you—it will be good practice for me. We can start on Thursday if you're free."

"I am."

Nicole rolls back over and adjusts her blankets. "Good night."

"Good night," Florence says, smiling in the dark. It's the closest she's felt to anyone since coming to the city. She doesn't sleep at all that night.

Nicole rearranges her schedule a few nights a week so she's home for supper, and as soon as they finish eating, they retreat to Florence's room for a quick lesson, even after the radiator's fixed and Nicole's bed is moved back across the hall. On the evenings Nicole doesn't come home for a meal, she assigns Florence homework that she marks in front of her at the start of the next lesson. By the time the weather starts to warm, Florence can print simple words and sentences on her own, and she can read the street signs, store signs, and newspaper headlines at the kiosks she passes on the way to work. The city opens up to her in a whole new way.

Their lessons taper off when Nicole's final exams approach and she even cancels a lesson at the last minute in order to prepare for her philosophy final, telling Florence to write something on her own.

"It can be anything. A story, a poem or two, or an essay on any topic you like," Nicole says. "I can look at it on Saturday." Then she's out the door again, heading back to campus.

The door closes and Florence is alone, and it shocks her when the first thing that comes to mind is a letter. A letter home. She ignores the impulse and instead writes an account of everything that happened at the King's Hotel that day for Nicole's review. But the idea takes hold and she can't shake it.

While Florence collects dirty dishes and sweeps floors, her mind works out on its own how she could do it. She could send it to Mrs. Duncan, who would let Clancy know, who would then tell Lillian. They could stop worrying, if they were, and she could include the money she took when she left. She could let them know that she's accomplished so much. So much more than what they planned for her, than what they'd thought she was capable of. The more she thinks about it and plans for it, the more it feels right. The more it feels like the right way to close, once and for all, that part of her life.

She starts the letter, erases it, starts again. Over and over. Nicole finishes her exams, receives her results, and is packing her things to head home for a break over the summer before Florence is finally done with her letter. She folds it into a neat square, tucks six one-dollar bills inside it, and places it in an envelope. She drops that into the basket that the sisters keep at the front door for outgoing mail and feels an immediate release.

OCTOBER 1946
Torduvalle, Saskatchewan

THE WEATHER HAS turned and Florence braces herself against the frigid cold, folding her collar up over her ears as soon as the first gust hits her. It's between the morning coffee break and the lunch hour in town, and though there are several cars parked on Main Street, most people are tucked behind steamed windows of stores and offices. Florence cuts across the street in the middle instead of walking to the corner and up Third Avenue. Nelson's bell chimes with her entrance.

"Good morning, I'll be just a sec," Hilde says without turning from her machine.

Florence removes her gloves and blows on her fingers to warm them, then distracts herself with an open catalogue on the counter while she waits. The machine stops whirring.

"Oh," Hilde says.

Florence hears the shock in her voice, then sees it on her face when Hilde steps away from her sewing cabinet.

"What can I do for you?" Hilde asks, her voice tight, strained.

"I've come to buy some scraps."

Hilde stays behind the counter. "Anything in particular?"

"Not really. They don't have to be pretty." Florence tucks her gloves in her pocket.

"For rags, then?"

"No, they're to line something."

Hilde watches her a moment, then reaches into a large bin standing against the far wall behind the counter. Pulls out handful after handful of scrap material, some folded into neat squares and rectangles, others firmly rolled into cylinders. "I can recommend something if you're able to tell me what they will be lining."

"A tea cozy. Two of them, actually."

"This cloth would be good for such a purpose. Would keep the heat in." She holds out a heavyweight cotton that's a pearl grey, like a mottled, earthy jewel.

"How much?"

"This would be plenty for two, maybe three. Five dollars."

Florence pauses. "Is there anything less expensive?"

"You're making these?" Hilde asks, tentative. She doesn't look up, continuing to search through the material, her movements brisk and sharp.

"I am." Florence swallows.

"You're learning to sew?"

"Sort of." Florence pauses, then: "I was actually taught. Long ago. I'm relearning."

"You never told me." Hilde pushes some scraps to the side.

"I was a child. I didn't think I remembered anything." Florence examines a piece of flannel.

Hilde pulls out another handful. "Sewing is something you never forget, though."

"There was a part of me that, perhaps, didn't want to remember." She lets this land as they continue to sort through the leftovers.

"It's just so strange not to mention it."

"So much time had passed, I didn't think it would matter so much." Florence looks up at Hilde. It's all over her face, disappointment and a distance. This is how her life will be from now on in this town. There will always be a line between her and everyone else. Over time, that line might grow thinner in places; it might wind and curve so it looks like Florence is a part of it all, but that line will rear up at times and remind her it's there. A length of thread that separates instead of connects.

Florence looks away. "How much for these two pieces of flannel?"

"A dollar each."

Florence looks into her change purse. "I'll take one."

"You'll need both for two cozies."

"One is fine."

Hilde starts to fold both up. "Most of this stuff was just going to the church for the kids' holiday costumes. I can give you both for a dollar."

"No, no. Just one piece, please." Pity masked as kindness is not what she needs.

Florence refolds the pieces they sorted through into neat piles while Hilde writes a receipt and wraps her purchase in paper.

"Thank you." Florence tucks the package under her arm.

"I've heard that the principal at the high school in Forsyth is looking to hire a secretary," Hilde says as Florence walks to the door. "It's a commute, but the distance might . . . be a good thing."

Florence's hand freezes on the door handle. Word might not have travelled that far yet, Hilde means. "Yes, thank you." She pushes the door and steps out.

Straight to the post office, head ducked against the wind. A woman's in there, back to the door, so it's not clear who it is. Florence keeps her collar turned up, gathers the items from her slot, tucks them inside the package under her arm, and scrambles back out. Goes up the street and home.

At the kitchen table, she sorts her mail. A phone bill for two dollars and thirty-two cents. A heating bill for nearly five dollars. If she wants to cover her mortgage payment next month, she can't afford both. Heat she needs more than a phone, and the phone company won't start charging late fees until next month's bill. Maybe she should call and ask for a grace period— she's been a reliable customer for over six years, never a late payment before. But it'd be better to call in the morning, when people aren't focused on trying to get home for supper.

Among three more flyers from local shops are two issues of the *Torduvalle Weekly*, this week's and last. She scans the classifieds in the latest issue.

Three jobs are listed: tinsmith at Karran's Plumbing, mechanic at Aitken's Truck Service, and a janitor at the elementary school. Nothing for her. But she'll call the high school in Forsyth tomorrow morning too.

Florence pushes the paper to the side. She'll line Hank's cozy, then put the finishing touches on Marguerite's and line hers. She unwraps the package from Nelson's and pulls out the single piece of flannel, which is already pilling in places. She spreads it out over the table to measure and cut it. Tucked inside the folds of the flannel is the length of thick, pearl-grey cloth. She puts the scissors down. There are too many things to take in at once.

COLD RAIN DRIZZLES DOWN, so cold it feels like it could turn to snow. The single window on Lillian's shack is steamed over on the inside, and when Florence steps in, scorching, humid air hits her. Colleen McKay, Margeurite and Norris's youngest, sits at the table sewing braided rags into a large oval.

"Boon zhoor," Colleen says, looking up from her work.

"How is she?" Florence nods towards Lillian, sleeping under layers of blankets on the bed.

"Better," she says. "The steam helps." Three large pots of boiling water cover the entire surface of the stove. Colleen rises and moves to the bed, her cheeks flushed and damp from the heat.

"No need to wake her," Florence says.

"She'd be mad if I didn't." Colleen nudges Lillian and speaks softly to her. There are two prescription bottles on the nightstand, one containing liquid, the other pills. When Lillian wakes, she immediately erupts into a coughing fit. Colleen hands her a kerchief and pats her back to help her bring up what's in her lungs. It's a deep, wet cough but settles quickly.

"Ma fii," she says, wiping her eyes after the effort.

"I finished the cozies for Hank and Marguerite." Florence holds up the package to explain her visit.

"Bring some chairs closer." Lillian motions to them both. "Li tea?" she asks Colleen.

"I'll make some more."

"How are you, Auntie?" Florence asks, shedding her outer layers, but she's already sweating.

"Ji bayn," she says, and taps her chest. She speaks some more but in Michif, but much of their meaning eludes Florence.

"She says she gave Clancy quite a scare," Colleen says to Florence, then picks up a pail and heads out of the shack. The frigid air pours in, offering a bit of relief, but the heat swallows it quickly.

"It's good he took you to the hospital," Florence says to fill the silence. "You'll recover more quickly." She points to the bottles on the nightstand.

"Clancy, boon keur," Lillian says.

"He is," Florence agrees, though *kind* is not what she'd consider him after he used her to make the illegal delivery. She wonders if Lillian knows he's doing that. She leans over and straightens the blankets on the bed, smoothing them tight around Lillian's legs.

"Kiishta," Lillian says.

"Me?" Florence asks. "I'm kind?"

"Wii. Maarsii."

Florence looks at her, confused.

"Maarsii," Lillian repeats.

"For what?"

"Clancy says you borrowed him some money. To help us move."

So he lies too. But somehow, his lie feels different than hers. "It was nothing," Florence says and continues to smooth the blankets. But Lillian reaches out for her hands and pats them. Holds them a moment.

"Do you have to go back and see the doctor again?" Florence says and stands up so her hands pull away from Lillian's.

"Only if it gets worse again."

"Did they say when you might be able to travel?"

Lillian shrugs.

"Soon, hopefully. It will be good to be in Winnipeg—you'll be closer to doctors there."

But Lillian isn't listening. "Clancy feels bad. Me too."

"Why?"

"Said you lost your job. Because you're Michif."

"That's not why—" But it comes out abrupt and she stops herself. The need to defend them is instinctive. "It was a misunderstanding—I shared information I shouldn't have." She pauses. "It wasn't because of... my background." She's not ready to admit the truth and it angers her.

"Did they know you were Michif before?" There's a look on her face that Florence can't read.

"I was good at my job. That's all they needed to know." Her anger is misguided but it continues to grow, long and sharp as a needle.

Lillian looks away. The heat in the room turns heavy, solid. Neither of them says anything until the door opens again and Hank hobbles in, Colleen following him with one hand on his back and the other carrying the pail, now filled with water. She helps Hank to a chair, then pours some water into the kettle and distributes the rest among the pots.

Florence sees Lillian's demeanour change as she exchanges pleasantries with Hank in Michif, pushing aside the strain that was growing between them before the arrival of other guests. Hank doesn't pick up on the mood in the room, and after greeting Lillian, he turns in his seat and pats Florence's knee. "I'm happy to see you again."

"Me too," Florence says, lifting the package at her feet, wanting to make her exit as quickly as possible. "Yours is the one on top."

Hank pulls open the cloth bag and reveals a Huntley and Palmers biscuit tin that previously held a lace tablecloth and a set of matching napkins Florence bought at an estate sale and never used. He lifts the lid and holds it against his chest with both hands as he takes in the cozy. His silence draws Colleen's attention from the stove and she steps up behind him to look over his shoulder.

"Lii pwayr," Hank says softly to himself, then takes a hand and runs it along the Saskatoon berries. "Mii seurs..." His voice breaks. "My sisters and I spent so much time picking berries together. I never liked them as a kid. Thought they were dry and bitter then. Still, we picked together, and that's what I taste now." He puts the lid under the bottom of the tin and lifts out the cozy. "Now I can't get enough." His eyes aren't wet but there's emotion in them. He nods over and over and over. "Mitooni kwaayesh." He looks up at Lillian. "She got this from you, didn't she?"

But Lillian stays quiet, letting him have the moment.

"Thank you, my girl," he says to Florence.

"Marguerite's is underneath," she says, indicating that he can lift the cloth that separates them in the box.

But Hank shakes his head. "She should be the first to look at it." He replaces the lid but holds his cozy in his lap as if it's a living thing.

"I should take it to her," Florence says, starting to rise.

"She's in the city. Left a couple days ago to meet up with family and make plans to move there."

"Can I leave it here? I'm not sure when I'll be back."

"I'll keep it for her." Hank reaches into his chest pocket and hands Florence a two-dollar bill.

"I didn't make this for money."

But he continues to hold it out.

It would cover most of her phone bill. "You need it for your move," she says.

But he places it in Florence's hand and turns to Lillian. "Have you told her?"

Lillian shakes her head, then motions to Colleen, who carries over an apple box that was under the kitchen table. She sets it on the edge of the bed closest to Florence.

Inside, more beading materials. More hide, more beads, and a man's vest at the bottom of the box. Tucked along the edge, an envelope. She glances at Hank, who winks at her, encouraging her to open it. She finds an order list of sorts. A request for two sets of moccasin vamps, another cozy, and items to be included on the man's vest—marigolds, pussy willows, violets, and buffaloberries. Folded around the list are four one-dollar bills and another two-dollar bill.

"We heard. Clancy told us you don't have a job anymore because you helped us—" Hank says.

"I can't—"

"Folks here worked hard for that money," he says, his tone almost admonishing. "They want to give it to you. In thanks."

"But this is a big order. It will take a while, and I'm not as fast as I was."

"That's fine, take your time. Everyone's just excited to have your beadwork—they'll be patient."

"But . . ." she starts, floundering. "I'm about to start a new job." She hasn't even had an interview. The lies never stop; they come too easy now. Lillian and Hank look surprised. "At the high school." She doesn't say which one, and they don't ask.

"That's good news," Hank says, patting her knee. "We didn't need to worry," he says to Lillian.

"So I just won't have time." Florence looks at the money in her hand, almost regretful. She puts it back in the envelope with the order and holds it out to Hank. His face falls, full of hurt. He turns to Lillian for help.

"Ma fii?" Lillian asks, both concerned and confused.

But Florence won't look at her. Can't. "But maybe I can find time on the weekends," Florence says, just to get out of the moment, and she slides the envelope back into the box with all the other items. She tucks a piece of cloth that's inside the box around everything like a lid. She stays for a cup of tea, listening to Hank and Lillian talk, nodding when they look at her despite not following the conversation. The lie didn't hurt anyone. Still, it needles. Besides, she should be thankful for the requests. Beading is the only time she's honest.

When she's back in her car on the highway, the dark clouds have cleared and the sun has come out, bright and beaming as if it's a new day. The rays reflect off the wet road and the glare is fierce. Florence's eyes dampen from squinting. She hears the siren before seeing the lights flashing in her side-view mirror. Slowing, she pulls to the side to let it pass. But it slows behind her, stops. A flutter in her chest.

Florence turns off the car and puts her hands back on the wheel, grips it like she's travelling over hazardous terrain. In her rear-view mirror, she sees the officer step out and walk towards her vehicle, pulling out a notepad from his pocket and jotting down her licence plate on his way. When he reaches her window, she winds the crank handle to lower it with one hand and loosens the knot of her headscarf with other so it slips it off. Brisk air pours in.

"Morning," she says, clasping her gloved hands in her lap. She doesn't recognize him. He's not from Torduvalle.

He nods and takes her in. Bright curls, fair skin. "You're coming from ... back there?"

"Yes, Officer."

"I see." But there's confusion on his face. He turns and looks back towards Seedy Creek, hidden beyond the trees. "You live out there?" he asks, perplexed.

"No," she says, laughing, then regrets it immediately. "I live in Torduvalle." She points up the highway as if he doesn't know where it is. "You must be from Forsyth, Officer ... ?"

"Keddie. Corporal Keddie. And yes, I am."

"Corporal," Florence says with an intonation to indicate she's impressed.

"What was the nature of your business out there?"

"Visiting."

"Visiting?"

"Yes."

"You know people out there?"

She nods. But he watches her as if trying to ascertain something.

"Relatives," she clarifies. "Distant."

"I see." He thumps a knuckle on the car, then steps away from it and looks it over. "Is this your vehicle?" He walks around to the back.

"It is." She leans her head out the window. "It's a little rough around the edges but it always gets me where I want to go," she says. "Is there something wrong?" She pulls her head back in and watches him in the rear-view as he opens the trunk. But there's nothing in there and he closes it again.

"Your back bumper looks like it's going to fall off, and that far rear tire needs air," he shouts. He starts to return to her window, scanning the interior of the car as he does. He spots the apple box in her back seat. "What's in that?"

"Beads."

"What?"

"Beads and other materials."

He watches her a moment, then steps to the passenger door. "Do you mind?" But he's already opening the door.

"Not at all." She steps out of the car.

He lugs out the box and sets it on the road, barely missing a puddle. He peels back the cloth and inspects the inside, rifles through the hide and other materials, pours beads into his hand until he's sure that's all that's inside the vials and containers. "These yours?"

"Yes."

"What do you do with them?"

"Make things." It sounds childish. "Tea cozies." She twists her scarf in her hands. "I've also done vests and hatbands and moccasins."

He stares at her, and she shifts on her feet but doesn't know why she's so unnerved.

He looks back at the box and spots the envelope. He bends to pull it out and sees the money inside. "You get paid for these things you make?"

"I've only just started making things again."

"You have a business licence?" He eyes her, scrutinizing.

"I didn't ask for payment. It was offered."

"If you're making things and people are giving you money for the things you've made," he says, holding up the envelope as evidence, "that's selling. And you don't have a business licence?"

"It's not a business—not really."

"It is if you're making money." He says it like she's not clever enough to understand.

"I've only made a couple of small things."

"Doesn't matter the size," he says, growing annoyed. "If you're selling, you need a business licence." He tosses the envelope back in the box.

She'd bet anything that the women in town who sell handknit items or homemade chokecherry jam at the weekend farmers' market do not have business licences. But she keeps this to herself.

"You could be charged for doing business without a licence." He nudges the box with his boot, a little too forcefully.

"I'm sorry—I used to work at the insurance agency in Torduvalle and handled various types of paperwork for several businesses. I should have known."

"Which agency?" he asks. He's testing her.

"Pratt's. I was there for the past eleven years."

"Was?"

"I . . . retired."

He nods and looks away as if calculating something. "Well, listen here," he says, "I'll let you go with a warning." He bends, picks up the box, and places it back in her car, as if he's being kind. "But you best sort out a licence before you sell any more of your items," he says. There's no kindness in his voice.

"I will, Officer. I will do that right away."

"And get this car seen to—it's dangerous."

"I'll take it to the shop this week," Florence says, knowing she can't. Then she climbs back behind the wheel, yanks the door closed, and heads for home, foot heavy on the pedal.

The vapour rises from the damp pavement as the sun beats down on it. Waves of steam, surging up.

SUMMER 1913

Regina, Saskatchewan

SEVEN DOLLARS IS too much to keep stashed in layers of clothing in her dresser drawer. During a lunch break on a Friday at the end of August, Florence walks from King's Hotel to the Imperial Bank next door and explains she's interested in opening an account but doesn't have identification at the moment. She says it was lost in a fire.

"Might there be any other options available to me?" she asks.

"I will need your husband's signature," the man behind the counter says.

"I'm not married."

The man looks at her left hand for confirmation. "Are you employed?"

"I am. I work at the King's Hotel," she says, pointing to the building beside them. "For nearly two years now."

"A letter from them confirming your employment and stating your home address will suffice."

"Thank you," she says, and heads back to work. During the afternoon shift she tries to find a moment to speak with the manager, but with the rush of those checking out at the end of the week and those checking in for the weekend, a moment never comes. Despite the busyness, she has more energy than ever. She imagines telling Nicole when she returns in the fall that she opened a bank account, something she never would have been able to do without Nicole's assistance. She realizes she's never properly thanked Nicole.

She will make a point of it when she returns to the city. She'll offer to take her out for a meal, maybe the Picardy Café or Monico's. She's never been to either place but she's heard guests at the King rave about them. Reservations are recommended. The idea excites her.

At the end of the day, Florence races to the manager's office on the main floor at the back of the hotel. Finds him behind stacks of papers and files trying to work an adding machine.

"What can I do for you, uh, . . ." he says, snapping his fingers and trying to recall her name.

"Florence."

"That's right. What is it you need?" He continues punching keys.

"A letter, sir. A letter for the bank so I can open an account," she says, adding, "so I can save for my future."

"How grand," he says, blasé. Then he points to a desk across the room. "There, that pad of paper there. Write your request down, all the details—name, address, which bank, et cetera."

Florence complies, finding a pencil among the scattered envelopes and rubber stamps. She writes down her name and address in Cathedral and what the letter needs to say, all in the precise printing she's practiced. She finishes and reads it over, but before she hands it to the manager, and without even realizing what she's doing, she quickly erases *Campeau*, replaces it with *Banks*.

"When do you think you might have it done?" she asks when passing him the paper.

"End of next week."

It feels so far away, but Florence says she'll return on Friday to collect it and save him the cost of postage.

He nods a perfunctory thanks.

Walking out the back door of the hotel to the alley, Florence is shocked at what she's just done, alarmed by her own brazenness. But more than that, she's electrified.

Instead of heading home, Florence walks around to the front of the hotel and goes to the Owl Café down the street to celebrate. She buys herself a bottle of ice-cold Coca-Cola and walks slowly home, window-shopping and moseying through Victoria Park on the way to Cathedral. The city's mushroomed this year. So many buildings going up here and there; there's a new one on nearly every block and some with two. She's aware that she slows as she passes each one, sweeping her eyes over every single builder and bricklayer. It's ridiculous that she still looks for him after all this time. She wonders if she'll ever stop.

That Sunday afternoon Florence hears voices across the hall and puts down the book she's reading to see if Nicole has been assigned the same room as last year, but when she opens her door, Miss Boxall is standing there helping a middle-aged woman bring her suitcases into the room. Miss Boxall introduces her as Miss Sylvia Everett.

"Nice to meet you," Florence says, disappointed that Nicole will have a room farther away this year. She asks Miss Boxall when Nicole will be arriving.

"I'm sorry, dear, did my sister not tell you?"

Florence shakes her head.

"Nicole informed us earlier this month that she will not be returning. She's engaged to be married and will be staying in her hometown."

Florence returns to her room and closes the door, the wind knocked out of her. Nicole was so committed to her studies and talked about finishing her training and starting a job somewhere in the province, maybe in a town up north so she could see the boreal forest. It pains Florence to think that Nicole's dreams have been cut off, abruptly ended. Nicole never once talked about wanting to marry or about staying in her hometown. But Florence was so focused on her own reading lessons and on keeping other people at bay, she never asked.

A sadness seeps in and keeps her tossing and turning all night. Maybe teaching wasn't Nicole's dream after all, maybe it wasn't her passion. Florence wonders about her own dreams and if cleaning up after people and living crammed in with those who are essentially strangers is where they end.

During the lunch break on Friday, Florence returns to the manager's office. He's not there, but another clerk is.

"He's taken some time off and will be back Monday," the clerk says. "Is there anything I can help with?"

"No, that's all right," she says, and starts to back out.

"What's your name?" the clerk asks.

"I'll come back to see him next week," she says.

"I still need your name—I'm to record every visitor." The clerk rolls his eyes, annoyed with the task, but reaches for a pen to make a notation.

"Florence Ca—" she says before stopping herself. "Banks."

"Florence Banks?" he asks, and when she nods, he reaches for an envelope. "I believe this is for you."

Florence takes it and opens it when she's out in the hall: It's the letter to the bank and says she, Florence Banks, is employed at the King's Hotel. Her eyes stare at the name, and it feels so official. She takes it straight to the bank and fills out a long application form that essentially repeats what's in the letter—where she lives, where she works, and for how long she has worked there.

"I know it seems redundant," the man behind the counter says, "but we do require completed forms."

"I understand," Florence says, signing her new name at the bottom. She hands the form to him along with the letter from the hotel.

"How much will you be depositing today?" he asks.

"I only have this on me now," she says, handing over the two dollars she keeps on her at all times in case of emergencies. "But I have more at home and will bring it in next week."

He completes the entries for her in a brand-new banking booklet and hands it to her. Her very own. She tucks the booklet into her bag as she exits the bank and heads back down Scarth Street towards the hotel. She slips the booklet into her apron pocket instead of leaving it in her purse in the maids' closet and glances at it throughout the afternoon. It's pleasing to see her new name in black and white. Official. Real. But she can't help wishing she could show Nicole.

She regrets not asking Nicole about her own hometown. Maybe it's like Quincy Lake. Or maybe it's as cozy as the Nest and that's why she didn't want to leave. Maybe Nicole has siblings too. Maybe she has a younger brother. A pain cuts through Florence, and she hopes her new life in the city won't always be as lonely as this. For the first time, she questions whether the city is even where she should be.

And it's as if the world has been listening to her thoughts all afternoon because when she arrives home, there's a letter waiting for her on her dresser.

Scrawled in the top lefthand corner: *Mrs. Lydia Duncan*. How had she found Florence? But Florence had left her letter in the basket for outgoing mail at the front door, and the sisters must have written her return address on the envelope, thinking they were doing her a favour.

She sinks onto the bed, a heaviness thickening within her, anchoring her down. Time passes but she just stares at the letter in her hands, not wanting to open it but knowing she has to. The sisters ring the bell for supper, but Florence doesn't go down. Claims a headache has taken hold when one of them comes and knocks at her door. It's not until everyone has gone to bed, when she knows she won't be disturbed, that she breaks open the seal.

It's a brief letter, five lines only. Mrs. Duncan thanks Florence for letting everyone know she is safe and has found meaningful employment. She has passed the message on to her family. Mrs. Duncan indicates she wasn't going to write back, sensing that Florence wasn't expecting her to, but she's doing so at the request of Florence's family. Maamaa has fallen ill again, but this time it's different. This time she's not expected to recover, and though Clancy and Lillian have not requested it of her, Mrs. Duncan suggests that Florence return home as soon as she can, even if only briefly. Even if just to say goodbye.

She's restless all night, then sleepwalks through the weekend, unsure of what to do. Certainly the manager at the hotel would understand if she asked for time off. The sisters would too, and she has enough to pay for her room even while she's not there—she doesn't want to go back to another precarious living situation; she's come too far for that. When Monday morning arrives, she's mustered the resolve for a trip back home.

Before leaving for work, she pulls the money from the folds of a camisole in her dresser, and she takes it all to the bank on a morning break when there are enough maids to cover her. It's busy and the lines are long. While waiting, Florence calculates how much she'll need for her trip home and decides to keep half, three dollars and fifty cents, and put the other half in the bank. Movement out the front window catches her eye. Labourers at the new building across the street are hoisting the business's sign up to the second floor. She watches the men working, examines their faces. He's not there, and she knows he never will be.

The line moves forward, and Florence moves with it, but she keeps turning back to look out the window. Eventually, the sign is lifted into place and held as another man on a ladder begins to secure it. *Queen City School for Secretarial Training.*

"Next, please," a teller says.

Florence stares at the sign.

"Next, please, miss," he repeats.

"Yes, sorry. I'd like to make a deposit." Florence pulls her bank booklet out and passes it to him.

"How much?"

She places four dollars on the counter. "Just three fifty today, please."

"Of course."

She glances at the sign again and something shifts inside her. "Actually," she says to the teller, "I'll deposit seven dollars today."

OCTOBER 1946

Torduvalle, Saskatchewan

FLORENCE BRACES HERSELF as she heads up the walkway to the post office, but is relieved to find no other customers inside. It'll be a quick purchase, in and out. She'll be no bother to anyone. She waits at the counter for Mr. Klein.

"One moment," he calls from a table behind the counter when he hears the door open. He rises and reaches for a cane to assist him.

"Mr. Klein, I hope you're well," she says as he approaches, her voice as professional as it was when she came here for Pratt's. This is just a business transaction like any other.

He grunts something unintelligible without looking up.

"I would like to send this letter by registered mail, please," she says, and pulls an envelope from her purse. Inside is her application for a business licence. She acquired the form at the town office yesterday from Mrs. Rondelet, who also barely acknowledged her. And Florence caught how she raised her eyebrow—just one—ever so slightly when she confirmed for Mrs. Rondelet that, yes, the form was indeed for herself. Also inside the envelope, attached to the form with two paper clips, is a cheque for twenty-five dollars, the application fee. A costly sum, hence Florence's desire for registered mail. Can't afford to have it get lost on its way.

"That's an extra two cents."

"Yes," she says, and counts six cents to cover the cost of postage.

Mr. Klein fills in the appropriate slip, and as he does, he not-so-subtly eyes the recipient's address—the provincial secretary's office in the city.

"It's for a business licence," she says. There's nothing to hide. And Mrs. Rondelet will ensure everyone knows anyway.

But he just grunts again, as if she offered up information he didn't want or need.

When he completes the registered-mail slip and is stamping the envelope, Florence closes her purse and turns to leave. As she reaches for the door handle, it opens, and she stops in her tracks.

Jennie stands in the doorway, also frozen. In the brief second, Florence sees her smile fade. The two of them stare at each other, neither knowing what to do—who should give way and who should proceed.

"Mrs. Broughton," Mr. Klein says behind Florence.

"I'll come speak with you later," Jennie says to Mr. Klein, trepidation in her voice, and she steps back out.

A rush of heat courses through Florence's body, making her skin prickle. There may never be an end to this.

She stands in the post office, letting the door close again, and pretends to fumble with her gloves to give Jennie enough time to escape down the street. As she does, an anger takes hold. Anger at Mr. Klein, at Mrs. Rondelet, and at Jennie. Anger at the stupid business forms and the officer who made her get them. Anger at the whole entire town.

"Thank you, Mr. Klein," she says, as affable as ever because she won't let on, won't let anyone know she's slowly being eaten alive.

Outside on Main Street, Florence quick-steps it to the bank and makes it the two and a half blocks without bumping into anyone else. At the counter, she informs the young teller in training she's here to meet with the regional bank manager. The trainee leads her down the hall to a room at the back of the building, occasionally used by the employees from the head office in the city, including the regional manager, Mr. Dixon, who visits semi-regularly to ensure things are running smoothly. The room is mostly bare aside from two desks, a few chairs, a wastebin, and a lamp. It smells mouldy and stale.

"Mrs. Banks is here for your meeting," the teller says.

Mr. Dixon, his back to the door, waves her in, and Florence takes a seat on a wooden chair, transferring her weight from one side of her posterior to the other, trying to find a comfortable position. She removes her scarf and runs her fingers through her hair self-consciously. She didn't dye it on Saturday; she wanted to bead instead, and, really, why bother at this point? But she regrets it now, sitting at the bank with the regional manager to discuss her mortgage.

Mr. Dixon sits at the second desk, which is perpendicular to the one she faces, reviewing her file. The skin on the back of his neck folds over his shirt collar. After a few moments, he swivels in his padded chair with wheels and uses his feet to drag the chair and himself to the desk that faces her. "Mrs. Banks," he says, extending a hand but not rising so Florence has to get up herself in order to shake it.

"Thank you for making time to meet with me today," Florence says, and sinks back down on the hard-surfaced chair. "Especially since I called only yesterday to schedule an appointment."

"The girls out front handle my calendar," he says, and swipes some crumbs from a folder in front of him. "But it's my job to make time for our clients. What can I do for you today?"

"I would like to inquire about a partial-payment plan for my mortgage. Just for a short time while I . . . sort through some things."

"I see." He examines the papers inside the folder. "I have, of course, heard that you are no longer with Pratt's," he says without lifting his head.

"That is correct," she says, maintaining the level of professionalism for which she is known. "But my situation is only temporary—I am pursuing some options. But until things are secure, I was hoping I could make arrangements for smaller, partial payments throughout the month rather than a single large payment at the start."

"The balance here," he says, reading, "indicates that you are able to make next month's payment, though." He keeps his head bent over the file but eyes her over the top of his glasses.

"That *was* the case; however, I have just placed a cheque in the mail that will reduce my balance."

"I see," he says, then leans back in his chair and interlocks his fingers, rests them across his thick chest. "And how much of your mortgage do you expect to cover on the first of the month?"

"Just under half," she says, then swallows because her throat feels thick and clogged. "But I plan to have more money later in the month so I can make another payment."

"How much later?"

"I don't have an exact date yet," she says, regretting that she didn't remove her coat because now she's starting to overheat. "Do you need an exact date?"

He doesn't answer, just looks away from her and sucks air through his teeth while he thinks. "You said you're pursuing options?"

"I have a job interview next week."

"But it's not certain?" he asks. He doesn't give her time to answer. "Are you at risk of defaulting on your mortgage, Mrs. Banks?"

The word *defaulting* hits her heavy and hard. "If a partial-payment arrangement can be made, it will not be an issue. You see, I am bringing in some income on my own," she says quickly. "Which is why I should be able to make another payment mid-month."

"*Should*." He says the word slowly, emphasizing it.

"Yes, I've started my own business—am starting," she corrects herself and hears how desperate she sounds. "That's what the cheque I referenced earlier is for—a business licence."

"Your own business?" he asks, finally leaning forward.

"I've been making things and people are paying for them." She regrets phrasing it this way; it sounds ridiculous. "Sewing," she says to clarify.

"There is a tailor in town now, is there not?" he asks.

"Yes, but it's not that kind of sewing—it's more . . . decorative." She looks away, frustrated with herself because that's not what it is, but how can she explain it to him? But it doesn't matter anyway because he just shakes the answer off, uninterested.

"Will it be enough to cover your payments?"

"I've only just started so I'm not sure yet . . ." she says, her voice fading out because she knows it won't—she needs the job at the high school. As if he picks up her thoughts, he flips the folder shut.

"Have you considered a lodger?" he asks.

"I don't have the room for a lodger." Imagine what the neighbours would think.

"Then perhaps I should have the girls up front put together some information for you to consider."

"Information?" Florence asks, a pinched smile on her face.

"There is a government program that provides funds to those in need."

"Unemployment insurance, you mean?"

"The funds are not intended to cover mortgages—they generally don't dispense that much—but it is money that may be available to you. Though you might want to look at the eligibility requirements, given your . . . unique situation." He sucks air between his teeth again.

"Is a partial-payment plan not something that can be arranged?"

He picks up a pencil and taps it on the desk. "It's not something that I can approve on my own—I will need to have some discussions here and at the regional office, and some assessments need to be made. Once that is complete, you will receive notification."

"How long will the determination take?"

"Each case is unique, but generally a week or so."

"Before the first of the month?"

"I will try to hasten things along, given the circumstances."

"That's very kind of you," she says, hiding the mild panic that's beginning to brew.

"Best of luck with your search for employment." Then he slides himself back to the other desk that faces the wall, ending their meeting.

Florence rises and exits. The panic continues to build and doesn't settle when she gets home. Not even after a cup of tea. She needs to busy herself, so she selects another scrap of hide from the pieces Lillian gifted her. A small piece, not much bigger than her hand. It could be used for a child's vamp or for a section of a small pouch, but she's making neither. Lemon-coloured beads for the cake, vermillion for the jam. There's even a perfect shade of green for the serving plate. Beading a Swiss roll will be similar to the spiral pattern for some buds and round berries, but this spiral will be a few rows thick—two or maybe three rows of yellow for the sponge and a single row of jam-coloured beads. She'll dust the top of it with a few white beads for the sugar.

She takes a break for supper and stays up past her bedtime to finish. When she's done, she pulls out the honeybee she previously beaded and looks at them side by side. Neither are the traditional Métis style. They don't fit and there's no balance, but they belong together somehow. She tucks them back into a drawer of a credenza and reminds herself that if beading has taught her anything, it's to be patient—trust that the design's meaning will eventually reveal itself. She staggers down the hall and collapses into bed, body and mind spent.

FLORENCE TURNS HER HEAD as she passes the road for Seedy Creek on her way to Forsyth, but the day is foggy and she can't see even the first shack in the line. The commute to Forsyth from Torduvalle would be a decent drive in the warmer months but certainly unpleasant in winter. There's talk of increasing the speed limits on the highways but her LaSalle can barely handle the fifty miles per hour now. The driver's-side door shakes and rattles, and a cold draft seeps in from somewhere in the footwell.

She turns at the town's welcome sign, follows the road on its periphery all the way to the south end, and parks in the school's gravel lot. A two-storey red-brick building. The red of the bricks is rich and dark like the ground they came from, and a large archway above the front stairs frames a glossy wooden door, so shiny it's like a mirror. So much bigger than the squat, single-floor stone building in Quincy Lake, a school she once tried to glimpse inside of before being caught and shooed away.

Florence approaches the school and pulls open the door. Follows the signs to the principal's office. A young, rather frazzled junior secretary is lost in a sea of paperwork strewn across her desk. She asks Florence's name and promptly forgets it when she knocks on the principal's open door.

"Mrs. . . . um, your next appointment is here," she says.

But Principal Aubrey is expecting her and is already exiting his office. "Mrs. Banks, I'm so pleased you're interested in our school," he says, extending his hand. "We are a remarkably busy one, I'm afraid, which is why it's taken some time for interviews." He pats the junior secretary on the shoulder, clearly trying to buoy her spirits.

"It's what I'm used to—I prefer to be busy." Florence pulls out an envelope from her purse with her neatly folded résumé inside. "I completed my certificate at the Queen City School for Secretarial Training and was with Pratt's for eleven years—"

"Yes, I've heard many sing your praises, Mrs. Banks." He takes the envelope and leads her into his office.

"Florence, please," she says.

"Florence. This is really just a formality. We're in quite a desperate state, and if I had my way, I'd ask you to start tomorrow. Unfortunately," he says, placing the envelope with her résumé on top of a small pile, "we've had several inquiries and do need to follow through with the process. For the board."

"Of course."

"Can I ask why you want to leave Pratt's?"

Florence takes a seat across from him, realizing that, indeed, he hasn't heard. "Pratt's has grown quite a lot since I began there. I've seen it through its stages of expansion and I've trained the secretaries who are there now—they're exceptional." She pauses. "And with the latest restructuring, I feel like I've accomplished all I can there." It's not the truth but it's not a complete lie either.

"You're looking for a challenge." An impressed look in his eye.

She nods.

"We can certainly offer you that." He laughs. "But you know we can't pay as well as Pratt's?"

"There's more to a job than its salary. An educational institution . . . well, it's meaningful work, isn't it?"

This time, he nods. "It is, and it doesn't ever seem to slow down. Like Pratt's, our school has grown exponentially in the past few years, but our budgets haven't grown at the same rate." He takes a moment and looks over some paperwork on his desk. "When Mrs. Lalonde left us earlier this fall, we simply didn't have the time to find a replacement, but now we don't have the time not to." He picks up a letter, shakes his head as he scans it. "You must have experience dealing with unhappy clients while at Pratt's?"

"Frequently. Not everyone is happy with their claims assessments."

"And how did you manage?"

"The crucial thing is to listen. Sometimes just a patient, kind ear is enough to calm a client. Often, they just need to vent and get their frustrations out. After, they still may not be happy with the results they were provided, but at least they've aired their views and that eases something, I think."

"You may need to listen to a lot of venting parents."

"I was aware that would come with the territory."

"More so than normal."

It'd be uncouth to pry so Florence simply waits for more, a neutral but attentive look on her face.

"I'm a liberal but I support many of the current provincial government's policies. But policies are effective only with well-thought-out plans for implementation."

"That's true for any workplace."

He watches her a moment, contemplating. "You might as well be informed now, then." He pulls a cigarette from a case on his desk and lights up. "With the decision of the new government to educate every child in the province, our school is expected to take in the children that are living in hovels around the outskirts of town. You're aware of these places?"

"I am." Her voice almost a whisper. What will he do when he finds out the truth? And he certainly will if she were to work here. This job is her last immediate option, and it already feels like it's slipping from her grasp.

"All children should be allowed an education—I believe that. An education is the solution to the problem. But it can't just happen at the snap of a finger." He puffs. "The condition of these places is deplorable. Our own Sergeant Buckley and other officers naturally go out to these hovels regularly and they barely have the words to describe what they see. The Division of Sanitation sent an investigator out to one of these places near Yorkton," he says, pointing to a letter off to the side on his desk, "and a six-year-old child was found to have trachoma. *Trachoma*," he repeats with emphasis. "Others had it too, of course, but a six-year-old child." He shakes his head. "It's unfathomable in this day and age for a civilized country, but here we are."

"Do you not want them to be students here?" Florence asks, trying to maintain her look of impartiality.

"No, that's not what I mean to suggest." He reflects a moment. "Education is the answer, of course. Education leads to better decisions and outcomes. But how we do it requires more thought. If we just open our doors, we expose all the other students here and everyone in the community. It's hazardous. Parents are already sounding the alarm, threatening to pull their children."

"You said Sanitation sent an investigator, but has a public health inspector been sent to Seedy Creek? To ascertain if there are health risks?" she asks without thinking.

His eyes flit to her and hold, as if assessing her. "No," he says and adjusts himself in his seat. "That's something that's been proposed, but again, what does implementation look like? Would a single inspection suffice or would regular monthly inspections be required? That's where the Sanitation and Communicable Diseases Division needs to weigh in, but the Department of Health is very reluctant to become further involved. Not everyone is rising to the task."

"Are the health concerns the only thing that's worrisome to Forsyth?" Florence says, even though she knows she should keep quiet.

Principal Aubrey stubs out his cigarette, having inhaled it rather quickly. "I fear I'm giving you the wrong impression of our school. There may be some parents who will pull their students even if there are no health risks posed." She watches his demeanour change in front of her, going from light and casual to stiff and stilted. "But contagious disease is a legitimate concern. Do you not agree?"

"Of course," she says but a rift has grown between them.

"I believe we should do everything we can to get those children into school. To give them an education," he says, emptying his ashtray into the bin beside his desk. "It's really the only way to resolve the problem."

"The problem?"

"The poverty, the deplorable living conditions. An education will give them opportunities to make different decisions."

Opportunities. Florence's mind hangs on to the word. That's all she ever wanted. It was what she was chasing. But in the moment, she also sees the connections that Clancy would make. The connections between the parents of these students, their grandparents, their great-grandparents. They're all connected to this problem, to the lack of opportunities for some. It's clear to her in a way that it wasn't before. Their outrage is misdirected.

"I feel like I should explain myself a little." Her voice comes out soft despite the nervousness bubbling up inside. "What I'm trying to say is that the families living in these communities . . . they don't have a choice either. They're not living in deplorable conditions because they want to."

"I'm in agreement with you there, Mrs.—Florence. I don't think anyone would choose to either. Maybe they didn't have the resources or tools to make other decisions, and that's where education comes in. Education will give them a chance to find employment, which—"

"Not if no one will hire them." It comes out louder than she wanted.

"Why wouldn't they be hired if they were properly educated?"

"For the same reason that some of the parents here will not be satisfied with health inspections, no matter how frequent they are."

A heavy silence fills the room and the two of them just sit in it. Neither knowing what to say or do. The ring of the noon bell startles them both.

"Well, Florence," he says, "thank you for taking the time to come in today." He rises and opens the door for her to exit, and the junior secretary jumps up and rifles through the papers on her desk.

"I have the typing test here somewhere," she says. "I'll take you to a classroom—"

"There's no need, Pauline," he says.

"Won't the board want—"

"It's not necessary in this case," he says. "Unfortunately, Mrs. Banks is far too qualified for the meagre salary we have to offer." He smiles, but it's disingenuous.

Florence knows that's a lie—she won't get the job because she challenged him too much—and she watches him head back to his desk.

"Thank you," she says to the junior secretary, and her heels clatter as she walks out the office door and down the hall. She trudges across the yard, her chest spasming. She climbs into the car and drives off, speeding over the gravel, racing for the paved road, eager to get back to the highway where it's straight and smooth. She presses harder on the gas and the door rattles like it'll come right off, like the wind will blow everything off its frame, but she needs the distance and she presses even harder.

FLORENCE PICKS UP THE receiver to try calling the bank, but again, there's someone else on the line. Surprisingly, it's not Mrs. Sanderson this time but Mr. Kilber on the north end of the street.

"I'm sorry, I'll try later," Florence says and hangs up, frustrated. She's tried the line four times this morning and every time it's been tied up by someone else. She was able to get through to the bank last week and spoke with Mr. Lesley, but he said he had no information on her meeting with Mr. Dixon and their discussion, which was quite off-putting—horrible customer service for an institution such as theirs. There should have been, at the very least, some notes in her file detailing their discussion. But Mr. Lesley, sensing her thoughts, offered to take it upon himself to call the regional office on her behalf and get an update directly. He said he'd call her back after inquiring, but by the end of the week she still hadn't heard, and today is the first business day of the month.

She heads to the fridge, peckish with lunch just around the corner. But she can't concentrate on food. It bothers her that the loop hasn't been closed, that they haven't followed through in the timely manner that was promised. She looks back at the phone but then goes to the front door instead, puts on her coat and grabs her car keys.

Of course there'd be a line at the bank today, but she waits patiently, purse hooked on her arm, hands clasped, eyes straight ahead. Her stomach growls. When she gets to the front of the line, Mr. Lesley is busy with Mr. Oborowsky but he waves at her to get her attention.

"I'll help you over here," he says to Florence, "if you just want to wait to the side."

"Certainly," she says, and steps out of the queue to let those behind her be served by the other tellers.

Mr. Lesley, in a sweater-vest of cream and brown diamonds and a brown bow tie, finishes counting some bills and stamping papers for Mr. Oborowsky. He turns to Florence when the counter is free.

"Mrs. Banks," he says, "I tried to call you this morning but—"

"The line was busy," she says, finishing for him.

"That's right."

"I've been trying to reach you too." Chatterboxes on her party line, but she won't say that out loud. "I thought, given the difficulties, I should just come in person."

"That's much appreciated," he says. "One moment, please." He walks to a desk behind the counter, grabs a file, and returns with it. He opens it, then inhales a large breath as if to prepare himself.

Florence's stomach cramps, but it's not from hunger. "Did you speak with Mr. Dixon?"

"Yes. Well, no," he says, correcting himself. "I did not get a hold of him, but I did speak with a member of his staff, and they spoke with him directly."

Florence sees that he's blinking rather fast, that he has trouble keeping eye contact, and her heart quickens like an alarm going off. "And?" she asks.

"I was told that he was going to reach out to you, but he hasn't?"

"I've not heard from him, no." Her voice is squeaky and high-pitched, as if not her own.

"Maybe he had difficulty too," he offers, trying to be helpful. "I know a letter is also being prepared and you should receive that shortly." He stops there and inhales again. "Unfortunately, the arrangement requested could not be implemented."

The floor seems to waver under her feet, and Florence steps to the side, then back, trying to recentre.

"I don't have the particulars as to why," he says. "I'm sure those will be outlined in the letter."

"So what does this mean?" she asks.

"Are you able to make your payment today?" he asks with a note of concern.

"The balance in my account is what I can apply, but, as you can see, that's only a fraction."

Mr. Lesley nods uncomfortably.

"I am in default, then, is that correct?" It's a statement of fact, that's all.

"Do you think you can come up with the remaining amount this week? I could hold off on notification . . ."

He seems genuinely concerned for her and it surprises her. Surprises her so much it almost overwhelms the fear that's setting in.

"I don't think I can, I'm sorry," she says, the apology a strange afterthought.

"Is there anything you can sell?"

The only big thing she has is the LaSalle, but no one would even want her jalopy, much less pay the amount she needs for it. Florence looks down at the floor that's still moving under her. "Thank you for your assistance, Mr. Lesley," she says and turns.

He says something to her but she doesn't hear it. She's too focused on keeping upright as she makes her way to the door.

Outside, the first snowflakes of the year have just started to fall. They're fat and wet and prick the skin on her cheeks when they land. She stands for a moment in the cold, feeling the sting, and before the thoughts have fully formed, she walks down the block to the corner and crosses the street. Heads to the *Torduvalle Weekly*'s office.

"I'd like to place an ad," she says to Miss Judith Shaw, who's snapping a large piece of gum in her open mouth and twisting a lock of her hair around a pencil.

"You can fill out this form," she says, passing Florence a sheet of paper from a stack filed in the slot beside her.

"Can it run in the next issue?" Florence asks.

"I'm afraid not—that issue is already full," Miss Shaw says, clearly not invested in her occupation.

"I can keep it short—just a line or two."

"Won't matter," Miss Shaw says. *Snap.* "There's no room."

"Are you certain? You can't squeeze it in with some formatting adjustments?" Florence has never worked on a newspaper layout, but she's put plenty of newsletters together for Pratt's and the church and it can't be much different.

"I'd have to ask Dennis but he's away until Thursday afternoon. It'll be too late by then, I'm sure." *Snap, snap.*

Florence clenches her jaw. Her insouciance is too much for Florence to deal with right now. She glances at the calendar hanging on the wall. If she's missed the November eleventh issue, her ad won't go out until the eighteenth.

She tunes out Miss Shaw's gum-chewing as she writes in the details of her ad. *Household items for sale.* She writes *Everything must go* but then erases it because it sounds desperate. Instead, she puts *Everything reasonably priced.*

"A sale?" Miss Shaw asks. "Before Christmas?"

She is unskilled and ill-mannered but Florence can't be bothered with that. "How much will the ad cost, please?"

"You'd be better off waiting until after the holidays."

"Perhaps, but I don't have a choice," Florence says, sharp. "How much do I owe you?"

"Two cents."

Florence's change purse is light but she finds the pennies and hands them over.

"Thank you," Miss Shaw says, though she clearly doesn't mean it, and she snaps her gum again, this time more loudly and on purpose.

Florence exits and heads back to her car, annoyed with the young woman but even more annoyed that she is, of course, correct—no one will want to buy anything before the holidays. They'll be saving to buy new items from stores in the city or ordered from catalogues.

She quickens her pace to her car. People know she has high-quality items, though. Maybe some of them will be looking for fine, enduring gifts. But can she sell enough to cover the costs of her mortgage? Both this month's and next?

By the time she reaches her car, the snow has already stopped falling and her throat has twisted into a knot and she tries to gulp for air but wheezes instead. She starts the car and heads back down Main Street for home, but instead of making the turn onto her street, she drives straight to the edge of town. She slows and comes to a full stop at the highway intersection. She cracks the window, hoping a cool blast of air will help. Her hands are shaking. She rubs them against each other, trying to knead out the tension, but it shifts somewhere else. Florence signals and turns onto the highway.

The lane that leads to the Hubers' house is long and lined with the boulders and rocks they salvaged when clearing their land. Florence parks at the end of the lane, not wanting to block their route. As she approaches the house, Mrs. Huber steps out onto the porch.

"Good afternoon, Mrs. Banks," she says and waves, then pulls her unbuttoned cardigan tight around her. "How are you?" She's smiling as if genuinely pleased to see Florence.

"I'm fine, Mrs. Huber." Because that's what you say even if the world is coming down around you. "And you?"

"Same," she says. "If you're looking for Clancy, he's at the barn."

Florence wonders if Mrs. Huber has always known it was her voice on the phone or if gossip has since travelled her away. Not that it matters now.

Mrs. Huber points to a plume of dark smoke rising in a column behind the barn. Florence waves her thanks, turns, carefully steps over the rocky border, and heads towards the fire.

She marches around the corner of the barn, footsteps heavy with anger. At the back, she finds Clancy standing between a large fire and an even larger pile of dry tree branches, old rags and towels, rotten lumber, pieces of broken furniture. He stokes the fire with a long crowbar, then throws in a chunk of refuse and uses the crowbar to poke it into the flames. He doesn't see her as she approaches, doesn't notice her until she's directly across the fire from him.

"Jesus," he says. "Scared the daylights out of me." He chuckles but stops, picking up on the mood in the air. "Florence, you okay?"

She shakes her head.

He leans the crowbar against the pile of trash but doesn't move towards her.

"You've ruined everything." Her throat is tight and distorts her voice.

He looks down.

"Everything I had, everything I worked for. I worked so goddamn hard. I cleaned up after other people—soiled sheets and stained towels, slops and spills that they couldn't be bothered to wipe up themselves. Morning, noon, and night. And when I wasn't working, I was learning to read and write so I didn't have to clean up waste my whole life. I scraped by—and just barely."

"I didn't know—"

"And I did it all on my own. Banks is just . . . a name I made up." She pauses. "I never had the courage to marry. Too afraid to be found out." She tries to pull the ring off, but it won't budge, vexing her further.

"I'm sorry," Clancy says, sounding like he means it.

"I finally saved up a bit. A pittance, really, but it was enough to pay for secretarial school and get my certificate so I could get a good job and move somewhere safe. Start fresh. This became my home. The home I never thought I'd have. It was good, Clancy. So good. Safe in ways that I'd never felt before. And it's not anymore. You came, and . . . why?" Her voice rises. "Why this town, of all places?" She's yelling now and he just takes it, and that fuels her anger even more. "Because of you, I've lost my job, and now I've missed a mortgage payment—and I have no idea how I'm going to fix that, Clancy. I could lose my house—I could lose everything!" She hasn't moved but her body is vibrating.

He picks up an armful of debris from the pile, steps towards her, holds it out.

She throws a branch into the fire and it catches right away. She throws another. Then a chair leg, then the end of a broken broom. The bristles sizzle. When his arms are empty, he tugs her to the other side of the fire, picks up a can of kerosene, hands it to her. She splashes some on the fire and it whooshes up higher, flames reaching for the sky. She throws more debris in. More. More kerosene. The fire grows almost as high as the barn roof. In its centre, the flames are blue. Then white and blazing. Chunks of wood crack and spark; embers fly out into the air, glowing with rage.

A long, intense hiss resonates as everything burns.

They step back from the heat and watch. It's a long time before the fire settles, and her anger deflates with it.

"The Hubers must think we're burning everything down," Clancy says, crushing the glowing cinders into powder with the crowbar, sending up little puffs of smoke.

"I hope she hasn't called the cops on me."

"Nah," he says, motioning to the house, "she wouldn't."

"How do you know?"

"You don't know about Agnes?"

"Know what?"

"She was born a Fleury."

"She's Métis?"

"French, if she's asked."

"Does Frank know?"

"He'll say she's French too if you ask him."

Florence glances at the house in the distance, and a sorrow starts to take hold, but she pushes it away. There are too many other feelings to manage.

She turns back to Clancy. "Doesn't it bother you that Lillian still lives in a place like Seedy Creek?"

"Because it's a shantytown? 'A scene of appalling squalor,' according to the papers?"

"That's how we lived when we were children. *Children.* On the edges and hidden and with . . . barely anything at all. And she's still there, after all this time. How does it not eat you up?"

He turns back to the coals, silent but contemplative.

"Thirty-five years have passed since then. Thirty-five years, Clancy." She pauses, digesting it herself. "And nothing has changed." She looks him in the eye.

"True," he says, and motions to the pile of smouldering ashes with his hand, "you still can't manage a fire."

She can't help but smile.

Even without the flames, the heat from the burnt rubbish rises up.

"I think you're right," she says, "I think Maamaa and Paapaa would be ashamed of me. And I think Lillian would be too."

Clancy momentarily stops tending the ashes. "I don't know about that—I said that in anger. But I do know you should never be near kerosene again."

"I'm serious."

Clancy looks up and meets her eye. "I think they'd still be proud."

"Would they?"

"Auntie sure as hell is now. Carries your bloody cozy around from house to house, bragging about you."

Florence looks at him.

"Christ, she won't stop talking about you and your beading. She's taking credit for it, though."

Florence laughs. "She should—she taught me." Moments pass; her smile fades. "She wouldn't be angry about the choices I've made?"

"They're choices many others have made."

"Would you have?"

"I don't know . . ." He squashes another ember. "I don't think I'd look as good blonde."

She laughs.

"You're damn lucky Auntie's losing her eyesight." He shakes his head. "You must use bleach the way you use kerosene."

She slaps his arm, and he laughs. Then he puts his arm around her and they stand there together, watching the remaining embers fizzle out.

"I should head home," Florence says when the last threads of light are trailing in the sky, and she steps away from Clancy.

"I'll walk with you," he says, and follows her to her car. "I really am sorry, Florence," he says when they reach it. "I didn't want all of this to happen."

"I know." She leans back against the LaSalle, slumping.

"What are you going to do now?"

"I don't know." She shakes her head.

There's a long moment of silence.

"How much do you need for this month's mortgage payment?" he says.

"Why do you ask?" Florence looks at him, but he's turning thoughts over in his head.

"I have an idea," he says. There's a stern look on his face. "It won't be for another week or so and you're not going to like it, but it could be a solution."

She knows what he's going to say. "Clancy, I can't—"

"I know, but it's the only thing I can think of to help you," he says. "What else is there?"

The answer is *nothing*, but she doesn't say it.

CLANCY SAID IT WOULD be forty minutes down this stretch of Highway 53, but forty minutes have long since passed. Now she's late and there's no sign of the marker. Maybe it blew away or is now hidden by the heavy dump of snow they had last week. What will she do with the crate if the man gets tired of waiting and leaves? She can't take it back to Seedy Creek. She wouldn't dare take it home. She should have asked Clancy more questions. What if the man she's to meet isn't there? But she wanted to know only the bare minimum. As if more information meant more culpability.

Her watch says she's closing in on fifty minutes now and still no marker. She must have missed it somehow. Or maybe the others who've come this way have driven faster. Been in trucks or vehicles better equipped. She never even considered that her car could break down, though it's always a distinct possibility with her LaSalle. So much she hasn't thought of. She removes her headscarf and cracks open the window. Lets the wintry air fortify her.

There's a break in the fence on the left. She lifts her foot off the gas. Two tire ruts, their indentations still visible in the snow, head southwest through overgrown bush, trees and slight rolling hills in the distance. Tied on the corner of one of the fence posts is a handkerchief, as Clancy described. It's navy, not red. In her head, it was red, but she'd never asked, just assumed.

Her tires sink into the ruts off the turn and bump over rocks, patches of prairie grass underneath the snow.

The instructions Clancy gave for what she should do after this turn were scant: Past the first thicket of trees, a small clearing. Beyond that, the road curves, but if you reach the hills, you've gone too far. The car jostles over the harsh terrain and she imagines having to walk all the way back to the highway to hitch if a tire blows. Bare branches on the side of the pathway poke out at the car, scratch at the windows. There's a sharp dip down and then back up, perhaps where a creek or a small river flows in the warmer months. On the other side, the trees clear, and there's an open field with tall grasses and shrubs blanketed in the freshly fallen snow, glittery in the sun.

Florence shields her eyes and presses the brake, comes to a stop. She scans the road ahead, sees a curve in the distance edging along the base of the hills, but there's no other vehicle in sight. She turns the car off and steps out. Silence, broken only by a cluster of chickadees warbling in the birches behind her. The stillness is captivating. Her sweaty palms cool, and the tension that cradled in her chest on the way here unfurls. A part of her hopes the man she's supposed to meet doesn't show. Hopes that she can just pull the crate from her trunk, set it on the path, and drive back as if this never happened.

Except that another notice would arrive, and it would be more serious. What if she had to leave the house? She might have to leave Torduvalle, but where would she go? Would she even have enough money to fill up the gas tank in her car? She's capable of starting over, but it requires planning and time and resources. None of which she has now.

Florence wanders up the road looking for signs of the man Clancy said she's to meet. She never even asked his name. She's late but only by a quarter of an hour, and surely that's too soon for him to give up on her. How long should she wait? She ties her scarf back on. She doesn't even know which way he's coming from. Maybe he's heading down the same path she just came from, but when she turns, barely anything is visible beyond the grove of trees and scrub that crowd around the ruts by her car.

But then, back at the hills, there's movement. The roof of a truck skimming along the top of a knoll, its body hidden by the mound of earth. Exhaust wafting up clouds behind it. Her own body puffs out a shock of adrenaline. It's just a crate. A single crate she only has to hand to him—that's it. Florence heads back to the LaSalle and waits. Where the knoll's slope descends, the whole of the truck eventually appears, just before the curve in the road. A half-ton the colour of caramel. Or maybe it's all rust and not paint at all. It slows around the curve, then comes straight towards her, headlights pointed like barrels. But it continues to slow as if losing gas. Florence steps to the side of her car so he can see her, see it's a woman. She waves, then feels silly; they're not friends or acquaintances. But you should still be polite.

The truck comes to a halt but there's quite a distance between them. At least two hundred yards. Florence steps forward again. Does he want her to drive out to him? He should just come the whole way. The door opens and a man hops out, truck still running. He's short and wiry, a cap on his head, and he's swimming in his lumber jacket. She waves again. He motions half-heartedly in response but doesn't walk any closer.

This shouldn't be so confusing. One crate, one handover; why this difficulty? The man's squat legs are braced in a wide stance on the road, a triangle on the horizon. Florence huffs out a breath and walks to the LaSalle's trunk. The bottles clank and tink against each other as she lifts the crate. Holds it tight to her stomach as she walks and watches her footing in the grooves. When she's halfway there, the weight builds in her arms and they begin to burn. She adjusts the load, shifting it over to her right hip. The change alleviates the strain in one arm but increases it in the other. The man's refusal to help also burns.

She sets the crate down on the ground, angled on a clump of grass and snow, so she can rest a moment. As she rises, she notices the man is no longer on the path in front of her. He's climbed back behind the wheel and is pulling the door closed. The sound of it shutting carries through the air, a small thunk. Coming to her aid, finally. Saving her the effort and both of them time. She places her hands on her hips, arching backwards to stretch her spine. But the truck's reversing. It reverses all the way to the curve, where it bumps its back wheels out of the ruts, pauses, swings its front wheels south, and takes off the way it came, moving at a good clip.

The rumbling engine fades, replaced with crunching footsteps in the snow behind her. More than one set. The ground seems to give way beneath her and she loses her balance as she turns. Three men march towards her, and there's a fourth at her car, already opening its doors and inspecting the seats, the footwells, the glove compartment. Behind him and through the gaps in the trees, she sees a twinkling, red beacon light.

The man closest to her, the only one not in a uniform, but in a suit jacket and tie and two-toned brogues, speaks to her. She can barely hear him; her mind's working too slowly and her hearing's tunnelling like her ear canals are clogged with cotton. He turns and speaks to one of the uniformed men beside him, who seems vaguely familiar.

"I recognized the car, sir," the man says. "Stopped her last month leaving Seedy Creek and had a feeling when I saw her again out in these parts."

"Good work, Keddie."

The other man in uniform puts Florence in cuffs and guides her back down the path to their vehicles. It's hard to keep stable with her hands behind her, and her left foot slips, her weight shifts, and then she's tipping to the side, but the officer catches her, holds her in a firm embrace. She steadies and the officer supports her the rest of the way, his hands firm on her waist. She resents him for confining her wrists but is also grateful for his assistance. Nothing is ever simple.

In the police car, parked near hers, the plainclothes officer peppers her with questions from the driver's seat. "What's your name?"

"Florence—" she says, then stops, not sure which name to go by anymore.

"Florence what?"

"Banks." It's the easiest in this circumstance—it's what's on her identification.

"And how do you know Norton, Florence?"

"Norton?" she asks, confused.

"That half-breed who ran away with his tail between his legs." He turns and looks at her in the back seat, maybe thinking she's playing some kind of game with him, but he sees her confusion, sees that she's being honest. "What name did he give you?" Then adds under his breath: "Sly bastard."

"He didn't—I wasn't given a name."

"You don't know who you were meeting?" he says in a tone that suggests he doesn't believe her.

"No, I don't."

"But someone told you to meet him, right?" He cocks his head.

Florence looks in her lap.

"You didn't make this moonshine, then," he says, turning away again.

"I didn't," Florence says.

"Who did?"

But she doesn't respond. Clancy said there wouldn't be any issues on this run. Even when he tries to help, he makes things worse. It was stupid of her to go along with this.

"Is the person who made it the person who told you to bring it here?"

Still she doesn't answer.

"Right." The officer scribbles in his notepad. "How do you know these people? You don't look like someone who'd be involved in this type of thing." He swivels again and eyes her closely, waiting.

"I need money," she says, soft.

"Don't we all?" He laughs. "You don't look like you need it, though. Look pretty well off to me."

But she just shakes her head—he wouldn't understand.

He softens a little. "Hey, listen, we all fall on bad times at some point, but this . . . this thing you're doing is not the answer."

A laugh escapes Florence, a little huff at his condescension.

"It's not funny—these are bad people doing bad things."

"They're not bad people," Florence says without thinking.

The officer stares at her, shocked that she's contradicting him. "What's that?" he says, an edge in his voice.

She lifts her head. "They may be doing bad things but only because they have to. That doesn't make them bad people."

"You know more than I do, then," he says. "How's that?"

She meets his eye. "Because I'm one of them," she says, defiant.

"You? You're a half—"

"I'm Métis," she interrupts, her desire to be polite having evaporated.

He sizes her up again with the new information. "I never would have thought," he says, but more to himself. "You look white . . ." Then he turns away from her and jots down more in his notebook.

The man who was examining her car walks up to the driver's-side window and speaks to the officer in the front seat. "There's nothing else in the vehicle," he says.

"Right, thank you. We'll meet you back at the station," he says to his colleague.

"We're going to the station now?" Florence asks.

"It's what happens when you get arrested," he says.

"What about my car?"

"You'll have to make arrangements to get it later." He starts the car, and the chickadees startle at the sound of the engine. They rise from the trees, scatter in the sky.

Florence's head spins as they drive to the station. All she can think about is undersides—the bottom surfaces of beadwork, where all the thread and knots are on display. Lillian used to examine the undersides of her beading. She'd test the strength of Florence's stitches to ensure the beads were snug but not choked. She'd inspect her knots to make sure they wouldn't come undone and that other stitches hadn't become snagged on them. So much can be understood from those messy undersides, but to most people, the undersides are ugly, a monochrome, tangled inverse to the vibrant, smooth design on the top. Less balance, less harmony. But it's by looking underneath that you can really see all the hard work, the effort. Both sides are part of the whole, but one gets covered up, hidden.

THE COPPER ASHTRAY OVERFLOWS, and the latest flick from the end of Staff Sergeant Buckley's cigarette causes an avalanche, and a small heap of ashes collects on the table. He wipes the ashes off the edge with the side of his palm, letting them fall to the floor. He takes another puff and rests his Camel in the tray, pushing even more ash onto the table, but he leaves the mess this time.

"So you didn't know anything about the man you were to meet?" he asks.

"I told you I didn't." She motions to Corporal Keddie, who's also in the room. "I told him too."

This is the second round of questioning since they brought her in.

The sergeant turns to Corporal Keddie. "Did someone call the neighbouring detachments about that rusted-out Dodge half-ton Norton was driving?"

Keddie nods. "Didn't ring any bells, but they'll keep a lookout."

Outside the window, the sky looks like a pebble, dappled brown and dusty. It's late afternoon, suppertime's approaching. The clouds had rolled in on the drive to Forsyth, and by the time they pulled into town and up to the station, the day had turned. They placed her in an empty cell right away and gave her a tin cup of water, but she didn't drink it. She just sat on the metal bench quietly until they came to collect her.

The sergeant turns back to Florence. "But what you haven't told us is where you got this home brew. You said you didn't make it, but you must know who did."

"I don't." Florence turns her gaze from the window, wishing she had used the time in her cell to nap.

"Okay," he says when Florence doesn't say any more. "Then let's talk about why. Corporal Keddie informs me that you're from Torduvalle, just west of here. Said you worked at the insurance place there—the one that bought up the outfit here in Forsyth."

Florence nods.

"You were there a number of years." He pauses, waiting. "But you lost your job and then needed money."

"It's not that simple."

"No, it's never simple when someone loses a job, but most people don't then turn to bootlegging."

"It was just going to be the once." She hears it, how weak and pathetic it sounds, a child's excuse.

"How'd you lose your job?"

"They said they were restructuring."

"They 'said'?" he asks, picking up on her emphasis of the word. "Were they not?"

Florence opens her mouth to explain but decides against it, says instead: "You'd have to ask them."

"We just might do that."

If they talked with Mr. Broughton, he could say she was slow or made too many mistakes. Or lazy. Or was a gossip and talked too much. Or didn't talk enough and wasn't friendly with the clients. It didn't matter. He can say anything he wants and they'll believe him because that's the way it works. He might even tell them she lies, is deceitful. And that is the truth, isn't it?

"You couldn't find another job?"

"Not many are hiring now." At least, not hiring her.

"But you knew others were making money at Seedy Creek and figured it was a way to make some quick cash."

"For my mortgage."

"I see. You didn't think to ask a friend or a family member?"

In a way, she did. "This was the only option."

"Look, we know some of the Seedy Creek folk are involved and we know you're connected to them." He reaches for his smoke and flicks it again but doesn't take a drag. "Family, right?"

"From a long time ago."

"But still family."

Florence nods.

"We've searched Seedy Creek a few times but haven't found the operation. The moonshine isn't brewed there, as far as we can tell. Where is it made?"

"I don't know."

"You don't know the man you were delivering to and you don't know where the brew's made." He drops his pen and scratches the base of his skull in frustration. He shoots a few more questions at her and then is interrupted by the rumbling of his stomach. After twenty minutes, he picks up his papers, says they'll continue later. Keddie takes Florence back to the cell.

On the bed, her purse. Returned, and rifled through and messy inside. She pulls it to her lap like it's a small animal. Sounds from the front of the station filter down the hall to her cell. Sergeant Buckley bellows that he'll be back in an hour or so, that he's heading home for supper with his wife. He exits, and then it's just the shuffling of footsteps, Keddie's and those of another young officer on duty. A cabinet drawer opening; the screech of a chair's legs across the floor as someone sits down or gets up. The clank and pop of the radiators as hot water courses through them to fend off the chill.

Her body feels weighted, each limb a heavy stone hanging from her. She could lie down on the bench, sleep for days.

"This is all we have to offer." The other officer is at her cell door holding a cup of coffee and a sandwich on a plate. "Baloney," he says apologetically.

"That's fine." Florence is starving. She missed lunch and had barely eaten breakfast this morning because of her nerves.

"I've got an apple if that's not enough."

"This will do, thank you." But after she finishes the sandwich, she regrets declining the apple. Nearly two hours pass before Sergeant Buckley returns. He's livelier; there's more energy in his movements. Maybe an impromptu nap after his meal, broken by his wife's poke at his arm, reminding him that his workday isn't over.

After he fixes himself a cup of coffee, he takes Florence back to the interview room, where there's now nothing visible outside the window. It's just a square of black with the sun gone down.

"Mrs. Banks," Sergeant Buckley says, voice more grave than before, and with a large crumb gummed to the stubble near his jawline. "Do you know the charges you are facing?"

"They were explained to me." She wants to meet his eye but can't.

"So you know it's a hefty fine?" He pauses. "Two hundred dollars."

She nods, but all her muscles feel weak.

"How will you pay it? You're already having difficulty with your mortgage."

"When would I have to pay the fine?"

"You'd have thirty days."

She shifts in her seat. That's hardly any time at all. "And if I can't?"

"That would be up to the courts. Sometimes extensions are granted or installments arranged. Sometimes people do jail time to avoid the fine."

"Jail time," she says out loud but to herself. "For how long?" The idea is absurd and she feels an odd urge to laugh, though it's not funny.

"You wouldn't take that route, would you, Mrs. Banks?"

"I wouldn't want to, but—"

"No, you wouldn't. But," he says, pausing to pull out a silver cigarette case from his pocket, "what if we drop the charges?"

Florence looks up at him. He's headed somewhere but it's not clear where.

He opens the case, looks at the white cylinders, then reconsiders and shuts it again. "You care about your neighbours, don't you, Mrs. Banks? The people in your town?"

"Of course." She steels herself for whatever's coming.

"I understand you felt desperate. You wanted to save your house, and who wouldn't? Torduvalle is a nice town. Been there several times myself—my wife drags me to the Christmas pageant every year." He smiles. "But this bootlegging operation poses quite a risk to your town and ours."

The case Clancy gave her was going somewhere else. Somewhere close to the border, he said.

"Just give us names. That's it. We know you're not the one behind all this. If you give us the names of the men involved, you can move on and forget about this."

"I don't know who makes it or where it's made or who's involved." Florence keeps her voice matter-of-fact. If she stays calm, they have to believe her. "I didn't want to know details."

He reaches for a cigarette again. This time he lights it. "But you know who does."

Her heart thuds in her chest, so hard it feels like it'll come right out. She takes a moment before speaking. "The person I know doesn't make the home brew either."

"He knows who does?"

She doesn't answer.

"This person you know—"

"He's barely involved."

"And he got involved for the same reasons as you?"

A small nod.

"Then we could probably offer him the same kind of deal. As long as he doesn't have any significant priors."

"He's a good man." She feels her insides shrinking, flattening out.

"Then it's easy."

He'd be at the farm now and probably finished with his nightly chores in the barn or the field, cocooned under blankets in his room at the back of the house, ready to wake early. Or maybe he wouldn't be sleeping right now. Maybe enough time has passed for word to have reached him. She would be giving him the chance to avoid charges. "Could I speak with him before you do?"

The sergeant considers this. "We can do that."

She pauses, a numbness setting in. "He's my brother," she says, voice weak.

"You're doing the right thing, Florence," Sergeant Buckley says, encouraging her. "What's his name?"

"Clancy Campeau." Then a hollowness fills her, and it grows, stretches out into something darker that she can't name, and it brings with it a horrible thought. She has become everything that society expected, everything expected of a half-breed—a down-and-out with nothing to show for herself. There's an odd comfort in that. She doesn't have to run anymore, doesn't have to lie or make up stories.

She sees two blankets folded on the bench when she returns to her cell.

"I couldn't find a pillow," the young officer says.

"How long will I be here?"

"The sergeant wants to hear what Mr. Campeau has to say first."

Florence steps into the cell. "Is there anything to read?" She won't sleep tonight.

The officer hands her a small stack of newspapers—the recent weeklies from Forsyth, Torduvalle, and Verden, and two editions of the *Regina Leader-Post* from earlier in the week. "We turn the lights out at ten, though."

"Any chance you could leave them on? At least for a bit?"

He looks over his shoulder to Corporal Keddie. "I'll ask him to leave them on."

"Are you going?" But he's already walking down the hall to the door.

She finally removes her coat. Slides it off her arms and drapes it over her legs. She props one blanket between her back and the wall for cushioning, and spreads the other over her shoulders like a shawl.

She flips to the back section of the Torduvalle paper first, knowing that it will be there but hoping it might have been missed, forgotten. It's not. *Household items for sale*. Only three days away. Before this she'd be lucky to get a few customers, but now she can't imagine anyone will show. She forces herself to read the articles, focus her mind on something else. Updates from the 4-H Club meeting; local blood donors interviewed and honoured; Mr. Klein the postmaster is experiencing a very busy month and expects it will only get busier as the holiday season approaches.

She drifts in and out of sleep, restless, and after midnight, she hears people arrive and rises from her seat.

"This way," an officer says to someone, "the door on the left."

Florence steps to the bars and looks out. Clancy, handcuffed, is being guided by the officer who gave her the newspapers. Clancy's hair is tousled and coiling in all directions, not slicked back as it usually is. No time when the police are at the door. They enter the room where she was questioned. The officers obviously drove to the Huber farm in the middle of the night. Would've woken Frank and Agnes, who would've been scared, pulling on their robes and seeing officers at the door. Florence had assumed the officers would wait until morning—there was no immediate danger. Clancy doesn't see Florence, and she doesn't call out. It would seem too desperate, even though that's exactly how she feels.

The young officer speaks to Clancy, then steps back out, closes the door behind him. "Sergeant Buckley still here?" he asks Corporal Keddie, who nods.

The young officer gets Buckley, and the two of them head into the room. A flash of Clancy's black hair as the door opens, closes.

"Excuse me," she calls out to Corporal Keddie, who's still at the desk. "I was told I could speak with him first."

"Pardon me?" He swivels in his chair but doesn't approach.

"Sergeant Buckley told me I could speak with Clancy—Mr. Campeau—"

"They'll question him first, ma'am."

"But that's not what he said."

He shrugs as if powerless to do anything about it.

"Please, I need to speak with him." She has to tell Clancy why. He needs to understand.

"You don't call the shots here, lady."

"Just for a minute. That's all."

He watches her a moment, hesitating, then walks to the interview room and knocks on the door. He's inside for several minutes before finally emerging and unlocking her cell.

"Thank you."

"No, ma'am," he says when she heads across the hall to the interview room. "We're releasing you." He picks up some papers from his desk. "And I'll need your signature."

"I need to speak with Clancy."

"You can't do that right now."

"Then I'll wait."

But he ignores her and hands her a pen. "Please read over everything first."

Four pages of notes and forms. The handwriting in the papers is so scrawled and messy it's almost indecipherable. They provide scant details of the reasons for her arrest, but nothing is incorrect and they do reference why they've released her without charges. Once she signs, he gives her back her car keys and she wonders how she'll collect her car. She takes a seat on a wooden bench against the wall, underneath a large clock, its second hand ticking loudly and somehow unevenly.

She asks for another cup of coffee and he begrudgingly brings her one. She'll sip it slowly, keep herself alert, though she's so on edge, the caffeine isn't needed. Before she's halfway done, the door opens and all three men exit.

"Clancy?" Florence says, and rises as the younger officer leads him to the cells in the back. Clancy half turns in her direction, glaring at her, then shakes his head in disgust and steps into the cell.

Florence follows, but Keddie puts his arm up, barring her entry. "The sergeant said I could speak with him," she says.

"It's best if you just leave," he says as the other officer locks Clancy in.

"Just for a second, that's all." Florence steps forward.

"Ma'am," he says, blocking her way.

"But why are you locking him in? Does he know about the deal? Has he been told about the deal?" Her words come out fast, panicked, and she tries to step around Keddie but he grabs hold of her arm.

"Ma'am, stop!" he says, jerking her arm forcefully when she fights his grip.

Florence relents. "I just want a minute with him, that's all," she says, voice quiet this time, pleading.

"He doesn't want to see you," Keddie says, and finally lets go of her arm.

"What?" Florence says.

"Leave, Florence." Clancy's voice from the cell.

It knocks the wind of out her.

Florence steps back, then stumbles to the door. She pushes out into the black night where a layer of slippery frost has settled over everything. This is not how it was supposed to be. What has she done?

PART FOUR

STEMS

NOVEMBER 1946
Torduvalle, Saskatchewan

THE GREYHOUND SMELLS faintly of sweat and mould. It's strangely comforting.

Florence wandered the streets in Forsyth in the cold until the shops opened at nine, refusing to go back to the station to seek warmth. She had enough in her purse for a ticket home and a nickel left over for a cup of coffee, which she nursed until noon, numb and depleted, when the bus departed. It's a long meandering trip back home, with a detour north through Radford, then Verden, then back south through Waterton before the bus pulls into Torduvalle. It's nearly five when she walks into her house and collapses into bed.

On Friday morning, she calls the station and asks to speak with Clancy, but he refuses to talk to her. Tomorrow's the sale. No one will show. She goes to the washroom and reaches for the towel she drapes over her shoulders when using the bleach, but she glances at herself in the mirror. Examines her dark roots. They're glossier than the bleached parts, richer. Thirty-five years ago she started this ritual. It was both ages and a blink ago. But instead of mixing the bleach with water, Florence carries the towel to the living room and cuts a section from it. She doesn't need to go through that process; there's no point. She sorts through her beads, looking for the colours she needs.

She starts with a long line of vertical brown beads on the scrap of blue-

and-white-striped cotton. The material's not sturdy and it's difficult to handle, but even on stronger fabric, straight lines are harder than curves. The eye detects the flaws in a straight line more easily than it does in something round. Maybe it's the sense of motion or flow that a curve suggests that is easier for the eye to absorb. Maybe it's because there doesn't seem to be anything in nature that's perfectly straight. The bark of a tree is rough and pocked. A horizon is always marked with the hump of a hill, a patch of trees, or even a slight slope in a section of land. Florence would bet that the strands of a spider's web have little flits of thickness here and there upon close inspection, just like the thread in her needle. Perfectly straight is just an idea—it's not actually attainable.

Until now, she's never beaded a straight line. The beadwork she was taught was inspired by nature, so there's flow, there's motion. Even the colours sprout, grow. Burst. They fill the eye. But this piece is different: A bottle. Only two shades of brown. One for the bottom, dark and rich, and then halfway up, she switches to a lighter shade, like nutmeg or cinnamon, because the bottle is only half full. The label is the trickiest, a cream rectangle with tangerine print: *Solution of Hydrogen Peroxide, 16 fluid ounces, U.S.P. 3%.*

AT TEN PAST NINE on Saturday morning, her doorbell rings, startling her. Florence opens the door to Mrs. Sanderson and four other women hovering behind her, all of them bundled against the weather and handbags dangling from their arms.

"It is today, isn't it?" Mrs. Sanderson asks when Florence is unable to hide her shock at them on her doorstep.

"Yes, it is . . . Nine thirty to one thirty," Florence says, trying to gather herself.

"You won't mind some early birds, will you?" Mrs. Sanderson is already stepping forward.

"Not at all. Come in," Florence says and makes room for them to enter. They all troop in with demure nods, artificially pleasant smiles.

"My, my." Mrs. Sanderson turns on the spot, a full circle in the living room. "Beautiful items. Which ones are you selling?"

"Everything." Florence apologizes for not having marked the prices but tells them they can pay what they feel is fair for whatever item they want. A quiet unease ripples through the room. No one wants to underpay, but they certainly do not want to overpay. The women begin perusing, murmuring to themselves. Florence steps into the kitchen, cuts up pieces of paper, and folds them into small tented cards. She returns to the living room, circling it and jotting down prices she hopes will be enticing and still bring in a good amount of money.

Mrs. Sanderson points at the delft vase Florence has just priced. "That's a steal."

"I'm keen to sell things quickly," Florence explains.

"Of course you are," Mrs. Sanderson says, meeting Florence's eyes briefly. "It's understandable." Then she picks up the vase, turns it slowly in her hands. "When will you be moving?" she asks, voice light and casual as if she's asking an innocuous question.

Florence steps to the cabinet to price the items on its shelves, refusing to let Mrs. Sanderson or any of the other women see the panic the question instills. The question she's been avoiding asking herself. "Moving?" Florence says, mimicking Mrs. Sanderson's tone.

"I only assumed," she says, tucking the vase under her arm and running a finger over the table it was displayed on. "After all that's happened and . . . well, when we saw the ad, we figured it was the next logical step, didn't we?" She looks to the other women in the room for confirmation and they nod in unison.

Assumed. The word lodges in Florence's mind. But it's the wrong one. Mrs. Sanderson isn't assuming, she's suggesting, and that's the real reason they've come to the sale.

"Maybe I was wrong?" Mrs. Sanderson raises her eyebrows.

"I hadn't thought about it," Florence lies, keeping her anger hidden. "Would you like to buy that?" she asks to change the subject. "I can wrap it up for you."

"On second thought, no," Mrs. Sanderson says, setting the vase back down. "I have so many already."

"How are the twins?" Florence says before she can stop herself. "I assume that now your boys are back in school, they're staying out of trouble?"

A sharp inhale from a woman in the corner while the others fall silent. Mrs. Sanderson watches her a moment, her thoughts unreadable. "They are, yes, and we intend to keep it that way." Another subtle suggestion.

Though Mrs. Sanderson refuses to buy anything herself, her entourage does, and by the time they leave, at nearly ten o'clock, the seascape paintings, the embroidered footstool, the four framed bird illustrations, and the grandmother clock have all been sold. And not long after, the bell rings again. More people coming for morsels of gossip they can chew on. But Florence doesn't care because they buy things too. By eleven, she's had a steady stream of people, and the cabinet, the china and silver serving tray inside it, her doilies, and all her jewellery, including the wedding ring she twisted off her finger and placed alongside the other items, have been purchased.

By noon, she's sold the magazine rack and the floor lamp. The wax flower arrangements that sat atop the side tables have also been purchased, as have cookie jars and various canisters. Two wool rugs. Sheet sets and the patchwork quilt. Embroidered tea towels she was saving for the right time to showcase but that never came out of their paper wrapping. Two ceramic vases. A round mahogany footstool with needlepoint roses. Shortly after one, when everything she priced and more has been sold, the last patrons in the house leave, and Florence locks the door and puts the kettle on for tea.

While waiting for the water to boil, she uses the kitchen chair to reach the topmost shelf in the cupboard above the counter. Reaches in and picks up the milk-glass candy dish. The one she bought for Jennie's Chicken Bones candy. She'd left it up there and didn't put it out with the other items because it was the one piece she wanted to keep. Couldn't put a price on it. But holding it in her hands now, she realizes she doesn't want it. It has another purpose.

Florence turns the stove off, puts on her winter coat, and tucks the dish into the crook of her arm. She goes out her door, down her walkway, takes twelve steps on the sidewalk, then goes up to Jennie's. Rings the doorbell.

It's several moments before the door unlocks. "Hello," Jennie says, opening the door, a look of surprise on her face at seeing Florence. She's a little unkempt. "What do you want?" she asks, but it's more distracted than mean.

"I had a sale today," Florence says.

"Yes, I saw the advertisement in the paper." She wraps her sweater around herself.

"I kept this, though," Florence says, holding out the dish. "I want you to have it."

"For me?" she asks, staring at the dish. Her eyes are tired and a little puffy.

"Yes. Please, take it," Florence says. "It's just a gift I want you to have." She pauses. "I never meant to hurt you." Then the words come out quickly, as if bubbling over. "You might think that our friendship wasn't real because I hid things from you . . . but it was real to me," Florence says. "More real to me than anything else."

Jennie stands there a moment. She opens her mouth to speak but doesn't. Instead, she reaches out for the dish and takes it from Florence.

"I'm sorry for lying to you," Florence says. "I always wanted to live like"—she motions around the neighbourhood—"this. To live in a town like this, and have my own house with my own things. It seemed so much easier than the way I grew up." Florence pauses, looks away.

Jennie doesn't speak but she doesn't close the door either. She's listening, and Florence continues.

"But I couldn't do it without becoming someone else. Half-breeds don't get to live like this."

The words get trapped in the air between them, and neither of them says anything for a moment.

"I didn't know when I first started to . . . lie"—Florence pauses on the word, feeling it, but then pushes on—"that I'd be hurting so many people. Or maybe I did, and I didn't care." Her honesty stings, but there's relief there too. "But I do care now, Jennie, and I'm so sorry."

The two stand there, unsure of what to do next.

Then Jennie nods, and there's a soft look on her face. Florence feels hopeful.

"Could we talk some more?" Florence asks.

Jennie shakes her head. "Not now."

It's then that Florence realizes how quiet the interior of the house is. No sounds of the children laughing or shouting. No sounds of Garth moving from one room to another. No sounds at all coming from inside. "Another time?"

"I don't know..." Jennie trails off.

"Are you okay, Jennie?"

But Jennie steps back inside and closes the door.

They're not those people anymore. Those people who confide in each other.

Florence returns to her house and stands in the hollowed-out space. Takes in the naked walls, the exposed corners of her home. Her whole life, emptied out.

The only place left to sit in the living room is the settee, where Jennie sat that first night she came knocking. The first night they chatted as real friends and not just neighbours. Jennie perched on one end the way the model did in the catalogue that Florence ordered it from.

Jennie didn't refuse to talk more with Florence. Didn't decline outright. But even if Florence does get another chance, she knows their friendship will never be the same. It will be like starting from scratch. Sadness floods in.

Florence grabs her shears from the kitchen, snips out a large section of upholstery from the settee, and carries it to the bedroom along with her beading materials. She selects a few strings of white beads in different shades and finds the jar of icy-pink beads. She begins with the candy dish. The milk glass. First its solid base, then the short stem that blooms up to the bowl like a flower itself.

Jennie had told Florence she wanted to bring something baked—a pie, a sweet loaf—but they'd just returned from her parents' house on the east coast and hadn't yet unpacked, so she simply brought over something she'd purchased during their trip—a bag of Chicken Bones candy. Still, Florence was grateful. It was the first gift she'd received in her new home. The first gift from a neighbour in her new home. She'd held on to that bag of candy for weeks, treasuring it. She didn't even open it until she saw the dish at an estate sale and knew it was the perfect one for the candy. As soon as it arrived, she poured the Chicken Bones into the glass dish, and she allowed herself to eat only one a day.

Hours later, her neck kinked, Florence begins on the short, rectangular candies themselves. She picks up a few pink beads on her needle at once. She hopes that Jennie views the candy dish as a keepsake. A way of remembering what they had. Florence looks down at the replica she's beaded. Her eye holds on a piece of pink candy that's falling from the overflowing dish. The one that's slipping away.

THE SUN IS STARTLINGLY bright against the fresh layers of snow. Florence wipes the water dripping from her eyes. *Woopht, woopht*—the snow lands on the small mound that she's piled up as she shovels her walk. It came down fast and hard during the night, but she waited until everyone was at church before venturing out to clear it. *Woopht.* She tried calling the station again today but the person who answered said they don't allow calls on Sundays and quickly grew annoyed with her. Told her he had important business to attend to and that she should come down and speak with someone else in person tomorrow. Then hung up. *Woopht.*

Her walkway done, she begins on the sidewalk. Her lower back is stiff and painful; she feels as if one sudden move would crack it in half. Still, she heaves up as much snow as she can scoop and tosses it aside, almost enjoying the pain. As if daring her back to break.

"Please don't bother, Florence."

Florence straightens and sees Jennie standing in her open doorway. Not at church today, and even more dishevelled. Must be sick.

"The twins are coming over after lunch and they can shovel it then."

Florence looks down at the path she's cleared. She's gone well past her own house and the edge of her own property. It was the pain she was chasing, not a neighbourly gesture. "You sure?"

"Yes, they'll handle it."

"I'm nearly done," Florence says.

"Just, please—stop!" Her anger startles them both, then Jennie steps back inside and closes the door.

Florence carries the shovel back to her house, leaves it outside the door, then enters, and removes all her winter clothing. The bell rings just as she's taking off her beret.

"I didn't mean that," Jennie says when Florence opens the door.

"That's all right." It comes out too fast and eager.

"I'm just . . ." Jennie shivers with only a sweater thrown over her shoulders. "There's a lot going on right now," she says, a strain in her voice.

"Please come in," Florence says, and drapes a headscarf over the hole in the settee that she'd cut out. "Have a seat." She goes to the kitchen and brings out a chair for herself.

But when she's seated across from Jennie, without even a table between them, without even the tick of her walnut grandmother clock to distract them, Florence is at a loss for words. Doesn't even know where to start. Should she ask what's going on? Does she have a right to? She should let Jennie set the pace. Shouldn't press or pressure.

Florence asks about the latest Eaton's catalogue. About any new recipes Jennie has tried. About what roles her kids will have in the upcoming Christmas pageant. But everything rings hollow. They're both self-conscious and rarely make eye contact. They can't pretend it's like before. The strain between them grows taut.

"I didn't know they would do that," Jennie suddenly bursts out. "Let you go, I mean."

The mood in the room changes as the layers of forced effort peel away.

"I was angry with you," she says. "I was so angry, and I vented to Garth. I told him everything."

"It's okay, Jennie." The words come out automatically but she means them. Even with all that's happened, she's missed this, missed her friend.

"But he said they needed to . . . to protect the company and its clients."

"Protect them." Florence scoffs at the words.

"Is that not true?"

"In their eyes, I suppose," Florence says.

Jennie looks confused. "But didn't you give out confidential information to the people living at that . . . what's it called?"

"It's a road allowance."

"Right."

"That's not really what happened," Florence starts, but she stops herself. "Or it is . . . but I did so only because I thought if I told them about the plans, Clancy and the others would leave Seedy Creek and it would help Pratt's." She pauses, reconsiders. "Or more accurately, because I thought it would help me." The truth satisfies and sears at once.

"I'm not sure I understand it all, but I'm just . . ." Jennie clears her throat. "I'm sorry, Florence. I'm sorry I told Garth and I'm sorry you were let go."

"Thank you." It's their first real moment this visit. They sit with it for a minute.

"It's nearly lunchtime. Can I make you something or do you have to go home for the kids?" Florence asks.

Jennie flinches, just slightly, but Florence catches it. Garth and the kids weren't at home last night when she stopped by, and it would be strange for him to take them to church by himself. "Or are they at the farm again?"

"Garth and I are . . . going through a difficult time." She looks away, pained.

"Oh, Jennie."

"It's been brewing ever since he got back from the war. You know I gave up my job when Mr. Klein came back."

Florence nods.

"At the time, I wanted to find another job, but Garth said no. Put his foot down, and I just went along with that, even though I loved working. Like you." Jennie stops, and Florence waits for her to continue. "Well, last month Mr. Klein decided he's going to retire from his job at the post office after the holidays—that's why I was there that day I saw you." Jennie looks at her, rueful, then continues. "After Mr. Klein and I spoke, the regional manager called me to see if I wanted the position." She pauses. "I said yes without a second thought."

"And Garth didn't want you to?"

Jennie shakes her head. "He told me I had to call them back and rescind my acceptance. He wouldn't listen to me, wouldn't discuss it." She pulls a tissue from the cuff of her blouse and wipes her nose. "But I loved that job. I felt different when I was working there. More me, in a way."

"I'm sorry, Jennie."

"So I didn't call them back to rescind. I thought if Garth just had some time to think about it, he might come around. But when the regional manager called to discuss my start date and Garth answered . . . he was furious. He took the kids to his parents' and told me to think long and hard about what I was going to do next."

"What did he mean by that?" Florence asks, shocked.

"He meant he wants me to choose between the job and my kids, but how do I do that?" Jennie lets out a sob.

"I'm so sorry." Florence reaches out and puts her hand on Jennie's.

"Florence, it's not the same situation as yours at all . . . I know that. But a part of me, a small part of me, understands what it's like to want something for yourself. To want something that others deny you for reasons that don't make sense." She looks Florence in the eye. "I regret how I reacted after I learned about your past. I was thinking about it only from one side . . . and I'm sorry."

Moments pass as Florence digests this and understands that this moment might be the closest she and Jennie will ever be.

"Ugh," Jennie says, dabbing at her eyes with the tissue. "Enough snivelling. I've done too much lately and I'm tired of it."

"Do you know what you're going to do?" Florence asks.

Jennie shakes her head. "I hate being without the kids," she says, "but I need some time to figure things out for myself. You know, life comes at you so fast, and it seems fun and exciting, but you don't really know it's happening until you look back, and then you wonder how you ended up where you are. You know you made certain choices to get here, but they didn't seem like choices at the time . . ." Jennie trails off.

"I know exactly what you mean," Florence says.

She arrived in Torduvalle as Florence Banks, and though that's not her anymore, she's not really a Campeau either. Who is she now? It's a question in everyone's eyes. In her own in front of the mirror. She's stuck between two different identities. Suspended, and there's nothing to grab hold of.

STEERING THE STUDEBAKER ALONG the highway feels like sailing a boat over smooth waters. Fat, plump tires and a fat, spongy seat. Florence barely feels the lumps and bumps in the road. Even the steering wheel is fat, wrapped in soft leather. Everything cushioned. Some lives are like that too, she thinks as she parks Jennie's car in front of Forsyth's police station. Kind of Jennie to lend it and save Florence another lengthy bus trip.

Inside the station, the young officer who gave her materials to read looks up.

"I called this morning, but no one will tell me what's happening with my brother. He was supposed to be let go, but he's still here," she says, pointing to the cells in the back.

The officer looks around as if for help, but he's the only one there. He just shrugs—he's not in the know.

"Can I speak with Sergeant Buckley, please?"

"He's not here."

"Corporal Keddie, then."

"He's not here either."

She swallows her irritation. "Do you know when they'll be back?"

He looks at the clock. "Before lunch or . . . maybe after." He shrugs again.

"Can I please speak with my brother, then?" she asks, voice as nice as she can make it.

The officer hesitates, unsure if he should grant the request, but he gives in and motions for her to step around the counter. "Just for a moment, though," he says as Florence passes him and heads to the back.

Her mouth dries as she approaches the cell. Clancy is lying on the bench on his back, eyes closed. Hands folded across his belly, which expands and contracts with his breath. She steps up to the bars. Waits. His unlaced boots sit side by side on the floor at the end of the bench, and a newspaper rolled into a neat tube sticks out of one of them. Oddly tidy. When he was a boy, he left a trail of damage wherever he went. It annoyed her then, but the tidiness now is worse in a way because it makes the few feet between them feel like miles.

"Clancy," she says, tentative.

"I have nothing to say to you," he says, eyes still closed.

"Why are you still in here?"

He ignores her.

"Haven't you taken the deal?"

He opens his eyes but remains still.

"Didn't you give them names?"

"I don't know what you're talking about." He closes his eyes again, blocking her out.

A spike of panic in her chest. "You don't have to stay in here, and there'll be no charges if you give them some names of those involved—" But she stops because he's laughing.

"Is that what they told you?" he asks when he settles down.

"It's the only reason I told them about you," she says weakly.

"There are two things wrong with that. First, I'm not a rat. Second," he says, turning to look at her, "you're more gullible than I thought if you believed them." He punctuates that with a scornful huff.

"He said . . . Sergeant Buckley said they'd do the same for you . . ." She's trying to absorb what he's saying.

Clancy sits up. Plants his feet on the floor and braces himself on the edge of the bench with his hands. "I can't believe you did this."

"Clancy." Desperation sets in. "They said there'd be no charges," she repeats. "I couldn't afford the fine and—"

"And now I have to go to jail!" He glares at her. "Four months." There's venom in his voice.

"No." Shock through her system. "I'll speak to Sergeant Buckley." Her thoughts scramble for a solution. "If you give me the names, then you haven't ratted." It's puerile, she knows it. And she knows she's been fooled.

"Those aren't the names they want, Florence," Clancy says. "That's not what they're after."

But Florence isn't following.

Clancy rises and steps forward. "The only names they want from me are the names of people involved in the Métis Society and its locals," he explains. "The bootlegging? That annoys them. But us organizing? That threatens them." He pauses. "That's why there's no deal for me and there never was."

Florence shakes her head in disbelief.

"For someone who's lived like one of them for so long," Clancy says, "you know so little."

"But you can't . . . you can't go to jail."

"You should have thought of that before."

"What about Lillian?"

"Don't." His face fills with silent fury, then he turns and paces as if to get away from her. "You don't get to say that to me." He walks to the far side of the cell and smacks the wall in frustration. "Jesus Christ!" He turns back around. "You didn't care about worrying her before, did you? You only cared about yourself and that's why I'm in here now. You're still the same."

"Please, Clancy."

"You have to go tell her," he says, shooting towards her from across the cell. "I'm serious, Florence—you have to go tell Lillian what's happened. You have to tell her I'm going to be locked up for four months. And that it's because of you."

The breath is knocked from her body. Florence looks away, absorbing the weight of what he's said. She opens her mouth, but nothing comes out.

"I wish I'd never seen you that day in August," he says. His voice is lower but his anger is fierce. "I wish it with everything I have in me."

She lets the words wash over her. It shouldn't hurt to hear them—after all, she felt the same way—but it does.

AT SEEDY CREEK, FLORENCE sits in the car a moment, hands still on the wheel, summoning courage. Then she heaves herself out and walks up the uneven pathway to Lillian's. She knocks on the door lightly, too lightly for Lillian to hear. She knocks harder but still gets no response. She steps to the window but can't see anything; the glass is all white and furry with frost. She goes back to the door and raps again. Still nothing.

She presses the latch on the handle with her thumb and pushes in. There's no lock. They didn't have one at the Nest either, their lives exposed and unguarded, as if they were inviting in everything that could harm them. It's vexing, how vulnerable they were, how vulnerable Lillian is now—a sleeping mound on the bed, unaware there's someone else inside her home. Florence could steal her things, break them. Smash her plates and bowls, shred her towels and blankets, tear up her sweaters. Anyone could. But instead she stokes the fire until it sputters and crackles louder than Lillian's rattling lungs. She sets to making a pot of oatmeal. Extra cinnamon and a splash of milk to make it creamier. Two large handfuls of raisins.

When Lillian wakes, she's happy to see Florence and joins her at the table to eat instead of staying in bed. But Florence doesn't have an appetite—her stomach is full of pins and needles—and so she lies, says she ate breakfast already. But Lillian will have none of it and makes her dish up a bowl for herself. Florence forces a few spoonfuls down before her insides rile, threaten to spurt it back out.

"Miitsho, ma fii, miitsho."

"Auntie," she says, "Clancy asked me to come see you." She pushes the bowl away, unable to stand even the smell of it. "He won't be able to come by for a while."

"How long?"

"I don't know. It may be quite some time." Four months. He'll be out in spring, before the thaw and before Seedy Creek is cleared.

"He always comes."

"And he will again . . ." She trails off. "Colleen is still here to help you out, right?"

Lillian nods.

"Is there anything you need now? Anything I can do while I'm here?"

But Lillian ignores her, confused by this information. "The Hubers have been good to him—always give him time off to come visit."

"It's not the farm. That's not why he's not here." Florence falls silent, fear setting in.

"Piikishkwew," Lillian says, her mood changing.

And Florence does tell her. She tells her everything. Lillian nods along at first, listening intently, but she looks away when Florence explains why she gave the cops Clancy's name. "They told me they would let him go. That they'd give him the same deal as me."

Lillian continues to gaze off into nothing, expression blank. Then she hands Florence her empty bowl to wash. "You've lost a lot more than your language."

Florence stares into the hollow of the bowl, lets the words sting. Lillian rises from the table and goes back to the bed. "I thought they were telling me the truth," Florence says. She's been so naïve.

"Kaaya," Lillian says, then switches to English: "No." She reaches under her bed, takes out her bag of rags. "You were always running," she says, pulling out a braid that's already begun.

"Running?"

Lillian folds length over length. "The only time you weren't was when you were beading. Then you could sit still and be. The only time. But without a needle in your hand, you were unsettled and always looking for something else. For a long time, I thought you were dreaming, like kids do. Dreaming of a good life for yourself. But it wasn't that—you weren't running towards something, you were running away." Lillian stops braiding, stares at the strands in her lap. "You were running away because there was a part of yourself you hated. I don't know how it grew there or why, but it was always there, and it still is." She lifts her eyes from her work. "And that part of yourself that you hate, it's the same part that holds Clancy and me."

"Auntie, that's not true." But her words hang in the air between them.

Lillian ties a loose knot at the end of the braid. "I need to rest now." She places the braid on the mattress beside her.

"Auntie..."

She leans back against the pillows. "Shipwayhtay shaymaak."

"I can wait until you wake up."

"No," Lillian says. "Shipwayhtay. I don't think it's good for you to come back."

Words rise up Florence's throat but they catch and tangle. Moments pass but Lillian has rolled away from her.

Florence pulls on her coat and walks out the door, wondering if the reason she always leaves everything behind is so she's never the one to be left.

THE COURTHOUSE IS A squat, two-storey brick building across the street from the detachment, with crumbling front stairs and a portico once painted white but now dirty and chipped. Inside, there's a mildewy smell that tastes like iron in the back of Florence's throat. A guard at the front desk tells her the room she's looking for is on the second floor, and she climbs the narrow stairs and takes a seat in the gallery, which soon fills and raises the temperature in the room. It's not long before Clancy and the other detainees are led in by another guard through a side door, and he takes a seat on a bench along a wall.

Florence watches him, can't take her eyes away. When he glances around the room, she waves, then regrets it when he throws her a resentful look. A door on the other side of the room opens and yet another guard leads in the judge, a tall man with thin, wispy hair that floats around his head like antennae.

Clancy is the fifth defendant called up, and when his name is read, the lawyer assigned to him motions for Clancy to join him at the table before the judge. As Clancy makes his way there, the judge reads through the file in front of him, and Florence straightens in her seat, hesitant. She wants to approach

Clancy's lawyer, but when she stands, the looks she gets from the others seated around her force her back down.

"Mr. Clancy Campeau," the judge says, "do you want the charge read to you again?"

"No, sir," Clancy says, but he's nudged by his lawyer, who then whispers in his ear. "No, Your Honour," Clancy says.

"You waive the reading of the charge?"

"Yes, sir." Another nudge but the judge doesn't wait for Clancy to correct himself.

"Are you ready to enter a plea?" the judge asks.

"Yes, Your Honour."

Florence rises, feeling weak.

The judge looks to Clancy's lawyer for confirmation, and the lawyer nods.

"How do you plead?" the judge asks.

"Guilty."

The judge looks shocked and amused at the same time. "Are you sure?"

Florence steps into the aisle, and murmurs rise.

"Yes, Your Honour," Clancy says.

"You're not going to explain to me why you had to do it, why you didn't have a choice?" The judge slightly cocks his head up from his desk to look at Clancy. "That you were actually a victim in this scenario?"

Clancy shifts on his feet and looks off to the side for a moment as if contemplating. Then he faces the judge straight on. "It wouldn't make a difference if I did."

The judge snaps his head all the way up now, glares at Clancy. Then he turns to Florence, who's slowly approaching. His attention makes her stop in her tracks, and she feels others turning to look at her, but she doesn't dare look back—she'll lose her nerve for sure.

"Your Honour," Clancy's lawyer says, hastily stepping in to do damage control, "my client is remorseful for his part in the crime and wants to put this behind him. You see, Mr. Campeau is having trouble finding his feet after returning from overseas—from fighting abroad—but he genuinely and vehemently regrets the actions that brought him here today and is committed to starting fresh on the right path."

This seems to mollify the judge a bit. "Are you aware of the fine, Mr. Campeau?"

"I am."

Florence starts walking again and when she reaches the front row of the gallery, her legs are so unsteady beneath her, she rocks side to side to keep upright.

"You're aware that it's a two-hundred-dollar fine with sixty days' imprisonment if you default on paying the fine," he says. "And if you cannot pay the fine, it will be four months in jail." He waits for a reaction from Clancy.

"I am, sir, and I'll do the jail time."

"Excuse me," Florence says, but so quietly only those sitting close to her hear.

"Are you sure?" the judge asks Clancy, then looks at Florence, who has raised her hand as if in a classroom. The judge's curiosity about her turns to annoyance. A guard is now crossing the room to intercept her. "Ma'am," the judge says, "please take a seat—we are in session."

"I'm sorry," she says.

Clancy turns and sees her. His expression immediately turns to disgust.

"You can't interrupt our proceedings here." The judge is more than annoyed now.

"I know, my sincere apologies. I don't know the process ... I just wanted to say that Clancy will pay the fine. He doesn't need to do the jail time."

Clancy shakes his head and the lawyer leans into him to speak.

"You will pay his fine?" the judge says, looking back and forth between Florence and Clancy.

"No," Clancy says.

"Did you not discuss this with your client?" the judge asks Clancy's lawyer.

"No. This"—the lawyer motions to Florence—"is new to us."

"I was told I could pay in monthly installments," Florence says to the judge.

"No," Clancy says again, louder this time.

"Enough!" the judge says, angry now. "Who are you?" he asks Florence.

"I'm his sister."

"Mr. Campeau," the judge says, "your sister here is volunteering to pay your fine, which seems a wise and generous offer." He stops when Clancy scoffs at this, then continues. "Do you not think so?" But it's more of a warning than a question. "Well, however you two work this out, let me inform you, sister of Clancy Campeau, that this is not the process—the charges are laid out here in the courtroom, and the fines are handled downstairs. This disruption was not needed. However, given Mr. Campeau's sensible plea, which has sped things up a bit, I'm happy to overlook this interference. So," he says, snapping the file closed, "no hearing date will be required and we are done here." He waves to the lawyer, indicating that Clancy may go.

The lawyer speaks to Clancy as another guard arrives to guide him away.

"Wait." Florence takes a step forward, and the other guard who is watching her moves to block her. "Isn't he free now?"

The lawyer turns to her. "Not yet. Wait in the administrative office down on the first floor. As soon as I'm done here, I'll talk to Clancy and make sure he accepts the money."

Florence waits over two hours before a clerk calls her to the counter and asks her to sign a series of papers and hand over the first twenty-dollar installment. Once the paperwork is stamped, she's directed to another room, where she waits nearly another hour before Clancy is finally released. But he walks right by her without acknowledging her and goes straight out the front doors. Florence follows.

"My car's over this way," she says as he heads in the opposite direction.

"I'll walk," he says over his shoulder.

"Where? To Seedy Creek?" Florence starts after him. "That's ten miles away and it's freezing."

He stops and looks at her dead-on. "I can handle the cold and the walk. I can't handle being around you." Then he turns and stalks down the street.

"Clancy!"

But he doesn't stop. Florence strides to her car and follows him, driving slowly. She trails behind, not knowing what else to do.

As she nears, he turns and sees her. He bends and picks up a stone. "Just leave me alone!" he shouts, and rips the stone towards her car. It doesn't hit it—it wasn't meant to—but the message is clear.

Florence finally lets him go and turns off down another street. She doesn't feel any of the relief she was hoping for now that he's released. When she returns to Torduvalle, the sky has grown dark with black, heavy clouds. So dark it feels like night, and she turns the headlights on as she drives through the town's streets. Some houses have their interior lights on and glow from the inside, adding a kind of sorrow to the day that Florence can't explain.

She pulls the Studebaker into Jennie's driveway and drags herself out of the car to the front door, her body deadened and weak. It takes effort to press the doorbell.

"Oh, my," Jennie says when she answers the door. "What's happened?" She holds the door open, inviting her in.

Florence steps inside, takes a seat in the living room, and tells her everything. She tells her about Clancy and that she's the reason he was arrested. She's honest and tells her that he was only trying to help her make money for her mortgage, and she repaid his kindness by turning him in.

Jennie watches and listens, listens without judgement. She doesn't react in shock and doesn't jump in with questions, just lets Florence get it all out. "I'm sorry," she says at the end.

"Not as sorry as I am," Florence says. Neither of them speaks for a long time, both lost in their own thoughts.

"I should go," Florence finally says, breaking the silence.

"What are you going to do now?" Jennie asks.

"I'm not sure." Next month's mortgage payment is due on Monday. Two defaults in a row, and the bank can begin the foreclosure process at their discretion anytime after that.

"Is there anything I can do?"

Florence shakes her head. "Thank you, though." She rises from her seat and goes to the door.

"One moment," Jennie says. She disappears into the kitchen and then joins Florence at the door. "I went to the post office today to sign my papers and saw your mail was piling up." She hands Florence a small stack of mail. "I hope you don't mind I picked it up for you."

"Not at all. I just haven't been able to get there." It did cross her mind, but she knew it would only be more bills and notices. She pushes them into her purse. "Wait. You signed some papers?"

Jennie nods. "I start full-time next week. Just in time for the Christmas rush." She tries to hold back a smile.

"Does this mean . . . you and Garth are . . ." Florence doesn't know how to finish.

"Maybe . . . I don't know. I still hope, but . . ." She shakes her head and shrugs.

"Well, congratulations on the job," Florence says. "I know it's what you wanted and I'm happy for you." And she is, despite the trajectory of her own life.

"Thank you. Call me if you need anything," Jennie says as Florence exits.

At home, Florence drops the mail on the kitchen table, and an envelope's return address catches her eye. The provincial secretary's office. She opens it and pulls out the Hawkers and Pedlars licence she applied for. Her number is typed at the top righthand corner: 1272. Bizarrely, it makes her laugh, though it's not funny. She doesn't need the licence, never did. Knew it first thing when the officer told her. But still, she jumped through the hoop because she was told to. It's what she's done her whole life, one meaningless hoop after another.

She puts the licence aside as her stomach cramps. She can't remember the last time she ate. Food would probably make her feel better, but as hungry as she is, it's not what she wants. She reaches for her beading materials instead. Selects two shades of grey, slate and gossamer, the lighter for the metal coin purse, and the darker for the finely etched flowers. Then she finds some milky-white beads and begins with the mother-of-pearl oval that was inlaid in its centre. Her first purchase when she was pretending she wasn't a half-breed, when she thought her life would amount to something more than it has.

"CAN I SPEAK WITH Mr. Hicks, please?" Florence asks when Mary Beth Watkins answers the phone.

"I'm sorry, he's not in," Mary Beth says. "Can I take a message?"

"When do you expect him back?"

"I'm not sure, I'd have to check with the senior secretary. She looks after his calendar. If you leave your name and number, I can call you right back."

Senior secretary—of course. Florence shouldn't be surprised but it still catches her off guard. "Is that Shirley Owens?"

"Yes, may I ask who's calling?"

"Mary Beth, it's Florence."

"Oh . . ." Mary Beth clearly doesn't know what to say next.

"Can you patch me through to Shirley?"

"One moment."

Florence imagines Shirley up on the second floor at the desk that Florence picked herself from the catalogue, her Remington Rand centred on its top. She should feel slighted. Hurt. But maybe it's the lack of sleep or the lack of a decent meal, or maybe it's something else, but she doesn't. Instead, Florence thinks about the typewriter and how she might be able to bead it. The challenge of it is compelling.

"Flossie?" Shirley says.

"Yes, it's me." Florence can't help but smile at Shirley's informal ways, but she feels a pang too.

"What can I do for you?"

"I'd like to make an appointment to speak with Mr. Hicks about putting my house up for sale." There's nothing else she can do. If she sells it herself now, that might prevent a foreclosure and she could avoid that on her records. It's something, at least. And she could also use some of the money from the sale to cover Clancy's remaining fine payments. "I know the juniors are capable of handling this, but Mr. Hicks has connections, and I would like to do this fairly quickly."

"Of course," Shirley says. "He's in the city now but I can fit you in next week."

"Thank you." Florence hears Shirley writing through the line.

"I've got you in for Tuesday at nine a.m."

"Thank you."

"Wait," Shirley says, but there's only silence on the other end. "So you're going to move too?"

"I suppose. I don't know. I'm just taking one step at a time. Sell first, then figure out what comes next."

"You're not going with them?"

"With who?"

"Your . . . family," Shirley says.

"What do you mean?" A twinge in Florence's gut.

"Don't you know?" Shirley's voice is faint.

"Know what?" Florence says, unable to hide the fear that's rising. "Shirley?"

"The government is moving them all to a farming settlement up north."

"I know, but not until the spring."

"No," Shirley says, "they've changed the timing. Because they were worried . . ."

"Worried about what?"

"They were worried about the people there organizing, and with"—she pauses—"with the bootlegging, some people were putting pressure on the mayor and the government. I think they've already been given notice."

"What? What did the notice say? When is this happening?"

"I don't know, give me a moment."

Florence hears Shirley set the phone down, then the sound of papers being shuffled.

"There are some notes from Jeremy here from a telephone call." Shirley pauses to read it. "It says they were told they could vacate voluntarily or be moved by the government. There are no dates here, but it says they were given a week."

"But when was notice given?"

"I don't know, it doesn't say." All the rustling stops. "But I thought it was last week. I thought that's what I heard Jeremy say."

"Thank you, Shirley," Florence says, then immediately hangs up and calls the Huber farm—the only place with a phone that she thinks Clancy would be. Mrs. Huber answers.

"It's Florence," she says, "is Clancy there?"

"I'm sorry, he's not."

"Could I leave him an urgent message?"

"You can but I don't know if he'll be back. We haven't seen him since he was taken . . ." she says, stopping there. "But I can speak with Frank when he returns this evening."

"That may be too late, but thank you," she says.

"You're welcome."

Florence hangs up and grabs her coat, handbag, and scarf. Heads straight to Jennie's. "Can I borrow your car again?" she asks without a greeting when Jennie answers the door.

"Of course. What's going on?"

"I have to go to see my aunt, and it's urgent."

"Your aunt? Near . . . Forsyth?"

"That's right," Florence says.

Jennie grabs her car keys, then gathers her own things. "I'll drive and you can explain on the way."

"You don't need—"

But Jennie steps out the door and looks Florence in the eye. "No offence, but you look awful, like you haven't been sleeping well. And besides, I could use the company myself."

A moment passes. "I would appreciate that."

They're both quiet in the car on the drive. Jennie turns the radio on low and they listen to crooning country music. Florence stares out the side window, at the line that divides field and sky.

It's not until they near the turnoff for Seedy Creek that Florence sits up, alert. "This is it," she says. Police cars are parked at the exit, blocking it, so Jennie has to park hers behind them.

Jennie looks up the road, apprehensive. "What's going on?"

"It's happening now."

Up the path and near the shacks, there are more police cars and farm trucks for transporting equipment, hay, and animals.

"What is?" Jennie asks. "What's happening now?"

"They're clearing them out. Moving them to a government-run farm up north."

"Are you sure?" Jennie's brow furrows, a mix of concern and confusion.

"That's what the trucks are for," Florence says.

Jennie lets out a little laugh in disbelief. "It's the middle of winter." But she sees that Florence is serious.

"I need to find my aunt and my brother," Florence says, climbing out. Jennie gets out too.

Doors to the shacks are propped open, and men and women carry out trunks and luggage, pack it into their wagons. Some kids help, carrying their own bags and boxes of things. It's oddly quiet despite the commotion. One child stands alone on a path between shacks, a wool blanket around her shoulders, her face blank. While the residents hastily pack, men in suits stand and watch, monitor it all from a distance.

"If you don't have your own transportation," a government official yells while striding along the path, "we can take you in our trucks, but you must pack lightly. Essentials only!" He turns on his heel as if shouting at a battalion. "One trunk per family! One trunk only!"

"Excuse me." An officer approaches Florence as she heads towards the shacks. "Can I help you?" But his manner is brusque, not helpful at all.

"I'm looking for my family."

"We're in the middle of . . . an operation."

"I just need to find them—"

"I'm sorry but I can't let you pass." He holds up his arm to stop her. Near the end of the line of houses, Sergeant Buckley and Corporal Keddie are speaking with some residents. Corporal Keddie notices Florence but quickly looks away.

"I need to find my aunt." Florence tries to swerve around the officer, but he blocks her.

"Ma'am!"

"I'm sorry, Officer," Jennie says as she follows behind Florence but more slowly. "We won't be long." She watches her footing in the blanket of snow that covers the lumps and bumps in the road. The belt of her wool wrap coat is cinched tight around her waist, her leather gloves shiny in the dull day. Her crisp, clean lines are incongruous with the surroundings. "Two minutes. That's all we need." Then Jennie throws him a smile, both pleasant and flirty. The type of smile Florence is familiar with, having used it often herself.

The officer watches Jennie a moment, as if trying to understand her presence here. "Be quick," he says finally, and steps to the side.

Florence heads up the path to Lillian's home, Jennie following close behind her, their bodies almost touching. The wail of a child erupts from a shack. A boy bursts out the door clutching a stuffed lion.

"There's no room," his father says, following him out the door. But the boy races around the shack, then into the trees behind it. Disappears in the branches. The father watches him run off, arms hanging at his sides, helpless.

"Let's move quick, people," an official yells. "The train won't wait for you!"

Florence hurries to Lillian's shack. Neither Lillian nor Clancy are there. Two officers rummage through her storage boxes and shelves, and her blankets have been torn from the bed and are now in a pile on the floor. Beside it, her mattress is folded like a clamshell. The door of the stove is open, but it emits only a thin trickle of smoke, the fire long gone out.

"What are you doing?" Florence asks. "Are you taking her things?"

"No, ma'am." But they both look like boys caught in the schoolhouse after hours.

"You have no right to be in here."

"This is actually an illegal construction on government property—"

"This is her home," Florence says, stepping forward and taking the bag of braided rags from the hands of the closer officer. "Get out!"

"We're under orders to search each and every structure here."

"Search for what? You're already forcing them out."

"We're looking for dangerous goods, ma'am." The two men continue their work.

"You know who lives here? A woman in her eighties with bad hearing and infected lungs. What kind of dangerous goods do you think you'll find?"

"Ma'am," the taller officer says, stepping forward. "Please vacate the premises. Now." He towers over her, waiting.

"Florence," Jennie says, placing a hand on her elbow. "She's not here."

Florence stares at the man, at the pimples speckled on his nose and cheeks, the steely glint in his eye. She lets the bag drop to the floor and leaves, closing the door behind her as if to lock the men in.

"You okay?" Jennie asks.

Next door, Hank is exiting his shack, half carrying, half dragging a suitcase and using a branch as a cane to keep his balance.

Florence rushes over, Jennie following, and takes the case from him. "Have you seen Lillian or Clancy?"

"Colleen helped Lillian pack up earlier. Norris is up there," he says, then points with his lips. "Clancy went south."

"South? Where?"

Hank shrugs. "He left after supper last night. Went looking for work but that's all I know."

"How come you haven't gone to your sister's in BC?" Florence asks.

"No one from here was headed that way, and I had no money for a ride myself. Have to take the ride that comes along."

"Can you help him?" Florence asks Jennie, who takes the case from her.

"Joke's on them, though," Hank says. "Can barely peel a potato, never mind drive a plow."

Jennie holds out her free arm for Hank.

"Bureaucrats can't do anything right." He laughs, taking Jennie's arm.

Back on the main path, Florence weaves through families carrying their possessions to the wagons. Their faces look heavy, burdened. They pack their belongings in the trucks and in their own wagons, speaking only when the authorities are out of earshot. Near the very end of the line, the McKays load their own wagon, now almost full.

"Marguerite." Florence rushes up, breath jagged. "Is Lillian with you?"

Marguerite passes an apple box up to Norris, who's cramming items into the wagon, filling every small opening.

"She is."

"Where?" Florence walks to the head of the wagon but the driver's bench is empty.

"With Colleen," Marguerite says.

"Don't think she wants to speak with you, though," Norris says while securing a box.

"I know. I just need to see her for a moment." Neither one responds. "Where'd Colleen take her?"

"Hurry up, folks! You should have been packed already!" The officer blows a whistle, as if that will speed them up.

"Please," Florence says to Marguerite.

"They're going in the government truck," Marguerite says. "Much faster than the horses."

Florence heads back to the other end of the path, maneuvering around people, a rocking chair, kids on a trunk, a table. When she reaches the truck, Hank's first in line to climb in, Jennie beside him still holding his case, a fretful look on her face. As they wait, an officer removes jerry cans from the bed of the truck to make more room for the residents and their belongings. He sets the cans to the side, then turns to Hank and helps him in, seating him beside the Petit family, all six of them, who are already squished in tight. A young couple, the woman pregnant, sit with their toddler near the Petits. And next to them are Colleen and Lillian, a plaid blanket over both their laps.

"Lillian!" Florence calls. "Lillian!" she says again, even louder.

Colleen nudges Lillian and speaks in her ear. Lillian nods but doesn't move.

Florence scrambles to climb into the truck and Jennie helps, pushing her up by the waist.

"Is there a problem, ma'am?" the officer says, turning around to get off the truck. He's older than the others, but not by much.

But Florence ignores him and steps around him, apologizing to the people seated as she squeezes by.

Florence squats down in front of Lillian. "Does Clancy know this is happening?"

Lillian shakes her head.

"Do you know where he went last night?"

She nods.

"Then if you come with me, we can call him. Let him know what's happening."

"Leave him be. You've done enough," she says, accusatory.

Florence feels the sting. "Do you want to go to this farm up north?"

Lillian nods.

"I thought you wanted to go to Winnipeg. To your cousin's. With Clancy. That's what the two of you were planning."

"Clancy has fines to pay," Lillian says, pulling the blanket up higher. "He can't move now."

"I'll help with the fines, and you can stay with me until he is able to move."

Lillian considers this, and Colleen turns to her, waiting to see how she responds.

But Lillian shakes her head. "I don't want to live with you. Not now."

Florence's stomach wrenches—she's done too much damage.

"You don't have to stay with me forever, Auntie," Florence says. "Just until he's ready to move."

"Auntie," Colleen says softly, and she leans towards Lillian and speaks in Michif.

"Truck's full. We're leaving soon," the officer says to Florence. "If they don't make today's train, they'll have to wait at the station two days for the next."

"Yes, sir," Florence says but continues to plead with Lillian. She puts a hand on her knee. "Please. Don't you think Clancy would want that?"

A moment, as Lillian considers this, then she nods. "Kiiyaam," Lillian says, and she starts to rise.

Florence helps her up and off the back of the truck, where Jennie's been waiting. Before Florence steps out, Hank taps her leg, throws her a nod of approval.

"Hi, Lillian, I'm Jennie, a friend of Florence's," Jennie says, and she puts an arm around Lillian's waist and leads her to the Studebaker.

"I'll get her things," Colleen says, hopping up.

"That's it," the officer says, clearly annoyed. "No more to-ing and fro-ing. We're heading out."

"I have a ride," Colleen says to the officer, who shakes his head but lets her off before closing the gate on the truck bed.

From their wagon, Norris and Marguerite dig out a trunk and a suitcase and hand them to Florence and Jennie. Marguerite gives Lillian a kiss on the cheek. Tells her she's always welcome to join them up north. "You let us know and we'll find a way to get you there," Marguerite says to Florence. "Let Clancy know as well."

"Taapway," Lillian says, squeezing Marguerite's and then Norris's hands. She pulls Colleen into a hug and speaks in her ear before stepping away.

Florence and Jennie each take a handle of the trunk, and Florence hooks her free arm through Lillian's. Jennie carries the suitcase, and the three make a slow procession back down the path to the highway. The trucks that are leaving honk at them, forcing the three of them to step to the side and into a bank of snow. Just before they reach the car, an acrid, harsh smell fills Florence's nose and stings her throat.

"La bookaan," Lillian says, stopping.

"Is that smoke?" Jennie asks, looking back.

Florence and Jennie set down the luggage and all of them turn around.

Dark plumes rise up from the site of Seedy Creek. Florence's mind flashes back to the jerry cans stacked by the side of the truck. They weren't pulled out to make room for passengers.

The three of them stand together, arms linked, and watch thick black columns of smoke snake to the sky. Below the smoke are eight fires, one for each shack, red flames lashing the air.

"Those were homes," Jennie says as she watches, growing pale.

Lillian faces the site of Seedy Creek, eyes squinting to focus. "Lii jhyaabs."

"Why burn it all?" Jennie says. "There were still things left behind that could have been collected."

"So they don't come back," Florence says.

Jennie falls silent as she takes this in.

Lillian's the first to turn and head to the car, hands bunched into fists the whole way. Florence follows and helps her in, but when she gets into the passenger side in front, Lillian pulls a handkerchief from her pocket and hiccups quiet sobs into it. Florence gets out and joins her in the back, sits close to her, sides touching, while Jennie chauffeurs them home.

WHEN THEY GET BACK to Florence's, Florence tracks down the phone number for the poultry plant where Lillian said Clancy went to find work, but the man who answers says he can't interrupt the men when they're on the factory floor and will pass the message on to Clancy when he's done with his shift. Florence warms some soup and makes biscuits, and the three of them eat over their laps in the living room, Lillian on the settee and Florence and Jennie on two kitchen chairs that Florence carried in. They eat in silence. After the meal, Florence makes them tea, extra sweet, and the three of them drink in silence too—no one knows what to say.

Nearly an hour after Florence left the message, Clancy calls back.

"She's safe" is the first thing Florence says. "Lillian's safe here with me." Then she tells him everything that happened.

There's a long, quiet moment. "I shouldn't be shocked," he finally says, his voice low but full of rage too. "I shouldn't, but how can they sleep at night treating people like that?" He lets out a slow, uneven sigh, the air catching in his throat as he fights emotions.

"She's okay, Clancy," she says. "Would you like to speak with her?"

He responds with a weak yes.

Florence steps to the doorway of the kitchen and sees that Jennie is already helping Lillian up.

"Taanishi," Lillian says into the phone when Florence hands it to her, then Florence heads back to the living room with Jennie to let them speak.

When Florence sits down again, the sky is darkening outside. She reaches over to the only remaining lamp in the living room and switches it on. The day is done and gone. Over. She's suddenly overcome with a sense of finality, like something more than just the day has ended. It moves her to tears.

"Florence?" Jennie asks when Florence wipes her cheek.

But Florence only shakes her head because she doesn't have the words to explain. Jennie tugs her chair closer and puts a hand on Florence's knee. The tears come faster.

By the time Lillian finishes speaking with Clancy, Florence has settled down. She returns to the phone.

"I can't talk much longer . . . Christ!" he says, frustrated. "I just got here! I lucked out landing this job—someone fell ill and they were desperate. It's good money too." He pauses, thinking. "But I've got no choice. I'll let them know, then find a way to get to your place to get her."

"And then what?" Florence asks, calm now after her release.

"Hitch to Winnipeg, I guess," he says. "What choice do I have?"

"Why don't you stay there longer?" she says before her thoughts have solidified. "Lillian can stay here with me and you can save up some money."

There's a long pause. "Can you do that?"

"They haven't started the foreclosure process yet, and even if they do, I'll have a month before they can evict me. I'm going to try and sell it before that can happen, though. Regardless, I'll have a few weeks left here so you can stay there and work. If you want." She waits as he ponders this.

"Maybe," he says, noncommittal, as if there might be a better idea.

Through the line, Florence hears a voice in the background, then a muffled sound as Clancy turns away from the phone and responds.

"I have to go, but let me think about this," he says. "I have Sunday off so I'll try to find a way there and we can talk."

He hangs up before Florence can say goodbye. She places the handset back in its cradle and returns to the living room.

"It's getting late," Jennie says. "Is there anything I can do before I go?"

"No, you've done so much today already." Florence follows her to the door.

Jennie slides her feet back into her boots, then turns to Florence and asks, her voice low, "Are you going to be okay?"

Florence nods and stifles a yawn at the same time.

"What happens next?" Jennie pulls on her coat and begins to button it.

"Clancy's coming on the weekend. We'll talk about how he and Lillian can get to Winnipeg," Florence says. "He has a friend there who can help set them up."

"And you?" Jennie asks, a look of genuine concern on her face.

"Maybe I'll hitch to Winnipeg too." She shrugs. "I don't know."

Jennie's look turns to one of worry.

"I'll figure something out," Florence says with more confidence than she feels. Another yawn surfaces and she can't hold this one in. "But after I have a good night's rest."

"It's been a big day," Jennie says, opening the door. "I'm just a call or a few steps away if you need anything else," she says.

"Thank you," Florence says and closes the door behind her. When she turns around, she sees Lillian is also fighting to stay awake. "Let's go to bed, Auntie."

She leads Lillian down the hall to the bedroom where Jennie placed the trunk earlier. It's on the floor in the corner and Lillian searches through it for her nightgown while Florence changes into her own. Because the bed is higher than what Lillian slept in before, Florence helps her climb in. As she walks back around to climb in herself, she sees that the lid of Lillian's trunk is still open and inside, poking out from under a sweater, is a corner of the black stroud tea cozy, the double line of white stems with mouse tracks along their length. Of all the things in the shack, things more useful or practical, Lillian packed the cozy Florence made her.

A small swell beneath Florence's ribs. She waits a moment before getting into bed.

"Good night, Auntie," she says, and turns off the light.

"Boon swayrii, ma fii."

Then, when the room is dark and it's just the sound of the two of them breathing, another phrase returns to Florence: Ni miyeuytayn. She whispers it.

"Kaykway?" Lillian asks, lifting her head from the pillow to hear better.

"I'm happy," Florence says. "I'm happy you're here—that you came home with me."

Lillian puts her head back down and closes her eyes. A moment passes. "Niishta," she says.

Florence expects to sleep lightly, given all the years she's been sleeping alone. She expects to be easily roused with someone else's breathing next to her, with the undulating of the mattress as Lillian turns over in bed, the different smells. But she sleeps soundly, deeply. Not waking once through the night. It's not until the sun starts to rise at eight thirty the next day that Florence finally stirs. Lillian is still snoring beside her, so she's careful not to jostle the bed as she climbs out.

As Florence stands over the kettle waiting for it to boil, her mind whirrs over all that's happened and that's about to happen. With the house, with her life. She's in a weird limbo, not here and not yet there. The pressure to fit the mould she created for herself and the mould that everyone else expected of her is gone. When the tea is ready, she carries it to the living room and sinks onto the settee. She has no idea what she's going to do, even who she's going to become. It should worry her, but it's freeing, in a way. She decides to approach this next part of her life the way she does her beadwork—she'll let instinct guide her.

The idea moves her to reach for the toolbox of materials on the floor. She slides it closer and lifts the lid. Black beads for the frame. Grey for the roller and the carriage return and also for the space bar because her thumbs wore the shine off the black paint. Red and black for the ribbon, and forty-four white beads and three red beads for the keys. This one feels more complicated than the others, and she hesitates before putting the needle through the hide for the first stitch. But she reminds herself that she's already beaded straight lines on the peroxide bottle, and with a few adjustments, she can bead the roller just like the lines on the honeybee's back. Besides, if it doesn't work, she can simply cut the threads and start again, because knowing what doesn't work is helpful too. Another lesson she forgot.

She works slowly through the morning, both a catharsis and a yearning taking hold as she beads the very thing that was, in its own way, a replacement for beading. While it's satisfying to pick up each bead, to tack them down, the beads don't clack and there is no margin bell. She wonders if she'll ever work in an office again.

It's nearly noon when she hears Lillian stir down the hall.

"You slept through breakfast, but I can make us some lunch," Florence says when she steps into the bedroom.

"This bed is like a cloud," Lillian says, patting the mattress. "Wrapped itself around me and wouldn't let go."

"Or maybe Clancy's right," Florence says, stepping forward to assist Lillian as she climbs out, "and you've just become lazy?"

"Mooshchipiikishkwayhk," Lillian says and swats Florence away when she's on her feet. But when she moves off towards the washroom, Florence catches her smiling.

Florence turns the radio on for Lillian in the living room, then heats up some canned beans and toast for lunch in the kitchen.

"It's nothing special—" Florence says when she returns and hands her a bowl, but Lillian shushes her.

"Can you turn it up?"

Florence adjusts the volume. It's a daytime soap, one that Florence has never listened to because she's always been at work. It's about a widowed female attorney who's fighting corruption while raising her young son. It draws them both in and they listen to all four of the fifteen-minute episodes the station runs in a row. The next program is a recording of a light concert-music program and Florence gets up and lowers the volume. When she sits back down, Lillian is holding out a single black bead.

"Have you been beading some more?"

A sudden nervousness bubbles up in Florence, like she's a child again and she's just been caught doing something she shouldn't. It's a silly reaction and she laughs it off, but the laugh is forced and awkward. "Sort of," she says.

"Taanishi maaka?" Lillian asks.

"I'm not really sure." She shouldn't feel so uneasy, there's no reason to, but she's almost shaky. "I'll show you." Florence pulls out the piece she started that morning and hands it to Lillian. "It's a typewriter. Or at least, that's what I'm hoping it will be when I'm done."

Lillian brings it up to her face, then feels the beads with her fingers. Florence has completed the rows of keys in the centre and a boxy outline surrounding them for the frame. She planned to work on the roller and the carriage return next but she's embarrassed to continue now that Lillian's looking at it.

"It's not traditional," Florence says, apologetic.

"Kaykway ooshchi?"

"I'm not sure I can explain, Auntie." It's true, but Lillian waits for an answer anyway. "Typing wasn't just something I excelled at and loved to do. It was something deeper than that." She pauses, then pushes past the moment. "But . . . it's silly, really."

"It's not silly if it means something to you." Lillian passes it back to her. "And if you're beading from here," Lillian says, tapping on her chest, "that's traditional."

Florence clasps the beaded typewriter in her hands, holding it tight as something in her releases. "I have more too. Can I show you?"

"Wii kaa kaashkihtaan."

Florence gathers the pieces, which are all wrapped up together in a length of cloth. She shows her the coin purse and tells her about Hollinger's and what happened there the first time she went in. She tells her about her first time passing and why she bought the metal coin purse. She shows her the honeybee and tells her about all the lies she told Clancy. All the lies that led to the moment at the Aylesbury café and the slice of Swiss roll and what it meant to her at the time, what it means to her now. She tells her about bleaching her hair at the boarding house in Regina and her various positions as a maid. About putting herself through secretarial school while still working, then about her interview at Pratt's and her move to Torduvalle. About Jennie and how, despite Florence having lied to her too, Jennie was the closest thing she had to family. Until now.

Florence lets everything out and Lillian listens to it all. To all the moments that brought Florence joy and the difficult and ugly moments that Florence is ashamed of. When Florence is done, she looks away, awaiting Lillian's response. She expects judgement, admonishment, but Lillian is quiet for a long time before she finally speaks. "Maarsii, ma fii," she says. "Kishchi maarsii."

OVER THE NEXT COUPLE days, the two of them find a comfortable rhythm together. Lillian continues to sleep through much of the morning and rises for lunch, when they listen to more radio dramas. When the programs are over, Florence reads aloud, first from *Murder on the Orient Express*, then from *Rebecca* when Lillian requests another mystery. In between, they reminisce and mindlessly chatter or simply sit quietly in each other's company as if they had never been separated. In the mornings, when Florence is alone, she beads. She finishes the tricky typewriter; then, when she doesn't feel compelled to begin another piece from her past, she beads something for Clancy.

Using the last of the hide, she fashions a roll-up pouch like the toiletry kits the men used when overseas, but this one is much smaller and intended for his pipe, matches, and tobacco. On the front, she beads a prairie crocus. A hardy flower that grows close to the ground, so close it's easy to miss. It's the first to bloom after winter, often before the snow is even gone, and it withstands the cold winds and nighttime frosts because of its deep roots and the woolly-white hairs that cover it like a coat, protecting it. A prairie crocus for Clancy. For his strength and resilience. The purple petals are soft and subtle and surround a centre that's a faint yellow, the shade of shortbread. Dusty grey-green beads for its leaves, with a cotton-white-coloured bead here and there for strands of its hair. Everything about it is muted, subdued, completely belying its strength.

She finishes it on Saturday afternoon, and late that evening when it's nearly time for bed, a car parks on the street outside the house and footsteps crunch on the walkway. Florence opens the door for Clancy before he knocks.

"Auntie," he says as soon as he enters and goes straight to her without removing his coat or boots. He helps her up from the settee when she opens her arms for an embrace.

"Ma niveu," she says.

Florence remains near the door for a moment, giving them some space.

"Are you okay?" Clancy asks when she finally releases him.

"Wii, ni miyaayaan." Lillian settles back onto the settee while Florence switches off the radio program they were listening to.

"I was worried about you," he says, unbuttoning his jacket.

Lillian shakes her head—he didn't need to. "Florence has been taking care of me. Taanishi kiiya?" she asks him.

"Si kwaarayk," he says. "Better now." He removes his jacket, and Florence steps forward to take it from him.

Clancy finally notices all the things missing from her home, the sparseness of it, and clearly pieces it together but doesn't say anything, just throws Florence an understanding look.

"You borrowed a car?" Florence asks after hanging up his jacket in the closet.

He nods.

"Did you eat supper?" Florence asks.

He shakes his head. "Came straight from work and only stopped once for gas, but it's late now."

"It's no trouble." Florence moves into the kitchen. As she warms some soup on the stove and butters some crackers, Lillian's and Clancy's voices drift in from the living room. They talk about his arrest and about the monthly fine payments he needs to make. There's a long silence at one point, and when they start talking again, they speak in Michif, then there's another long silence. It's broken when Clancy finally says, "I know she does."

The conversation is over, then, and Lillian tells him to turn the radio back on. A piano recital airs, the music contemplative and heartfelt without being melancholic.

While Clancy eats, Florence sets up the camping cot that Jennie brought over that morning in case it was needed and places some blankets from the hall closet on it. Then, because no one seems ready for bed despite the late hour, she makes another pot of sweet tea.

"Auntie thinks I should forgive you," Clancy says when Florence hands him a cup.

A small bubble of gratitude for Lillian blooms inside Florence.

"But I'm still pretty mad," Clancy says, though not angrily.

"Well, you never listened to her before," Florence says, "you don't need to start now."

Lillian laughs, and Clancy, caught off guard, smiles too. The mood in the room lightens.

"I find it interesting, though, that you've forgiven her so quickly, Auntie," Clancy says to Lillian. "You still haven't forgiven me for eating all your berries when I was seven."

"I remember that," Florence says. "She beat you with her broom."

"Beat him good," Lillian says, nodding. "Deserved it too."

"But you didn't need to," Clancy says. "I had cramps for days after gorging myself, that was punishment enough."

"Wasn't just cramps either," Florence says, teasing.

Clancy hangs his head in shame but laughs too.

The three of them stay up late into the night, losing track of time and not caring about it.

∞

"WHAT'S THIS?" CLANCY ASKS the next morning when Florence hands him the roll-up pouch. He sits up on the cot.

"It's for your pipe."

He holds it a long time before he undoes the wooden button she sewed on as a clasp and looks at the pockets inside. He takes his pipe from his shirt pocket and tucks it in the pouch, rolls it back up. "It's a perfect fit." He continues to stare at the beadwork.

"It's a crocus." But she doesn't tell him why she chose that flower for him. She'll wait until he asks, if he does.

"Did Auntie ask you to make this for me?"

Florence shakes her head.

"When we were kids, she always said you were one of the best beaders she ever knew, but I didn't believe her—you were so young and I thought she was exaggerating because you were her niece," he says, then pauses. "But I was just jealous. And I always wanted you to make something for me."

Florence looks away, uncomfortable with the honesty between them.

"It means a lot to have this. Our people, our history, our future . . . taanishi, Nimish."

A moment passes.

"I'm glad you like it." The words feel weak and insignificant, but everything she wants to say is in the beadwork.

"It makes me feel hopeful," Clancy says, then leans back against the wall and unrolls the pouch again, this time to light up his pipe. "I also feel hopeful because it looks like the Métis Society is going to be having a big meeting soon." He pauses. "With Mr. Tommy Douglas himself."

"What?"

"It's true." He strikes a match against the cot's frame. "Apparently, he's open to it, and they're discussing dates."

"The premier is going to meet with Métis people?" Florence asks to make sure she heard correctly.

"He wants to talk about the 'poverty and socioeconomic ills of the Métis people in the province.'" He inhales from his pipe and continues to speak. "I think he's finally heard the message that he can't just run roughshod over us anymore. It's not going to work."

Florence listens in disbelief.

"The society's even hired a law firm that supports our cause," he says. "They're going to prove that we have rights to this land." His eyes are bright and alive.

"I never . . ." Florence says, absorbing the information.

"Would have thought?" Clancy finishes for her.

"When is the meeting?"

"Don't know yet."

"But you want to go?" she asks.

"Doesn't matter," he says, staring into the bowl of his pipe. "I'll be long gone by then."

"Then why don't you stay?" The question shocks them both.

"What do you mean?" he asks.

Something settles quickly in Florence. "I think I want to stay too."

Clancy watches her, a confused look on his face.

"Over these past few days," she says, trying to find a way to explain, "with Lillian. And you too . . . this house has never felt more like a home."

A moment as this lands.

"Is it possible?" Clancy asks.

"I don't know, but I want to try."

Clancy nods, considering. "I can stay at the plant and come back here on the weekends. Like I said, it pays well, so I can help out a bit."

"It will depend on whether I can scrape some money together too, but I've been thinking . . ."

"I can also call Mr. Huber. Just see if he'll need any help on the weekends when I'm back here."

Florence nods, both excitement and anxiety filling her.

∞

"**I THOUGHT YOU'D BE** in your Sunday best," Florence says when Jennie opens the door to her. Jennie's hair is up in a kerchief and she's pulling rubber gloves off her hands.

"It's been made known to me that many people in town seem to be on Garth's side of things," she says. "I think I will be avoiding church for a while."

"That makes two of us," Florence says, and they share a commiserating smile.

Jennie invites her in, and Florence takes a seat in the living room while Jennie disappears into the kitchen.

"Good timing," she says when she returns with tea and a tray of snacks. "I've been cleaning like mad since the crack of dawn and could use a break."

"It looks spotless," Florence says, noticing the lack of children's fingerprints on the coffee table and the absence of toys strewn about.

"Garth's parents are bringing the kids by later this afternoon and will pick them up after supper." Jennie stuffs a cheese-laden cracker into her mouth but continues talking. "It's silly to clean before they get here. The kids certainly won't care but"—she pauses to swallow—"it's nervous energy, I suppose."

Florence sees she's a little frayed at the edges. "Jennie," Florence says, "the kids are going to be so happy to see you."

Jennie's eyes well up and she reaches for another cracker and pops it in her mouth to stem the tide.

"It's going to be an adjustment," Florence says, "but with some time, you'll all find a way to muddle through it together."

Jennie reflects on this, then nods. "You're right, I'm sure we will," she says, shaking off her mood and picking up her tea. She gulps it down.

"Which is what I'm also trying to do—in my own way," Florence says. No need to beat around the bush.

"Yes, how are things with you and Lillian? And your brother?" Jennie asks.

"Good. Really good. Clancy's leaving shortly to head back to work, and Lillian's enjoying the radio and not having to stoke a fire all day long." Florence smiles, wanting to tell Jennie about Lillian's reaction to the bed and how much it fills Florence to care for her. Instead, she pulls Lillian's cozy from the bag she carried in and places it over Jennie's teapot.

"What's this?" Jennie reaches out to touch it but then hesitates.

"Go ahead," Florence says.

Jennie lifts it off the pot and holds it in her lap. "It's so beautiful. I've never seen anything like it."

"I made it for Lillian."

"You . . ." Jennie trails off as she studies Florence's handiwork.

"I was wondering if you might want one, or something else—I could bead a picture frame or a wall pocket for your keys and sundries." The words come out faster than she'd like, her own nerves rising.

Jennie looks up from the cozy, puzzled.

"I don't want to move." Florence comes out with it. "I don't want to sell the house, but in order to stay, I have to—"

"Yes, I'd like a cozy," Jennie says, understanding what Florence is saying. "I'd like two, actually, because I could use one at the post office. And a wall pocket would certainly be handy."

Now it's Florence who reaches for a cracker.

THAT AFTERNOON WHEN FLORENCE arrives back home Clancy's already gone and she regrets he didn't stay long enough for her to say goodbye, but she's also feeling charged. She looks for the letter from the provincial secretary she left on the kitchen table. She pulls the business licence from the envelope and stares at it. For a brief second, she thinks about tearing it up. She thinks again of all the farmwives who make and sell jam and who don't need licences. She thinks of the long line of beaders she came from who didn't need licences. But instead, she folds it neatly and tucks it away into a safe pocket in her purse in case anyone questions her again. On the one hand, she's glad she ordered it, but on the other, it rankles. She shakes it off, though, and begins to jot down ideas for Jennie's pieces in a notebook. She's not familiar with the plants and flowers on the east coast, where Jennie is from, so she makes a note to ask her and see if she has pictures. If she doesn't have pictures, perhaps a trip to the library is in order. It excites her to bead new things. For new people, and new reasons. It still might not work; she and Clancy still might not make enough to cover expenses, but there's a spark of something inside her that feels good. It feels right.

Florence puts the notebook away and joins Lillian in the living room to take stock of her materials. She'll need more of everything—more cloth, more beads. For cloth, maybe she'll speak to Hilde about scraps again. For beads, there must be a store in the city and she'll ask Jennie if she can tag along the next time she drives in. When Florence was younger, she remembers Lillian and other women using beads from items that no one wanted. Florence can do the same. She can visit the Goodwill store and even go to estate sales—damaged or out-of-style clothing and things are always sold for pennies. She's going to find a way.

She's about to close the lid on the toolbox when the phone rings. It can't be the bank. They wouldn't call on Sunday.

"Hello?"

"It's me—"

"Clancy?"

"I'm all right," he says, because the fear in her voice is obvious. "I just stopped by the Hubers' before heading back. They invited me in for a meal so I'm just about to leave now."

"Did you talk to them about work?"

"I did. Frank thinks there could be a few things over the winter that I could help out with, and come spring, there'll be plenty."

"That's good." The spark takes hold again.

"And also," he says, "Mrs. Huber would like to speak with you."

"What?" But there's only muffled sounds as Clancy passes the phone.

"Hello?" Mrs. Huber says.

"Yes, hello, Mrs. Huber. How are you?"

"Agnes, please."

"All right. Agnes," Florence says.

"I'm doing fine. I'm hoping for a mild winter, but we never seem to get one, do we?"

"No, but we're sure due for one, so who knows, this could be the year."

"From your lips," Agnes says, but ends the saying there and changes her tone. "I wanted to speak with you because Clancy showed us the pouch you made for him." Then silence through the line. "I'd forgotten . . ." she says, letting the words fade.

"Forgotten?" Florence asks, prompting her for more.

"I haven't seen beadwork like that in ages. And Clancy told us that you . . . well, I was hoping you could bead another pouch like it. For my brother. We're going to see him in the new year and I know he'd be just as moved to have something like that."

"Yes, I could do that."

"And maybe," she says, her voice softer, a little more hesitant, "something for me too?"

"Of course, I would love to. Is there anything in particular you'd like?"

"My grandmother used to have a beaded leather cover for her Bible. I don't know what happened to it, but she treasured it." She stops there as if she's said too much.

"I'll bead one for you, Agnes."

A sharp intake of breath on the other line, then: "Thank you."

When she hangs up and returns to the living room, she doesn't tell Lillian about Agnes and the new order because she needs to do something first. Florence pulls out all the little pieces she beaded for herself and lays them out on the floor in front of her. All the pieces that explain her life, that mark definitive moments in her past. She sits with them for a while, Lillian watching her from the settee but not saying a word. Florence starts to see a way to join them together and she threads a needle. Begins to sew. Once all the various materials are joined, she reaches for the beads, and, using long, twisting vines that curl and stretch across the different fabrics, she connects the candy dish to the bee, and the bee to the coin purse. The coin purse to the peroxide bottle, and the Swiss roll to the bottle, then to the typewriter. It won't be balanced and there won't be harmony, but it will hold meaning.

She beads through the evening and the entire next day, and Lillian watches without interrupting her. When Florence finally finishes, Lillian points to the coin purse. "If that one's the beginning of your story, which one is the ending?"

Florence looks at the strange, mishappen piece. "I don't think it's done," she says, and knows immediately that she's going to bead the business licence next. She's not ready to tear it up. Not yet. But she doesn't have to bead just the past anymore—she can bead the future too.

ACKNOWLEDGEMENTS

THIS BOOK CAME to life because of the support of many people and organizations. First and foremost, I want to thank Wilfred Burton. He generously shared so much of his knowledge and expertise on Métis/Michif histories and culture, and he carefully (and enthusiastically) read draft after draft. His input was invaluable and deeply appreciated. Years prior to the writing of this book, Wilfred was my jigging teacher and I'll be forever grateful for his guidance both in writing and in life.

I'm profoundly touched by and beholden to the amazing Métis women beaders and beadwork artists who opened their homes and hearts to share stories of their lives and their beading practices. Kishchi maarsii to Jennine Krauchi, Katherine Boyer, Audie Murray, Merelda Fiddler-Potter, Amy Briley, and Phyllis Poitras-Jarrett. Those conversations meant the world to me. And thank you to all the people involved in organizing the Ziigimineshin and Radical Stitch Beading Symposiums—those events were joyous little worlds unto themselves.

Thanks to the Gabriel Dumont Institute and the Gabriel Dumont Institute Press and all the people who work there for everything they do to preserve our culture and support the community. GDI's programs, publications, and virtual museum have been enormously helpful to me personally on my reconnection journey and in the writing of this book. Through GDI I've begun to learn the Michif language, which is truly a gift. Thanks also to my instructor Samson Lamontagne for his kind, encouraging lessons (please note, though, that all language mistakes in this novel are solely my own).

Thank you to SK Arts for funding the research and writing of this novel; the support was immensely helpful. And to Rita Bouvier, who saw something in the initial concept and supported my application. Funding was also kindly provided by the City of Regina Writing Award, administered by the Saskatchewan Writers' Guild; the Saskatchewan Foundation for the Arts' Colleen and Allan Bailey Memorial Fund; and the Hnatyshyn Foundation's REVEAL Indigenous Art Awards.

To all the readers of early drafts, including Jane Warren, Harry Tournemille, Elizabeth Philips (Sage Hill Writing Fiction Colloquium), Gail Anderson-Dargatz, and Jennifer Ashton (Indigenous Editors Association): Your thoughtful, incisive feedback helped make this novel a better one.

My agent, Sam Haywood, is a force and her unbelievable passion and support for this novel moved me. I'm a lucky writer to have her in my corner. I'm also terribly lucky that Eva Oakes, who initially read my submission, saw its potential. Big thanks to you both and to everyone else at Transatlantic Agency.

It's been a dream to work with Simon & Schuster, and I extend my eternal thanks to Nita Pronovost, who first connected with the story. I've especially loved working with my editor, Brittany Lavery, who has a unique ability to provide critique that is as insightful as it is inspiring. The novel and I couldn't have been in better hands. And what a joy and an honour to work with katherena vermette, whose talents and humour are unparalleled.

Finally, I want to extend my deepest thanks to all those in my life who help to keep me healthy so I can write: Dr. Pushpika Karunatilake, for taking care of my body. Dr. Megan Tuttle, for taking care of my mind. And Gavin de Lint, for taking care of my heart and soul.